content warnings

This book is intended for an 18+ audience. Attached at Heart contains explicit sexual content. It also contains references to a drowning incident, not depicted on page, as well as mentions of cardiac medical conditions, alcohol usage, and adult language. This book discusses toxic and unhealthy (& healthy) family dynamics, particularly with parents, and has overall mature themes.

ATTACHED AT
Heart

attached at heart

WILDFLOWER SERIES
BOOK 3

AMELIE RHYS

Cover Design: Caitlin Russell

Character Art: Alie Reighard at alies_artwork

Editing: Sandra Dee at One Love Editing

For more information about Amelie's books, check out her website:

www.amelierhys.com

playlist

You Are In Love - Taylor Swift
Death Wish Love - Benson Boone
Everything We See - Khalid
Linger - The Cranberries
After Midnight - Chappell Roan
Mess - Noah Kahan
Risk - Gracie Abrams
But Daddy I Love Him - Taylor Swift
Heaven II - Julia Michaels
Nothing's Gonna Hurt You Baby -
Cigarettes After Sex
Dress - Taylor Swift
that way - Tate McRae
Juno - Sabrina Carpenter
Wait For You - Myles Smith
Homemade Dynamite -
Lorde, Khalid, Post Malone, SZA
False God - Taylor Swift

To anyone still waiting for all the pieces to
fall into place...
One day they'll create the most beautiful picture.

eight years ago

BLAKE

I listened to the phone ring while drumming my fingers on the steering wheel.

The thought, even the anticipation, of hearing her voice made me smile to myself. Fucking pathetic.

And then I actually heard her voice, and my stomach did the violently pleasant flip that should only happen when talking to the person who was going to be your wife.

A slightly problematic and sobering thought, considering there was no way Delaney Delacroix was ever going to let me marry her.

"Hello?"

Her sleep-coated voice made it all too clear that, once again, I'd woken her up, and I found way too much satisfaction in knowing I got to be the first one to talk to her every morning before clinicals. That I was the one who knew how she liked her BLTs and had packed an extra one for lunch today. Because Delaney never woke up in time to pack a lunch on Mondays.

"What the hell are you going to do when I'm not around every day to be your alarm clock?"

A ruffling noise cut through the phone, and I bit down on a laugh as I imagined her springing out of bed.

"What do you mean 'not around anymore'?" she huffed, sounding more awake with every word. "I thought when you signed up to be my best friend, you knew that this shit was for life, Blake."

I laughed but didn't respond.

Mostly because I both loved and hated being categorized as her best friend.

CHAPTER ONE

delaney

G ETTING A TEXT MESSAGE from your ex-fiancé in the middle of the workday might put some people over the edge, especially when it was about the date he had planned for later that night. But I responded with an encouraging thumbs-up before pocketing my phone and looking up to see the real wrench in my day.

The brown-haired, brown-eyed, cardiologist-sized wrench.

A handful of weeks had passed since the end of my engagement with Austin Long, but it had been one hundred twenty-seven days—not that I'd been counting—since the last time I'd seen my best friend. Since that night on the hospital bench when the first snow of the season fell in Minnesota, covering the city of Rochester in a blanket of white.

One hundred twenty-seven days since he'd abruptly moved out of the state.

I'd planned to stay at the Mayo Clinic after finishing our fellowships in cardiology. He had, too. Until he hadn't, accepting a position in Boston instead. He never told me why, but the sight before me had to be a clue.

Because Blake London was here.

In the hospital lobby.

And he was sitting by a woman, bouncing a baby girl on his lap.

A *baby*.

I supposed it made sense; he'd always been that guy, the one who looked for a wife in every girl he took out to dinner. But this was extreme, even for him, to already have a baby cradled in his arms. Was it even *possible*?

I mean, of course it was possible. I couldn't manipulate the situation in my head to be *probable*, but of course it was *possible*.

Especially considering how he looked at the girl opposite him, smiling.

Smiling.

Blake didn't smile all that often. Not really, not in a way where you could see his teeth. Usually, it was just a close-lipped tilt of his lips that I kept telling him looked condescending, but he didn't believe me.

No, Blake didn't smile like this often.

Usually, he only smiled like that at—

"Do you think you'll get Noah into the boxing ring some more?"

Boxing? Noah?

I straightened at the woman's voice as she asked Blake about his brother, otherwise known as the New England Knights' quarterback and the hottest football player in Boston. According to the internet, of course. If tattoos and muscles were your thing, he'd be considered objectively attractive. And considering the way this woman's eyes lit up at the mention of Blake's brother, tattoos and muscles were definitely her thing.

I gritted my teeth, crossing my arms over my chest. I'd had to watch more than one woman use Blake to try to get to his brother, and if this—

"I'll force him, even if he doesn't want to."

Blake's voice soothed my raising hackles, making me forget all about the woman opposite him. I'd needed to hear that voice in the past few months. Needed to hear that calm cadence,

2

needed him to give me some of his no-nonsense advice, but he'd left.

He said his family in Boston needed him. He didn't tell me anything. After ten years of friendship, *ten years* where we'd navigated medical school together in Chicago, supported each other long distance through residency, and reunited at Mayo for our fellowship, he'd simply left me. Without even telling me the details of the hospital he planned to work at as an attending physician. The very thing we worked for so many years to do. Together. He didn't tell me it was this one. And definitely didn't tell me he had a *baby*.

How had we not run into each other until today? How had I not known about any of this?

Seeing the scene before me shouldn't have made me feel sick to my stomach, but it did. When Blake told me his family needed him, I'd assumed he meant his brother and single-mom sister. They both lived out here in Boston, too. I never could have imagined that he'd meant a completely different kind of family.

"Good. You should because I'm just a little worried about him," the woman replied to Blake before dropping her voice, clearly wanting whatever she had to say about Noah London to be private.

My frown deepened as I studied Blake's expression. His brows furrowed as he listened. He reached out, squeezing the woman's arm affectionately, and I wondered if *he* was worried for his brother or if he was worried about how worried *she* was about his brother.

I didn't like it either way.

I continued to watch as Blake rocked the baby up close to his chest. Then he cocked his head to the side, brushing an absent-minded, tender kiss over the top of the baby's head like it was the most natural thing in the world.

My stomach did a weird flip.

When the woman stood a moment later, Blake leaned in for a brief hug before passing the baby to her. She was tall, I realized.

About as tall as me with blue eyes and fair skin that wasn't so different from my own. But that was where our similarities ended; her pretty face hosted a smattering of freckles, and her copper hair draped around her shoulders in lovely, loose waves. My blonde hair, on the other hand, hung in a limp braid down my back.

The woman tucked her baby girl into a carrier, chatting softly to Blake as she gathered her things. And then she walked the other way with a little wave.

Odd.

The whole thing was odd, and I tried to make sense of it as I turned to watch Blake's girlfriend, or whoever she was, walk away with such an offhand goodbye.

"Delaney?"

I froze at the sound of Blake's voice.

On a scale of one to ten, how obvious was it that I'd been standing here the entire time? Probably at *least* a seven. *Shit*.

"What are you...Delaney?" He said my name again, his voice growing louder, closer, infused with confusion, and touched with disbelief. He was trying to figure out why I hadn't responded. Or why I was here.

I should have told him, my best friend, that I'd moved to the East Coast, to the same city he'd moved to. But after the way he'd left, I hadn't even been sure we *were* best friends anymore. And the last thing I wanted him to think was that I'd *followed* him here. Especially considering the emotional distance he'd placed between us that far rivaled the physical separation.

Attempting to gather myself, I waited a beat longer before turning to face him.

"Blake," I said breathlessly, hoping that maybe I sounded more surprised and less like I'd been spying on him for the last five minutes.

I mean, I *was* surprised. Surprised to see him here, probably on a break between rounds. Surprised we hadn't crossed paths before. Surprised to see him with a baby in his lap.

"What's—what's going on?" Blake was standing in front of me now, his intense gaze scrutinizing my presence. His eyes swept over me, taking in every inch of my being here, standing right in front of him. When his attention flicked back to my face, he reached out like he was going to touch me, maybe pull me in for a hug, but then he seemed to remember that he'd put distance between us and stopped. "Why are you here? How long have you been standing there?"

That last question grabbed my attention, sounding an awful lot like Blake was worried he'd just been caught.

I lifted a brow. "Long enough that I have some questions of my own, Dr. London."

"Oh?" Blake crossed his arms over his chest and gave me a look I recognized from med school. *A challenge.* "Why am I not surprised, Dr. Delacroix?"

"That makes one of us."

Blake frowned, his face twisting with confusion. "I'm sorry, but *I'm* the one who moved to Boston. *You're* the one who's supposed to still be working in Minnesota but is, for some reason, standing here. In Boston. The person who should be surprised is me."

"True," I allowed. "But you could have at least told me the real reason why you moved." I waved a hand at where he'd just been sitting with the baby and the woman. "You could have told me about...that."

A ghost of a smile passed across Blake's lips. "You want to know about that, Lane?"

I looked at him like he was losing it. "You were holding a *baby.*"

Of course I wanted to know about it.

"Mm, so you *were* standing there for a while."

Oh, goddamnit.

My mouth opened and closed, but no words came out.

A twinkle lit up Blake's eyes now. "Care to share exactly how long you were spying on me, or would you rather try to lie?" He leaned forward and added with a whisper, "You're a terrible liar."

I rolled my eyes and gave in. "I watched long enough to know that you once again found a woman who'd rather talk about your younger brother than about *you*."

I expected Blake to react to that, but he just straightened and shrugged. "Maybe my brother's more interesting to talk about."

"Stop it." I swatted his arm, annoyed and confused as to why he thought this was funny. He usually hated when girls asked him about Noah. "Seriously, Blake. You're annoyingly smart, unfairly handsome, and usually nice. You can do so much better than someone who only cares—"

Blake's laughter cut off my rant. "*Usually* nice? Really?"

"Sometimes you do come off as a condescending asshole."

For some inexplicable reason, Blake's grin grew. Not that full-out smile I'd missed or the tight-lipped, condescending tilt, but something different. A sly one. A crooked one. His eyes shimmered with mischief as he leaned back against a row of chairs, perching on the top of one. I couldn't remember the last time I'd seen him looking so goddamn amused, and it was irritating as hell. Because the more I thought about how that woman had just zoned in on Noah like that in front of him, the more bothered I became. And Blake, clearly, couldn't give less of a shit.

"I'm serious, Blake," I pressed, somehow withholding a childish stomp of my foot.

Why wouldn't he want to be with someone who appreciated him for who he was?

Blake nodded, his smile holding strong. "I can see that, Lane. Very serious."

I scowled at him.

"You really think I can do better?" he mused. "I don't know. At thirty-three, sometimes I feel like I'm starting to push past my prime for the dating market. Not to mention, I have a crippling addiction to caffeine and absolutely no fashion sense, as you've pointed out before. But if you say so..." He chuckled softly as he trailed off and then didn't say anything for a long moment, just sort of stared at me. I was about to tell him off again when he sighed.

"Her name is Gemma," he said. "Gemma Briggs, soon-to-be London."

"Oh my God, you're marrying her," I muttered, more to myself than to him.

I knew one day Blake would find someone to settle down with, but I just hadn't expected it to happen so *suddenly*.

Blake's smile grew, and I wanted to punch him for being so cavalier about this when my heart had just momentarily stopped, stunned.

"No," he said simply, and the floor felt like it opened beneath me. "I'm not. But Noah will be soon, I'm sure. And that was Noah's daughter, Delilah. My niece. She had her checkup this morning. The newborn phase has been a little tough for the whole family." He dropped his voice to a whisper again—an annoying, condescending whisper. "Gemma was talking to me about Noah because she's dating him, and he's my brother. If you had walked up a few minutes earlier, you would have seen him walk out to get the car."

Embarrassment washed over me as my brain processed his response, and I closed my eyes to try to hide it, pinching the bridge of my nose.

"But I'm so glad to hear that you think I'm *usually* nice," Blake added with another velvety laugh.

I swallowed past the weird mix of mortification and relief before opening my eyes and apologizing.

"I'm sorry." Both of Blake's brows lifted like he couldn't believe those two words had fallen from my lips so easily. "I jumped to conclusions, and I'm sorry."

I would have been *more* sorry if he didn't look so damned pleased with himself. I was sure it had to do with the slight competitive streak we'd harbored for years. He clearly felt like he had just won a point in the imaginary years-long game we always seemed to be playing, but I couldn't even care at the moment. Because I'd never been happier to be wrong.

Blake nodded, accepting my apology without wasting another breath on the subject. He was a man of few words on most occasions, so it didn't surprise me. Instead of talking, he looked over me again, like he was still struggling to believe we'd bumped into one another. His eyes stopped as they lowered, zeroing in on my hand.

My ringless hand.

His smile fell, his mood shifting. His gaze was unreadable when it lifted back to my face, but I could feel it, sharp and acute. Intense.

"Why are you here, Delaney?"

I swallowed hard. "I work here."

He took a moment to work through that fact in his head. I could almost see how he repeated it to himself, maybe once, maybe twice. And when he finally spoke, it was slow and measured. "You told me I was acting rash when I decided to leave Minnesota, and now here you are, too?"

"You know my plans were always to return to the East Coast."

"But you were going to stay on at Mayo as an attending for a few years first. Did you already get your inheritance?" he questioned, because he did know—he knew exactly what my dreams had always been: to use my grandparents' inheritance to found a cardiac clinic close to home. Close to my brother. "I thought you wouldn't get the money until your next birthday."

"I don't have it yet," I admitted. "But I wanted to be closer to home."

"You wanted to be with your family."

His words were stunted, confusion lingering in them. Fair, considering the poor relationship I had with my family outside of my brother. Something else he was well aware of.

"Yes," I said. Better to keep it succinct.

"And Austin?" Blake's gaze flicked down to my ringless hand again. "Did he want to be closer to your family?"

"He..." I shifted on my feet before clearing my throat. I never felt more guilty than when talking about Austin with Blake. Because I should have told him the truth about my fiancé a long time ago, but I'd always talked myself out of it. "Did not. We're not engaged anymore."

Blake's eyes met mine, his stare hard, and I suddenly really wished they'd taught mind reading in med school. There was a noticeable tick in Blake's sharp jaw as he slowly unfolded himself and stood again. His tall, built frame towered over me, but like usual, I drew myself up to match him.

"What the hell did he do?"

A low tremor ran through his words. I'd never been afraid of Blake London before. Not once in my whole life. But if I didn't know him better, I might be right now. His usually light complexion had flushed red, and his eyes had hardened with a brand-new intensity.

"How do you know *he* did something? Maybe *I* did something."

I felt immediately defensive over Austin because none of this was his fault, and I didn't want him to seem like the bad guy. It wasn't fair to him. I didn't love Austin, but I liked him well enough.

Blake scoffed like the idea was preposterous. He muttered something under his breath that I didn't catch before taking a step closer to demand answers from me. Answers I knew I owed him.

"Either way, it doesn't matter," I said quickly.

Blake didn't like that response, either. "Of course it fucking matters, Lane—"

"Because it was never...*real*, Blake," I confessed with my heart in my throat.

God, that felt good to get out. Not telling Blake that had been eating me alive for months.

Blake's brows furrowed as he tried to decide what to make of that statement. Some unnamed emotion flashed across his face, and I let him absorb my words while I breathed in the scent of woody vanilla and musk. It was familiar, it was warm, it was Blake.

The bustle of the hospital surrounded us, but no one noticed the two doctors standing in the middle of it all. We blended in. Just a few more people in scrubs, looking like any other exhausted physician in this building.

When he finally spoke, his words were careful. Like they were the weightiest ones he'd ever said.

"*What* was never real, Lane?"

I swallowed. "All of it," I admitted shamefully. "Me and Austin. Nothing about it was real."

Blake shook his head like he refused to believe that and then looked me over, a scrutinizing effort to figure out the truth and assess me for damages, the way any person might if their friend showed up and announced a broken engagement. Which made me wonder if he'd completely misinterpreted my words.

"Who ended things?" he asked, confirming my suspicion.

"He did," I said honestly. "But—"

"Absolutely unbelievable," Blake muttered, flicking his eyes up in...vexation? Anger on my behalf? I couldn't be sure. Then he looked down at his watch, pulling his sleeve up to see the time properly. He stared at the ticking hands for a little too long before he finally met my gaze again.

"I'm sure you're busy," I said so he wouldn't have to come up with an excuse to exit this conversation, which had turned down a road we maybe didn't have time for at the moment. Was I trying to put off telling him the whole truth? Possibly. But it was hard to spit out after I'd held on to it for so long. "Maybe we can catch up some more soon," I added, giving him a pained smile.

God, how I wished things weren't so pained between us.

"I'd like that," Blake said in that solemn tone of his. He gave a perfunctory nod before cocking his head to the side. "What are you doing tonight?"

"I—oh, tonight?" My brows rose with surprise. "I'm not doing anything tonight."

"Dinner, then." Blake took another look at his watch, pursing his lips as he slowly started to back away. Maybe he really did have somewhere to be. "Seven o'clock. Giovanni's."

"Giovanni's? That sounds like a place I should wear a dress. Should I wear a dress?"

"Wear a dress, Lane." Blake's expression shifted, his lips in a slight tilt, the start of a secretive smile. Something I wasn't actually supposed to see. "The black one with the buttons you wore at graduation would be perfect."

I tried hard to school my reaction at Blake remembering a dress I wore years ago, but I doubted I managed. And then Blake threw me a wink before striding away, and I *knew* I didn't manage. Fuck, he got *way* too much satisfaction from being a know-it-all who remembered every little thing, and I should definitely *not* prove him right and wear the dress I wore to our graduation.

Definitely not.

But it was one of the only dresses I'd made sure to hang up when I'd moved into my new place, and the rest were still crumpled up in boxes scattered around my slightly damp apartment. I'd planned to wear it to the hospital benefit coming up in a few weeks.

So fine, I'd wear the dress for our dinner date.

Well, not date.

Dinner, full stop.

Just dinner.

With Blake London, my kinda, sorta best friend who hadn't talked to me in months.

I should have been apprehensive, but instead, a sense of familiarity washed over me. A sense of ease. Because even though

I grew up on the Cape and traveled to Boston regularly over the years, I'd never felt more at odds than I had in the last weeks as I'd settled into my new routine here at Suffolk County Medical Center.

And I had a feeling that Blake being back in my life would help even me right out.

CHAPTER TWO

DELANEY WAS NOT ENGAGED.

She was *not* getting married.

And she was *here*, in Boston, yelling at me because she'd thought *I* was getting married.

Had I dropped into some other dimension?

Fuck me, I didn't know what to make of any of it. I was still processing this earth-shattering revelation that Delaney was once again single. I had questions—*so* many questions. But I hadn't wanted to overwhelm her while we stood in the SCMC lobby, especially considering Delaney's evasion of the details. Normally, she would have offered them up for me without any hesitation, and I hoped that her shift in behavior didn't have something to do with how I'd left Minnesota—left her when maybe she'd needed me.

But I hadn't known. All I'd known at the time was that she was marrying Austin fucking Long, and I—well, I'd needed to get the hell away from that.

My thoughts continued to tumble, even as Delaney walked up two minutes before our dinner reservation, wearing the little black dress of all little black dresses. It was *the* little black dress. The only one that existed in my mind.

Her graduation dress.

The fabric curved over her hips, which swayed as she walked, capturing my attention. *Fuck me.*

"Why are you staring at me like that?" She reached my side and smacked me in the arm with the small clutch she had in her hand. "You *told* me to wear this dress."

"I'm just...surprised you actually found it." I cleared my throat, hoping she wouldn't notice the heat rising up my neck at being caught staring. I was usually so much better at keeping myself in check, but I was out of practice. And feeling a little greedy and desperate. I hadn't seen Delaney in months, and I'd been deprived of looking at her. "You look...nice."

She snorted. "That sounded convincing."

I bit my tongue, forcing myself not to respond to that. I *could* be convincing, but she hadn't asked for that.

"Nice," she repeated beneath her breath as she slid past me and into the restaurant. I curled my fingers into fists in my pockets to keep from stopping her and rephrasing myself to make sure she understood just how *nice* I thought she looked. But before I could do or say anything, Delaney pulled up short after opening the door to Giovanni's.

"Wow, you want to talk about nice—look at this place. Good thing I wore my dress."

As I stood staring at her backside, I thought the opposite. Maybe it *wasn't* a good thing she wore this dress. Not if I wanted to keep my shit together enough to have a conversation.

"Don't worry about it." I placed a hand on the small of her back and gently urged her forward. "Dinner's on me."

"I wasn't worried about it." She peeked back over her shoulder. "And you don't need to pay. Unless I find out you're making more money than me simply because you have a dick. In that case, I'll allow it."

I shook my head, biting down on a smile. God, it was so fucking annoying how much I'd missed her. "I know I don't need to pay. I'm paying because I want to, Lane."

She turned on me with a mock gasp. "Has Boston turned you into a gentleman?"

I scowled, resisting the urge to demand she tell me at least one time that I had been *un*gentlemanly. Trust me, where Delaney Delacroix was concerned, I was very much a gentleman. Fucking killed me at times, but maintaining our friendship had always been the most important thing to me.

To no surprise, Delaney ignored my scowl and turned toward the hostess, giving her my name before clasping her hands behind her back demurely. I found it satisfying that although I hadn't told her I made a reservation, she'd known I'd taken care of it. Meanwhile, I traced the buttons on her dress with my eyes, following them up the straight line of her back and marveling at her perfect posture. When the hostess gestured for us to follow her, Delaney moved with grace in every step like the retired ballerina debutante extraordinaire she was.

"I just want to celebrate the occasion," I clarified as we settled into opposite seats at a table tucked in the corner of the restaurant. The quaint space glowed with ambient lighting, and I realized how awfully romantic it felt. I knew I could play it off, but this was the kind of shit I should really be more careful about. Especially until I figured out the rest of the details surrounding her broken engagement.

She said it hadn't been *real*. What the hell did that mean?

"The occasion?" she parroted.

I shrugged, attempting nonchalance. "You know, you moving to Boston."

You being single.

She laughed, but it was slightly strained. "I've been here for nearly a month."

I paused at that, the air getting choked out of me as I decided how to respond. *A month.* How hadn't I known? After a beat, I settled on, "When the fuck were you going to tell me?"

Chill. Real chill.

Did Delaney not *want* to be around me? Because that was probably something I should figure out, and quick.

"I don't know." Delaney's gaze lowered as she focused on her menu a little too hard. "I was getting settled and everything, and I didn't even realize you worked at SCMC. I have no idea how we went this long without—"

"Oh, I don't." I'd forgotten to clarify that earlier. I didn't work there, but my sister, who was a trauma surgeon, did. "Nat works there, and I was having lunch with her."

"Oh." Delaney glanced up from her menu before burying her gaze back inside it. "Well, that makes more sense."

"I work at Boston Medical." I raised a brow, mostly at how she was avoiding eye contact. "I've still been in Boston, Lane. Like I told you."

Heaving a loud sigh, she put down the menu. But instead of meeting my eyes, she began toying with her water glass, sliding the tip of her finger around the rim and watching it with an annoying amount of concentration.

"Yes, but that's *all* you told me. Just...Boston. We left things weird, Blake." She flicked her gaze to mine—all accusatory—before adding with a mumble, "Or rather, *you* left things weird."

I shifted slightly in my chair before clearing my throat. "I don't know what you mean by that."

"Yes, you do."

Okay, fine. I did.

Delaney's expression dripped with exasperation. "You *clearly* didn't support my engagement to Austin—"

"You'd only been dating him for like a month, Delaney," I interjected dryly. I mean, come on. What friend wouldn't point out that it was moving a little too fast? Especially when she'd spent years telling me she didn't even *want* to get married one day.

"Okay, yeah," she conceded. "But also...no, because we never actually dated at all."

"It certainly didn't seem like it," I agreed. "You went to, what, like one football game with him? Dinner twice?"

I ran into her at one of Noah's football games in Minneapolis, and finding out she'd been there with him had put a damper on the whole goddamn day.

But she shook her head. "No, Blake." She took a deep breath before releasing it slowly. "That's not what I meant."

I frowned, feeling a knot form in my gut. "What do you mean?"

"I mean..." Her eyes shifted away from mine. "We never dated. We were never engaged. It wasn't *real*."

"You keep saying that, Lane, but I don't know what that means. Did he do something? Because if he did, I swear to God—"

"He fell in love with someone else," she blurted, and I reared back, assaulted by the thought.

"He *what*?"

My brows drew together as I raked a hand through my hair, needing to do something to keep from running out of the restaurant to find Austin Long and demand to know what the hell was *wrong* with him. Fell in love with someone else? Fell out of love with *Delaney*? When he *had* her?

How could he so easily do the one thing I'd tried all my goddamn life to do? The one thing I'd failed at so miserably.

"He fell in love with someone else," Delaney repeated calmly. Why was she so calm? "Which is *fine*, Blake."

I blinked at her in disbelief. "It's fine that your fiancé fell in love with someone else? What are you talking about? That's absolutely not fine. It's the *opposite* of fine, Lane. It's—it's impossible."

Literally impossible. And if she wasn't going to be angry about it, I would be. Because what the *fuck*?

She sighed. "It's fine because it was..." She dropped her head back, and my breathing suspended while she figured out how to end that sentence.

"Because it was what?" I probed, anxious.

Delaney looked up again, startled to find that I had leaned in, moving closer. A sort of shiver worked through her before she threw her hands up and confessed, "Fake. It was fake."

"Fake?" I repeated, sounding hollow.

"Yes," she confirmed. "Falsified. Fictional. Like I said...not real. That's what I was trying to tell you."

I mouthed the word one more time silently, attempting to understand it.

"My inheritance..." Delaney hedged, and the puzzle pieces slowly started to fall into place, causing my heart to pound. "I actually have to be married for a year to get it. Because in the dictionary, next to *old-school*, you'd see a picture of my grand-parents."

I shook my head, trying to keep up.

"So you have to turn thirty-five and *then* get married for a year?"

"No, I, um..." She scratched her head and winced. "I made the birthday thing up. It was only ever the marriage thing. By the time I told you about it, I just knew both would coincide, timing-wise. Austin was simply a means to an end."

Something about my expression—probably my jaw that had dropped—made Delaney quickly add, "But he knew. He knew about it. He was going to get a cut, and then we'd get a divorce after a year, and he'd get to pay off his student loans and run happily into the sunset debt-free. He was a very willing partici-pant, I promise."

Of course he fucking was. He got to be married to Delaney while getting paid for it. I was sure he thought he'd won the goddamn lottery.

"So, what I'm hearing is you were never *really* engaged."

"*Yes*." She slumped in her chair, looking both relieved and exasperated. "Thank you for finally understanding."

"Jesus fuck, Delaney," I swore beneath my breath, my eyes fluttering shut at her affirmation.

I massaged the back of my neck, trying to get a grip on this new reality. One where Delaney had never been in love with

Austin Long, where she'd never even wanted to marry him, not in a real sense, and one where she wasn't *going* to marry him. But most importantly, a reality where she'd needed a husband, and for some goddamn reason, she hadn't asked *me*.

Austin was just some guy from our cohort in med school who'd also ended up at Mayo for his fellowship but in a different specialty. All I really knew about him was that Delaney had thought he was funny and kind because he bought her lunch, like, one time, and if that was the bar to ask someone to marry them, then Christ, what had I been doing wrong for our decade-long friendship? Did I need to tell more jokes?

Delaney worried her bottom lip, and I internally groaned, trying not to look at her mouth. Now was not the time. *So* not the time for my brain to go there.

She drummed her fingers on the table anxiously. "Can you please say something else?"

I released a slow breath before pinning my gaze on her and asking, "Why?"

Her brows pulled together. "Why was I getting married? I told you—"

"No." I shook my head, running a hand over my face. "No, why didn't you tell me? Or better yet, why didn't you just ask me?"

"You were dating someone," she said, hasty to clarify that.

Only it didn't clarify anything.

Someone?

I crossed my arms over my chest because we both knew she was being vague on purpose. I'd taken girls on dates, if only to see if anyone might break through the spell Delaney had on me, but I'd never seriously dated anyone.

Fine, though. We could go with that reasoning for now. I wasn't going to risk pushing her for the truth about this when I'd just gotten her back. It wasn't the important thing at the moment.

"Well, who are you going to marry now?" I asked instead.

Because that *was* the important thing. I knew Delaney still had plans to get that inheritance money. And I needed to know what those plans were. Needed to know what I should brace myself for.

Delaney blew out a breath between her lips. "I don't know. I decided to move closer to home and focus on work for a bit while I regrouped. Maybe push my grandparents' executor, see if there's any other workaround. Thought it might be easier to do while I'm here since he's local to Boston."

"He does know you want to use the money to do a good thing, right?"

"He knows," she said, and I pursed my lips in irritation.

"I see."

I hated that Delaney had to go through this just to follow her dreams of making the world a better place. But at least I knew about it now. And I wouldn't let her go through it alone, even if there were still some things up in the air between us. Even if maybe there were certain aspects of this situation I still didn't understand. I understood enough. Enough to make up my mind about what I was going to do next.

The easiest decision I'd ever made.

"So..." Delaney tucked a piece of hair behind her ear, giving me a side-eyed look. "That's why *I'm* here."

Then she stared at me expectantly. Waiting for me to pick up where we'd left off in the conversation before, as though she hadn't just shattered my world in some of the best and worst ways possible.

But fine.

"You *know* why I'm here," I said.

"Do I?"

"I told you my reasoning for moving to Boston," I said with a sigh. "I wanted to be closer to my family."

"You lived an hour away from your parents and two brothers in Minnesota," she countered.

"My *other* family."

Delaney flicked the corner of the menu, chewing her bottom lip in contemplation. "It just seemed so sudden. So...insincere, in a way."

"Like your engagement?" I muttered, but she ignored me.

"Blake, don't hate me for saying this, but you rarely even *visited* Noah or Natalie before. And now you're so compelled to be close to them that you abruptly changed your career plans and moved across the country?"

Shit, she hit the nail on the head. And it kinda hurt. "That's exactly why I moved." Well, not exactly. But it was exactly the reason I would be telling her. Because she knew all about the big, loving London family—of which I might have been the worst member in the last years—and it could be an excuse she believed. "I realized I'd been a shitty brother," I explained when she furrowed her brows in confusion. "Okay, *I* didn't really realize it. Gemma might have called me on it."

Delaney stilled. She was almost always in motion in some way, so when she stopped, it was like the whole world stopped, too. Her intense gaze wandered my face. "Gemma?"

"Noah's girlfriend," I reminded her.

"Oh." Delaney perked up at that, sitting back in her chair with a contented look. "Now I'm feeling bad for misjudging her. She sounds exactly like the kind of sister-in-law you need."

"She is," I agreed. "Noah better get to proposing soon."

"Why hasn't he? I mean, considering they have a child together."

"Delilah is not Noah's biological daughter, but he'd hate I'm even mentioning that. He's stepped up to be her dad in every way that counts, and I think they're just focusing on being parents at the moment. But I know it's only a matter of time before he pops the question."

"Wow. That's great." She smiled, and it was soft. "I can tell you're really happy for him."

"I am," I said honestly. "Now, if only I could find some of that happiness for Nat. I've actually seen her and Chloe more than Noah lately."

As a recently divorced single parent with an incredibly busy work schedule, Natalie had relied on Noah a fair amount to help with her nine-year-old daughter, Chloe. I hadn't realized *how* much until Noah bowed out of uncle duty for a bit to focus on dad duty, and I'd stepped in to take his place.

"That's sweet that you were getting lunch with her today."

I nodded, not really wanting to get into the thick of my conversation with Natalie and the reason we met up for lunch, which was to talk through a legal mess involving her shithead ex-husband.

"How's your family?" I asked instead.

"Oh, you don't want to hear about them."

"Fine." I chuckled and amended, "How's Bry?"

Delaney's whole face lit up at the mention of her brother, the one family member she adored with everything in her. Bryan was born with Down syndrome and consequently had experienced a myriad of heart trouble growing up. Now in his early adulthood, he was doing well health-wise, which was a relief. But regardless, he was the entire reason Delancy was a cardiologist.

"He's great. I mean, my mom isn't very happy with him at the moment because he tried to sneak out of the house this past weekend to go meet up with his girlfriend, but I told her that was actually the best news she's told me in a long time."

I watched her continue to talk animatedly about her brother and knew, without a doubt, that even though what I planned on doing would fuck me up from the inside out, it was the right thing to do, considering the circumstances.

And also considering the determination that fueled this woman from the moment she woke up until the moment she went to bed.

If *I* didn't marry Delaney Delacroix so she could get her goddamn inheritance and chase her dreams of opening a specialty cardiac clinic, she'd find someone else to attach herself to for a year. Fake or not, I had no interest in going through that again. I'd have to find a new city to move to, and despite how much my fucking brothers liked to tease me for running away from my feelings, I was starting to like Boston.

The waiter interrupted Delaney before she could finish talking about Bryan, and Delaney sheepishly ordered a glass of chardonnay before falling silent.

I chuckled to myself. "What other mischief has Bryan been getting into?"

"Oh, nothing. You know, the usual. I don't want to ramble too much about it."

The waiter returned with the wine, and she immediately picked it up, all but downing the chardonnay.

"Since when do you care about what I think of your rambling?" I asked with a frown.

She flicked her eyes up in pretend annoyance and traded her wine for my glass of pinot noir—since *I* hadn't drained my drink the moment I got it—and took a sip, making a face.

"I don't know." She put the glass back down with more force than necessary. "Maybe you moved to Boston to escape my rambling. Otherwise, you would have at least called."

I sighed and took a drink of the wine myself, hating that hurt look in Delaney's gaze. "I'm sorry I didn't."

She watched me expectantly, no doubt waiting for an explanation. But I didn't have one that I could give her.

I was trying to get over you.

"You know I'm not really a phone person," I added because it was the best I could do. "I don't know, there's something about not seeing a person's face when you're talking to them."

"Blake." Delaney put both her hands on the table and leaned forward conspiratorially. "I don't know if you've heard of this or not, but there's something called Face—"

"Okay, *okay*." I threw my hands up in defeat. "You're right. I'm *sorry*."

She sat back again, looking smug as hell.

23

"Say it again."

I pursed my lips, trying not to let them curve into a grin at how victorious she looked from hearing me say those two magic words. But it was a losing effort, so I picked my wine back up instead and took a long sip, studying Delaney over the glass's rim and drawing out the moment.

Her eyes met mine, bright and alive.

"You can't hide in that wineglass forever, Dr. London."

I raised a brow, taking another slow gulp of wine. Her eyes flicked down to my throat as I swallowed before lifting back to my gaze again.

If she could chug a hundred-dollar glass of wine, then so could I.

Delaney leaned forward, resting her chin on her hand as though watching me down this glass of wine was the most interesting thing she'd seen all day. One of her brows lifted as if to say, "*Are you done yet?*"

But I was a fucking glutton for her attention, so no, I wasn't done.

When I'd drained the last drop of wine from the glass, I set it back on the table and licked my lips, feeling a dribble of pinot escape. Delaney's lips parted as she stared at me in some kind of unspoken disbelief before she abruptly sucked in and repeated herself, her voice lower.

"Say it again, Blake."

The waiter returned, saving me from repeating the words Delaney desperately wanted to hear. He looked at our drained glasses of wine with surprise but was well trained enough not to say anything.

"Another glass of pinot?" he asked me first, a placid expression on his face.

"I think maybe we'll just take a bottle of the chardonnay she's having for the table," I answered, and Delaney made a face at me. One of those *you didn't have to do that* faces.

If she was making that face at me now, I couldn't imagine what kind of face she would be making in the next few minutes.

"What's your schedule look like tomorrow?" I asked after the waiter left.

"I'm pretty booked with *being right* all day."

"Hmm," I pretended to consider. "No breaks in the day to do something a little bit...wrong?"

Because that was no doubt what this proposition was. Wrong, for so many reasons. And maybe rushed, but I didn't want to take my chances and let her slip away again.

But Delaney's brows shot up, and I realized too late what my proposition had sounded like.

"What did you have in mind?" she questioned.

Fuck, she really didn't want to know the full answer to that question. So I stuck to the one that would shock her the least.

And that was saying something.

"I'm thinking I could sneak a visit to the government center into my schedule."

"The government center?"

"For a marriage license, of course."

"For a—" She broke off, her eyes growing wide. "*Blake*—"

"But I guess I should ask properly first." I cleared my throat, both reveling in this moment and hating it in one breath. This was not how I ever imagined proposing. To anyone. I wasn't exactly a creative person, but proposals were supposed to be... better. So much better than this.

This wasn't a goddamn fairy tale, though. And I knew better than to imagine anything other than reality. So I flashed my best friend a grin and did my best to play it fucking cool.

"Delaney Delacroix, will you marry me?"

CHAPTER THREE

"I —*WHAT*?" I SPUTTERED. "Blake, you don't—"

"What?" His lips twitched as he pretended to be affronted. "I'm sorry, did you want me to get down on one knee?"

He started to push his chair back, and I reached across the table to put a stop to that immediately.

"Don't you *dare*," I threatened through gritted teeth.

Blake stilled and put his palms up to signify surrender. I thought maybe I was in the clear and this conversation would get pushed aside completely, but then he leaned forward again, flashing me a tilted smile.

My pulse, which had picked up its tempo as soon as the words *marry me* had left Blake's mouth, thrummed loudly. I could hear it pounding in my ears as Blake lowered his voice and asked, "What's wrong? You don't want to marry me, Lane?"

"Oh, stop." I fidgeted nervously with my empty wineglass, *really* wishing the waiter would make a reappearance with that bottle. I couldn't believe Blake had the nerve to tease me about this. I mean, *maybe* I deserved it for lying to him about my engagement, but still. "Blake, this is—"

"You did tell me I was handsome earlier today," he cut in, his smirk growing.

"That's what you took away from that?" I cried incredulously.

Blake lifted a brow, his gaze boring into me, making my cheeks heat. Oh my God, I hoped he couldn't tell. The last thing I needed was for Blake to remember he had the ability to make me *blush*.

"'*Unfairly* handsome,'" he added, and I wanted to melt into the floor immediately. "I think that's what you said."

"You're unbelievable," I groaned, squeezing my eyes shut for a moment because I couldn't keep looking at him when he was staring at me like that.

"True." Blake nodded solemnly before adding conspiratorially, "And I'm *usually* nice, too."

I flailed, trying to find the words to combat Blake's absurdity.

Blake seemed to be enjoying himself too damn much, which was not helping me collect my thoughts. "All in all, not bad for a husband, huh?"

As the word *husband* fell from his lips, Blake's attitude dropped. And in its place was a quiet calm that housed sincerity.

I looked at him, the person who'd been my closest friend for over a decade now. The person who'd kept me alive in med school and let me cry over the phone to him in residency about how I'd never become a cardiologist. The person who told me my dreams were going to be worth it.

And now he stood here, still pushing me toward them.

Because I realized...he was serious.

Oh. My. God.

"No," I admitted when I found my voice. "Not bad for a husband."

That was exactly the problem, though.

And precisely why I hadn't told him about any of this before.

Because of course Blake would offer to fake-marry me if he'd known what I'd needed. I would have thought he'd need at least a *little* more time to think about it, but he was just that kind of friend. When I'd told him in med school that I was a hands-on learner, he let me draw all over his body and then hadn't even

27

complained when he realized I'd used a permanent marker. He'd had "frontalis" written on his head for nearly a week. I bought him a whole selection of hats out of guilt.

But I couldn't fake-marry Blake.

Blake wasn't the kind of guy you fake-married. He was the kind of guy you married-married. I knew that because he'd been looking for someone to marry since I'd met him. He wanted that life, that settled-down, minivan life. I couldn't let him postpone it for me.

"So it's settled." Blake clasped his hands together in front of him on the table as though it was as simple as that. "We're getting married."

The waiter took that moment to reappear with our wine, pouring us both a glass as Blake and I sat staring at each other, a heavy silence hovering overhead. As soon as his glass was full, Blake picked it up almost lazily, an air of indifference in the movement like he wasn't freaking out at what he'd just proposed. He lifted the glass higher, like a toast. "Cheers," he said lightly.

I shook my head, struggling to understand how he could be so calm about this.

He understood that he'd just *proposed*, right?

Oh my God, Blake London just proposed to me.

I mean, he didn't *really* propose.

I knew that.

But my mind wasn't connecting with the rest of my body, which was reacting like he really *had* proposed. If I could somehow get my rapid pulse to slow, maybe I'd be able to process this like a rational person.

The problem was, though, that this wasn't rational. This was...impossible. This wouldn't work. Most of all, it wouldn't be *fair*. To him.

Blake wanted to save me. That was the person that Blake was. Someone who wanted to save others, save *everyone*. But he did *not* need to do this.

I cleared my throat and said his name with as much authority as I could muster. Because he liked to tease and goad, at least with me, but I needed him to be serious for one goddamn minute.

"Blake."

He lowered his glass and cleared his throat, mimicking me.

"Delaney."

His tone was as serious as mine, low and almost gravelly. But something danced in his eyes.

"I know you're trying to help, but we can't..." I sighed because I truly wished it could just be that easy. But it just wasn't. "We can't get married."

Blake nodded like he'd expected me to say that and took another sip of his wine as he thought. That teasing spark had died from his expression, and now he was considering me more carefully.

"Correct me if I'm wrong, but I thought you needed to get married to access your inheritance. That's what you told me earlier."

I pursed my lips before admitting, "You're not wrong."

"And that's why you were going to marry Long, correct?"

I didn't miss the slight bitterness with which he said Austin's name but decided it was better not to comment on it.

"Correct."

"But you can't marry me?" Blake questioned, giving me a look that, if I wasn't mistaken, harbored a bit of wounded pride.

Fuck.

He didn't understand. If I could have picked any man under the sun to fake-marry for a year, it would have been Blake. But there were reasons I never said anything about it to him.

"Correct."

Blake narrowed his eyes on me, but he didn't say anything more than, "I see."

The waiter returned, interrupting me before I could say anything further to explain myself. I tapped my fingers on the pristine white tablecloth as Blake ordered a cut of meat I didn't recognize, and then I hurriedly ordered the first thing I spotted on the menu because I hadn't even had a chance to look at it. I hadn't seen Blake look at it, either, but knowing him, he'd probably checked it online before we came and already had the whole damn thing memorized.

I felt his eyes settle back on me when the waiter left, and I took a deep breath before leveling him with a look.

"You don't want to marry me, Blake London."

His brows lifted in surprise at that, as though I had said something utterly shocking and not the simple truth of the matter.

"I'm your friend," he said as soon as he recovered. "Friends help friends when they need something. You need a husband for a year. I happen to not have a wife. I don't see what's so wrong with the idea."

"Because," I said, trying not to grow frustrated with him when I knew he was just trying to help me. "You can try to hide it all you want beneath that big brain—"

"I've never heard you give me so many compliments in one day, Lane. Are you *sure* you don't want to marry me?"

"—and teasing grin of yours, but I know you're a romantic softie who wants a wife to settle down with," I finished, ignoring him.

"I mean, I believe I just asked *you* to be my wife."

I rolled my eyes. "A *real* wife."

He leaned forward and flicked my arm before brushing his fingertip to my wrist and lightly circling the bone there.

"You feel real to me."

"That's—" My words descended into a growl of annoyance that hopefully covered up the way his touch made me shiver. "That's not what I meant."

Blake chuckled, and his hand dropped to the table next to mine.

God, he was irritating sometimes.

"I'm being *serious*, Blake."

He cleared his throat and shifted in his seat. "Right. Serious. You're very serious today, aren't you?" He took another sip of his wine before smacking his lips lightly and adding, "It's just you called me a romantic softie, and it's pretty hard to take you seriously when you say ridiculous shit like that."

"Oh, I'm sorry, did I damage your street cred?"

He rolled his eyes. "I'm not the hopeless romantic you seem to think I am."

"The twenty dating apps you're on with the bio *'looking for someone to build a life with'* could have fooled me."

"I do not have *twenty*, Jesus Christ." Blake shook his head while muttering, "She stalks my dating apps but doesn't want to marry me."

"Yes," I said before going on to clarify, "I don't want you to give up a year of your life that you could be using to meet someone who you really want to marry. Like, *actually*. Someone you can start a family and build a life with. I can't ask you to make that sacrifice for me."

Blake shrugged. "I need a break from the dating scene anyway. It wasn't getting me anywhere."

"You don't need to do this for me," I said more forcefully since it wasn't getting through his thick skull and into that big, or so I thought, brain of his. "I can't ask this of you. It's way too much."

"Well." Blake paused, tapping his finger on the table thoughtfully. "Maybe I want to. Because maybe I want you to get that inheritance money just as much as you do. After all, you want to start your own cardiac clinic. And I just so happen to be a cardiologist, too."

"You want to..." I cocked my head to the side, unable to keep the surprise from my voice. "You're interested in the clinic? But your plan has always been to—"

"Plans change, Delaney," he said, cutting me off.

He wasn't wrong; he'd already changed the plan he'd always recited to me. He'd already left Mayo, his dream hospital, prestigious and close to where he'd grown up. He was already here in Boston instead.

"I mean, of course. I'd love to have you on board at the clinic if that's what you want."

He gave a solemn nod. "I want to work somewhere that's innovative and leading change in the medical community. Is that not what you're aiming to do?"

"Of course it is."

He clasped his hands on the table again, as though things were settled. Which they were beginning to feel like maybe, just maybe, they were.

"You have to stop telling me what I want," he said, and there wasn't even the tiniest teasing glint in his gaze anymore. "I want what you want. We're friends with similar career goals who work well together as a team. We push each other to be better; we always have. We can spend the year doing just that, and when we come out on the other side, we'll be in a position to take big, life-changing steps. This is a good idea, Delaney. You don't need to feel guilty about it. You can just accept it."

The tightness in my body began to relax, and I melted back into my seat, doing exactly what Blake told me to. I started to accept it. It made me feel a hell of a lot better knowing that he had a vested interest in my goals and that his proposition wasn't just charity. Working together as a team because this was something he wanted too made it a lot easier to get on board with the idea.

The idea of getting married.

Holy shit.

I'd obviously already gone down this road with Austin, but that marriage was nothing more than checking off a box on a list. Marrying Blake was major. There was so much more at risk.

But with what Blake just said, it also left me feeling like there was so much more that could go *right*. And while that was terrifying, it was also exhilarating. Blake made my pushed-aside dreams feel attainable again. He put things into a perspective I could understand, which shouldn't surprise me. He'd always been able to do that.

"You're right. It's a good idea," I finally said, agreeing with him.

His lips spread in a slow smile. "Yeah?"

"Yeah."

He lounged back, crossing one leg over the other and draping his arm over the back of his chair like he owned the fucking room. "I'm right?"

Ah, that was why.

I pursed my lips but decided to give in to him.

It was the least I could do, considering what he was about to sacrifice for me.

"You're right." I raised my glass to mimic the toast he'd given me earlier. "Cheers, Dr. London."

He happily clinked his glass to mine, took a sip, and then set it back on the table.

"Excellent." Blake steepled his hands in front of him. "So tomorrow?"

"Tomorrow?" I parroted, my head spinning from the decision we'd just come to.

"Marriage license," he prompted. "That way, we could be married by this time next week if you wanted."

"Uh, sure. I mean, there's no..." Feeling flustered, I stopped to clear my throat before continuing. "Yeah."

Okay, so maybe I didn't quite know what to say. I was *going* to mention that there wasn't a real rush, but that would have been a lie. I already had to wait a year from the date of our marriage before I could access my inheritance, so the sooner we could start the clock on that, the better. When Austin and I had come to an agreement on *our* version of a fake marriage, he'd asked to have a little time to spend together ahead of eloping—just to test the waters. It had been a reasonable request.

But Blake and I didn't need that.

Clearly, considering how he was trying to expedite the process.

"Are there any other stipulations in your grandparents' will that we should be aware of?" Blake asked, cutting into my thoughts.

"There is a line about approval," I admitted. I hadn't looked at the will in a couple of months, not since Austin and I had made our plans, but I'd all but memorized the damn thing. I'd spent months picking it apart—first to try to find ways around what I eventually recognized as the inevitable and then to ensure that there would be no hiccups once I tied the knot with someone. "My grandparents were supposed to approve the match for me to obtain the inheritance, but since they've passed, their executor will make the call. And I think Mr. Anderson will do anything to get me off his back. I suppose there's always a bit of risk, but..."

I trailed off as my gut twisted at the thought of our fraud being exposed.

What if I put Blake through a fake marriage only for all my plans to fall apart? I'd prepared endlessly for this, but all it took was one slipup.

But Blake simply shrugged. "No risk, no reward, Lane."

"That's easy for me to say. But *you*—"

"Don't worry about me," Blake interrupted, sounding solemn and sure. How was he so sure? "Why do you think marriage was so important to your grandparents?" he asked, quickly changing our conversation's direction.

I shook my head because it was a question I'd asked myself a million times. My grandparents both passed when I was still in the early years of med school. And before their decline, despite how close we *weren't*, they'd still been incredibly disappointed in my decision to ignore all the "womanly" pursuits my mother had imposed upon me growing up so I could chase my dream of becoming a doctor instead.

I couldn't really be upset about their stipulations. It was their money to do with what they wanted, and I was still grateful to them. But it really was unfortunate that their way of thinking was just as old as their money.

So sadly, the answer to Blake's question was just as simple as

"Because, in their world, women aren't cardiologists. They're wives."

Blake sighed, just as annoyed by that reasoning as I was.

"Well, Lane. I guess you'll just have to be both."

My lips pressed together in a silent reaction as flutters tickled my insides. Whether it was anxiety or anticipation or excitement that the doors to my dreams were open again, I wasn't sure.

But I could figure that out later.

"I guess I will."

Our food showed up a moment later, and the waiter put a plate of something that smelled alarmingly fishy in front of me.

Blake looked from my food to my face, one of his brows rising in amusement.

I grimaced. "Is this really what I ordered?"

"I was going to say something, but..." He shrugged. "I thought maybe you developed a sudden taste for uncommon seafood."

He gave me a look like he couldn't wait to watch me suffer through dinner.

"I can't believe I actually missed you," I scoffed.

Blake's lips curved into a familiar smile.

And then, he offered to switch meals with me, which I politely declined.

He'd already offered marriage tonight.

He wasn't allowed to do me any more favors for the rest of the year.

ten years ago

BLAKE

"Bold move sitting in the front row of a lecture hall that has a capacity of several hundred people. You could sit anywhere, and you chose right here in the middle, huh?"

The voice was close to me. Too close, actually. I usually sat in the front row in lectures because it meant no one dared to sit next to me, but a backpack clunked down in the chair one over from mine, and I had a feeling this girl was here to stay.

"I'm not paying thousands of dollars for this course just to fuck off in the back during lecture," I muttered without looking up from my computer screen. "I don't think that makes me bold. Just makes everyone else look like they don't take shit seriously."

A soft laugh rang through the air, trickled over me like a spell, and I couldn't help it; I lifted my gaze to see who plopped down next to me. And damn, what I found was not going to be good for my GPA.

Looking over at me was a sapphire-eyed goddess with an ironic twist of her lips and long, blonde braided hair that had me dumbfounded. I'd never seen a woman this gorgeous in my entire life and certainly had never had one talk to me before.

"Well, that's something we have in common," she said, unfazed by *my brusque reply. I wasn't used to that. But I...liked it? "I'm not paying to fuck off in the back, either."*

I stared at her, because honestly, what else was I supposed to do? I couldn't ask her to move; I'd already been passive-aggressive—a Minnesotan's worst quality—about it, and she hadn't gotten the picture. I couldn't outright ask her to move, and I sure as hell didn't want to make conversation and encourage her to stay. So I just...stared.

Fuck, I needed to stop staring.

"Don't worry." She put her hands up in a defensive move, her lips curving into a knowing grin. "I'm not going to distract you."

But that was exactly what she did.

For the rest of the class.

And then the rest of the year.

And eventually, the rest of my life.

CHAPTER FOUR

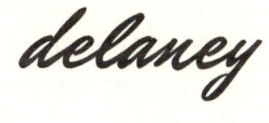

A DARK BLANKET OF night had fallen over the streets of Boston by the time Blake and I emerged from Giovanni's. Indulging in so much wine meant that putting one foot in front of the other felt criminal, but I couldn't remember the last time I'd drank something of such quality and laughed so much.

That was the thing about being around Blake; he knew how to let me be me.

The same couldn't be said for my family. Anything that involved too much emotion was somehow inappropriate. Anything that reminded them of tragedies outside their little bubble was uncomfortable. And anything that brought me happiness usually made them roll their eyes.

But with Blake, I didn't have to act a certain way or avoid talking about things that were uncomfortable. I could laugh loudly if I wanted to laugh loudly, and I could break down a difficult day at work if I needed to. We experienced the same pressures our career brought, and he got it. He got *me*.

It only took us a single dinner to get back to a place of understanding, back to this level of comfort. Which was good, considering what we'd decided on. We *had* to get here if we were going to be married—well, fake-married—for the next year.

"Where did you park?" Blake scanned the street outside Giovanni's. "I'll walk you to your car."

"Oh, I walked. My apartment's not far."

He nodded. "Then I'll walk you to your apartment."

"You don't need to do that." I tipped back against the door to the restaurant. The world careened to the side a little bit before Blake caught me by the arm and straightened me again. "Although, you might actually need to *roll* me to my apartment," I admitted.

His breathy chuckle warmed the skin on my neck, and I realized just how close he was and just how much I didn't mind. My body strained toward his, seeking an escape from the spring chill in the air.

"Come on," he murmured. "I'll drive you home. No walking or rolling needed."

"Oh, I'll be fine. I'm just being dramatic." I swatted at his chest, trying to push him away, but he was all hard and solid and wouldn't let go.

"It's late, and you drank nearly an entire bottle of chardonnay." Blake started to guide me in the opposite direction of my apartment, and I let him, feeling too warm and fuzzy to put up my usual fight. "You're not walking home alone, Lane."

"Such a gentleman today," I laughed, leaning far too much of my body weight into him as we walked. But he didn't complain.

"I don't know why you keep saying that as though I've ever *not* been a gentleman around you." He sounded affronted, and I couldn't help a giggle from escaping. But then I thought about what he'd said a beat longer, and my laugh died.

"Around me?" Something turned in my stomach as his words bounced around my buzzed brain. "Are there other girls out there getting a different treatment than me?"

He sighed, his breath ruffling my hair in a way that made a shiver work down my spine and goose bumps pebble my skin. It was just what happened when warmth invaded the chilled senses. Nothing more.

"You always get the best treatment, Delaney."

My weird, momentary jealousy slipped away at his words, and I grinned up at him. "So you're saying I'm special."

Blake laughed. That wavy McDreamy hair flopped down over his forehead as he glanced down at me. "I haven't asked any other girls to marry me today, have I?"

I pursed my lips. "You better not have."

Blake stopped walking abruptly, and I realized we'd reached his car. He kept his grip on me while reaching for the car door, as though he thought I'd fall over if he let go. For the record, I wasn't *that* drunk. But I didn't entirely mind the way he tucked me into his car, buckling me in like I was incapable of doing it on my own.

It was a rare moment. Usually, I'd fight this. But I was too tired and fuzzy-feeling to care right now. There were a lot of things I did for myself, by myself—especially in the last months since he'd disappeared. I hated to admit it, but loneliness had definitely been a factor in moving back to the East Coast. But then I got here and realized that being in Boston wasn't much better; besides Bryan, my family wasn't exactly great company. So I was still alone, still doing everything on my own.

But now, Blake was here.

And while I'd hate to make it a habit, I'd let myself rely on him, let him take care of things, for just a few minutes. Just until I got home.

He slid into the driver's seat a few seconds later, and I impulsively slid my hand over his as he grabbed the gear stick, stopping him in his tracks. Blake glanced over, his brows furrowed.

"Thank you. I realized I hadn't said that yet." I leaned my head back against the headrest because it felt too heavy to keep upright. Looking over at him from beneath my lashes, I felt my eyelids begin to droop. Damn wine. I cleared my throat and repeated, "Thank you, Blake."

His lips curved ever so slightly. "You're the one who paid for dinner while I was in the bathroom and then wouldn't let me pay you back."

I gave him a look. "I mean, it's the very least I can do, considering..."

Blake held my gaze for a long moment, strung with a tension I didn't understand. There wasn't enough light in the car for me to be able to fully see his expression, but I noticed when his eyes dropped to my hand, which still rested on top of his. I tried to quickly move it back to my lap, but Blake grabbed it before I could.

"You'll need a ring," he muttered to himself, inspecting my fingers as though he could size them out just by staring at them.

I slipped my hand out of his grasp with a shake of my hand. "You don't need to do that."

"I disagree," he said before handing me his unlocked phone to put my address into and training his attention on the road. He pulled out of the parking spot, and I started the directions. "We can't take any chances with your grandparents' executor, so you need a ring," he added.

"Fine," I sighed, knowing he was right. "But it can just be something cheap. And you need one, too."

Blake frowned, but he didn't argue. The car grew silent as he obediently followed the directions back to my apartment, and I watched the lights zip by outside the window in a blur.

Blake began to incessantly tap his finger on the car steering wheel, drawing my attention, and I looked over to see his concentrated expression. I'd always found it to be sort of adorable, the way his face scrunched up when he was trying to figure something out.

"What?" I laughed, wanting to know what he was thinking so hard about.

He blew out a breath. "Exactly *how* believable do we need to make it?"

"The more believable, the better, but I don't want you to have to do anything you're uncomfortable with."

"Did your parents or Mr. Anderson know about your engagement to Austin?"

I shook my head. "I hadn't told any of them yet. I was too worried my parents would try to put a stop to it. I knew they'd be suspicious, even though they didn't really know anything about my life in Minnesota. My plan was to call them up after we eloped and tell them the joyous news."

He nodded, taking my words in. "Is that your plan this time?"

I considered. "I hadn't really had a chance to think about it, but probably. At least they know you exist, though."

A light laugh left his lips. "What an honor."

"I know you're closer with your family," I said with a hard swallow. "So if you want to tell them the truth about the entire thing, that would probably be okay. It makes me a little nervous, but I'm sure it would be a lot harder to convince them that you eloped with a random girl who you've never even dated."

Blake laughed again, but it was humorless. "I think I can convince them," he muttered as he pulled up to the curb outside my building. "You're not a random girl, Delaney."

I shrugged as I unbuckled my seat belt. "Whatever you want to do is fine with me."

Blake nodded as he put the car in park and unbuckled his seat belt, too.

"What are you doing?"

He opened his car door and got out, calling over his shoulder, "Walking you to your apartment."

"Oh, that's really not necessary." I flew—okay, maybe stumbled—out of the car after Blake, who walked confidently to the building's front doors, holding them open for me. "I got it from here."

The stumbling aspect of my quick escape did not go unnoticed by Blake, who simply looked at me with a raised brow.

I understood he was trying to be considerate, but I really didn't need Blake going anywhere near my apartment. I was embarrassed enough that he'd seen the outside of the building, which definitely didn't have a single fleck of curb appeal. The inside of the building wasn't much better, with its chipped paint and decor that may or may not have been thrifted from the set of *That '70s Show*. And my apartment, which was almost entirely still in boxes with the occasional rodent visitor, was definitely not something I wanted anyone, *especially* Blake, to see.

"What floor are you on?" he asked as I fished out the key fob to get into the second set of doors, accessing the building.

"First," I said absently as I beeped us in. "I got it from here. Really. It's just around the corner."

"You shouldn't be on the first floor." A crease formed between his eyes as he ignored my insistence and brushed past me into the building. "You're at more risk for break-ins being street level."

"It was the cheapest option," I huffed, resisting the urge to push him back out through the door. I'd never manage. He was way too big and broad and annoying.

"You and I both know you could afford a higher floor," Blake said with a roll of his eyes.

"I could," I allowed, "but then I wouldn't be able to put most of my paycheck into savings for the clinic. Figured it would be a good idea after the whole Austin thing fell through."

Blake's gaze swept over the building entry, his lips pulling tight as he surveyed every little detail. He was always so *scrutinizing*; I knew he'd get like this. And this was just the fucking foyer.

When he reached a hallway that ran both right and left, he glanced over his shoulder at me, seeking directions.

I sighed before relenting. "Right. Apartment 117."

He waited for me to catch up to him before taking off to the right, marching down the hallway before stopping in front of my door.

"Thanks," I said breathlessly as I leaned against the entry to my apartment, hoping to bar him from entering. "You really didn't have—"

"I swear to God, if you tell me I 'didn't have to do that' one more time, you might have to find another man to marry."

"Don't make me do that," I groaned, tipping my heavy head back until it thunked against the door frame.

Blake shook his head, a smile playing on his lips again. "I'd never. Now, let's get you inside."

I sighed, knowing he wouldn't leave until I walked through this door. So, after taking a quick moment to gather myself, I turned and let us into the apartment, holding my breath the entire time.

When I didn't turn on the lights, hoping that if the unit stayed shrouded in darkness, Blake wouldn't be able to see how crappy it was, he flicked them on for me.

Fuck.

I felt his presence still behind me as the buzzing light illuminated the space. Then he cleared his throat. His voice was hard and unrelenting when he spoke.

"Delaney."

"Hm?"

I didn't dare look back at him.

"There's a rat on your stove."

I trailed my gaze over to the kitchen, and sure enough, Blake was right.

"Oh, that's Fred." I forced a laugh through my lips. "I think he's just cooking himself some dinner."

"Delaney," Blake said again, groaning this time.

"What?"

I chanced a glimpse over my shoulder to see him pinching the bridge of his nose. When he dropped his hand, his eyes met mine, and they were dark, irritation swimming in them.

"Grab your stuff," he grunted. "Let's go."

It took me a moment to register his words. "*What?*"

"It looks like it's all still packed anyway. Just tell me which boxes to load up tonight. We'll come back another time for the rest."

"What are you—" He strode past me, beelining for a stack of

boxes in my kitchen. He ignored Fred scampering across the countertop and popped open the top of one.

"Pots and pans," he muttered to himself. "I've got plenty, so don't need those."

"*Blake.*"

His head jerked up, looking surprised by my tone. And then he frowned at my indignant expression that probably told him all he needed to know about how stubborn I was going to be about this.

"You can't live here, Lane," he said forcefully.

"Well, I don't have anywhere *else* to live."

"You can move in with me. I have an extra bedroom. It's fine."

Everything about his tense tone did not make it sound *fine.*

"I can't just—just *move in* with you, Blake."

His eyes flashed with determination. "Well, I'm sure as hell not going to let *my wife* live in a rodent infestation. And no one will believe that we got married but have separate apartments. Come on."

Fuck, he was right.

Of course he was right.

But I wasn't going to tell him that. Not again. He might be doing far more favors for me than I felt comfortable with, but I was only going to allow him one *you're right* a day. Still, his logic about keeping up appearances for our marriage made an irritating amount of sense, and because the last thing I wanted was for my grandparents' executor to have *any* reason not to give me my money, I sighed and stomped my way to my bedroom to grab my stuff.

Ten minutes later, I was walking back out of my apartment, a suitcase wheeling behind me.

"I'm going to miss Fred," I grumbled.

"Is your relationship with Fred going to come between our marriage, Delaney?"

I shrugged. "It might if you keep me away from him."

A laugh filtered through Blake's sigh as he followed me out of the apartment again.

"You can see whoever you want while we're married," he said, sounding resigned. "But not Fred."

"Oh." I almost stopped walking at that comment, surprised by it and unsure what to say. I hadn't really thought that far, but I supposed there was only really one way to reply. "You too, of course. You can see whoever you want. Keep all those dating app girlies fed with a healthy serving of Blake London."

I expected Blake to laugh, but he didn't. His expression was tight as he led me back to his car. He loaded my suitcase into the trunk before opening the door for me.

"No, Delaney," he said finally. "I already deleted them."

I heard a gasp slip out of me. "What?"

"The dating apps."

"When?"

"When you were packing your things."

And with that, he closed the door, leaving me to wonder, as I was on my way to move in with my best friend, how fake this fake marriage actually was.

Definitely fake, of course.

I mean, he'd been my friend for years, and he'd never made a move, even though I'd been single the entire time. He'd go on dates with other women instead, trying to find someone to settle down with. And sure, we'd had our moments, little comments that some people might misconstrue as flirting. But that was just us, our humor. That was just Blake. And he had said that he wanted to take a break from dating for a while, so this was probably just a convenient excuse to delete his apps.

Living together and getting married wouldn't change a thing. I'd stayed over at his place before—during med school and our fellowship at Mayo. Sometimes the roads heading home would be bad, or getting off his couch to drive across town seemed like too much work. Sometimes he'd have nightmares—I knew because I heard them, not because he told me about them, not at first—and then I'd come up with excuses to stay over more often. Sleep on the couch, in case he needed me to pull him out of the past.

So, sure, Blake and I had never been married before, but we certainly knew how to coexist. Knew how to be there for one another. And this was just that. It was real, in the sense that our friendship was real.

But the marriage?

It was definitely fake.

Totally fake.

Totally.

ten years ago

BLAKE

"What is your why?"

Delaney clicked her pen as she said each word, her lips forming the pronunciations deliberately.

I really shouldn't have been staring at her mouth—again—but here we were.

"I hate this icebreaker shit," I grumbled. A lie. I didn't mind them. Actually, I kind of liked them. It meant I got to talk to her at the beginning of every class.

But I hated this specific question.

Because I didn't want to answer it.

I'd just say something cliché, something surface-level, something about how I got a scholarship to be here and couldn't turn down a funded education in this day and age, and leave it at that. I mean, it was the truth. Part of it.

Baring my soul in the front row of a lecture hall was not something I planned on doing today. And to Delaney Delacroix? I didn't need her to know this about me.

"The future Dr. London doesn't want to get to know me, huh?"

49

I sighed. "I already know you. We've been sitting next to each other the entire semester. You'd think she'd stop with the daily cohort questions already."

"But do you know my why?"

Delaney's lips spread in a smile because she knew I didn't.

Gritting my teeth together, I admitted defeat. "What's your why, Delaney? Why did you decide to go to med school?"

Her grin faded before she answered softly, "My brother. He has AVSD, atrioventricular septal defect, which means he was born with a hole in his heart. So I decided a long time ago that I want to learn everything there is to know about the heart. For him and for other people who have Down syndrome."

Her words were a punch to the gut and a reminder that I was being an ass.

"I'm sure you will," I said with sincerity. I could tell that Delaney would blow the medical world out of the water one day.

"Thank you," she murmured before looking at me expectantly. Waiting for my answer—the one I'd been planning to lie about. But I couldn't do that now, not after what she said. After she'd been honest about something that clearly meant a lot to her. The whole world to her.

"I failed to save someone once." I choked the words out. "And I'm trying to make sure that never happens again."

Delaney stared at me, unfazed by the intensity of my answer. She was never fazed. Not by me. "I'm so sorry, Blake," she said, and I could tell she meant it.

"Me too."

"Do you have a specialty area in mind?" she questioned, and I was just grateful she didn't push me to explain more about what had happened years ago.

"I've actually been thinking about cardiology, too."

"You can save a lot of lives by fixing hearts, can't you?" she murmured, her voice like a soft, reassuring hug. Like she wanted to tell me that I would save lives.

I studied the sincerity of her expression. And the hue of her eyes as she watched me back.

"Yeah." *I swallowed the lump in my throat.* "I think I'd definitely like to know more about hearts."

CHAPTER FIVE
blake

DELANEY FELL ASLEEP ON the short trip from her apartment to mine, a natural result of how much wine she drank and her long-standing ability to pass out in any kind of moving vehicle.

She left me alone with my thoughts, alone to face the slow-sinking realization of our situation.

I needed to get a fucking grip. I needed to make a firm distinction in my head between the role I had just signed up to play for the next year and reality, which was that Delaney was my *best friend*, and nothing between us had changed or was going to change. The last thing I needed was for this fake marriage to go to my fucking head.

But clearly, it already had. Otherwise, I wouldn't be carrying a sleeping Delaney in my arms as I maneuvered my way into my apartment. She'd only squirmed once when I picked her up out of the car, and maybe, just maybe, I could get her into my guest bedroom before she woke. That way, I could avoid saying any more shit tonight that would reveal too much about the reality of my thoughts and how they differed from the reality of our arrangement.

God, I wasn't going to make it through the next year.

"What's happening?"

Shit.

I could hear the fuzzy confusion in Delaney's voice and sighed at how my chest ached when I looked down at her.

"You fell asleep in the car. Like you always do."

The words came out sharper than I intended, but only because I was upset with myself. With the situation. With how much I liked the situation when I shouldn't. Specifically our current situation, with her curled in my arms.

"Sorry," Delaney muttered, a bit sheepish. Her cheeks flushed as she rubbed her eyes and glanced up at me. "You can put me down."

That would be a good idea.

A very good idea.

But I had the undeniable urge to clarify to Delaney that I wasn't upset with *her*. I wasn't really sure *how* to be upset at Delaney. So I flashed her the best grin I could muster, considering the circumstances, and walked her through the apartment to the guest bedroom.

"But I'm carrying my bride over the threshold."

She laughed the way I'd been hoping she would. "I think you're supposed to wait to do that until after the wedding."

I shrugged. "We're a bit nontraditional, aren't we?"

"Very true." She glanced around the room, which was tragically basic but clean and tidy. The only person who had ever stayed in this room before was my niece, Chloe, who was probably the most pragmatic nine-year-old to ever exist. When I asked her what color throw pillows I should get for the bed, she replied they should be black to match the rest of my lifeless style. "Nontraditional, like having two separate beds," Delaney added. "I'm assuming this isn't your room, otherwise you *really* need some decor, Blake."

"It's the guest room that you can have," I said, but the words

53

scraped my throat as they emerged. "I think nontraditional will work out best for you, considering I...snore."

"Really?"

No, not really. I didn't snore.

"Why do you sound surprised?" I shrugged. "It's not like we've slept together before."

The minute the sentence was out, I regretted it. Heat licked its way up my body as I tried desperately to keep my thoughts in check and not let them linger on my words—on the idea of sleeping with Delaney.

"Well, no. Not in the same room." Thankfully, she brushed off the comment without another thought. Not surprising since I was sure that Delaney, for one, had never once thought about sleeping with me. "But you're *you*."

"I'm *me*?"

"All pretty and annoyingly perfect."

"I'll take perfect, but never call me pretty ever again."

"*Annoyingly* perfect," she clarified.

"*So* many compliments today, Lane," I mused, which caused Delaney to smack me in the chest.

Her hand lingered there, fingers drumming on the buttons of my dress shirt before she demanded, "Put me down, you annoying man."

I nodded and tipped her feet toward the ground. Delaney dragged her fingers up my chest before wrapping her arms around my neck, holding on for balance as I released her. The result was her body slithering down mine as she found her way to the floor, and I gritted my teeth so hard that my jaw twinged with pain.

I should have immediately tossed her on the bed when we'd walked in so I wouldn't have to endure whatever this torturous dismount was. It wouldn't have been terribly out of character for us; harmless pranks were our sense of humor, and I was sure she would have just huffed with fake indignance and then laughed.

But as Delaney kept reminding me, I was a gentleman tonight.

Too bad the thoughts running through my mind at the feel of her curves pressed against me were not getting that fucking hint.

Jesus Christ.

Delaney seemed oblivious, looking around the room with an impressed expression. I swallowed a feeling of pride as she said, "No wonder you recoiled at the sight of my apartment. This place is nice, Blake."

"Thanks." I cleared my throat. "Feel free to have a look around. I'll go get the rest of your things from the car."

Delaney opened her mouth to protest, but I was gone before she could say anything.

I needed to get my fucking shit together, and I sure as hell wasn't going to be able to do it while standing in a room with Delaney Delacroix and a bed. My head needed to be clear, nothing in it before I fell asleep. I didn't need any dreams tonight. Not about Delaney. And certainly not about any of my other demons.

Moving to the coast, just miles away from the ocean, had brought back nightmares I hadn't had for a long, long time. And the last thing I needed was for my best friend and future wife to know about their return.

"What's with the emergency boxing date? It's fucking early."

Noah groaned as though he wasn't a professional athlete who basically signed up for a lifetime of waking up early to work out. Although, now my younger brother was not just a professional athlete. He was also a dad to a newborn baby.

Which was exactly why we were here this morning.

Well, sorta.

I slipped my hand into my glove and pulled the wrist strap

tight until it was exactly right. Then I gave it a little slap for extra measure and turned to the next glove.

"We're here this early because I have patients later," I replied, trying to hide that it also felt too early for me, considering how little sleep I got last night with Delaney staying down the hall. "Gemma said it would be good for you to get out of the house, and Gemma knows best."

I'd needed to get out, too. I'd walked into the one bathroom in my apartment this morning to the overwhelming smell of Delaney's perfume. Her soap. Her...*everything.*

Noah watched me warily, like he could sense there was something I wasn't saying. His green eyes flicked from the boxing gym around us to the gloves on my fists.

"Gemma does know best," he admitted. "Gemma will also kick your ass if you mess up my pretty face."

"You should be more concerned about your hands than your face. Those are your moneymakers," I chuckled, facing him once my gloves were both in place. "Don't worry, we'll skip sparring and stick to the bags. Focus more on footwork and agility. Wouldn't want to fuck up your knuckles too bad before the season starts."

Noah rolled his eyes, a bit of competitive spark in them. "Look, I know you've gotten all buff and shit lately, but you're not made of goddamn rock. And I'm not *fragile.* I think my bones can handle giving you a few punches."

"I know you're not fragile," I admitted. As much as I liked to give him shit, Noah had grit. He played *hard* in every single one of his football games. He'd built a legacy playing for the Knights the past seven seasons. "I've seen you get tackled more times than any quarterback really should. Any chance they drafted you some new offensive guards?"

"Nah," Noah replied before picking up the gloves I pointed him toward. He cleared his throat and gave me a look. "What's up with you today? You're extra...I don't even know how to describe it."

I sighed and gave him a bullshit excuse. "Work's been a bit much lately, that's all. Entering into a field that you've been training to do for the past ten years shouldn't be so fucking stressful, but it is."

Noah seemed stumped by my words. "I know the job is new, but haven't you been a cardiologist for, like, years now?"

"No, man." I laughed at his expression. "The three years at Mayo were my fellowship in cardiology. It wasn't the same." I gave him a tight smile. "There was a different kind of weight on my shoulders." Noah raised a brow, but before he could say anything, I added, "That's why I'm here. Gotta work off some steam."

I turned away from him and focused on a hanging bag, intending to give it a good punch.

And then Noah's words stopped me.

"You sure it's not because Delaney Delacroix is in Boston?"

"How the fuck—"

I whirled around to find Noah giving me a shit-eating grin.

Fucking hell.

"Gemma turned back to ask you something yesterday and saw you having quite the, uh, conversation with another doctor, and I knew immediately who it was. You, smile at work? Not a chance. Not unless it was—"

"Fuck off, Noah."

Noah's eyes practically fucking glowed with glee as he ignored me. "I told you I saw her, remember? The day Delilah was born. She passed by our hospital room. You and Nat told me I was imagining things. But I showed Gemma a picture of her last night, and she confirmed it. So don't bother lying, Blake."

Shit, I'd forgotten about that. Noah *had* texted something in the blur of all his other anxious messages about Delilah's birth. I'd just blown it off since he'd clearly been on the verge of a new-dad mental breakdown.

"Well, I figured she would have told me if she moved out

here," I said, feeling defeated at the reminder that she hadn't. "Guess I was wrong."

"Damn," Noah said with a wince as if he felt my pain. "Still engaged, then, too?"

"Actually, no," I said tentatively, fighting to hide my reaction to that and the roller coaster of emotions his words evoked. Immediate irritation that Delaney had been engaged, followed by instant relief as I remembered it had been fake, and then, of course, annoyance that I hadn't *known* it was fake.

And then there was the little reminder of who she was engaged to now.

Me.

That sparked a whole different set of emotions.

"Oh?" Noah's lips spread in a sly smirk. "So, that means..."

I hadn't precisely thought I'd be broaching this topic with Noah when I'd texted him to meet up; otherwise, I probably would have thought my next words through a little more. But as it were, I simply spit out the truth.

"So, that means she's currently sleeping in my bed."

Noah's jaw dropped before he recovered and let out a celebratory whoop that drew the attention of the few other people in the gym. It wasn't a big space, just big enough for a few rings and a slew of bags for practice. I liked it because it was low-key, designed for people who loved the sport but weren't overly competitive. So no one really seemed to give a shit about the hollers my brother just let out.

"I can't believe you actually got yourself together and made a move," Noah laughed. "I've never been prouder to be your brother." Then his grin instantly fell as another realization hit him. "Wait—I take that back. Why the hell are you *here*, then?"

I focused my attention on my gloves, adjusting the straps with my teeth as I tried to figure out what to say. I fucking hated lying to Noah. However, I didn't say anything that wasn't true. She *was* in my bed, just not the one I slept in last night. And I *did* make a move, just not in the way he thought.

And Noah's next assumption wasn't necessarily untrue, either.

"Come on, man. Don't fucking run away from your feelings now, not again." Noah grabbed my hands, undoing the straps on my gloves and shucking them off. I'd be annoyed if I didn't know how well-intentioned he was. "It's not too late. Just go grab some coffee, maybe some of her favorite flowers, and—"

"Noah," I sighed, bending to pick up my gloves again.

His brows pulled together as he watched me. "I mean, if you don't know her favorite flowers, anything will—"

"Tulips. She loves tulips."

"Good. Okay." Noah nodded with satisfaction. "Maybe you can still make it back before she wakes up. Is she an early riser?"

I shook my head, deciding to just let Noah work this through unnecessarily. "She sleeps as long as she physically can. When we had early mornings on rotations, I'd always call her to make sure she was awake for them."

"Perfect." When I didn't move, Noah urged me with a little push. "Well, get the fuck out of here, then."

"You did hear me say she sleeps as long as physically possible, right?" I checked my watch. "Give me at least twenty minutes to work up a sweat."

"Didn't work up enough of one last night?" Noah asked with a smirk.

I gave him a light shove to avoid answering, my body going rigid with the thought. I didn't bother correcting him, though. If I was going to convince my family that Delaney and I had eloped, then I might as well start now by letting my brother think things about our relationship that weren't true.

Things that would never be true.

Delaney was already married to her work. She had no interest in a real relationship with anyone. I had a feeling it stemmed from her emotionally stunted parents, combined with the need to prove herself and provide for her brother, but still. It was what she had always said she wanted, and I respected her as a friend enough not to push it. And I respected our friendship enough not to risk changing it or try to bring anything else into it.

Like the sex that Noah thought we'd had last night.

My brother relented enough about Delaney to let us get in a quick workout, and then he was pushing me out the door again. I wished we'd had more time, maybe a chance to actually talk about how *he* was doing, but Noah was right about one thing: it probably wasn't a good idea to leave Delaney for too long, even if I had put a note on the counter before heading out the door earlier.

Vowing to check in with my brother again soon, I walked back through the Boston streets, making two quick stops on the way back to my place.

A quiet calm permeated the air when I entered the apartment, which was a good sign. I put the tulips I got for Delaney in a drinking glass because I was a grown-ass man who didn't own a vase and then put her coffee on the counter next to the flowers, hoping she'd see it.

My next stop was the shower, but before I could even make it to the bathroom, I ran right into Delaney as she popped out of the bedroom, looking exactly as I imagined she would in the morning: sleepy-eyed and fucking gorgeous. Her blonde hair was slipping out of the messiest bun I'd ever seen, a huge scrunchie tied haphazardly around her hair. Sapphire eyes blinked up at me as surprise slowly spread over her features. Soft fingers were wrapped around my arm from bumping into me, and they stayed there like a grasp on reality as it came back to her.

Seeing me at work yesterday. Dinner last night. Our trip to her apartment. Me bringing her back here. I could practically see it running through her mind like a movie, and it was slightly adorable.

"Morning, Lane," I said, trying to keep my amusement to myself but failing. A smile slid onto my face.

She rubbed at her eyes before shooting me an accusatory look that likely would have had me backing down if it weren't for the way her bun flopped from one side of her head to the other when she moved.

"What's so funny?"

"Nothing," I said, biting down on my grin. "Absolutely nothing is funny." She narrowed her eyes, and I interrupted her interrogation by adding, "I got you a coffee. It's on the kitchen counter."

She snapped out of it at the mention of coffee, smiling. This girl was a glutton for caffeine, almost to a concerning degree. It paralleled her love of wine and my own caffeine addiction.

Delaney let go of my arm as she turned toward the kitchen, looking down at her fingers in a melting sort of confusion. Her gaze then snagged on my outfit, seeming to realize for the first time that I was fully dressed, shoes still on my feet.

"You're all *sweaty*," she said, her nose wrinkling.

I winced because, well, she was right. And now my sweat was all over her fingers.

"I went to the gym," I said apologetically, but Delaney didn't appear to be listening. Instead, her gaze was hooked on me, trailing over my body. I felt it, hot and acute, and it made my breath hitch. Her attention lingered on my biceps as though realizing I *had* biceps for the very first time. I mean, in her defense, they'd definitely gotten bigger lately. But still, they'd always been there.

"Would it make you feel better to know that I'm about to take a shower?" I asked, drawing her out of her intense study.

"A shower?" A fierce blush suddenly erupted on her cheeks for a reason I couldn't quite figure out. The morning sun filtered through her bedroom, hitting her face in a way that made sure I could see every shade of red. And for that, I was fucking grateful. The flush spread up her face, highlighting her cheekbones. "Oh, I, um, yeah. Sure, a shower is a good idea."

She tucked a piece of hair behind her ear before flashing a soft smile and sidestepping her way toward the kitchen. "I think I need some coffee."

Delaney disappeared down the hallway, and I released a breath of relief.

She needed a coffee, and I needed a fucking cold shower. An icy one. It would be a shock to my system, but I needed to get used to it. I had a pretty good feeling I'd be taking a lot of them from here on out.

Because in a matter of days, I'd be married to my best friend— the same woman who I hadn't been able to get out of my head since the day I met her.

seven years ago

DELANEY

"What's wrong?"

I didn't even look up from the puzzle pieces on the floor of my apartment when I replied, "Nothing's wrong."

"You've been working on that puzzle for almost four hours."

"I love puzzles." I shrugged. "You know I love puzzles."

"I do know you love puzzles." Blake's voice grew louder as he sat on the couch. I almost forgot he was still in my apartment. He'd been sitting at my kitchen table studying while I trained my focus on something I could control. Just for a little bit. "But since when does it take you so long to do this puzzle?"

I wrinkled my nose. "You say that like I do this puzzle often."

"Delaney..."

Okay, fine. This was my favorite puzzle, and sure, maybe I'd done it before. Many times. But there was something to be said for that—the satisfaction of puzzling through something you knew you could solve because you'd done it before. I needed to feel accomplished about something today.

"I just think the colors are pretty. Can you imagine seeing that many rows of tulips in real life?" I stared thoughtfully at the picture on *the lid of the puzzle box for a moment, wondering what it would be like to indulge in the little things in life instead of sifting through never-ending piles of homework. Like wearing pretty dresses and going to see tulip fields. Then I snapped out of it, because that just wasn't my life or my life goals, and looked up at Blake. "You wouldn't understand. You don't like color."*

"I like color," he said in immediate defense but didn't elaborate because he knew he didn't have a way to prove it.

CHAPTER SIX

delaney

B LAKE AND I ARRIVED at the courthouse separately, as two people getting married to satisfy an inheritance clause would. I found him leaning against a marble archway that branched off the atrium just inside the courthouse's main entrance. And goddamn, he really *was* unfairly handsome.

It had always been a fact that I'd known, that I'd been aware of in the back of my head. Just like how newborn babies have the fastest heartbeat. Or that cardiovascular diseases are the leading cause of death globally.

Blake London was an attractive man.

But that fact felt a little bit different today as I took him in while he waited for me to show up so we could get married. He stood there, the picture of nonchalance with his hands shucked in his pockets and his shoulder resting against marble. And yet, he didn't even have a hair out of place. His McDreamy waves were sculpted perfectly on his head, and his crisp, black suit had been tailored precisely to his fit physique.

My stomach flipped in a mix of emotions I didn't dare try to unpack. Not right now.

As though Blake could sense my gaze, he straightened, head swiveling to find me just inside the door. Something flickered in his eyes before he masked it and strode toward me with a wave, acting like this was the most natural thing in the world. Like we were meeting up for drinks after work or getting together to study for a final exam.

To an extent, it did feel natural. And to be completely honest, I *had* thought about this moment before.

The marriage clause was fresh on my mind when I initially met Blake in the front of a lecture hall, looking as solitary as I was at the time. He'd seemed kind of perfect for the role: an equally driven partner who had similar career goals to me.

But then I got to know Blake more and realized his goals in life were not, in fact, the same as mine. Because they went beyond a career. He came from a big, loving family, and he *wanted* a big, loving family. It made sense, something I was sure many people with normal, healthy upbringings could relate to.

Unfortunately, I was not one of them.

I was raised in the same fashion a prized thoroughbred mare might have been. Except I *did* possess enough autonomy to select not to join the race when it came down to it, and the disappointment that caused was likely as traumatic to me as it was to my family. My dad had been raised in a supremely traditional sense. He was born to manage money, whatever that really meant, and he'd found a wife who'd liked the idea of marrying into that money. My parents' partnership was as superficial as they came, and if what they had was love, I didn't want it.

The only scraps of tenderness my parents possessed were reserved for Bryan, but I wouldn't change that for the world. It was the least they could do.

So no, I'd never wanted to follow a traditional path the way that Blake did. We were two best friends aligned in every way except that one. At some point, I'd always known our lifestyles would split and go down different roads. He wanted a wife, a family, and I'd never really wanted a husband. And yet, for some reason, we'd still somehow ended up together in a courthouse.

"I'm looking for a blonde girl in a white dress. Said she

wanted to get married today," Blake teased with a crooked smile as he walked up. "Maybe you've seen her?"

I gave Blake a shaky smile. The last week had flown by, and it was hard to wrap my head around the fact that we were really here. It should feel rushed or rash. It should feel uncertain. But the truth was...it didn't. Standing here with Blake seemed like the only logical conclusion at this point.

That didn't mean I wasn't a little nervous, though.

"Don't get too disappointed, but you're lookin' at her," I muttered beneath my breath.

Blake's demeanor immediately shifted as he sensed my anxiety. He reached out to grab my hand and squeezed it.

"Never, Lane." His gaze lowered, slowly taking me in. My cheeks heated with the attention, even though I knew he was eyeing me up for show, trying to drive home the point that I wasn't the disappointment I felt like. When his eyes lifted to my face again, he held my gaze, even though it seemed to pain him slightly to do so. The slight clench of his jaw didn't go unnoticed as he dropped my hand and took a single step back. But his words were sincere when he said, "I could never be disappointed to see you. You look amazing."

I couldn't handle Blake's intensity, not today, so I dropped my focus to my shoes for a moment, clicking the pumps together while I got my shit figured out.

"Thank you. It's my debutante dress." I smoothed my hands over the silky fabric, which cinched around my waist with a tiny bow detailing before flaring in an A-line fashion, stopping halfway between my knees and feet. "But I altered it enough that I doubt anyone could tell." I cocked my head to the side as I studied the dress. "In fact, I actually kind of like it now."

I gave a half-hearted laugh before looking up to see Blake wearing a funny expression as he watched me.

"What?"

"I'm just thinking it's too bad you don't love it. You should love your wedding dress, Delaney."

"Well, it's not, you know, a *real* wedding. So whatever works, right?"

I smiled at him, but Blake's features grew tight.

"Right." He gave a tight nod. "Whatever works."

I forced an even brighter grin onto my face as I held out my hand for him to take. "Wanna go get married?"

His expression softened as he shook his head, hiding a slight grin. He took my hand and said, "Yeah. Let's go get married."

We walked together through the courthouse, my heels clacking on the marble floors as we made our way to the correct room, following the directions they'd given us when we'd made the appointment.

And then there was no looking back. Everything moved in a whirlwind around me, and before I knew it, I was standing before a judge with Blake across from me. The elderly officiant was saying words that would tie us together, at least for the next year, and asking us to exchange rings.

My pulse had been hammering since I'd walked in to see Blake waiting for me, but now it was *racing* as Blake pulled a ring out of his pocket. And then it stopped. My heart, the thing that kept me alive, that organ I'd spent years of my life studying, halted. Because the ring that Blake presented to me was the most extraordinary piece of jewelry I'd ever seen in my entire life.

There was something about it so perfect, so precious, that I couldn't hold back my gasp. It echoed through the courtroom, making the judge chuckle in delight, and I slapped a hand over my mouth, slightly horrified that I'd let that slip.

When I looked up at Blake, an unrestrained grin spread over his face, one that told me he felt damn good about shocking me, trying to best me as usual.

Well, I'd give it to him this time. The wedding band I'd gotten him was nice but nothing compared to the extravagance of the ring he slowly slid onto my finger. I marveled at how perfectly it fit, at how confident Blake seemed as he pushed the band into place, at how lucky I was in this moment. And not just because of the ring.

"Blake," I said, my voice a mix of admonishment and awe. I had no idea where he had gotten a vintage sapphire and diamond-encrusted ring, but it was too much. Way too much. "Blake, I can't—"

"Shh," he murmured, his voice brushing against my senses like velvet. Soft and smooth. "You think anyone would believe I wouldn't get my wife a ring as stunning as she was?"

He winked at me before shooting a glance at the judge as if to remind me that we were being watched.

I cleared my throat and nodded as I pulled out his wedding band from the hidden pocket in my dress. He let me slide it on his finger, smiling as I fumbled with slightly shaky fingers.

I'd been the one who'd been preparing for a fake marriage for years, but for some reason, *he* was the one who was so calm and collected about it, even though this had only been his reality for all of a week.

Especially when the judge told Blake he could kiss the bride, aka *me*, and Blake didn't even blink in response. Meanwhile, panic bubbled up inside me because while I'd thought of the dress and the ring and the marriage license, I had not given one single thought to the very real possibility that *this* could happen. Which was ridiculous, as evidenced by how Blake leaned in, clearly prepared to seal our marriage with a kiss.

People kissed at weddings.

I wasn't sure why this hadn't crossed my mind before, but now it was the only thing in it as Blake's palm slid across my cheek, cupping my face and angling it up toward his.

"Hey," he breathed, and the sound of his voice instantly put me at ease.

"Hey." I blinked up, our eyes meeting in a moment of mutual understanding. What that understanding was, I couldn't really pinpoint. But I felt it. I felt *him*, and I leaned into his touch, letting him guide us closer together.

"I'm going to kiss you now." His words were a low murmur brushed across my lips, and my body reacted on autopilot, seeking the kiss. Suddenly *wanting* the kiss. We were so close, and the proximity was intoxicating in a way I didn't understand but didn't care to.

"Okay?" he checked when I didn't reply, and I barely nodded before Blake's mouth slanted over mine, capturing it.

A feverish need flooded my senses in a way I never imagined possible as Blake kissed me. His tongue swept into my mouth as if that was where it belonged, tangling with mine in a way that made it seem like he'd always wanted to do this, like he'd always wanted to taste me.

I groaned, which should have embarrassed me, but instead, I instinctively wound my arms around his neck, pulling us closer, *needing* us to be closer. Blake broke the kiss, but only for a moment, only to brush his lips over mine in such a tender caress, one that completely contrasted with the way he swore gruffly under his breath and the way he dove back in for a deep, unrestrained kiss a second later, dipping me back with a dramatic flair.

When he tipped me up again and broke the kiss, we were both breathless. The kiss hadn't been long, but it had been inexplicable and unexpected, and Blake's rough breaths against my lips caused an unbidden desire to pool in my gut until he moved away. Disappointment bloomed inside me, and I frowned with confusion that got swept away as Blake's mouth trailed to my ear.

"Figured we'd need the practice if we have to be convincing newlyweds for a year," he said, his husky voice making my skin pebble with the awareness of him. It sent a jolt of heat through my body that I desperately wanted more of. But Blake pulled away, and then I felt adrift.

"I think we're gonna nail it," I somehow managed to whisper in response.

He leaned back, and there was something I didn't expect to see in his face—a wretched sort of despair that he quickly blinked away, masking it with a light smile, the twinkle in his eye return-ing. He took a deliberate step backward while simultaneously grabbing my hand, keeping me at arm's length.

"I think you're right."

There was something off about him, but when he said those words, I couldn't detect anything that wasn't just...Blake.

My best friend.

My husband.

His grin grew as it was announced that, on this random Tuesday afternoon in the last week of April, we were now Mr. and Mrs. London.

CHAPTER SEVEN

> MOM: We're SO excited for you, honey!!

> MOM: I forgot to ask on the phone this morning. Did she like the ring???

> DAD: It's about damn time, son. Happy for you.

> She loved it, mom.

At least, I hoped she did. But my mom didn't need to know just how much of yesterday felt a little unclear.

> And thanks, dad. Appreciate it.

I sighed, ignoring the bad taste in my mouth from telling my parents half-truths. We didn't always get a chance to talk regularly; they were just as busy as me, my mom running a pet rescue organization in the Twin Cities that kept her going all day long to save as many animals as possible and my dad working as a security guard with long shifts. But still, I'd never purposefully kept things from them. I was their oldest of five, and our relationship had always been really transparent.

But this was just how things had to be. At least for now.

I switched over to a different thread, the one with all my siblings.

Hey guys, I wanted to let you know some news.

NOAH: Oh, I think I know what this is.

NAT: Do I know what this is?

Neither of you know what this is.

Well, Noah kinda knows.

NOAH: Fuck yeah, I do.

NAT: Why does Noah know and I don't?

SULLY: Oh, thank fucking God you texted us. Otherwise I was about to spill it myself.

Wtf? You don't even know what I'm going to say.

SULLY: Yes, I do. You called Mom, and then she got lunch with me to gossip about it.

I rolled my eyes at the direction this conversation was going, but I wasn't surprised. The whole reason I'd pulled my phone out to text my brothers and sister was to tell them before my mom spilled the news. And it looked like I was already too late.

SULLY: Am I mad you've deprived me of a reason to party? Absolutely. But am I even happier that you finally got the girl so you can stop depressing everyone with your moping? Hell to the fucking yes.

SULLY: Congrats, bro.

SULLY: How'd you do it?

SULLY: I need details.

NOAH: Sul, no. Just no.

SULLY: What? You don't want to know how he proposed?

NOAH: PROPOSED?

THEO: Wtf is going on?? You're blowing up my phone in the middle of a lecture. 120 college kids aren't learning right now because of you.

NOAH: I told you to pick up her favorite flowers and some coffee, not a RING.

SULLY: Oops, I'm gonna shut up.

SULLY: But first, speaking of rings...you should maybe work on that yourself, Noah.

Delaney and I eloped. Here's a picture of us yesterday at the courthouse.

I sent the picture in the group chat, wanting to get to the point before the entire conversation unraveled. And save Noah from having to reply to Sully.

NAT: OMG, BLAKE.

NAT: Congratulations! You both look stunning.

I looked at the picture of the two of us, taking in our happy expressions. We'd taken the photo for evidence and had posed to look like newlyweds might right after tying the knot. Delaney had her hand on my chest, ring on display, her chin tipped as she looked up at me, eyes sparkling. And since her smile was the most contagious thing in the world, I had a wide-stretched grin plastered on my face as my eyes cut down, looking over her as she stood beside me in her wedding dress.

The picture was fake, but I liked to think some bits of truth were woven into it.

THEO: Wow. Congrats, man. I think I'm missing some pieces to this story, but I don't even really care right now. Happy for you.

NOAH: Holy fuck.

NOAH: Okay, I'm with Sully.

NOAH: I want to know the details now.

SULLY: See??

I shook my head, undeniably a little entertained by their reactions. I probably should have called them all separately to tell them about it, but we were a busy crew. It would have taken ages to get each of them on the phone, and then it probably would have resulted in a ridiculous argument that one of them knew before the rest.

I'm at work, but we'll have to catch up. I can tell you all more about it soon.

> NAT: I'm calling an emergency sibling dinner. This weekend. Chloe and I will host. Bring Delaney and Gemma!

> NAT: And Delilah of course.

> SULLY: Some of us don't live in Boston, Nat.

> NAT: You and Theo can join virtually. 7pm Saturday. See you there!

Christ.

I slid my phone back into my pocket, sighing as the lies I'd just told sunk deep in my gut. They undoubtedly thought this was sudden—any sane person would. But they'd be happy for me anyway. My siblings were well aware of how much Delaney meant to me. They knew that it had wrecked me when she'd gotten engaged to someone else. So as wild of a lie as this was, I'd known my family would believe it.

Which said something about how truly fucked I was.

I tried to pull my attention back to my charts. I'd never had a harder time concentrating at work than I did today. It didn't even have to do with the fact that my pocket kept buzzing as my siblings continued to plan the family dinner that would be an absolute terror to get through without slipping up.

No, even if my phone was dead silent, I still wouldn't have been able to concentrate. Because I was fucked in so many ways besides lying to my family. It was entirely my fault, considering I'd been the one to propose to Delaney. And that proposition had led to the events of yesterday, the ones where I'd married my best friend and kissed her in a way that wasn't the least bit friendly.

I shouldn't have done that. I should have given her a chaste kiss that wouldn't have given anything away, like how much I'd been dying for that—dying for her mouth on mine, her taste on my tongue, her breath hitching because of my touch.

Fuck, I'd wanted it, had been wanting it, and the reality of it, of *her*, was beyond anything I ever could have imagined.

Just *thinking* about that kiss and what she'd tasted like made me hard to the point of goddamn pain, and I didn't know what the hell I was going to do about it. I'd never touched myself while thinking about Delaney before because I respected her too fucking much. I put her in a box labeled *"friend, best"* in my head and didn't go near it or dare to open it with any thoughts in mind except for appropriate ones.

But that was before I knew what her lips felt like. That was before we'd gotten married and kissed—things that didn't belong in a box labeled *"friend, best."* And now I was going wild, drowning in desire without any relief.

But I'd had to kiss her like that.

For one, it was the only opportunity I'd ever probably get to kiss Delaney Delacroix—scratch that, London.

Delaney London.

Oh my fucking God.

I dropped my head into my hands in the spare exam room and groaned. A goddamn name wasn't supposed to put me into this much of a spiral. My cock wasn't supposed to twitch in my fucking pants from just the thought of her name. But it wasn't just her name anymore; it was *our* name. Delaney thought it was best to take my name—with the exception of remaining Dr. Delacroix at work—to make this seem as real as possible, and fuck, did it feel real. Too real. And that was what undeniably drove me wild. That and the memory of that kiss.

I shouldn't have given it to her, but I didn't want our one and only kiss to be something she wouldn't remember or something I'd regret. Not to mention, she'd shown up at that courthouse looking so fucking despondent, like she wasn't sure if she should be making me do this, like this was the best and only wedding she would ever have, and maybe that *did* make her a little bit sad— even if she didn't want to admit that to herself.

There'd been a wistfulness in her; I'd seen it when she looked down at her dress, one that she'd worn before and reminded her of an upbringing that she despised. And all I'd wanted to do was kiss those thoughts away. I couldn't go back in time and make sure she wore the wedding dress of her dreams or had a ceremony that wasn't rushed through in a courthouse. But I could kiss her like any girl deserved to be kissed on their wedding day. It was the least I could do.

And then, Delaney had done something that I still couldn't wrap my head around.

She'd responded.

She'd groaned into my mouth, and that little sound was going to reverberate through my entire being for the rest of my fucking life.

I'd known for years that Delaney and I had chemistry—chemistry that she viewed as a compatible friendship. And having proof that maybe that chemistry was a little bit more than she expected was both satisfying and destructive to my sanity.

I dragged a hand down my face and forced myself to stop thinking about it. I needed to get through the rest of the workday without losing my shit, and then I needed to figure out how to spend the evening in the same vicinity as Delaney while pretending I wasn't simultaneously elated and depressed about being her (fake) husband.

I hadn't exactly done a great job last night; I'd spent so much time preparing for the wedding—ensuring I had the ring, the license, the balls to kiss her—that I hadn't thought much about what would happen immediately *after* the wedding. The result had been to order our favorite combination of pizza that we'd relied on so many times as starving med students—pineapple and pepperoni—while sitting on the couch in our wedding clothes and binging the last season of *New Girl*. Which was, arguably, the worst one.

Not a stellar first night as a husband, fake or not.

Checking my watch, I stood and took a deep breath. I'd been lingering in here for too long after my last patient and was going to be late for my next one if I didn't pull it together. So I tucked Delaney deep in the corner of my mind in a box labeled *"wife, fake"* and *"friend, best"* and strode into the hallway, maneuvering around the nurses and other physicians until I found where I was supposed to be next.

This was a new patient, but I'd met her dad on a number of occasions. It was one of those tricky things about being a doctor; you never really wanted to see someone you know end up in one of your exam rooms because that rarely meant something good for them.

But I was providing a second opinion today, and from what I knew, the first opinion was good news for the patient.

I heard the sound of a giggling toddler before the door was even open, and I smiled as I greeted Gracie Elez-Everett first, bending down to say hi before turning to her parents—her very famous, very high-profile parents, who were also some of Noah's best friends from college.

"Hey, man," Grayson said first, shaking my hand with a firm grip. "Thank you so much for fitting us into your schedule."

"Yes, thank you *so* much," his wife, Nessa, echoed. "We're so grateful that you were able to meet with us."

"It's my pleasure," I said honestly. I'd always liked these two. "I'm sure your schedule is a hell of a lot busier than mine." I paused in thought, cocking my head at Grayson, who played in the NFL like Noah. "Have mini camps started for you yet? I know they haven't for Noah, but I don't know enough about it to know if they are all at the same time or how that works."

"Not yet," Grayson replied with an easy smile. "I've got a few weeks still. Get to spend more time with the kids and be Nessa's number one fanboy at her upcoming shows."

He glanced at his wife, his expression so full of adoration that the moment suddenly felt intimate.

Noah had told me that it was always like that with them, and since he'd said that pre-Gemma, when he'd been a cocky playboy, he'd mocked their obsession with each other a little bit. But all I felt when I looked at these two and their daughter bouncing on Nessa's knee was envy.

But I swallowed that envy and smiled. "Where's your other little one today?"

"Gabe's back home with his Uncle Beau and Aunt Collins, getting undoubtedly spoiled," Grayson replied.

I chuckled, recognizing the names as more of Noah's college friends. Then I turned to Nessa, also known as the indie pop sensation Wednesday Elevett. Delaney listened to her music sometimes, but I'd never told her I'd met Nessa years before she grew into fame.

"Any of those shows around here?" I asked.

"Sadly, no," Nessa said. She had a twinkle in her eye like she knew that was probably for the best. Like I wasn't *actually* interested in going to one of her performances.

But it would have been fun. I could have brought Delaney. Surprised her.

"Just a few in New York," Nessa added, which piqued my interest.

That wasn't *that* far away.

I nodded before turning my attention to the real reason we were here: their daughter.

I'd been prepped on their history before their appointment today, so I knew that Grayson was born with a congenital heart defect, coarctation of the aorta, which had been passed on to their older son, Gabriel. Only the defect hadn't been detected at birth, despite Grayson's perseverance in having him scanned for it. His aortic coarctation wasn't discovered until Gabriel was four or five when Grayson took his son back to his own childhood physician for a second opinion.

Gracie's early scans did *not* show evidence of a heart defect. This was what her doctor back in California had told Grayson and Nessa after her birth, but they were skeptical, understandably. And they wanted a second opinion.

Coarctation of the aorta was manageable and treatable, as

evidenced by the existence of Grayson, a star athlete in the NFL. I had my own slight concerns about that, especially as Grayson pushed toward thirty, but that was beside the point of why we were here today.

If aortic coarctation was left undetected, there was a high level of risk, which was also evidenced by Grayson, who suffered a stroke and fell into a coma when he'd been in college with Noah. Such as in Grayson's case, it was possible that even after corrective surgery, re-coarctation could occur, resulting in constricted blood flow and forcing the heart into overdrive. But in most circumstances, correcting the defect when patients were young provided good outcomes for a healthy childhood and adulthood.

"So I took a look at Gracie's scans," I said, settling into the desk space in the exam room and swiping my badge on the computer to pull up her file. "And I have good news."

I could practically hear how both Nessa and Grayson held their breath at my words, and I looked over at them with a reassuring smile before Gracie drew my attention with a gurgling giggle. She was an adorable mix of her parents. Her dark brown hair, matching Nessa's, sprouted from her head in ringlets, reminding me of a hobbit child. And her piercing grayish-blue eyes were the same ones boring into the side of my head, coming from the chair where Grayson sat.

I looked over at him, meeting his concerned gaze.

"I didn't see anything that's a cause for worry," I said before pulling up the scan to show them myself. I wasn't sure if their previous doctor had done this, but I liked my patients to know my reasoning and feel confident in what I shared with them. When Grayson and Nessa seemed convinced with that, I added, "But we can absolutely run another set of tests for me to take a closer look. I could also, with your permission, pull in my wife to review the results of the new scans. She's a cardiologist at SCMC who I know has had experience with cases such as yours, and I'm sure she'd be happy to consult with me on it."

I'd expected it to be hard to remember to refer to Delaney as someone more than a friend or a colleague, but the words came out with so much ease.

My wife.

She was my wife.

Even if it was just a legality, I didn't fucking care.

Grayson's expression shifted at the mention of Delaney, like he couldn't decide if he should have known that I had a wife. I could tell he was wondering if it was something Noah had told him, and he'd forgotten, or if congratulations were in order. Ultimately, he decided not to say anything, staying focused on Gracie.

I was fine with that—less faking for today.

"I would like that," Grayson said, and why wouldn't he? Money wasn't an object for them, and he came with baggage that I could tell weighed on him. There was guilt in his eyes, guilt that he could pass on something that could possibly harm his children. "Anything we can do to make sure nothing is missed."

"Sure," I said with a nod, "let's see what we can get scheduled for today. And then after I consult with Dr. Delacroix on the results, I'll reach out to you to discuss."

Grayson gave me a grateful look before I turned back to the computer to get everything set up so I could put his mind at ease.

Delaney didn't hear me walk into the apartment when I got home from work, even though she was sitting on the couch, well within earshot. Her attention stayed trained on the puzzle spread across the coffee table, a wineglass dangling between her fingers. She stared without touching it or moving the pieces.

She did this sometimes, zoned out. She got lost deep in that beautiful brain of hers, and I couldn't even blame her because I'd spend my days there, too, if I could.

But this evening, I took the opportunity to study her profile, the graceful curve of her nose, her long, windswept bangs framing her heart-shaped face, and the slight rosiness of her cheeks—likely from the wine.

My eyes dropped to the ring on her finger, and my stomach twisted into knots.

Would I ever get over that?

I hadn't been sure if she would wear it all the time or just when the occasion called for it, and to see that it was on her finger now, when there was no one else around, made a smile creep onto my face.

I took a careful step forward, not wanting to startle her. It was probably inevitable at this point, but I'd still try.

"Lane," I said softly, dropping my keys on the kitchen counter.

She jolted a little, as I knew she would, but recovered quickly, turning to face me with a friendly smile.

"Oh, hi." She sounded breathless. "I didn't hear you come in."

"Thinking about work?" I asked. "Long day?"

That was usually what it meant when she brought the puzzle out. She was doing her favorite one, too—the one with the tulip fields.

"Thinking about..." she repeated like she was processing the question. Her cheeks flamed brighter, and she quickly sipped her wine before nodding. "Yeah, just some work stuff on my mind." She sat up straighter, folding herself onto the couch and tucking her bare feet beneath her bottom like she always did. "How was your day?"

"Pretty good." I hooked a finger into my tie to loosen it and then walked over to Delaney, feeling her gaze trail me across the room as I sat on the couch next to her. "I got permission to run this case by you. Can I?"

"Of course." She cleared her throat and put her glass of wine on the coffee table before us. "Tell me about it."

Her eyes turned eager, as sharp as her focus suddenly became, and I launched into a rundown of Gracie Elez-Everett's case and shared the scans with her. Even though I got written permission from Nessa and Grayson to divulge everything, I decided to keep their identity to myself. Delaney wasn't the kind of physician to let a patient's high profile distract her from providing sound medical advice, but I didn't want to take any risks or derail the conversation from the point.

Delaney tracked the details easily like I'd known she would, and I was happy, but not surprised, that her consensus was the same as mine after she reviewed the results from today. As her original doctors in California had determined, Gracie had *not* inherited her dad's congenital heart defect. There really hadn't been a question in my mind about the results, but if Delaney's input could provide Grayson even further relief, this conversation was necessary.

"Coarctation of the aorta *is* more commonly found in males than females, so it isn't terribly surprising that her brother was born with the heart defect, but she wasn't," Delaney commented thoughtfully before picking up her wineglass again with a note of finality.

"I was thinking the same thing," I said, nodding. "Thanks, just wanted to make sure I wasn't missing anything."

That, and I'd wanted to talk to her about something that would bring us back to our roots, to where our friendship belonged—intertwined with medicine and professionalism and our careers.

She gave me a thoughtful look.

"What?"

"Since when do you miss anything?"

"Don't act like I don't make mistakes, Delaney. I'm not perfect. My flaws go far beyond being a condescending asshole sometimes."

If she knew some of the things that went on in my head, especially where she was concerned, she'd undoubtedly agree.

"Oh, stop." She ran her finger up and down the fringe on one of my throw pillows, her eyes watching the movement instead of me. "Do you still feel like yesterday wasn't...a mistake?"

"I don't have any regrets about yesterday," I said without a second thought. I should have regretted the kiss, but I didn't. My only regret was that I hadn't done more to commemorate the day, even if that might have alarmed Delaney, considering our marriage wasn't *real*. "Do you?"

I held my breath as she took longer than normal to respond, but then...

"Of course not. It's really more than I could ever hope for."

I nodded. I might have spent the better part of the day in agony while replaying the events of yesterday, but that didn't mean that it wasn't also incredibly satisfying to help Delaney chase her dreams. She deserved them.

"You might change your mind when I tell you about our plans for the weekend," I said dryly.

Delaney's head popped up, curiosity glittering in her gaze.

"*Our* plans?"

I sighed before admitting, "London family dinner at Natalie's."

"Oh." She tipped her head to the side, adorable confusion still playing out on her features. "But I'm—"

"A London now," I finished. "And my siblings have a lot of questions about that fact."

Her lips popped apart in both understanding and surprise, and I couldn't help but trace the curve of her mouth with my eyes, my thoughts immediately deteriorating into a place they shouldn't be. Heat licked every nerve ending in my body as I remembered how eagerly that mouth had met mine yesterday, and I had to drag my attention up to her eyes. But fuck, they'd been watching me. And there was something I hadn't seen before in her gaze, something...alive.

"You told them already?" she said after a tension-filled beat of silence.

"It would have killed my parents if I didn't tell them right away, so I called them this morning," I replied. "But news travels fast in the London family, so I knew it wouldn't be long before my siblings knew anyway."

Delaney took in the information with quiet consideration.

"Okay." She flashed me a nervous smile. "Dinner with the London family it is, then."

I went to grab her hand, wanting to reassure her, but thought better of it. Touching Delaney right now when I still hadn't gotten over touching her yesterday seemed like a bad idea. So I gave her a relaxed grin instead.

"It'll be fun," I said, hoping I could speak that fact into existence. "My siblings are all way nicer than me anyway."

"I'm sure that's not true," she scoffed.

"It is," I argued. "I'm only *usually* nice. They're always nice."

Well, they weren't always nice to *me*. But they would be nice to *her*, of that I was certain. Especially since it was the first time Noah and Natalie were meeting her, considering we used to live in different states until recently.

Delaney gave me a teasing little shove before returning to her puzzle, leaving a spark of heat in her wake. My body tingled from that touch, and I wondered how the hell she didn't feel it, too.

But I'd been wondering that for years, and just because there was now a ring on both of our fingers didn't mean that was about to change.

Nothing between us was going to change.

But for some reason, I just couldn't shake the feeling it already had.

CHAPTER EIGHT

delaney

I'D EXPECTED THINGS TO feel fundamentally different after Blake and I got married, but they didn't. And I couldn't decide if I was grateful for that...or disappointed.

A week ago, there would have been no decision. I would have been grateful, end of story. Period. In this scenario, what could I possibly be disappointed about?

But a week ago, I'd never kissed my best friend.

A week ago, my lips had never touched his, and my body had never ached for the feel of his hands.

And a week ago, I didn't have to try to figure out how I felt about that.

Blake, on the other hand, seemed completely unfazed by it all. I'd moved into his apartment, put his ring on my finger, and life had moved on. It was like we were still in school together, except years had passed, we were legally bound together for the next year, and the patients we were discussing were real and not case studies.

And that was *fine*. Great, actually. But considering the way my brain hadn't stopped spinning since our lips had broken apart at the courthouse, I needed to set some parameters for this fake relationship. Otherwise, I was going to get too far into my head about it all.

"I think we need some ground rules," I said as soon as we got into the car to head to the London family dinner. My stomach was already tied in knots at the prospect of spending the evening with his siblings, and the thought of having this conversation was not helping, but it needed to be done.

Blake lifted a brow as he checked behind him for any traffic. "Ground rules might have been an important conversation to have *before* we tied the knot."

"Yeah, well..." I shrugged. "Before we tied the knot, I didn't know you were going to kiss me like that."

Blake went momentarily still before he swung one arm behind my seat and single-handedly backed out of the parking spot. Humidity flooded the car—a sweltering heat that I would have blamed on East Coast summers...except it was only spring.

I leaned forward to turn on the air-conditioning.

"Kissed you like what?" Blake asked once we were situated on the road. There was a light, teasing quality to the question that I recognized.

"Like—" I bit down on my tongue, forcing myself to filter my thoughts for once.

Like you wanted to kiss me.

Like you wanted to do more *than kiss me.*

Blake cleared his throat and took pity on me, not forcing me to finish my sentence.

Or maybe he realized what I was going to say and didn't want to confirm or deny it.

Either way, my silence was for the best.

"So you want to have ground rules about what? Kissing?" he prompted, sounding suddenly serious. His eyes landed on mine for just a moment, grounding me with his sincerity, before they flicked back to the road. "I won't do it again if you don't want me to, Lane."

Oh, God. And now he thought I was *upset* about the kiss.

Was I upset about the kiss?

It certainly would have made things easier if he hadn't kissed me, so maybe I was upset about the circumstances *surrounding* the kiss. But the kiss itself?

No, I wasn't mad about that.

I shook my head. "Not just about kissing. Ground rules about what we're both comfortable with, I guess. When we have to fake things over the next year."

Blake swallowed. A crease deepened between his brows before he finally asked, "Did I make you uncomfortable?"

"No," I groaned, dropping my head into my hands to hide for a second. I was starting to wish I hadn't brought this up, but it seemed important. Especially considering how we were going to have to spend the night trying to convince his siblings that this marriage was real. And there were four of them. Four people who knew Blake better than anyone.

"Delaney..." Blake urged softly when I still hadn't emerged from my hiding spot in my hands.

I sighed and lifted my head. "No," I repeated. Clearly, so he wouldn't misunderstand. "You didn't make me uncomfortable. I just think we should be, I don't know, on the same page about that sort of thing."

He nodded slowly, like the words were coming into his head at a slower pace than I was saying them. "I agree," he concluded. "Tell me what you're comfortable with, then."

I shifted in my seat, for some reason taken aback he'd asked me for specifics when in reality, it was a perfectly sensible follow-up question. But it wasn't that I was uncomfortable with anything he had done or likely would do. He had *surprised* me. *Confused* me. *Shocked* me to my fucking core.

"Can I hold your hand?" he prompted when I didn't say anything, and I couldn't help but laugh because of the sheer ridiculousness of this conversation. Blake had held my hand a number of times. Waiting for exam results. An encouraging squeeze at the end of a long shift. A steadying touch when he could sense I was about to lose my balance. But now, because of two little rings on our fingers, we were overthinking everything.

Or maybe it was just me.

When I looked over at Blake, his expression was just as serious as the last time I'd checked.

"Yes, you can hold my hand," I answered because he seemed to be waiting.

He gave a perfunctory nod. "I want to know what you feel okay with, Lane. And I'm just starting at the bottom and working my way to the top."

I couldn't fault him for that or for what he was trying to do. I'd asked for it, after all. But that didn't mean I knew what to say except for, "What's at the top?"

I immediately regretted asking the question. Especially when Blake's gaze momentarily met mine in the rearview mirror, and I couldn't understand the look in them. All I knew was that it made me cross one leg over the other and clear my throat as I waited for his reply.

"Whatever you want to be at the top," he said, his lips twitching before his gaze darted away from mine, focusing out the window instead.

I gave his arm a playful smack. "You are *not* being helpful."

"I'm trying to be *considerate*."

"Such a gentleman lately," I murmured beneath my breath, and Blake rolled his eyes. But when he didn't say anything further, I shot back, "Why don't *you* tell me what you're okay with to make this marriage believable? You're the one who was dragged into this, and it's your family that we're going to see tonight."

Blake sighed heavily.

And then, without looking away from the road, he said seven words that shocked me almost more than the kiss had. Seven words that made it feel like lava had replaced the blood flowing through my veins. Seven words that absolutely could not mean what they sounded like.

"You can do anything to me, Delaney."

His voice was low, barely audible above the thrum of the car engine. But there was no hesitation, no consideration. I traced the angles of his handsome face while he stared straight ahead, searching for any signs that he might not be telling the whole truth. But I couldn't find a shred of evidence that he wasn't.

"Careful what you sign up for," I said with a laugh for levity. "I'll end up writing medical terms all over you again."

But Blake just shook his head, remaining as serious as ever.

"Fine by me. And any public displays of affection that you think will help are okay with me, too," he clarified. "Physical touch doesn't make me feel uncomfortable, not from you."

I nodded because that made sense.

"It doesn't really feel weird to me, either," I said honestly.

"Good," he husked, and I noted how relieved he looked.

A pang of guilt hit me; I hadn't meant to make him feel like he'd done anything wrong. Being close to Blake wasn't strange. And it didn't make me feel uncomfortable. In fact, it had always been the opposite. I could relax around him in ways I couldn't with anyone else.

But being romantically close to Blake, even if just an act, was *different* than I was used to. And I didn't know how to handle it.

I cleared my throat and asked, "Can you maybe just give me a warning if you're going to kiss me like that again?"

"Wow," he chuckled, but it was humorless. "It really bothered you. Fuck, I'm sorry."

"No, it didn't—" I broke off with a grumble of frustration. "I'd just appreciate a heads-up, that's all."

Blake frowned. "Saying '*I'm going to kiss you now*' wasn't enough of a heads-up?"

"You're right." He was absolutely right. He *had* warned me. I'd known he was going to kiss me, but that wasn't the problem. Blake clearly wasn't getting it, and I didn't want to spell it out for him that the issue wasn't the kiss; it was that it had felt real. Because maybe the reason he wasn't getting it was that it hadn't felt real to *him*. He'd probably thought it was unextraordinary. This was apparently a *me* problem and nothing more. "Never mind. I'm just going to...shut up."

A dreadful silence settled over the car before Blake spoke up again.

"You, uh, sure you're okay? I've never seen you so flustered before," he commented lightly, but I heard the deeper questions in his tone.

"We've never done this before," I tossed back, trying to keep my tone just as casual. But I was sure Blake noticed the way I squirmed in my seat as he pulled up to the curb outside of a brownstone I assumed was Natalie's. "I don't really know how to act."

"That's fair." Blake put the car in park before turning in his seat, giving me his full attention for the first time since we'd started this conversation. I felt my cheeks heat as his eyes roamed my face, searching it for...something.

He seemed to find whatever it was because when he spoke next, it was businesslike. Authoritative.

"How about you follow my lead, then. Does that sound good to you?"

I nodded.

"Okay, here's what's going to happen." He paused to rake his hand through his hair, and I watched it flop perfectly back into place afterward. Magical. "We're going to go in there, say hi to everyone, ask Natalie if she needs any help, and after she says no because Natalie never lets anyone help, we're going to go sit down. Noah will probably have some kind of sports playing on the TV. I'll sit down on the couch, pull you onto my lap. You'll put your arm around me. We'll pretend to be sickly obsessed newlyweds until it's time for dinner, where we'll sit next to each other. I'll scoot even closer to you than is necessary before tucking your hair behind your ear and staring longingly at you instead of remembering to eat." His lips tipped up in amusement before he shrugged and finished with, "Before we know it, it'll be time to leave, and we'll say our goodbyes. Are you okay with all of that?"

A flush had worked up my neck as Blake spoke, but I couldn't exactly say why. He wasn't saying anything scandalous; in fact, everything he was saying was very matter-of-fact. A perfect plan, all laid out. I could appreciate that because it was how he spoke about medicine, and it put us back into a realm that my brain could make sense of. Even if the words themselves didn't make any sense at all.

"Yes."

It was the one word I could manage. Truly pathetic after how many words Blake had just said.

"Good." He met my gaze with his usual intensity, but it felt stronger than normal. "Don't worry, okay? I won't kiss you again. And of course, I'll only touch you if the occasion calls for it. If there's an audience. How's that for ground rules?"

"That sounds good," I acknowledged, thankful I was able to say more than one syllable now that I'd recovered from his rundown. "But Blake, I wasn't *worried* about the kiss. I'm committed to making this believable. And if the occasion calls for it..."

My voice trailed off, but Blake understood.

"Alright. If the occasion calls for it," he repeated, an agreement of sorts.

And then he got out of the car, leaving me to wonder what kind of occasion that might actually be.

But I didn't get too long to think about it because my phone rang. Looking down at the number, I froze.

"Do you need to get that?" I heard Blake ask, his car door still open.

"It's my grandparents' executor. I sent him our marriage license earlier this week, so..."

"So you should probably get that," he confirmed.

Fuck.

As if I didn't have enough to be worried about at the moment.

93

Grimacing, I looked down at the screen for a moment before answering the call.

"Ms. Delacroix?"

The older man sounded more panicked than I would have expected, which did not help the feeling that had settled in my gut.

"Mr. Anderson." I tried not to audibly gulp down my nerves. "It's actually Mrs. London now, but how may I help you?"

I glanced at Blake, who was now leaning down to look into the car, right at me. His gaze flared bright.

Was he nervous, too?

"Yes, that is...why I called. I received the copy of your marriage certificate in the mail. And while I know it is not business hours, I didn't want to wait to reach out and verify with you."

I nodded, aware that Blake's eyes were glued to my movements. "Yes, we eloped earlier this week. My husband and I were just going to celebrate with his family."

"I, um..." The sounds of shuffling paper broke through Mr. Anderson's words. Then they stopped, and I could picture his dark brows furrowing as he stroked his salt-and-pepper mustache. "I wasn't aware that you were intending to wed, Ms.— Mrs. London. This has just come as a surprise."

A humorless laugh broke through my lips, and I looked outside the window, studying the traffic as it drove by in front of Natalie's home. "Well, that is the point of an elopement, isn't it? To be a surprise."

"Yes, I suppose it is."

Mr. Anderson didn't sound entirely convinced, so I lowered my voice to add, "Blake and I have been very close for many years. And when we finally realized how we both felt, we didn't want to waste any more time than we already had. Surely you understand."

He cleared his throat. "Of course. Yes, of course. Congratulations on your marriage, Mrs. London."

"Thank you." I smiled to myself, hoping it came through in

my voice. "You should know that I have not yet informed my parents but am planning to do so soon."

"Oh, good." His relief was palpable, even through the phone. "I'm sure they will be glad to hear it from you."

I frowned. Was *he* thinking of telling them? In that case, I was glad that we'd had this call. I didn't need a surprise from my mother tonight as well.

"Yes, I know you are often in, um, business with my parents, so I will let you know when they are aware of the elopement."

"Perfect." More relief. "That works perfectly. We will be in touch, then."

I hung up the phone with a weird feeling in my stomach but struggled to place it.

Mr. Anderson didn't give the impression that he intended *not* to approve our marriage in terms of the inheritance, but he didn't seem entirely convinced, either. Or maybe he just didn't like the idea that his approval would undoubtedly put a wrench in his working relationship with my parents since they'd oppose it—we both knew that to be true.

It was something I hadn't quite considered until now.

"Everything good, Lane?"

I nodded, putting those thoughts away for now, and turned toward Blake, who I'd almost forgotten was there.

"I think so, yes."

"Ready for dinner?"

Taking a deep breath, I forced a smile. "Ready."

I was even more glad we were doing this now, pretending for his family. We needed to cover all our bases, just in case Mr. Anderson came poking around.

Natalie's home was a brownstone apartment with bay windows that I would die for. It was small and a bit dated but had crown molding and a fireplace with books stacked on top of the mantle. The coziness made me want to curl up on the couch, and that was precisely what I did.

But with a six-foot-two, finely muscled doctor beneath me.

Everything happened as Blake predicted, and now I was sitting on his lap in his sister's living room. A baseball game was on in the background, but no one was really paying attention to it.

The only thing I could pay attention to was the man whose lap I was on.

We were on the end of the couch, and I'd leaned back, wrapping my arm around his shoulders like he'd told me to. His arms circled around me. One was settled securely around my waist like he thought I might flee, and his free hand rested casually on my thigh. His fingers kept grazing my bare skin as he fidgeted with the hem of my dress, and I was so acutely aware of him in a way I never had been before. Every tiny shift of his body was as obvious as an earthquake with deadly magnitude.

Blake, on the other hand, was unfazed. He'd introduced me as his wife to his sister, Natalie, and his nine-year-old niece, Chloe, without batting an eye. They'd both given me hugs like we'd known each other forever, even though this was our first time meeting.

I'd heard a lot about Natalie over the years, but we'd never crossed paths before; from what Blake told me, she was an incredibly busy woman between parenting as a single mom and working as a trauma surgeon. He also said she'd been busy and overworked her entire life, starting in high school when she'd taken so many PSEO courses that she almost had her bachelor's degree completed by the time she'd graduated.

After our introduction, Natalie had ducked back into the kitchen and shooed us toward the living room, where the infamous football player, Noah London, sat with his family. His girlfriend, Gemma, whom I recognized from the hospital, gave me the warmest greeting, and I immediately felt guilty for how I'd judged her that day. Then, Noah smiled broadly and held out his hand to shake while his other arm was preoccupied with holding the baby I'd thought was Blake's. Her name was Delilah, and she was precious and sweet and couldn't have been much more than a month old.

If it weren't for Noah, I might have felt weird about sitting all wrapped up in Blake in front of his family. But Noah had immediately pulled Gemma into his side when they sat back on the couch, and he hadn't once moved his available hand away from her. Blake's gentle affections only matched the vibe of the room, and I was grateful for that.

It only took me a few minutes to decide I liked Noah. I couldn't lie; for years, I'd held a slight distaste for Blake's younger brother simply because of his reputation and how people treated Blake when they found out he had a famous athlete for a brother —like he was a stepping stone of sorts. But in real life, Noah seemed charismatic and kind and *clearly* devoted to his girlfriend and daughter.

He also seemed *very* curious about his brother's spontaneous marriage, which in any other circumstances would have been sweet. But it only put me that much more on edge.

"You could have called me, you know," he said, a twinkle in his eye as he glanced at his brother. I recognized that twinkle. It was the same teasing spark Blake had, except Noah seemed to have it more openly. Blake's only appeared when we were alone. "I could have been a witness."

Blake chuckled, and I felt the vibrations of it through my entire body, making me tingle deliciously. I bit down on my lip, trying not to react as Blake carried on like nothing had happened. Like we weren't suddenly connected in a way we never had been before.

"You don't need a witness in Massachusetts," he said with a shrug.

Noah shook his head, grinning. "Sully's still mad you've deprived him of a party."

"I'm sure there will be another reason for the Londons to celebrate soon," Blake said, his smooth voice more pointed as he looked between Noah and Gemma, who began blushing furiously at the comment.

"Very true," Noah hummed, glancing over at his girlfriend with stars in his eyes. *He* wasn't embarrassed by the comment. It actually looked like he was melting inside from the thought of it. My cheeks started to heat just from watching the two of them.

Or maybe it was from the way Blake's hand slid across my rib cage slowly like he was trying to feel for the bones and count them to make sure I was real and alive. He dragged his hand all the way across my abdomen, skirting just below my breasts before letting his touch vanish, his hand dropping to his side.

That was for the best. The more Blake touched me, the more I worried that he would realize how my pulse ticked up. He was a doctor—a very good doctor—trained in looking for subtle differences in the body, symptoms, and signs of distress. I was exhibiting too many of those at the moment.

"How did the two of you meet?" I spit out, looking for something to say to distract from Blake, from his woody scent overwhelming me and the compelling job he was doing of making his family believe he wanted his hands on me as much as his brother wanted his hands on his girlfriend.

Gemma's head popped up like she'd been abruptly pulled out of a trance. Noah turned his attention toward me more slowly, as if he had to be dragged away from looking at his girlfriend.

Gemma managed to answer me first. "Noah is a close friend of my brother," she said sweetly. "Julian and Noah played football in college together, but we reconnected more recently because Chloe is one of my figure skating students," she explained, nodding to the nine-year-old who'd just entered the room in a ball of energy, making a beeline for the baby. She walked straight up to her uncle, bent down to inspect her cousin with soft eyes before she looked up, and they widened into the perfect puppy dog plea.

"Can I hold her?"

Noah's grin kicked to the side. "Sure, Lo. Sit next to me, okay?" She hopped onto the couch next to Noah, settling in and holding her arms out, ready for a baby deposit.

I smiled at the scene, watching Noah carefully place his daughter in Chloe's arms, who held very still. She seemed practiced, like they'd gone through these motions before, and it was so precious that my heart felt like bursting.

Noah observed Chloe holding Delilah for a few moments before switching his attention back to me. "Yeah, these two are quite the skating stars," he said, warmth in his tone. "Chloe actually has her first show next week."

"I've always wanted to learn how to figure skate," I admitted, smiling at Chloe, who had lifted her head, realizing we'd been talking about her. She wore a sheepish smile that told me she loved the attention but would never admit it. "It's so fun to watch. I bet you'll do amazing in your show, Chloe."

"You should come!" she encouraged, her eyes alight with a glow now. "And then Gemma can teach you how to skate!"

I laughed, feeling infected by Chloe's contagious enthusiasm. Before I could respond, Gemma chimed in.

"It's never too late to learn, you know."

"I'm sure Delaney would pick it up quickly," Blake added, his breath warming the exposed skin on my shoulder. But my body responded like a bucket of ice water had been dumped over me; goose bumps pebbled where I felt him. Which was everywhere. "All the years of dance would help, right?"

"Oh, absolutely." Gemma perked up. "What kind of dance?"

"Ballet," Blake answered, seeming eager to share that about me. Seeming eager to play the role of a husband wanting to show his wife off. I'd never been particularly proud of my years as a dancer because it only reminded me of the things I did to make my parents happy, but in this moment, I suddenly felt differently.

"She's a ballerina," he added, as if it weren't clear enough. And then he brushed his lips over my shoulder, in the exact spot I'd felt his breath a moment ago. Where goose bumps had pricked my skin. He smoothed his lips there like he was trying to get rid of them. But all he was doing was making it worse.

"I *was*," I clarified, "but I'm not anymore," I said, trying not to sound as breathless as I felt. "And I'm sure dancing on solid, dry ground is a lot different—easier—than dancing on ice."

I could feel Blake hovering over my shoulder. More accurately, I could still feel his lips. The ghost of them. His breath fanning over the spot he'd just kissed. A shiver worked through me, and Blake pulled me in closer. There wasn't an inch of separation between us.

"Classical ballet training is absolutely an advantage when learning to figure skate," Gemma said sincerely. "Let me know if you ever want to try it out."

I smiled at Gemma, trying to focus on Blake's sweet family and not the confusing way my body reacted to his. "I will, thank you."

"Are you cold?" Blake whispered in my ear. Once again, I could feel his lips, but this time, he didn't let them touch me. I couldn't decide which was worse, having his mouth on me or wanting his mouth on me.

I shook my head, not trusting myself to look back at him.

Natalie entered the room a second later and announced it was time for dinner. Noah helped Gemma to her feet and then took Delilah from his niece. The four of them started to make their way to the dining room, but I didn't know how to move.

"Did this make you uncomfortable?" Blake asked quietly once his family was out of earshot.

I shook my head again.

Uncomfortable and confused were not the same thing.

"You still okay with me taking the lead?" he asked, trying to get more out of me.

I nodded, twisting to look at him for the first time since we'd sat down. His dark eyes were earnest.

"You're very good at it. You're doing a better job than I probably would."

Blake chuckled lowly at that. "Yeah, well..." He trailed off. "My family is affectionate. I know what they probably expect to see."

I nodded again. That made sense.

"They like you," he added when I was silent. "I can tell."

"It's nice to meet the rest of your family after so many years."

"Yeah." Blake's lips lifted in a small smile. "It's nice."

He looked at me, and there was something different about it. But then he shifted beneath me, and I realized it probably had something to do with the fact that I was still sitting on his lap. I still had my arm around his shoulder, like I was holding him captive. So I slid to my feet with as much grace as I could muster, tugging the hem of my dress down as I started to walk after his family.

We'd only been playing this game for a matter of days, and I was already forgetting when I could stop acting. I had a feeling that might become a problem, but I couldn't spend my time worrying about it now.

Not when I had a family dinner to perform through.

CHAPTER NINE
blake

I WATCHED DELANEY WALK away and blew out a breath between my lips, willing her not to look back. There would be no hiding the tent growing in my pants from the way she'd just slid off my lap, her ass rubbing against my dick as she dismounted.

Fuck, I'd been doing so good at keeping myself in check.

Yeah, maybe I'd let myself get too carried away for a bit there because holding her felt like the most natural thing in the world. But overall, I'd kept my shit together. Somehow, I'd managed to keep my thoughts far away from the reality of the situation. I didn't think about how good she felt. Didn't think of how perfectly she fit in my lap. Didn't think about how dizzying it felt to breathe her in. Didn't think about how soft her skin was. Didn't think about what she felt like beneath my lips.

I didn't think about any of that because Delaney would have instantly known that I was thinking about it. I'd be having the same problem I was having now. She undoubtedly would have felt it, felt *me*, and I couldn't risk that.

But now? Now, as she was walking away, her hips swaying as she flicked that sweet-smelling hair of hers over her shoulder?

Yeah, I was thinking about it now.

And I needed to stop.

We still had dinner to get through, a dinner where I had to convince my siblings that this was real.

When Delaney disappeared into the dining room, I stood and adjusted myself before following her. I could hear Sully's voice from here, saying hi to Delaney and welcoming her to the family. Theo said something next, but I couldn't quite make it out. His voice was softer, his tone deeper. When I rounded the corner, a flash of blonde hair drew me in, and I found my way to Delaney's side. I pulled out the chair for her, and she smiled at me over her shoulder before sitting.

"Theo is a Dr. London, too, right?" she checked, speaking softly while the rest of my siblings carried on around us. "He has his doctorate?"

I nodded. My younger brother was a professor at the University of Minnesota.

"And what does Sully do again?"

"Software developer. He could have a PhD, too, if he wanted." I snorted. "But he couldn't be less interested in schooling." I picked up a bottle of wine off the table and poured her a glass. "You'll need this," I said, handing it to her with a wink.

"What a gentleman," Sully drawled, his voice growing louder to capture my attention. He clapped his hands mockingly, and I glared at the laptop propped on the corner of the table where Sully's and Theo's faces floated on the screen in a video call.

"Fuck off, Sullivan," I muttered, and my brother laughed.

"What was that, Blakey? I couldn't hear you all the way over here in Minnesota."

Settling in my seat next to Delaney, I turned to my sister. "Nat, there's this annoying buzzing coming from your end of the table. I think it's the computer. Could you maybe close it for me?"

"No!" Sully leaned in, plastering his face far too close to the camera. Next to him, Theo was shaking with laughter. "I promise I'll be nice. I won't even complain that you didn't invite me to your wedding."

Gemma cleared her throat as she gave Sully the side-eye. "I don't know if you know this, but we actually all gathered here today to discuss *your* love life, Sully. How's that going again?"

Sully threw himself back into his chair dramatically, pretending he was mortally wounded. Then he recovered, his face coming back into view with a grin on it. "Gemma, you're always such a sly little—"

"Careful how you finish that sentence," Noah grunted, but there was a curve to his lips because Sully would never cross that line. Gemma knew how to keep the London boys in check, and we loved her for it.

The first time she came to visit in Minnesota, she wasn't even dating Noah, but she called me out for acting like a jealous asshole to him all the same, and honestly, I think she saved our relationship a little bit. I loved my brother, and while I had no interest in his fame or money, the people I met always did. And since that sometimes got a little old, my bitterness showed. Gemma was right to call me out on it.

"Sully's too busy pining over his ex to have a love life," Theo said, which caused Sully's jaw to drop and the rest of my siblings to raise their eyebrows with interest. It was typically an unspoken rule not to bring up exes at the dinner table, especially not Ellie, the woman everyone thought at one point that Sully would marry.

"Hey," he said defensively as soon as he recovered. "As it would turn out, hopelessly pining for years works out for some people. Take a look at—"

"Okay, that's enough," Natalie intervened, and I'd never wanted to hug my sister more than I did right now. I had no doubt in my mind that my name had been the one about to come out of my brother's mouth. "Chloe, can you start passing the salad around before your uncles derail the entire dinner?"

Chloe giggled as she picked up the salad bowl and passed it to Gemma, who gave her a little wink when she took it. I chanced a glance at Delaney as Theo switched the conversation to the NFL draft, asking Noah for his thoughts on the Knights' picks. Delaney gave me a reassuring smile, and I reached over to tuck a piece of hair behind her ear just like I told her I would.

Except no one was really watching us, and it was probably bad timing if the point was to be convincing newlyweds. I needed to be better about this, more intentional, instead of just taking advantage of all the opportunities to touch her.

I'd spent years tiptoeing around my attraction to Delaney. *Years* carefully ensuring I never crossed a line that would ruin our friendship. And while I was selfishly enjoying this little scenario where I got to pretend she was mine—even if for only a few hours here and there—I was cognizant that I could still accidentally cross that line.

When she brought up boundaries in the car on the way here, I thought that was exactly what had happened. I'd been momentarily gutted when she'd brought up the kiss, at least until the groan of frustration she let out told me I was reading the situation wrong. But I wasn't sure I read the situation right, either, and I was still on edge, still worried I'd do something wrong, even though all of this felt so right.

"Hey," she said because I was still looking at her.

I liked that I had an excuse to do that now.

"Hey," I murmured, my lips tugging up into a smile that she owned. She saw it, too. I could tell by her expression that she saw the difference between how I looked at her and how I looked at everyone else. She knew we understood each other in a way no one else did, and to her, that was all this look was—an inside joke, a trading of secrets, an insider glimpse that only two people who'd known each other for years and had gone through the worst of it together would understand.

Funnily enough, she was the only one who didn't know my biggest secret—as evidenced by how Sully had almost just blurted it out like it was common knowledge.

It practically was.

"What are you newlyweds doing for your honeymoon?"

I froze. Delaney's eyes grew wide, and I forced myself not to react before turning toward Noah, who had asked the question.

"Oh, I..." I hesitated to clear my throat, hoping the answer would come to me. And, of course, my youngest brother took that opportunity to pounce.

"You didn't plan a wedding, so I sure as hell hope you're planning a honeymoon, Blakey."

"*Sullivan*," Natalie hissed, and I decided I owed my sister an entire week of babysitting. Maybe a month. "You're about to get kicked out of family dinner."

"I'm sure he has something planned," Noah cut in, trying to smooth things over, and then Delaney attempted to do the same thing, which genuinely pained me.

"You know, it's not easy for two cardiologists who just started new jobs to find time for a honeymoon. It's just not really in the cards for us," she said with a dazzling laugh, attempting to appease my family and give me an out. And she wasn't wrong; Natalie nodded across the table with sympathy, knowing the truth of Delaney's words all too well.

But something about it didn't sit right with me. The way Delaney shrugged off the idea of ever being able to go on a honeymoon reminded me of how she talked about her wedding dress, the one she liked but didn't love because it was a repurposed debutante gown. I knew this marriage was fake, but that didn't mean it had to be a disappointment. I didn't want it to be a disappointment.

"But we'll have to manage it because I already booked our flights for next week," I lied before I could think too much about it, and Delaney whipped around, her eyes scrutinizing me in a way the rest of her expression couldn't in front of our audience. But her shock was still apparent enough that I had to smother a chuckle and add, "It was going to be a surprise. Sorry, sweetheart."

Her lips parted as her eyes bored into mine, trying to figure out if she could lie over my lie. She reached out, her hand slipping onto my thigh in a way that caused a jolt of heat to course through me. She squeezed my leg, and while it probably looked affectionate to the rest of my family, I knew it was a *what the fuck* squeeze.

Her lips pulled into a confused grin, and I had to give it to her —she was playing the part well. "What are you talking about, Blake?"

All I did was smile. "You have a passport, right?"

She nodded slowly. "Yes, I have a passport."

"Perfect."

"Where are you going?" Noah asked through a bite of chicken, and Gemma promptly elbowed him hard enough that I heard him grunt.

"Maybe he wants it to be a surprise," she hissed.

"It's okay," I laughed because there was one place I'd always wanted to take Delaney. And suddenly, I didn't have to worry about what to say at all. "Delaney had an obsession with this puzzle all through med school."

"It was not an obsession," she muttered, even though I glanced over to see her looking a little dazed. She still had her hand resting on my thigh, and I reached down and curled my fingers around hers, squeezing them.

"It was, but it was a cute one, Lane. You did that puzzle until the cardboard edges were fraying."

Her lips twitched like she wanted to smile but was too confused about what was going on to let herself.

"The puzzle was a picture of a tulip field," I continued. "There's one lone windmill surrounded by thousands of tulips in all different colors. One time, she asked me if I could ever imagine seeing that many rows of tulips in real life. I didn't have an answer at the time, but things are different now. And it just so happens that the tulips are in bloom this time of year. It's just getting to the end of the season, but I think we can still get there in time."

Delaney stared at me. And then she started to shake her head, in denial of everything I'd just said. The room was quiet, the silence eating us alive, until Natalie broke it.

"Shut up, that's so cute."

Still, I didn't look away from Delaney.

Not until my sister gasped, yanking my attention away.

"Oh, and the *ring*," she crooned, leaning forward to get a better look at Delaney's hand, the one that wasn't in my grasp, from across the table. "Blake—"

"One thing at a time, Nat," I laughed. Nervously, hoping my interjection would distract Natalie from bringing the ring up again. "So, what do you say?" I asked Delaney, even though there was really only one thing she could say right now, considering the circumstances. There would be a car conversation later, I was sure. But I couldn't help but hang on to her response all the same.

"Blake," she said breathlessly, a smile creeping onto her face to mix with slight exasperation. She couldn't believe what I was spinning this into, and I could also tell that her speechlessness wasn't fake. And I was maybe enjoying that a little too much. "Yes."

I squeezed her hand in response, and all she could do was shake her head with a growing grin.

This was the third time I'd gotten a yes out of Delaney Delacroix since she'd moved to Boston.

Marriage. Moving in. Honeymoon.

And I knew they all had asterisks next to them, but at the moment...frankly, I didn't care.

I followed Natalie into the kitchen after dinner, even though I knew she would argue with me about doing the dishes. But she'd already done enough as a hostess tonight, and my sister was tired. I could see it in her face, and while I might not be able to fix all her problems, I could clean her kitchen.

"Thanks for dinner, Nat," I said as I plucked the empty salad bowl out of her hands and took it to the sink. "I've got it from here."

"Oh, Blake." She sighed, her eyes rolling up. "Thank you, but you know better than to leave Delaney at the hands of our siblings. Go back out there with her."

"She's not with our siblings," I said pragmatically. "She's with Gemma, Chloe, and Delilah in the living room."

Natalie nodded her head from side to side, satisfied with that answer and coming to the conclusion that Delaney would, in fact, be okay given her current company.

"Get yourself a glass of wine and relax, Nat," I encouraged, and that seemed to be all I needed to say. Natalie grabbed a bottle of pinot off the counter and filled a glass with it, sighing heavily for the second time.

"Thank you." The words were muttered into a wineglass, and I chuckled before starting to load the dishwasher.

"That asshole still causing you problems?" I ventured lightly, not sure if she'd want to talk about her ex-husband right now. But I also knew that Natalie didn't have a whole lot of people to talk to. She didn't slow down enough to talk, not unless it was carefully scheduled into her life. So maybe now was the perfect time.

She nodded, glancing at Noah as he walked by her carrying a load of dirty plates. "He's filing for more custody of Chloe, and I need a new lawyer."

"Why?"

"My previous divorce lawyer is no longer practicing."

"I could just kick that asshole's ass," Noah muttered beneath his breath as he lowered the plates into the sink.

I nodded, on board with this plan. "Noah and I could show up at his office. Have a nice little chat."

"*Don't* do that," Natalie said pointedly, glaring at the both of us above the rim of her wine glass.

Noah's shoulders slumped, relenting because we both knew Chloe was what was at stake here.

"Fine, then at least let me find you a lawyer. I think Julian and Juniper are visiting Juni's sister in New York this week, but when they get back, I can get you in touch with them."

Natalie frowned. "Thanks, but I'm not sure I can wait a week before at least getting the process started and having contact with someone about it."

Noah slipped his phone out of his pocket. "Then I'll ask them if they know anyone else who can help."

Natalie nodded, and even though she didn't say much, I could see the mixture of distress and relief on her face. Noah crossed the kitchen and pulled her into a hug, which she detached from her wineglass to return until Noah's phone buzzed with a response. Pulling away, he looked at the message and then said, "Oh, duh."

Natalie cleared her throat and went to retrieve her wine again. "What?"

"Julian said to reach out to Cameron, which I should have thought of."

"Do I know him?" Natalie asked, rubbing her forehead like she had a headache coming on. Or maybe she already had one.

Noah pocketed his phone and pursed his lips as he thought. "I don't think you've met Cam. He went to law school with Jules, and now they work at the same firm, but we originally met because his sister, Collins, went to undergrad with us."

Natalie rubbed her forehead again, and I couldn't blame her. Keeping up with Noah's friend list that mostly stemmed from his college experience was exhausting sometimes.

"Got it," she muttered. "Well, if you could send me his contact info, that would be amazing."

"Will do," Noah said as he pulled out his phone again.

"We'll get this sorted, Nat." I wiped my hands on a nearby towel, abandoning the dishes for a second to wrap my arm around my sister's shoulders and give her a squeeze. "It'll be okay."

"It will," she agreed with a nod I could tell was fake. "But don't worry about it. We're here to talk about *you* tonight." She gave me a little elbow nudge, her lips stretching into a smile as she glanced over at me. "You finally got the girl. I'm happy for you, Blake."

I grinned back at her, but I knew it was lacking. I didn't *really* get the girl. And the realization of that was so much heavier when my family kept giving me that look and congratulating me on something that wasn't real.

Natalie immediately clocked me. "What's wrong?"

I shook my head, prepared to feed her some lie or another, but then changed my mind and said something that had a semblance of truth.

"I'm worried I made a mistake."

When Noah's head snapped up and Natalie's brows rose straight into her hairline, I quickly amended, "Not because I don't want this. It's the opposite. I want this—her—*so* much, and I don't want to mess it up. I hope I didn't mess it up."

Natalie's expression softened. "I don't think you messed it up. It's clear how deep your connection with Delaney goes, even though you got married so quickly. You think we didn't notice that you were having whole conversations with your eyes?" A gentle laugh fell from her lips before she pursed them, and I knew there was more she wanted to say that she wasn't.

"But what?"

"Just..." Nat shrugged. "Well, I just think there's something to be said for the dating phase. And even though you're already married doesn't mean you should skip it."

"In other words, you better take that girl on a date," Noah said, jerking his head toward the living room. "A lot of them."

"Thank you for explaining that for me, Noah." I rolled my eyes before glancing through the doorway. I could see a sliver of Delaney from this angle, her shiny blonde hair and flowery dress, and felt my lips cracking into a smile I couldn't control.

Fuck me.

I inched closer to the doorway and realized that Delaney was holding Delilah in her arms, looking down at her sleeping form.

This time, it wasn't my lips that cracked; it was my chest. It cracked wide open.

"My career keeps me so busy that I could never imagine my life with kids," I heard Delaney say. Her voice was a soft hush, a rare little confession directed at Gemma, who sat on the sofa beside her. "But I also..." Her voice dropped, but Gemma gave an encouraging look, and Delaney shrugged with a smile. "I never really imagined I'd be married, either."

Those words had haunted me for over a decade. Those were the words that kept me in check all these years. Delaney never wanted a husband. We'd only made it here by happenstance. But regardless, it was nice to see Delaney have an authentic moment with Gemma. Maybe they'd become friends. That would be good for Lane. For both of them.

"Sometimes things don't go as planned," Gemma said with a warm look at her daughter. "And sometimes that really is for the best."

I hoped to hell that Gemma was right about that. Just because it had worked out for her and Noah didn't mean it would work out for us.

"Go ahead." Natalie's voice startled me from behind, and I whirled to face her. "Don't worry about the dishes. Go get your girl and get out of here."

I grinned crookedly. "Kickin' me out already, Nat?"

"I'm kicking you out *with love*," she laughed, and I knew it was the truth.

I walked into the living room as Delaney was handing my niece back to Gemma. She heard my footsteps and turned as soon as Delilah was out of her arms.

"Hi," she said breathlessly, her vibrant gaze flicking over me in a way that got my blood pumping faster and fucked with my head. Thank God that look was for the benefit of Gemma because I could barely handle it without exploding.

"Hey, sweetheart," I murmured, and a flush of color spread over her cheeks. Had no one ever used a term of endearment with this woman before? She was watching me like she wasn't used to such romantic softness, and fuck, I hated that when I'd been wanting to give it to her for so long. "Ready to go?"

She nodded and stood, taking my outstretched hand. I was ready for the heat of her touch this time, but that didn't mean I didn't feel it. I felt it everywhere. You'd think I'd be used to it after years of proximity, that maybe it would fade, but it only ever burned stronger, brighter.

Delaney took that moment to flash a shy, seductive smile at me, almost like she could feel it, too. Like she knew what she was doing to me.

That couldn't be the case, but that still didn't mean that I wasn't fucked.

Especially considering the honeymoon we had ahead of us— the one I was suddenly determined to take my best friend on.

ten years ago

DELANEY

"Can I ask you a question?"

I had no business asking this question, but it was one o'clock in the morning, and I couldn't study anymore.

Blake looked up from the textbook he still had his nose in.

"You can ask me anything, Delaney."

His immediate answer, so confident and sure, made something skip inside me.

"It's...personal."

"Even more personal than one of Dr. Keilly's icebreaker questions?"

"Actually, it's a follow-up question to one of those."

Blake closed his textbook and sat straighter in his chair at my kitchen counter. He cleared his throat. Preparing to answer me, maybe. Or shoot down my question, more likely. Because he clearly knew what I was about to ask.

"Who..." I started before clamping my mouth shut. I didn't have any right to bring this up. "Never mind."

"It's okay," he said, but he didn't look like it was okay. He looked exhausted, and I hated my impulsivity for speaking thoughts aloud that I should have kept inside. "I didn't know them."

"What?"

"The person I couldn't save?" he prompted.

I nodded slowly, letting him know that we were on the same brain wavelength. Still, I wanted to stop him. Tell him he didn't need to say anything more. But then he kept going, the words spilling out of his mouth like he'd been waiting to release them.

"I didn't know them," he repeated. "She was just a stranger, a young woman, at the beach when I was nineteen. My first spring break, first time at the ocean. I'd gone down to Florida with some guys from my freshman dorm. I watched her get pulled into a riptide. Well, I didn't realize that was what it was at the time, but I watched her... struggling. Jumped in without a second thought. I was a strong swimmer. I grew up spending summers on the lake." He paused. Looked down at his closed textbook. "A lake is different from an ocean. I thought maybe I was going to get swept away, too. I couldn't—"

"Blake." I leaned across the countertop, putting my hand on his. "You can stop. You don't have to tell me."

He shook his head, seemingly determined. "I got her out, but it was...I didn't know what to do. I mean, I understood the basics of CPR, but I wasn't trained in it. I hesitated before starting chest compressions. She was lifeless. The lifeguards made it to our side within a minute or two and took over, but it...she didn't make it, Lane." His voice trembled as he finished.

The confession that I suspected Blake hadn't spoken in years hung between us. My pulse raced, and I could feel Blake's hammering in his wrist.

"Blake, you have to know that wasn't your fault," I pressed after a beat of silence.

"I hesitated."

"Not when you jumped in the water, you didn't. That was a big risk, and you took it anyway."

He stilled, considering my words. But then he shook his head.

"A risk that meant nothing. I should have been able to save her."

delaney

B LAKE PUT HIS HAND on the small of my back as we walked out of his sister's brownstone, and I felt it hovering there until we reached the car, making my pulse feel like it was on a roller coaster.

It was good we were leaving. Not because I didn't have a good time, but because it was starting to be too good. Too comfortable. Too real. I was married to Blake, but I wasn't *married* to Blake, and I never *ever* imagined I'd need to give myself so many reminders of that.

Blake opened the door for me before I could reach for it, and when I turned to comment about his uptick in impeccable manners, he put a warning finger up.

"Don't."

"What?" I laughed as I slid into the passenger seat.

He tried to glare down at me, but his lips kept curving without his permission, and it ruined the effect he was going for. "Stop saying shit about how I'm suddenly a gentleman because it's making me feel like I've been an asshole to you for years."

He leaned over me, resting one elbow on the car and the other on the car door. I had to tip my head back to look up at him. "You've never been an asshole to me," I said because it was true.

117

Blake's expression smoothed at my words, but then I added, "Just everyone else." At that, his lips pulled taut, gaze flicking up the sky as if he couldn't bear to look at me any longer. Then he strode around to the driver's seat.

"I'm *kidding*," I assured as he slid into the car beside me.

He raised a brow at me. "Somehow, I don't think you are."

"*Everyone* else is definitely an exaggeration."

"Sometimes people deserve to be put in their place," he muttered as he started the car, and the air blew through the vents. I angled them so they hit me square in the face. I'd been over-heating since Blake pulled me onto his lap a few hours ago.

"I would agree," I said with a nod.

"Like when Dr. Arnold tried to tell me the best course of action for that endocarditis patient was to—"

"I know, Blakey," I interrupted before he started down a long rabbit hole of doctors he'd clashed with during residency. It was a conversation I was more than familiar with, and we didn't need to rehash it right now.

His eyes cut over me, glittering. "I'm never letting you hang out with Sully again."

"Aw, but I really like Sully."

Blake narrowed his gaze in a silent accusation. He had one hand on the steering wheel and the other on the gear stick, but we hadn't moved from our parking spot. Blake was too busy glaring at me.

"Stop," I laughed, patting him on the arm. "I like my London men all broody and contemplative. Don't worry."

But that didn't seem to appease him. "Does that mean I have competition with Theo?" he asked, his sharpness still targeting me. "You said *men*."

"No. I think he still smiles too much for me."

"*I smile*," he argued. "I smiled all damn evening."

"I know," I said with a grin. "But you're different around your family."

"Than I am at work?" He cocked his head to the side. "Well,

yeah. I think a lot of people are, Lane. I think the problem is that you think work me is default me. But I think most would consider it to be the opposite."

I frowned at his words. My work was so intertwined with everything I did and who I considered myself to be that I never really considered that someone might have a split personality like that. Dr. Delacroix was who I was. I didn't just...turn that off when I left work.

Then again, I'd never really had a reason to turn that off.

Blake watched me patiently, but I could tell he wasn't waiting for a response. He knew I was working through a reality that wasn't mine. Eventually, he cleared his throat and said plainly, "It was a nice night. Thank you for doing that with me."

"Of course. Your family is..." My throat tightened with wistfulness. "So wonderful."

Putting his hand on my leg, Blake gently squeezed it before returning to the steering wheel. He finally maneuvered out of our tight parking space and pulled onto the road as we headed home.

"They're your family now, too," he said after a beat of silence.

I shook my head. "You know that's not true."

"It is," he said forcefully. "Even if you're not always a London in name, you'll always be my friend, Lane. And you'll always be welcome at the London dinner table. Or anywhere else we are. So is Bryan, if you want to invite him sometime, too."

"I don't know about that," I sighed, turning my attention out the window. My stomach was doing all sorts of weird things because of what he'd said, and I didn't want Blake to see it on my face.

"What do you mean?"

"One day, you'll get married for real, and somehow, I doubt future Mrs. London will want former Mrs. London coming to the family dinners." I forced a laugh out, but I knew it wasn't very convincing. I wasn't sure why I was even struggling *to* be convincing. I'd always known Blake wanted to settle down and marry. It was why I'd never asked him to fake-marry me before—so I wouldn't ruin that for him. But for some reason, the thought of him marrying someone else irked me more now than ever.

Blake was quiet for a long moment, probably trying to figure out how to reply in a way that wouldn't hurt my feelings.

But eventually, he just said, "I'm not worried about that."

"Are you ever worried about anything?"

"I worry about you," he said without missing a beat.

I scowled. "You don't need to do that."

"I do," he insisted. "Because you won't."

I crossed my arms over my chest. "I take care of myself."

"You're very self-sufficient, Lane. But that's not what I meant."

I sighed because I didn't have a comeback. Not a very believable one, especially since he'd seen with his own eyes the mess that was my cheap, rat-infested apartment that I picked because it was the only option that left me with income to invest in my future clinic plans. And while I was surviving just fine in that apartment, I couldn't exactly say I was thriving or even doing moderately okay.

"I, uh..." Blake started, and I swiveled my gaze toward him, mostly because I was curious about the odd tone of his voice. His expression didn't give anything away, though. It was focused on the road. Serious. Attentive. Very Blake-like. He cleared his throat. "I heard what you said to Gemma. And I just want you to know that you can have your career, save the world, *and* live for yourself, Delaney. If you want marriage and kids...I just don't think you have to pick. Or if there's something else you want, you can have it."

He pressed his lips together to signify he was done talking. Or maybe it was to force himself not to say anything more. There was a part of me that wished he would keep talking so I would have an excuse not to respond. An excuse not to think too hard about what he said.

But Blake remained quiet.

And so I said the only truth I knew at the moment.

"It's easy to want a family when you were born in one like yours, Blake." I swallowed, trying to soothe the sudden scratchiness in my throat. "It's more complicated for me."

Blake nodded with understanding. I didn't elaborate, and he didn't push me for more. He never did. I didn't like talking about my family, and he never made me unless I offered it up willingly. And thinking about my family after spending time with his felt so much more painful.

There was a reason I wanted this inheritance so badly. My brother was the only one who loved me with the kind of love the Londons had for each other, and I was doing this for him. Outside of Bryan, my cousin Ophelia was the only friend I had to talk to growing up, but my aunt sent her to a boarding school in Europe when I was ten, and I rarely saw her after that. We still stayed in touch, and even now, I considered her one of my only friends, but we lived in different worlds. And that would never change.

"You're right," Blake finally replied. And he sounded so serious that I didn't even tease him for admitting I was right about something. "I can't and I won't pretend that your upbringing wasn't different from mine, and I can only imagine how that has impacted you, Lane. But I just want you to know... my family? We're not perfect, either. I've never really admitted it before, but my parents getting a divorce wrecked a part of me. I mean, yeah, for the most part, it was an amicable split, but it was still a split. A divide. A shift in the way our family operated. And it felt so wrong because I never saw it coming."

His words felt like a sucker punch because, to be honest, I'd forgotten that Blake's parents were even divorced. His family seemed so effortlessly put together that it was hard to believe that, in some ways, they'd been ripped apart.

"I'm sorry, Blake." I found myself aching to touch him, to reassure him, but I wasn't sure that was a good idea. I'd touched him a lot today, and that touch was growing more confusing by the minute. "I didn't mean to undermine your experience like that. I'm sure that must have hit you hard."

"It was just a shock," he admitted. "I grew up wanting a love like what they shared, to build a family like they had. And it felt a little like I'd been lied to because suddenly, they just...weren't in love anymore? I didn't understand it, even though I found myself in the middle of it. Saw my parents act in ways I didn't think was possible. I don't think Nat or Noah even realize everything that happened. That's okay, though. I'd rather they didn't. I think our family has stayed together so well because my other siblings don't realize."

I couldn't help it. I reached over and put my hand on his leg, wanting him to know I was there. Blake automatically covered my hand with his, giving my fingers a squeeze.

"But that didn't change your thoughts about marriage at all?" I asked thoughtfully. "I feel like children of divorce are sometimes more like...me."

"You mean, scared of commitment?" Blake challenged, giving me a side-eyed look.

But I shook my head. "I don't think commitment is what I'm scared of."

Blake thought about that for a moment before saying, "True. You're actually incredibly committed as a person. Just not to dating."

I was thankful that at least he could acknowledge that. I stuck to things, and I wasn't scared to stick to things. I hoped my friendship with Blake stuck for a very long time. It wasn't commitment.

"I'm more, I don't know, scared of a love that won't last," I said, my voice feeling a bit raw from what I was admitting. Vulnerable. "When you don't see it echoed in the way your family treats each other, it's hard to believe it's real. That we should risk our livelihoods for something that might ruin us in the end."

"You'd think I'd be like that, too." Blake shrugged as his lips pulled tight like he wasn't happy about either my words or his next ones. "But my parents' divorce became more like a personal challenge, in a way. Like I'm trying to defy that reality. Prove them wrong in some way. Which is ridiculous, but..." He drifted off with a shrug.

"You've always been a touch competitive like that," I said with a soft laugh.

"I *am* the eldest of four brothers and a sister who is literally the smartest person I know."

He smiled. I smiled. Then, both our smiles faded. I realized my hand was still in his, and I slowly extracted it. He let me go.

"Blake?"

"Yeah, Lane?"

"You know it's not a competition, though, right?"

"What isn't?"

"Love."

He blew a breath out between his teeth. "I know. Which is a good thing since I think Noah would have already won." Blake's words were said with the slightest edge. A touch of bitterness that I never would have expected. "Don't get me wrong, I'm so fucking happy for my brother. But he never even..." He broke off, shaking his head. "Never mind."

He felt guilty saying it aloud, but I didn't.

"He never even wanted a relationship or a family, and he landed himself with both."

Blake grimaced. "I'm a jealous asshole."

"You're not an asshole," I said with a sigh. "You're a good guy who deserves everything he wants and more. Maybe just...smile more at work. Be a bit more approachable, yeah? I bet you could have your pick of cute nurses or trauma surgeons or anesthesiologists. The hospital is a minefield of intelligent, hardworking women."

Blake pursed his lips like he was considering my advice. "There *is* this smart, pretty cardiologist, but I heard she's married."

I rolled my eyes, even as my stomach twisted unpleasantly at the thought of another woman working so closely with him. It was obviously inevitable, but I didn't like thinking about it. Or visualizing it. Or hearing him talk about it. I cleared my throat, trying to sound neutral. Slightly teasing. Our norm. "Stay away from the married ones, Dr. London."

Blake gave me a funny stare before he just shook his head. "Noted," he said. "Why don't we focus on one thing at a time? Starting with our honeymoon."

"Yeah, I hope you're good with Photoshop," I snorted, relieved that this conversation was taking a different turn.

Blake's brows furrowed. "Why?"

I thought that was obvious.

"Because you're going to have to photoshop a picture of us in front of a field of tulips to send to your siblings."

A soft chuckle slipped from Blake's lips. "No, I'm not."

"Then you'll have to figure out a different plan because you're the one who decided to tell them you're taking me to Europe *next week* to see my favorite flowers." I gave him an accusatory look, but he didn't notice, his gaze still trained on the road, remaining focused on the bumper-to-bumper traffic. "I don't know what you were thinking with that, Blake."

"Don't worry," he said simply. "I have the perfect plan."

"Thank goodness for that," I mumbled. I truly didn't like the idea of deceiving the London family any more than we had to. "What's your plan?"

"I'm taking you to Europe to see your favorite flowers."

"Oh, shut up," I laughed, lightly smacking his arm.

But for a second, I imagined it. I imagined the flowers come alive, the ones I'd seen so still and lifeless on those little puzzle pieces. I imagined them swaying in the breeze while I walked through them, letting my fingers graze the petals. I imagined having the time to do that. To enjoy that.

It was a nice thought.

But it wasn't reality.

Blake wore a playful grin, his eyes darting to mine before training back on the road. "You think I'm kidding, Lane?"

"I *know* you're kidding."

But his grin only grew, and I felt myself falter for the first time. He *was* kidding, right?

I'd better check.

"There's absolutely no way you're taking days off work to go on a fake honeymoon."

"Actually..." he started, drawing out the word in a way that heightened my senses. "There's no way I'm getting fake-married and not taking my wife on a fake honeymoon." He shrugged. "I'll take off as many days as I can figure out."

My jaw dropped. I actually felt it falling open, hanging on its hinges. I stared at Blake, and he stared at the road, and he *had* to be kidding, right?

"Who are you, and what have you done with the Dr. Blake London I know?

"You knew the best friend version of Dr. Blake London," he replied pointedly. "I'm just introducing you to the husband version of him." When all I could do was gape at him, Blake added, "Besides, I think you forget that while I take work seriously and love my job, I've never been interested in being a workaholic. That's you."

"Rude," I scoffed.

But I didn't deny it.

"I think it's time I introduce you to a little work-life balance," he finished. "As your husband, I think maybe that's my responsibility now."

My jaw dropped even further. I might have even dislocated it. "Are you taking me on a honeymoon as an *intervention*?"

His lips twitched with amusement, and I'd never wanted to punch him like I did right now.

"If that's what you want to call it...sure."

"Blake, give it up." I needed him to stop. Now. "Pulling pranks isn't your style."

"You're right," he agreed, which only made me grind my molars together. "I'm not much of a jokester. I'm actually a terrible one. Being dead serious is much more my style."

Oh my God.

"Blake."

"Delaney."

"Stop."

"Not a chance." We stopped at a red light, and Blake looked over at me for the first time. Our gazes connected, and I realized he *was* serious about this. "I'm booking our flights to Amsterdam as soon as we get home. We can send your grandparents' executor pictures from the trip, too. That ought to help."

"You don't need to do that," I insisted, switching my tactics now that I knew he wasn't kidding. Blake always had this need to save things, fix problems, make everything perfect, but this just wasn't something that needed solving. We could figure out another way around faking a honeymoon. "You've done *more* than enough for me with this whole marriage business."

"Did it ever occur to you that I *like* traveling?" He raised a brow before switching his attention to driving as the light turned green. "Also, you heard Sully. My family already thinks I'm a chump for not giving you a proper wedding. I'm not going to let them think I'm doing the bare minimum for a honeymoon, too."

"Oh, so we're doing this to save your bruised ego?"

His dark eyes cut to mine, crinkling around the edges. "You know how important my ego is to me, Delaney."

"As much as I *do* know, we can't just go to the Netherlands."

"Why not?" he pushed.

But I didn't really have an answer for that outside of the responsible ones I knew he was likely expecting. Answers that revolved around work. And I didn't really need to add any more fuel to the fire surrounding Blake's belief that I was a workaholic, considering he'd already brought it up multiple times in this conversation.

"Because that's just...that's just silly." *Wow*, great. That was probably the worst reasoning I could have given, but it was also true, right? This was *ridiculous*. "And you and I don't do silly things."

"We did just get married on a whim."

Fuck.

"Well, that's...that's different. It wasn't entirely a whim. I'd been planning for it. To an extent." I was losing this argument and fast. "Also I have a...thing coming up I can't miss."

"A *thing*," Blake repeated. He raised a brow. "Tell me about this thing, Lane."

"A benefit thing." I cleared my throat. "One of the hospital's biggest donors is hosting. You know, the usual."

"Sounds very important," he said, his tone both serious and mocking at the same time.

I elbowed him because he deserved it. "I have to make an appearance, you know that. I can't miss things like this when I just started. And I especially can't unexpectedly take time off *and* miss something like this all in one week."

He nodded, and I knew he understood, even if he wanted to give me shit about it. "When is it?"

"Thursday."

"Then we'll leave after Thursday."

"Blake," I groaned, exasperated. But my heart wasn't really in it. The more I thought about it, the more I wondered if a fake honeymoon would be so bad.

On principle, I knew that I shouldn't let it happen.

But the tiniest part of me was aching to just give in. To stop and smell some fucking flowers—for just once. I shouldn't. I *really* shouldn't, but...

"I think doing more silly things is exactly what we need," Blake cut into my thoughts.

I shook my head because I knew it was hopeless at this point.

"This *is* an intervention, isn't it?"

"It's whatever you want it to be, Lane." He grinned, and there was something electric about it. His expression was animated in a way I wasn't entirely used to. He was *excited*. He really *did* want to go on this trip. And if there was anything I could get on board with, it was giving Blake something he wanted. "But we're going," he added, and the finality of his words sealed the deal.

"Okay, Blake." There was no denying it at this point. "We're going."

But first, I had to figure out how to get the time off for it, and then I had to survive my first fundraising event at work.

Sighing, I braced myself for the week ahead.

CHAPTER ELEVEN

delaney

I FIDGETED WITH THE scalloped neckline of my familiar black dress, feeling uncomfortable in my own skin.

It had nothing to do with the dress and everything to do with tonight's event. I hated these sorts of affairs, which felt like a parade of wealth—exactly the sort of thing that I hated from my childhood. I went into medicine to make a difference with my mind, not with my bank account, and I didn't like the reminder that my hard work truly meant nothing without money, without funding, without financial backing.

It was the whole reason I was married to Blake, after all.

Money, money, money.

I was well aware of how much of a privilege it was to grow up in a wealthy home, to even have an inheritance at all—a fact I reminded myself of often, whenever my resentment for my family grew just a little too strong. But I still struggled with knowing what I gave up in exchange for wealth.

Smoothing a hand over my dress, I checked the time on my phone. I should stop lingering in the hospital hallways and make my way to the benefit, but I *really* didn't want to. Anxiety balled in my stomach as I thought about having to make small talk with donors and wear a plastered smile all night. It wasn't that it would be hard for me; on the contrary, I was all too good at schmoozing. But I hated it, hated that I learned to do it so young, hated the memories it evoked.

Resigned to my fate, I pushed myself off the bench that had been my home for the last twenty minutes while I tried not to panic and headed toward the benefit. As I grew closer, voices grew louder. Music cascaded down the hallways. It was the kind of orchestral sounds that had flooded my home growing up, symphonies that my mom pretended to appreciate.

It did nothing to help me feel at ease.

I paused at the end of the corridor because I knew as soon as I rounded the corner, there would be no going back. Not until the evening was done, not until I'd played nice and smiled so hard it made my jaw ache.

The tension in my stomach knotted tighter.

"You look great, Lane."

And just like that, it loosened again.

Blake's deep voice was the last thing I expected to hear echoing between these walls. My heart leapt into my throat as I spun, finding Blake a few steps away, striding confidently toward me. He wore a crisp tux, one hand tucked in the pocket of black dress pants. His dark, wavy hair was perfectly tousled on his head, while an anticipatory expression rested on his face as he waited for me to piece things together.

"You always look good in that dress," he added as though he wanted to *add* to my speechlessness. But at least he didn't point out that I kept wearing the same old thing repeatedly—my graduation dress.

"What are you...what are you doing?" I choked out.

Blake rocked to a stop a pace or two away, raising a single brow. "I thought that might be obvious."

"But..." I scrunched my face up, and I knew that it was because, on some level, I was trying not to cry. "Why?"

Blake tilted his head, staring at me in a way that made my

head spin. "This is your first event as an attending cardiologist, Delaney."

I just stared back at him. Because I knew that. I was *well* aware of that fact. But it didn't help to explain what *he* was doing.

"I know, better than anyone, how hard you worked for over a decade to get to where you are now," Blake continued, giving me one of his intense, piercing gazes. "But I also know that you hate rich people events like this. Did you really think I was going to let you go alone?"

Hearing him confirm that he planned to come with me tonight nearly made me crumple with relief. Somehow, I managed to stay on my feet, but that was about all I was capable of. Words were too hard.

Blake nodded, comprehending my silence perfectly.

He closed the distance between us and grabbed my hand, the one that had been fidgeting with my neckline again. The tips of his fingers grazed my skin in the process, leaving little traces of heat and reassurance behind. He laced his fingers through mine and squeezed.

"Did you really think I wasn't going to show up for my wife?"

I swallowed past the lump in my throat, trying to enforce reason and logic and not let emotion completely trample me. "I'm not—" I started, but a finger—Blake's finger—stopped my words, pressing against my lips. His touch shut me up immediately.

I was used to Blake touching me, but I wasn't used to feeling him against my lips, and everything about how we were standing, everything about our body language, suddenly felt intimate. Out of place. Shifted to a different dimension where we were the type of friends who knew what each other's lips felt like.

Because we were now.

"Don't," he said, lethally soft.

So I didn't. I didn't point out the obvious. That I wasn't *really* his wife. Even though I wanted him to know that this wasn't something he needed to do, that I expected him to do. It wasn't part of the deal.

"That's not the point," he muttered as an addition. "Let's go, okay?"

And since I didn't have the energy to argue, not when my nerves were already fried, I agreed.

"Okay, let's go."

I'd never been to this part of the hospital before.

How much money did they spend to build this lavish hall with its high ceilings and rows of tables and classy decor only to use it to raise more money—money that they might have had if they hadn't used it on this?

"I know this is not your scene," Blake whispered in my ear as we walked into the gala, "but you should take notes on the things you *do* like for the future."

I frowned up at him. "For the future?"

"For your clinic," he answered as though it was obvious. When he noticed people glancing in our direction, he wrapped his arm around my back, tucking me close to his body as we entered. "Someday, there will be a wealthy donor who wants to invest in you, too, Lane."

My steps faltered at the thought, something that left me with a mix of emotions.

"It'll be a fundraiser that's on your terms," Blake went on, reading my mind. "And you call the shots. It might not be so bad when you control the narrative."

"*Will* I control the narrative?" I questioned. "Or will the person with the money still hold that power?"

Blake gave a little nod of acknowledgment to my point but then added, "But you get to decide who you want to work with and whose money you want to accept."

While that did give me some peace of mind, I shook my head.

"We're getting ahead of ourselves. I might not even have those kinds of options when we get to that point."

"You will, Lane," Blake said reassuringly, casting a warm look down at me.

"Dr. London! I'm surprised to see you here." A man I didn't recognize, with thinning blond hair and a congenial smile, practically jumped in front of us. He held out his hand, which Blake accepted, giving it a firm shake.

"Davis, nice to see you."

The warmth on Blake's face faded until he wore a placid expression, and he spoke in a tone I knew well. His voice came across strong but soft—an odd combination that could only ever explain Blake London. Or rather, Dr. London.

Dr. London was intelligent in a way that, to others in the medical community, sometimes made him seem like a know-it-all. He took things seriously; for some people, it was *too* serious. But it was only because he cared. Because he wanted to do right by people. Because he wanted everyone else to be just as much on top of their game as he was, knowing medicine was a collective effort. And the thing was, if, for some reason, you *weren't* ready and you *weren't* on your game, he'd help you get there.

Blake didn't have ambition in the same way I did. He didn't want to be the best. He wanted to be surrounded by the best. And fuck, did I admire him for that.

The blond man glanced from Blake to our surroundings with a puzzled look. "You haven't already left your poor staff over at Boston Medical, have you?"

Blake shook his head. "No, no. I'm here with my wife tonight." He nodded to me and then tightened his grip on my side, pulling me closer. "Dr. Delacroix is a cardiologist at SCMC."

"Pleased to meet you," I said, thrusting my hand out to greet the man with my own firm shake and wondering why Blake knew people here that I didn't.

"How lovely." Davis grinned, looking between me and Blake with amusement. "Two married cardiologists." He laughed to himself. "There's got to be a joke in there about hearts somewhere."

Blake gave a tight smile, but when he spoke, it was with a huskiness that sent a shiver through me. "After years of listening to other people's hearts, we finally took a second to listen to our own, and wouldn't you know what happened?"

He punctuated that statement with a brush of his lips against my temple, and I felt my body temperature rise.

"I love that," Davis said enthusiastically, clapping his hands together, getting a real kick out of Blake's little play on words.

Meanwhile, those words made my stomach flip, even though I knew Blake was just doing what we were here to do—schmooze. So maybe the sensations in my lower belly had more to do with the way Blake's fingers had trailed from my side to my lower back. They moved in soothing circles, like he was reminding me to relax.

It was a little hard to comply with that at the moment.

"You know," Davis directed the words at me, and I stood up a bit straighter, which caused Blake to flatten his entire palm on my low back, supporting me. "I have so appreciated your husband's CPR initiative. He's not only donating his time to provide these free CPR classes, but he's making it so accessible for all members of our community. This man is so determined to reach everyone that he can."

It was a good thing I'd already trained my face into a fixed smile tonight because otherwise, I definitely would not have been able to fool this man into believing I knew anything that he was talking about. Blake had been doing *what*?

When I opened my mouth but no words came out, Blake intervened. "Davis is the facilities manager I've been working with and has been kindly allocating space for the initiative at his clinic, which has ties to both the SCMC and Boston Medical networks."

"That's so great," I gushed, glancing between Blake and Davis.

I hoped it wasn't too noticeable that I was blinking more than was really necessary.

"It's my *absolute* pleasure," Davis said before he saw someone else he knew and went to give them one of his hearty, enthusiastic handshakes, which seemed to be his standard way of greeting people.

"CPR initiative?" I asked as soon as Blake and I were alone again, pulling back to look up at him.

He shrugged, his eyes not really meeting mine. "It's something I thought of when I first moved here. CPR can save lives, you know."

"So I've heard," I said, drawing out my words because I didn't know what else to say to that.

Blake nodded. "So the more people who know how to do it, the more lives will be saved."

He was spitting generic statements at me. There were things he wasn't saying, and I had a suspicion of what they stemmed from and why he'd kept this close to his chest. If we were at home, I might have pressed him for more, but this wasn't the place for diving into things that Blake kept under the surface.

"I think that's amazing, Blake," I said, earnest about that statement. Of course it was great. Of course *he* was great. "Why didn't you tell me? I'd be happy to donate my time as well and teach a few classes."

"It's not a big deal," he said, brushing aside my comment. "You're already so busy, Lane. I mean, you're putting together plans to open an entire specialty heart clinic. This is just...this is just a little something I wanted to do."

I frowned and reached for his arm, squeezing it. "It's not little. It's clearly making an impact in the community, and I want to help."

He nodded and finally met my gaze. "Okay. We can talk about it later, alright?"

"Sure," I agreed, even though it bothered me that he was

being so cavalier about the entire thing. But then again, that was Blake. Cool, calm, collected.

It's just that wasn't usually Blake *with me.*

"Let's get you some food," he said, switching the topic and steering me toward the crush of people, through the onslaught of sparkles and gems.

"Why are you saying that like you assume I haven't eaten anything today?"

"Because I am one hundred percent assuming you haven't eaten anything today."

"Actually, I—" I stopped short at the sight of a man with graying hair and bushy brows and sharp, blue eyes. *Shit.* This was not a situation I'd prepared for. But I quickly realized that had been an oversight on my part.

"Lane?" Blake questioned. I could *hear* his brows furrowing.

But I didn't look at him, too focused on the sight of my dad standing roughly ten feet away from us, surrounded by other men in identical black suits.

Of course he would be here—at an event that revolved around money and would make him look good at the same time, make it appear as though he gave a shit about anything that wasn't himself.

He started to turn in our direction, and I knew I had about ten seconds before he saw us to decide how I wanted to handle the situation.

A part of me wanted to run.

But it was only the start of the evening, and I wouldn't be able to make it through hours of this event without him catching a glimpse of me.

This wasn't really great, seeing as I was here pretending with Blake. I'd been hoping to keep our marriage to myself for a bit before having to face the music with my parents. The longer I could avoid that mess, the better.

But on the other hand, I wouldn't have very many opportunities to convince them that our marriage was real, considering I rarely saw them, so I might as well take advantage of this.

Besides, my dad was the easier target. Was I looking forward to his reaction? No, of course not. But he wasn't going to care that I'd eloped in the same way as my mom. I wasn't *his* pet project. I hadn't been bred to live out *his* dreams before dumping them to the side the minute I saw an escape. I wasn't the embodiment of *his* resentment. He wouldn't view my marriage as another act of rebellion and disrespect, but my mom would. Just because I didn't want to live the life she'd always wanted.

Maybe it was actually for the best if she heard about my marriage through my dad. Although Robert Delacroix was so wrapped up in his own world there was a good chance he wouldn't even remember to mention anything to his wife about his daughter's new husband.

Making a quick decision, I spun to face Blake.

"Okay, quick." I stepped into him, eliminating the space between us, and Blake, whether by instinct or by some other force, locked his arms around my body to hold me against his chest. "My dad's over there, and he's about to see us. It would be really, really great if you could just look at me like you're deeply in love or something."

Blake's brows rose slightly in surprise but then lowered again, and I waited. Waited for his expression to morph, to shift. I waited for him to play pretend.

But Blake just blinked down at me, his lips pressed tight with the tiniest curve, his brown eyes boring into my own with the faintest sparkle.

Exactly how Blake always looked.

Fuck, he'd been doing so good at this whole fake husband thing, and this was an awfully annoying moment for him to suddenly forget how to act.

I groaned.

"What?"

I shook my head. "Nothing. You're just looking at me like you always look at me."

Blake heaved a sigh. "Delaney—"

"Maybe the occasion calls for it," I blurted before I had a second to think about what I was saying.

He stilled. "You want me to kiss you?"

"Just a little."

"You want me to kiss you...just a little."

"Yeah, like just a peck or something. It is my *dad*." I was talking at the speed of light at this point, but I needed him to understand. "But he doesn't know we're married, and I'm sure he isn't going to believe it when I tell him in like two minutes, considering we weren't even *dat*—"

"Okay, Lane," Blake hushed me, forcing me to relax with his assuring tone. "Just a peck."

I nodded, trying to press myself closer to him, even though it wasn't really possible. I could already feel the beat of Blake's heart pounding against my chest. It was unusually quick, but then again, I'd suddenly put a lot of pressure on him to make believe in front of my dad when he'd never even met the man before, so I suppose that was warranted.

Blake cupped my cheek and bent his head, lowering his mouth so it was just a breath away. But then he hesitated, and now my heart had quickened its pace, too. I tried to tell myself that it was the circumstances, the ones I'd put us in, but I knew it was the anticipation, the excitement to feel the brush of Blake's lips again, to test whether the kiss at our wedding had been a fluke or if it was something that could be standard for us. A spark that was real behind the pretense of something fake.

My eyes fluttered shut as Blake's thumb caressed my cheek, like he was coaxing me into this kiss even though it had been my idea. I circled my arms around his neck, tugging him closer. So close I could feel his uneven breathing. So close I could feel his lips move as he cursed beneath his breath. So close I could feel my name when he murmured it against my mouth.

Was it this painful for him to just give me a peck on the lips?

Had he actually *hated* our first kiss, and I hadn't even realized?

"Delaney?"

My name sounded again in my brain, but it took me a second to place it. Because for a moment, Blake had encompassed my entire world. And I'd forgotten that my dad was even here, in this room. Or that anyone was in this room, honestly.

Blake ripped his mouth away before our lips even had a chance to touch, and the feeling that tore through me was indescribable.

"Dad," I said breathlessly as I turned, wondering if it was noticeable how hot my cheeks were. Blake's hand had dropped to his side, but he still kept one arm around my back as we both faced the man who had, supposedly, raised me.

"I've been looking for you," my dad said, coming to my side to pull me away from Blake and into an awkward, one-armed hug.

"I hadn't been looking for you," I replied honestly. "I didn't know you were going to be here."

My dad took a step back again, and his brows knitted together. "Didn't I send over an email about it? I could have sworn I did."

I shook my head and then tried not to roll my eyes. Because what father communicated with his daughter via email?

"Not that I saw."

I had a better relationship with my dad than my mom. He didn't pressure me the way she did growing up, but he also didn't stand up to her when she treated me like her plaything, and I'd never quite forget or forgive that. He just didn't care enough. Wasn't around enough. Couldn't be bothered to intervene and show up when it mattered.

This was the only time he'd cared about my work, and he'd forgotten that I was even involved in it.

"Huh." Seeming stumped by that and not sure what else to say, my dad turned his attention to Blake. His eyes narrowed as they looked him up and down. "And who do we have here?"

"Dad, this is Dr. Blake London."

"Ah," my dad said in an assessing, judgmental sort of way, even as he stuck his hand out for Blake to shake. "Another doctor, huh?"

I could tell he wasn't entirely impressed by that, but he wasn't outright offended. I'd take it.

"It's nice to meet you, sir," Blake said, gripping my dad's hand so hard my dad actually winced.

"Same, same," my dad replied, shaking off the greeting as though it had already bored him.

Then again, we weren't important people who he could impress and build connections with, which I was sure was the reason he was here tonight. I honestly couldn't believe that it never occurred to me that I might see him this evening.

"Dad, Blake is, um—" I cleared my throat and then shifted on my feet, not sure if I'd be able to spit out the next part of this sentence. Blake gave me an encouraging squeeze. "Well, I know you've heard me talk about him before," I said, deciding to ease into the reveal. "We went to med school together, remember? And we both did our cardiology fellowship at Mayo."

"Oh yes, yes."

My dad's attention had drifted, his gaze surfing the crowd for other people to talk to.

"Well, we actually e—"

"Oh, can you excuse me, honey?" my dad interrupted, pulling away from us before I even had a chance to respond. "I see someone who I've been trying to get in touch with for *weeks*. I'll be right back. Come find you in a few."

And just like that, he was gone.

I should have been upset, but relief swamped me instead.

My shoulders slumped as I dropped my weight against Blake. He seemed to be ready for it, holding me steady, unwavering in his support.

"Well, that was..." he started before realizing he didn't know how to finish that sentence. Or maybe he just didn't know how to finish that sentence without upsetting me.

But whatever he had to say wouldn't bother me. I was well aware of my family's reality.

It was, of course, the reason I didn't really want one. A family, that is. Because how could I be a good wife or parent when I'd only had emotionally stunted examples? I would hate to do to *anyone* what my family had done to me.

"That was my dad," I said with a sigh. "That's just how he is."

Blake echoed my sigh. His body swayed slightly like he was rocking me.

"Want me to get him to come back over here so you can finish telling him about us?"

"Nah." It might be enjoyable to watch Blake try, but it wasn't worth it. "This is probably for the best. At least for now."

I could put off our marriage announcement until after the honeymoon. That way, I might have more proof that this was real and not just something my best friend and I had cooked up.

Blake remained quiet for a moment before murmuring, "If you want to go home, I'll take you home."

Did I want to stay here while my dad ignored me and made stuffy conversation with hospital benefactors? Absolutely not.

But I *should* stay.

I hadn't made it this far just to let my dad dictate what I was going to do. I didn't let him get in my way back when I first applied to med school, so I wasn't going to let him now.

"I don't want to go home. Not yet."

I felt Blake nod. "Then let's get you some food."

This time, we made it across the room without any interruptions.

But for some reason, that made me a little disappointed.

CHAPTER TWELVE
delaney

MY BRAIN KEPT FLITTING in and out of work mode today, and considering that had never happened to me before, I wasn't sure what to do about it.

I needed to be at work, though. Being here with my patients and beeping heart monitors and charting to get done grounded me, and after last night and my looming travel plans for tomorrow, that was necessary. My attention, as always, remained undivided when it came to my patients and the consultations I had today, and that focus kept me going, kept my head on straight.

But the minute I stepped out of the exam room? That was when my mind slipped away to somewhere very different. Like the open suitcase I had at home, which had absolutely not been filled yet. Or the plane seat I'd be sitting in at this time tomorrow. And the person who would be sitting next to me.

Blake and I had never traveled together. To be completely honest, we didn't do *fun* things together, period. He was like a work friend who had become a real friend, a *best* friend, but the only thing we did together outside of work was talk about work. I mean, sure, technically, we did other things. We'd grab food and talk about work. Or meet for happy hour and talk about work. But food was a necessity. And sometimes, after a harrowing day of rounds, so was alcohol.

To be clear, that didn't make Blake any less of a friend. Honestly, it made him *more* of one. My career was everything, and therefore, so was Blake. He was, after all, the *only* reason I'd made it this far. He was the reason I was as balanced as I was and the reason I felt lopsided when he'd unexpectedly moved to Boston. Blake was one of the most important people in my life, tied right up there with Bryan.

But still—the truth was that our friendship existed because of a particular set of circumstances. And traveling to Europe together was certainly not included in those.

"I was surprised to see you had the rest of the week blocked off on your calendar."

I looked up from a patient's chart to find Jack hovering over my shoulder. He was my least favorite nurse in the cardiac center at SCMC. Not because he wasn't good at his job; in fact, Jack was a very capable nurse with a strong work ethic, and in most cases, I'd be considered lucky to have him in my unit. But he was also a terrible gossip, who always seemed to stand a touch too close to me for my liking. I hadn't decided yet if his insistent familiarity was just friendliness I wasn't used to or if it was something more. But either way, I couldn't deny it made me uncomfortable at times.

I snapped the chart shut, not liking the feeling of being spied on.

"I'm going on my honeymoon," I said, even though I knew I didn't owe him an explanation. I also knew I didn't owe him a smile, but I flashed a strained one anyway before moving back a step.

Jack only took that opportunity to sidle up next to me, like we were at the bar getting drinks instead of standing in front of the nurses' station. His eyes popped wide before they dropped to my hand resting on the countertop and the beautiful ring on it—the one I hadn't quite gotten over yet.

Jack discovering I was married was both annoying and perfect. He'd make sure everyone knew about it, which saved me a lot of *faking-it* work. However, I was still relatively new at SCMC and didn't exactly relish the idea of being a topic in the rumor mill.

"Have I just been missing that big rock on your finger this whole time?" he questioned, saying it like he already knew the answer. Like he definitely would *not* have missed this big rock on my finger.

"Not the *whole* time," I said tentatively.

"Damn." Jack whistled. "Were you even engaged?"

"Not for very long," a new voice cut in, and even though I didn't understand it, my whole body, once again, relaxed at the sound of his steady timbre. An arm wrapped around my waist, tugging me back a bit—away from Jack—and I melted into the body behind me because I knew whose it was. "We were impatient."

Even though I didn't need confirmation to know it was Blake, I glanced over my shoulder anyway, seeking a glimpse of him—that sharp jaw, acute gaze, and wavy, dark hair. Yep, it was him. He was here, at my work. Holding me possessively as though I would slip away. I didn't understand, but at this moment, I was grateful.

"Dr. Blake London," he said by way of introduction, extending his free hand for Jack to shake. "It's nice to meet you."

Jack gave Blake a nice, long look before he shook his hand. "Jack Henry, one of the cardiac nurses. Nice to meet you, too."

"If you don't mind, I just stopped by to talk to my wife real quick," Blake said, his voice hardening ever so slightly. It was his way of effectively ending the conversation with Jack, and to make it even more clear, he applied gentle pressure on my waist, encouraging me to twist to face him and turn my back on Jack.

I tried not to smile when my gaze met Blake's, but it was tough. Behind us, I could hear Jack's footsteps shuffle away. Blake didn't move, though. He kept his arm locked around me, caging me close to his chest.

"What are you doing here?" I hissed. "You're being ridiculous."

"Not as ridiculous as that guy," he muttered. His eyes flicked up, blazing as they trailed after Jack. "He was practically standing on top of you."

"I know," I sighed. "I hate when he does that."

Blake's eyes cut back to mine with alarm. His jaw ticked as that fierce gaze of his bored into me. "You mean that's a common occurrence?"

I shook my head because I didn't want to get into it—not when we were still standing amidst the bustle of the cardiac center and I had things I should be doing. "What are you doing here?" I asked again. "You sure are making it a habit of showing up unannounced. If I didn't know better, I'd think you were scoping out SCMC to see if it's better than Boston Medical."

Blake answered me by producing a brown paper bag and holding it out to me.

"Lunch." He gave me an assessing look, pursing his lips before adding, "I'm going to take a wild guess and say you haven't eaten yet."

I frowned. "Why are you so stuck on feeding me this week?"

"Because I'm starting to worry you didn't have a single solid meal in the months we were apart."

"I—"

Could not finish that sentence honestly.

Blake shook his head and stepped back, finally releasing his grip from my waist. The sudden loss of warmth sent a shiver down my spine, and I drew my white coat tighter around me. "I was meeting Nat for lunch to talk about some legal stuff with her ex, and I thought I'd stop up here and bring you my leftovers before heading back to Boston Medical."

"Oh, how *thoughtful*," I drawled, but my words had no real

bite. I'd happily eat leftovers. It would be much better than the rabbit food I packed this morning.

"No leftovers, I'm kidding," Blake laughed. "I brought you a BLT with extra mayo and a pickle on the side. Promise I didn't even take a bite."

"That's my favorite," I said absently, peeking inside the bag.

"I know. I also know that you've been packing shit lunches for work, so we're going to need to work on that when we get back."

I bit my lip because I couldn't even argue with him about that.

And when I looked up, Blake wore an expression of satisfaction because he *knew* I couldn't even argue.

"Are you ready for tomorrow?" he asked suddenly, clearing his throat. "You were holed away in your room for hours last night. I can only assume you were packing."

"Not even close," I groaned, thankful for the change in topic. "I still have to pick out at least four more outfits that don't look terrible."

Blake snorted. He thought I was kidding.

I was definitely not kidding.

I didn't buy clothes for myself very often, which meant my closet was full of things that went out of style a decade ago. I had at least a dozen peplum tops I should really just throw away.

"I'm sure none of them look terrible."

"Don't be so sure."

"Let me be the judge, then." He shrugged. "You can try on the options for me."

"Didn't realize you were a fashion show kind of guy," I said, shifting on my feet and trying to push off this idea. I would *not* be trying on my outfits for Blake.

But Blake just grinned crookedly, held my gaze, and said, "I'm whatever kind of guy my wife needs."

My brain knew he was being a lighthearted tease, but other parts of my body didn't, clenching at his words.

"If you're expecting a Victoria's Secret–type show, you're going to be disappointed," I said with a sigh.

He choked a little at that comment, which led to a cough. His voice sounded strained when he finally replied. "You know, funnily enough, I did not assume you'd walk out in your underwear."

"That's not what I meant." I waved that idea away quickly. "I was referring more to the level of hotness on the runway."

Blake gave me a funny little stare, and I wondered what he was thinking. But before I could find out, he simply shook his head.

"Don't sell yourself short, Lane." He tapped on the paper bag with my lunch. "Eat. I'll see you at home."

"Thank you for lunch," I called after him, and he grinned over his shoulder as I watched him walk away.

Like I actually stood there when I had a million other things to do, including scarfing down this sandwich, and watched my best friend walk away.

No, *husband*.

Blake was my husband.

And he was doing a very good job at reminding me of that a little more each and every day.

Not that I minded.

In fact, I was starting to wonder if I actually kind of liked it.

This dress was nothing like the other ones I'd tried on.

The first two pieces in this fashion show had been floral and flowy, the next had been solid and basic, and the one before what I was wearing now had been a linen shirtdress with buttons up the front and a tie around the waist. So far, Blake had surprised me with honest feedback about which dresses seemed to suit me better. I'd packed three of them and set one of them aside.

And now there was one more to try on.

This one.

I stared at myself in the corner floor-length mirror, which I was honestly shocked Blake owned but appreciated at the moment. I smoothed my hands down my sides, running my fingers over the fabric clinging to my skin. It was tight. It was red. It had a corseted bodice with ties in the back, giving me the illusion of having more curves than I did.

I'd bought this dress for Ophelia's bachelorette party, which had been a ritzy affair in the Hamptons, and even though my residency schedule ultimately intercepted my ability to make it that weekend, I'd held on to this dress. It was a nice dress. Maybe too nice? Maybe too...salacious. Like a piece someone who was actually going on their honeymoon would wear, and I wasn't really going on my honeymoon, was I?

"I think I'm done!" I called, loud enough for Blake to hear me over the boxing podcast he turned on every time I disappeared back into my room to change. I didn't understand the appeal of two men talking about punching each other, but then again, it was also nice to see Blake so into a hobby. He went to his boxing club at least three or four times a week, and I had to admit, he always seemed to come home mentally recharged. Every once in a while, it made me miss ballet. Or just dancing in general.

"You told me there was one more!" he shouted back.

"I, uh, made a mistake!"

"Since when do you make mistakes?" He laughed, but I wasn't sure if it was because of his comment or because of something the boxing dudes said. "I know you have a dress on. Just come show it to me."

It was annoying how well he knew me.

I gave myself one more look in the mirror, debated, and then gave in, walking straight into the living room and stopping in front of Blake, who had his head bent, looking at something on his phone. "Also," he started without looking up, "you know you don't have to clean the entire apartment every day just because you live here now. I don't know how you do my dishes so fast, but it's not necessary." He tossed his phone to the side a second later, glanced up, and froze. His entire body tensed. "Oh."

That was the only word out of Blake's mouth when he saw the dress. Actually, it wasn't even a word. It was a single goddamn syllable. Just a syllable. Nothing else except for the clearing of his throat. He eventually adjusted how he was sitting on the couch, leaning forward with a patient look, both elbows resting on his knees. It felt like he was preparing to let me down easy.

"Cleaning is the least I can do since you're letting me invade your space for the next year," I said, forcing out a laugh as I felt heat rise into my cheeks.

"I..." Blake's face contorted like he didn't understand my words.

"It's okay if you don't like the dress." I tried to say it casually, tucking my bare toes beneath the edge of the rug in his living room; years of ballet meant I had ugly, deformed feet. "Really, Blake. You don't, do you?"

"I didn't say I didn't like it," he replied, but his words were slow, as if he was thinking about them very carefully—thinking about how he could tell me the truth without hurting my feelings. Because Blake didn't lie just to soothe people's egos. It wasn't like him, so I could see the gears working in his head as he tried to figure out what he could say that would be both honest and kind. "You look..." He cleared his throat again. "Great. Really great."

"Thank you." I smiled hesitantly before cocking my head to the side. "But you still didn't answer the question."

His mouth opened and closed as he tried to find the right words.

"It's just, you told me this *wasn't* going to be a Victoria's Secret fashion show," he finally said, and my jaw dropped, flailing open from his comment.

"I'm fully clothed, thank you very much," I argued.

But Blake just sort of pressed his lips together and said, "Mhm."

"Are you confused because you forgot I had boobs?" I asked

because in glancing down at the surprising amount of cleavage this dress awarded me, I couldn't blame him. I'd *also* forgotten what they looked like when I put them in a dress like this. I'd always thought that I was on the cusp of being in the itty-bitty titty committee—like perhaps if they were feeling generous, they'd let me in—but this dress was making me think that I actually wouldn't have a chance. "Like, do you not like the dress because it's weird that you can actually see them for once? Because honestly, I think that's what's getting me about it, too."

"Delaney," Blake choked out, and I couldn't tell if he was mortified or laughing. His expression was hard to read, but his face was turning a shade I'd never seen before. "Stop. Just stop. I did not—fuck." He rubbed the back of his neck, wincing like I'd physically injured him with this question. "I am...aware that you have boobs," he rasped after a moment. "Always have been. And I did not say I don't like the dress."

"Okay, great. Then just give me your objective opinion," I said, trying to reframe his thinking. I did a half spin to give him a better look, and Blake watched intently, trying his damnedest to do what I asked. But it also meant I felt his eyes like hot little daggers, and a warm flush rose up my body as I said, "Pretend you don't know me and I'm not your best friend. You're just a random guy, and I'm a random girl. Would you walk up to me in a bar and ask for my number?"

He raised one brow. "Are you hoping to give out your number to a lot of guys on our honeymoon, Lane?"

I rolled my eyes. "No, of course not. I'm just trying to..." I sighed, throwing my hands up in the air and giving up. "Never mind."

I started to walk away, wanting to retreat to my room and hide my heated cheeks. But Blake saying my name stopped me in my tracks.

"Delaney."

I should have kept walking but instead turned on my heel.

Faced him again. Watched how his gaze flicked over me like he was deciding his fashion advice, determining the final verdict.

"You want to know what I think about that dress?" he finally asked, his voice hoarse, and I wondered if maybe this was a line we shouldn't have crossed in our friendship. He might have offered to judge my travel outfits, but perhaps this one in particular was making him feel weird.

"You don't have to tell me. I didn't mean to push it or make you feel uncomfortable." I bit down on my lip with a shrug. "I bought it for Ophelia's bachelorette party, but I never got to wear it. I thought it might be a good option for the trip, but maybe not."

"You're not making me uncomfortable," he said, and based on his earnest expression, I was inclined to believe him. "Not in the way—" He paused and looked away for a second before finishing. "I just wasn't sure if you really wanted my...honest thoughts."

"I do," I insisted.

Blake nodded as he took in that information. He ran a hand down his face before piercing me with a gaze that told me whatever his next words were, he meant them. But then he dropped his head, staring at some spot on the floor as he spoke.

"If I were some random guy, and you were some random girl, and I saw you wearing that in a bar, I'd ask for your number in a heartbeat. And then I wouldn't let you out of my sight for the rest of the fucking night. I'd chase off other men when you weren't looking, and then I'd insist on walking you home, holding my breath when we got to your door and hoping to God you'd invite me in. And if you did, I'd—"

He bit down on whatever the next words were going to be and looked up. I felt that look, that heated stare, that slight parting of his lips as words went unsaid, disappearing from his tongue. Whatever it was, whatever it meant, I felt it right down into my very being. It was terrifying. Exhilarating. I loved it because it felt good, but I hated it because I didn't know why.

"Yeah, Lane. I'd ask for your number. I like the dress, okay? But it might, uh, cause some problems."

"Because men are just going to start throwing themselves at me?" I couldn't help but roll my eyes. Now he was definitely taking it too far.

Blake remained quiet for a moment. "Something like that, yeah."

"Sounds like men are the problem, not my dress."

His lips finally cracked a smile again, like he'd snapped out of something. He leaned back onto the couch again, raising his hands in defeat.

"Men are most decidedly the problem, you're right."

I lifted my brows. "Blake Bennett London once *again* telling me that I'm right? Wow."

"I heard that's the key to having a happy marriage," he said, that teasing glint returning to his eyes. "And I'm pretty committed to that." He checked his watch. "You should finish up. We have a long day tomorrow."

I nodded and turned to head back to my room. I nearly made it inside when Blake called after me.

"So, do you think you're going to pack it?"

I paused, and I knew my gut reaction was to say yes. Because I couldn't get that feeling out of my chest, the one I felt when Blake had lifted his gaze and said he'd ask for my number.

But for that reason, maybe he was right.

Perhaps it could cause problems.

"It'll be a surprise!" I called back to him, deciding to keep my options open.

As I dropped to the ground to sort out the mess I needed to fit into a suitcase, I heard a soft curse leave Blake's mouth, followed by a grumbled, "Great."

Maybe he was mumbling about his podcast.

Maybe not.

Maybe I really didn't want to know.

CHAPTER THIRTEEN

blake

I'D BEEN SO CONFIDENT that taking Delaney on this honeymoon was the right move...until last night.

Was she trying to fucking kill me?

I might have volunteered to be the sole audience and judge of her pre-trip fashion show, but I never imagined she'd walk out of her room wearing a dress like the one she had on last night. I never would have signed up for that kind of torture had I known.

And then she'd wanted to know if I *liked* it.

Liked. It.

What a loaded question that I didn't know how to answer— at least not aloud.

Yes, Lane, I like your dress. I like that dress so much that my brain malfunctioned when I saw you in it. It made me momentarily forget that you have no idea how viscerally attracted to you I am, and I had to lean forward so you wouldn't notice how fucking hard you wearing it made me. So yes, I like the dress. But I also hope I never see you wearing it again. Because there's only so many times I can see you wear it before I'm on my knees, begging to take it off you.

Somehow, I managed not to say that.

But then she wanted to know if I would have asked for her number if I didn't know her.

First of all, it was hard imagining a world where I didn't know Delaney. But sometimes, I wished I could go back in time and ask for her number. I wished I had made it clear how I wanted to be more than her friend from the beginning. I wished I'd done exactly what I described to her.

But I also knew if I had done that, we would never have worked out how I wanted us to. Perhaps I would have found my way into her bed for a night, but then I would have lost her. She didn't keep men around like that. She'd never had any interest in serious or even casual relationships. And if I had to pick between one night in Delaney's bed or being in the friend zone for the rest of my life, I'd pick exactly where I was every time.

Especially where I was right now, boarding a plane with her in tow. For the next week, I got to have Delaney all to myself. I'd never been so fucking excited or terrified in my entire life, and that included taking the MCAT. All I could do was hope that I didn't screw this up.

I just wanted Delaney to have fun. Be happy. Be cared for in a way that her family never had. Actually experience an emotion that wasn't stress or worry or responsibility for once in her life.

At the moment, though, I wasn't sure I was achieving that.

"Oh my God." Delaney waved the plane's safety pamphlet in front of her face like a fan. "I think every orifice in my body has sweat coming out of it right now. Every single one."

How this woman could say things like that and I could still be so irrationally turned on by her was beyond me. I suspected it had something to do with the wave of perfume she sent in my direction with every flick of the pamphlet. She smelled like fucking sin. She smelled like how that dress looked. Edible. Having her near me in such tight quarters on this plane was intoxicating. Even though our first-row Comfort Plus seats had afforded us ample legroom, we were still shoulder-to-shoulder.

"It'll get better once we're in the air," I reasoned. "It's always stifling when people are boarding."

Delaney nodded idly and checked her phone. A smile immediately stretched across her face, hinting at who might have messaged her.

"Look what Bryan just sent me," she said a moment later, confirming what I'd suspected. "That's his girlfriend, Makayla. She's the sweetest."

She showed me a picture of her brother with a young, blonde-haired woman. Sun drenched their overpowering smiles and the towering cones of melting ice cream in their hands.

"They're cute together. Should we send a picture back?"

"Okay." Delaney seemed to like that idea, snuggling impossibly close to me as she held out the camera to take a picture of us. "But you have to look happy."

I rolled my eyes. "I *am* happy."

She had no fucking clue about the extent of my feelings at the moment.

Which was how I planned to keep it.

"Prove it," she said, nudging me with her elbow until a laugh slipped out of me. "There it is."

Satisfied with the shot, she lowered her phone, and I settled back into my seat. While Delaney kept her attention on the message with her brother, I decided to mind my own business, clicking aimlessly on the TV in front of our seats. But when Delaney tried to muffle an abrupt laugh, I couldn't help but look over at her, raising a brow when she tried to hide her phone.

"Did he roast our picture?" I asked because I knew Bryan got his sass from his sister. Or maybe it was the other way around.

Delaney shook her head. "No...not exactly."

I laughed. "I can take it, Lane. What did Bry say?"

"Oh, it's nothing."

She waved it off, but the flush working its way up her neck had me more than curious.

I watched her closely.

She ignored me, keeping her phone tucked between her legs.

I didn't dare try to look at it.

I should mind my own business, after all.

155

And not be looking between her legs.

Or thinking about things between her legs.

Or thinking about her at all, really.

"He asked if we were finally dating," she blurted out before shrugging and clearing her throat. "Well, that was the gist of it anyway."

I felt a grin tug on the corner of my mouth, and I was trying desperately to resist it. Delaney didn't need to know how I felt about her brother's question. "Had a little more flair to it, did it?"

I always liked Bryan.

"You could, uh, say that."

I laughed, wanting to pry more. But I could tell something about it had embarrassed her, so I didn't. Instead, I asked, "You haven't told him about the marriage?"

Delaney shook her head. "I haven't told my mom yet, to be honest. I want things settled with my grandparents' executor so she can't meddle. And I won't ask Bry to lie for me or keep that from her."

"You think your mom will try to mess things up?"

"I know she will," Delaney said with certainty.

"I'm not good enough for the upper crust?"

I might come from a family of doctors, developers, and professional athletes, but I knew I had nothing on the elitism of Delaney's background.

"It's not even that," Delaney insisted, and I could tell she wasn't just saying that to make me feel better. "She wants the money, so I'm sure she'll try to find a way to get it."

"Didn't your parents also inherit something when your grandparents passed?"

"They did." She pursed her lips with annoyance. "But it's never enough, is it? Frankly, I wonder if they're in a bad spot. I think my mom got a little too carried away with her spending, and my dad's investments aren't making as much money as they used to. But I think they're trying to hide it because it would be the end of them socially if they did something wild like noticeably cut back on their lifestyle choices."

I frowned, not liking the sound of that. People who were used to having money didn't do well when that money was taken away from them. "Is Bryan still doing okay living with them?"

"I think so," Delaney said, but the words fell from her mouth slowly, a clear demonstration that she wasn't entirely sure. She started waving the makeshift fan in front of her face again, more vigorously this time.

"I need to visit soon so I can assess everything better. But he seems happy whenever I talk to him. I will say that my parents have connected him with a lot of excellent programs that will support him as he moves into more competitive job opportunities, and Makayla's there, too. Otherwise, I'd be thinking more seriously about if he should move in with me instead. At least until he felt comfortable living independently or in a supported-living arrangement. Because as of last summer, he *is* officially an adult, and I think he can absolutely do that if he wants to. I mean—"

She gave me a sheepish look, like she forgot that we were married. I couldn't blame her for that, not really. "Obviously, *we* would have to rethink our living arrangements if that happened, but I don't think it will anytime soon."

"We would make it work," I said without thinking twice. "If it came to that, if you thought it was best for Bryan to be with you, we'd make it work, Delaney. Nothing to rethink."

I'd thought about it before. Of course I'd considered how a future with Delaney would involve Bryan to some extent, and I had absolutely no problem with that. If it meant we'd need to upgrade to a bigger apartment or find a house that would be better suited until our fake marriage was called off, I didn't care. We'd make it work.

"I think he's doing well where he is, but maybe I'll ask him." She looked down at her hands, fiddling with her thumbs. "He can make his own decisions, of course. I just, you know, want what's best for him."

"I know you do."

She gave another little nod of acknowledgment and then crossed her ankles, jiggling both of her feet impatiently. The movement reminded me of something I'd meant to ask her before our flight. Preferably before we'd left the apartment, but today had been more hectic than I'd expected, and after she'd retreated to her room last night, I couldn't risk talking to her again. For the sake of my dick, I'd needed a break from being in her presence. I thought if I took the night off from thinking of her or talking to her or breathing in her air, I might survive this flight.

I was most definitely wrong about that.

"Are you on the pill, Lane?"

Delaney's brows furrowed as her eyes cut over to me, giving me a look like she couldn't believe I'd just asked that question.

But I knew she'd understand in a second.

"Yeah, why? Afraid you're gonna come back from this honeymoon with a baby on the way, too? Trying to budget exactly how many extra bedrooms we need?"

Her eyes popped wide the second her words were out of her mouth.

"Please forget I just said that," she groaned, covering her face with the safety pamphlet.

No, I would never forget that she just said that.

Because now I was, once again, thinking about things I really shouldn't be. Like fucking Delaney until she was pregnant.

Jesus Christ. What is wrong with me?

"It's the heat." She dropped the pamphlet and began waving it in her now bright red face again. "It's doing things to my brain."

I shook my head with a laugh, letting her know she didn't need to be worried about it.

"First of all," I started. "That wouldn't scare me." Delaney's movement stilled, and she glanced over at me with those wide eyes again. Fuck, I shouldn't have said that. I should have just stuck to the point of the conversation. I cleared my throat and tried to get back there. "Second of all, which pill is it?"

Delaney gave her head a little shake as if she were trying to clear it. "Ocella."

I nodded and ran through the mental notes I had from pharmacology.

But Delaney got to the point before I did.

"Ohh." She patted me on the leg reassuringly. An innocent touch that affected me in not-so-innocent ways. "The answer is yes, Blake."

"Yeah?" I felt instant relief. "Show me."

Delaney understood, reaching down to tug up the hem of her athletic pants and show off her flower-printed compression socks.

"Good girl." I sank back in my seat. "You've been hydrating well this morning, too, which is excellent. If you didn't come prepared, I was going to make you put on the extra socks I packed in my backpack."

"I thought I was bringing the husband version of Blake London on this trip, not the doctor version."

I frowned. "Doctor and Husband Blake are equally worried about his wife's health. The clotting side effects of birth control are not something you should take lightly on a long-haul fli—" My words went dry in my mouth when I realized the way Delaney was glaring at me. "Right, you know that."

"We did take pharmacology together, *honey*," she said in an overly sugared voice.

"I know, *sweetheart*. Just..." I looked down at her legs. "Make sure you pump your feet every once in a while. And get up to walk around a few times on the flight."

"Blake." She dropped the fake wife voice. "Besides the pill, I don't have any other risk factors for blood clots. It's going to be okay." She pointed to my feet. "Are you wearing socks? Or do I need to shove some on your feet?"

"I'm wearing some," I said.

"Good boy."

Her satisfaction about that tickled something inside me.

"But *I'm* not the one on birth control."

"That's good. I'd have some questions if you were."

"Mr. and Mrs. London?"

I looked up with surprise at the flight attendant who had approached us and couldn't help but notice how quickly Delaney had reacted, too. I mean, sure, maybe it had more to do with someone appearing next to her aisle seat, someone who was clearly talking to us, but I chose to believe it was the name, my name, *our* name, that drew her attention.

"We're so happy to host you on your flight today," the attendant went on, flashing a pearly white smile at us that confused me. But her following words cleared everything up. "As the New England Knights' official airline carrier, we're so happy to have our favorite quarterback's family on board with us."

I smiled back politely. "Thank you. We're happy to be here."

She nodded enthusiastically at my minimally enthusiastic response. It was rare that random people in public connected me to my brother, but it did happen on occasion. People's questions and interest in Noah lately usually revolved around Gemma or Delilah, and like hell was I going to give anyone insight about them beyond the fact that they were his entire world.

"We meant to catch you earlier," the flight attendant started, her tone regretful in a professional, robotic sort of way. "So I apologize that you're already settled in, but we'd love to upgrade you to first class for your trip to Amsterdam today."

"Oh, that's not—"

"I insist. Your brother wanted to ensure you had an excellent start to your honeymoon." She blinked at me, trying to convey unspoken words with those eyelashes. It was like a new form of Morse code, but I understood it completely. I'd only make her life more difficult if I refused. And while I certainly didn't think it was necessary to fight being upgraded, there was something weird about getting special treatment because of your brother's job.

But this seemed less like preferential treatment and more like Noah called in a favor.

And I'd be more grateful—especially considering Delaney would probably get to recline and put her feet up now, which was better for her circulation—if I didn't feel so damn guilty about it, considering it was not my *actual* honeymoon.

"That sounds wonderful, thank you," I said, flashing another congenial grin.

"Thank you so much," Delaney echoed, pocketing her safety pamphlet fan and grabbing her bag from beneath the seat.

"Excellent." The flight attendant clapped her hands together. "Do you have any carry-on luggage in the overhead compartments?"

"I have a suitcase," Delaney answered.

The attendant nodded. "Perfect. I'll lead you to your seats, and Marcus here can grab Mrs. London's belongings if you point them out."

"I can grab my wife's luggage," I assured her with a tight smile, starting to feel a bit useless and like I was losing control of the situation. Which was ridiculous, I knew. But still.

Delaney wore a tilted grin and avoided my eye contact as she stood, following both flight attendants to the front of the plane. I retrieved her carry-on suitcase from the overhead bin before I joined them. Delaney was settling into a cushy first-class seat by the time I reached her, and Marcus directed me to a spot beside her, separated by what appeared to be a retractable wall.

I couldn't believe I was saying this, but I was grateful for the slight separation from Delaney that these seats would give me. Maybe by the time we deplaned in Amsterdam, I'd have my shit together where she was concerned.

It was probably too much to hope for, but I tried. I spent most of the next seven hours in the air trying to catch all of the inaccuracies in episodes of *Grey's Anatomy* and *not* peek over at Delaney's sleeping form every ten minutes. Surprisingly, time passed quicker than I expected, and we were landing before I knew it.

As soon as the wheels were down, I checked my phone, wanting to confirm the train details leaving from the airport. But I found a message from the host of the vacation home I booked instead.

A message that said there was an issue with flooding in the downstairs of the house.

A message that said that, because of that, they would be upgrading us to a nicer property.

It looked beautiful—the kind of place where honeymoons were supposed to happen.

But it made my stomach flip for two reasons.

One, it looked over the rolling North Sea.

And two, it only had one bed.

six years ago

BLAKE

"This is truly the last thing I expected when you said you wanted to watch your favorite movie as a reward for getting through finals."

Delaney scoffed. "I have no idea why this would come as a surprise. The Lizzie McGuire Movie *is iconic.*"

"And incredibly unserious."

"So?"

"You're the most serious person I know, Delaney."

"No, you *are* the most serious person you know, Blake."

I pursed my lips, hating to think that Delaney calling me serious was another way to imply that I was boring to be around. It would be really unfortunate, considering she was the only person I looked forward to seeing every day and basically my only friend.

Maintaining friendships in med school was challenging, especially with people who weren't in med school. But Delaney was in the trenches with me, so it was different. Some days, it felt like me and her against the world.

Some days, it just felt like me and her.

"Besides, this movie has very important themes." She sipped her wine. A dry chardonnay. Her favorite. Besides appletinis—although

163

she'd never admit to that. "Like don't trust strangers or handsome men."

"Wow." I slapped a hand to my chest. "Never been called ugly like that before."

"Stop." A laugh burst from Delaney's lips, and I caught myself staring at her mouth for a beat too long. "No, you're just an anomaly, Blake London."

"Damn right I am," I muttered, trying to keep my smile to myself.

Delaney shook her head, tucking her feet beneath her and curling into a tighter ball on the couch beside me. "But actually, do you want to know why I like this movie so much?"

"Naturally, I do."

"Because I can trust it just like I can trust you."

My body suddenly felt too small for my heart, science be damned.

"It's familiar and comforting, you know?" she added. "It's a reminder of the good parts of home."

I hoped that maybe she was still talking about me, too.

I'd do just about anything to be Delaney's home.

Which was why I didn't mind one bit when she fell asleep on my shoulder about thirty minutes into the movie.

CHAPTER FOURTEEN

delaney

T HE TRAIN RIDE FROM Amsterdam to the coast of the North Sea, where we were staying, didn't take long. I spent most of it craning my neck to see the views outside the window, even though my muscles were already sore from sleeping funny on the plane.

My parents traveled abroad a lot while I was growing up but never took me. Not even when they visited Ophelia at her French boarding school with my Aunt Violet and Uncle Tripp when I was fifteen.

I remembered crying that time.

I remembered Bryan asking me what was wrong and not knowing how to tell him our parents weren't the people he saw them as.

I told him I missed Ophelia instead, and he put on my favorite movie to make me feel better.

"This is us, Lane," Blake muttered when the train approached its next stop. "Here, give me your suitcase."

Too tired to protest, I rolled it toward him, and Blake grabbed our bags by the handles to carry them off the train. I watched in awe, trailing after him as he handled them with ease.

AMELIE RHYS

I suspected I was going to like traveling with Blake.

An Uber pulled up outside the train station just as we emerged with our luggage, reaffirming that thought. How Blake had timed that so perfectly, I wasn't sure, but I also wasn't going to complain.

"We're almost there," Blake said, a soft reassurance as he loaded my bag into the back of the Uber.

"I can't wait."

Smiling, I slid into the back of the car and tapped my toes eagerly as the driver took off.

"So I got a message from our rental host," Blake said once we were on our way, and I tensed, immediately sensing something was wrong. His tone was hesitant, which was unusual for him. "There was some flooding at the place I booked, so they moved us to a different property. The home is upgraded and seaside, and they also gave us a discount for the inconvenience."

"Okay." I glanced over at him, confused by his tone. "That's... good, right?"

I didn't know much about the place that Blake had booked for us to stay originally. He'd insisted on taking care of it, which had been fine with me as long as he allowed me to contribute to the cost.

"Yeah." He didn't sound convincing. "There's just one thing."

I chewed on my bottom lip, waiting for the other shoe to drop.

"There's only one bedroom."

Of course.

"And only one bed?"

Blake pursed his lips and nodded.

"Is there a couch?"

"It looks like it," he said. "Based on the pictures, there's a good-sized one in the living room. I can sleep there."

I gave him a sharp look, which he actively avoided.

"You can't sleep on the couch for the whole trip."

Another shrug. "Not a big deal. There isn't really another option, and we aren't here *that* long."

166

He was right; we'd only been able to get a handful of days off for the trip considering how last minute it was. But we both knew there was another option.

We could share the one bedroom.

And the one bed.

"How big is the bed?"

I mean, if it was king-sized, we could probably share it without any problems. Right? I could take one side, and he could take the other. There'd be an ocean of space between us. It didn't need to be weird. Blake and I had napped together before. We'd fallen asleep on the couch after I forced him to watch the best movie in cinematic history, the same one I'd watched that night with Bryan, aka *The Lizzie McGuire Movie*.

This was basically the same thing.

Blake's eyes finally skated to meet mine, and I realized that no, it was not basically the same thing. Falling asleep on each other's shoulders accidentally wasn't the same as planning to sleep together. Of course. That was why it was different.

That...or maybe it was the kiss.

The kiss that had been really so good, something I realized more and more every time I thought about it.

Not that I thought about it often.

Regardless, that kiss had made me more aware of Blake and every moment of our proximity than ever before. Had it made him more aware, too? He didn't act like it before, but now, I couldn't be sure. His jaw ticked, and his eyelids grew heavy as he considered my question. The air between us in the Uber thickened, and I cleared my throat in an attempt to make the closeness more bearable.

It didn't. But it got Blake to respond.

"I'm not sure," he said, but his tone made me think sharing a bed was not within his comfort zone.

And yet, I couldn't shake his words from our conversation about boundaries.

You can do anything to me.

He said I could do anything to him, but sharing a bed was too much? Was it because we weren't trying to convince anyone of anything?

"I can sleep on the couch," I said, pushing words out of my suddenly dry mouth. "I'm shorter. Makes sense."

He shook his head. "I can't let you do that, Lane. I convinced you to take this trip and booked this place; it's my mess-up. I'll take the couch."

I sighed, recognizing his stubbornness when I saw it.

"We can take turns."

Blake hesitated, his lips drawing in a tight line. But finally, he nodded. "We can take turns."

I mimicked him, giving a nod of finality as the car pulled up to an adorable thatched-roof house surrounded by a smattering of pink flowers and encased by a wooden picket fence.

"Is this it?" I asked, feeling my stomach tighten with anticipation.

Blake checked his phone and then surveyed the house like he was comparing the two. "Looks like it. I'm hoping the view around the back makes up for the lack of a bedroom."

"I think you're going to love it." The Uber driver tossed us a grin over his shoulder, his Dutch accent thick. "This is a beautiful stretch of the coast."

I smiled back at him. "Thank you. From what I've seen, it's gorgeous, and I can't wait to see more."

"Go check it out." Blake jerked his head. "I'll be right behind you."

I didn't need to be told twice, although I did stop to grab my suitcase from the trunk despite Blake's grumbling. I dragged it with me, charging toward the house. I felt reinvigorated. Maybe because we'd finally arrived at our final destination, or perhaps it had something to do with the way Blake had been looking at me. I didn't know, but I'd gotten a second wind. A touch of giddiness might even be flowing in my veins, but I couldn't be sure. Because that would be weird, right?

Either way, I couldn't remember the last time I'd felt this way.

Blake had the house's entry code, but I'd left him in the dust, rounding to the back of the house and promptly gasping. The rental home sat elevated from the coastline, which stretched endlessly. The dark waters crashed vigorously against an extended sandy shore, yet an undeniable serenity calmed my senses as I watched it.

Footsteps alerted me to Blake's presence, along with a prickling sensation on the back of my neck, an awareness of him I couldn't shake.

"I think the view definitely makes up for it," I said before sweeping my gaze around the rest of the backyard. My jaw dropped at what I found inside the glass wall that lined the patio's perimeter, walking through an opening in it. "Oh my God, is that a *hot tub*? And a *pool*?"

Blake's steps grew closer. "Did you pack your swimsuit?"

I turned to find him lingering a few paces away, his body tense.

"I threw it in at the last minute. I didn't expect to be *on* the sea, but I knew we'd be near it."

Blake's eyes darted to the shoreline and then back to me. His expression grew wary.

Oh, of course. *Shit*, I was an ass. Blake hated large bodies of water—ever since the drowning incident when he was younger. No wonder he was standing there looking like he might bolt back to the Uber.

"Blake..." I started, unsure of what to say. I didn't want to bring his trauma to the forefront if he wanted to keep it in the background. "Is this going to be okay?"

He nodded, but it was curt, and his eyes hadn't moved from the crash of the waves on the shore.

"We should message the rental hosts," I said. "I'm sure there are other property options that aren't by the water."

"No, Lane. It's okay," he insisted, more forceful this time.

"If you're sure." I stepped toward him. "We don't need to get

169

any closer to the shore than this. It's too chilly to go in the sea anyway," I reasoned. "The hot tub will be perfect for this weather."

His body remained strung tight enough that I worried if I plucked at the wrong cord, he'd break. But still, I inched closer, hoping I could reach him.

"Maybe we should head inside, Blake."

The wind was strong, billowing around us. It ruffled Blake's hair. He swallowed hard but shook his head. His eyes finally found mine, and I saw apprehension flash through them.

"I won't go in the sea," I promised. "*We* won't go in the sea. Okay?"

He exhaled, and when his body relaxed, so did mine. "Yeah, okay."

"If you don't want to go inside, I wouldn't mind dipping into this hot tub." I walked over to the edge of it, dropping to test the steamy water with my fingers before glancing back at him. "Join me?"

I hoped he'd say yes because I didn't want to leave him alone when he looked like he did right now, a bit like he might be sick. Although maybe rest was what he needed. Close his eyes. Take a load off his shoulders.

"Unless you wanted to lie down?" I added, desperately trying to deduce what he needed right now. "If that bed's calling your name, you can take it."

"No, I—" His voice was hoarse, and he clamped his mouth shut before trying again. "I don't think I could sleep right now. I shouldn't." His gaze shifted back to the sea, seemingly worried I'd disappear into it if he didn't pay close enough attention. "Because of the...jet lag, you know?" he added when he looked back at me. "The hot tub sounds really good."

"Make sense," I said softly. "Hot tub it is, then."

Blake's hooded eyes followed me as I straightened to walk back toward him, and it was at that moment that I realized how my proposition for him to join me might have come across. That realization should have made me second-guess it. All of it, all of this. But I didn't feel that way at all.

"Should we go put on our swimsuits?" I prompted when Blake remained unmoving, unspeaking.

He cleared his throat. "I didn't pack a suit, but I'll wear my shorts."

And then he turned to go change.

Blake and I had always done a good job of maintaining boundaries as friends.

But Blake and I had also always done a good job of remaining completely clothed in each other's presence.

Until now.

I'd already downed a whole glass of wine from the complimentary bottle the hosts had left us and let the hot tub jets lull me into semi-consciousness by the time Blake emerged onto the deck in his shorts and nothing else.

As soon as I saw him, I woke the fuck up.

I was aware that Blake London was attractive. I was also aware that I'd felt attraction to him before, even if I was good at burying it. Little flutters that I brushed off as a natural bodily reaction to someone who looked like he did. A spark that burned a little brighter than the others when we teased each other and he smiled that uncommon smile at me. *My* smile.

But it didn't *mean* anything. It was just a bit of chemistry that had always translated into friendship and nothing more.

But this—what I was experiencing right now—wasn't a flutter. And it wasn't a spark.

A fully formed flame lit inside me at the sight of him sauntering toward me with shorts riding low on his hips, the sinking sun shining a spotlight on every one of his defined muscles. He pushed a hand through his hair, trying to get the strands out of his face.

My cheeks flushed. Maybe it was the hot tub. Or the wine. Or the lack of sleep. Or, most likely, it was a combination of all of it that was making me so attuned to how fucking good Blake looked right now.

He was my husband. In most dimensions, it was considered appropriate to thirst after one's husband, right?

Except Blake and I lived in an entirely different dimension— one where marriage was simply a means to an end. And, in reality, we were just friends who shared a last name. And I shouldn't be looking at him like this or feeling less-than-friendly things.

"Delaney?"

"Sorry." I snapped myself out of it with a shake of a head, and my cheeks burned hotter. "Did you say something?"

Blake's lips tilted as he slid into the hot tub. "I asked if you wanted another glass of wine."

And because I needed something to do other than just stare at my husband, I waved away his question. "I'll get it."

But *getting it* meant I had to pass Blake to climb out of the hot tub, and my skin brushed against his beneath the water. I wasn't even sure which part of my body had touched which part of his because I felt that little bit of contact *everywhere*. There wasn't a single cell in my body that wasn't reverberating with heat at the moment, and while I wanted to blame the hot, steaming water, I knew I couldn't.

Blake, however, remained unfazed. He averted his eyes as I slipped past him, staring out at the sea, a haziness in his gaze. He was apparently the sane one between the two of us, and I took a few deep breaths as I walked back into the house, trying to get myself to his level of unbothered. After all, we had a whole honeymoon left to get through; I couldn't unravel the very first night.

When I returned to the hot tub with my full glass of wine, I retreated to my spot across from Blake, rubbing my sore neck as I lowered into the water, wondering if I could sink deep enough for the jets to hit my aching muscles. But when I realized it wouldn't happen, I flopped back against the seat with a sigh.

"What's wrong?"

Blake was watching me, a frown on his face.

I shrugged. "Just got a kink."

"A kink?"

"In my neck, from sleeping on the plane."

His attention dropped to my neck, studying it like he could heal me with his gaze. "Ah, so not the fun kind."

I lifted a brow, smirking without meaning to. "And what do you know about that?"

His gaze flicked to me before he looked away. "Know about what?"

"Kinks."

He rolled his bottom lip into his mouth before breathing, "We've never been the kind of friends who talk about our sex lives, Lane."

"No," I agreed. "Just the kind of friends who get married."

Blake cracked a smile before chancing a glance back at me. "Touché."

We fell silent; the only sounds of our conversation were the whirring jets of the hot tub and the more distant lull of waves. But my brain was anything but quiet. Blake's words kept repeating in my brain.

We've never been the kind of friends who talk about our sex lives, Lane.

Friends who knew each other on the level that Blake and I did talked about that kind of thing, though. Maybe not in explicit details or on the level of sharing kinks, but to *some* extent, right? But I knew next to nothing about Blake's sex life.

"Why is that?" I blurted out after a moment.

"What?"

"Why is it that we've never been the kind of friends who talk about our sex lives?"

Blake poked at the bubbles on the water's surface. "Do either of us have a very active sex life to talk about?"

"Touché," I muttered. "Even though you didn't have to call me out like that."

He shrugged. "I called us both out."

His logic quieted my thoughts, but only partly. Maybe we didn't have much of a sex life *now*, but surely that hadn't been the case for the last decade.

"Here, turn around," Blake said, motioning for me to spin in my spot. "Let me take care of that neck."

I did as he said. Mostly because my neck was throbbing but also because I was worried if I didn't, I'd start asking more intrusive questions that would threaten our honeymoon. But then I felt the pad of Blake's thumbs graze the base of my neck, and I realized that him touching me was probably not going to make our situation better. I nearly opened my mouth to lie, to say it felt better, to claim I needed more wine, anything, *anything* that kept just a bit of distance between my already on fire senses and my hot husband.

Before I could come up with an excuse, though, Blake dug his fingers into the knot in my neck, and a groan flew out of me. My body surrendered to his touch, needing the relief he was readily supplying.

"That the spot?" he asked, his voice sounding more carefully controlled than it had been minutes ago. I recognized it as a part of his concentration state, the way he sounded when he was dialed into something. I certainly hadn't expected Blake to be this passionate about massaging my neck, but I was *not* caring at the moment.

"Yeah," I gasped as he dug in even deeper. "Right there."

"Mmm," he hummed. "Good."

My head felt too heavy to keep upright, so I rested it on the edge of the tub, letting Blake have full range of my neck. He took advantage of this, caressing a path up my spine and then kneading his fingers back down it. I closed my eyes, feeling lost to the sensation of his touch, the water, and the thick air around us. The combination had me dozing in and out of heaven.

"Oh my God, *Blake*," I moaned as he found that spot again. The one that had originally sent me into a spiral.

"Jesus Christ," Blake rasped as I tried to hold in another groan and failed. "Hey, Lane?"

His direct question drew me out of the stupor he'd temporarily put me in. "Yeah?"

"I might be your friend who happens to also be your husband..." he started, his words suddenly husky and strained, alerting something inside me. "But I'm also just a man. And if you keep moaning my name like that..."

He didn't finish the sentence.

Why didn't he finish the sentence?

Why did I *want* him to finish the sentence?

"I'm sorry," I breathed, my lungs struggling to find the air I needed to think clearly. "You can...stop."

"It's fine," he murmured after a beat, his hands still working into me. I bit my lip to keep quiet when his fingers passed over that spot again.

"Blake, I don't want to make you uncomfortable."

God, this was embarrassing.

"I'm not uncomfortable." Blake huffed a humorless laugh. "Not like that," he added in a hushed voice. He was close enough that I felt his release of breath as he exhaled. It hit the sensitive hollow below my ear, and now I was holding in my sounds for another reason. "I'm sorry."

His apology was almost inaudible, but I heard it.

My body pulsed. The steam swirled around us. I didn't know how to breathe, let alone think about what to say next. All the words we'd said rolled around in my brain, and I tipped my head to the side to whisper the only realization that surfaced.

175

"This is why we don't talk about our sex lives, isn't it?"

"Yeah, Lane."

His hands vanished, making me want to protest. But I could tell by the sound of him pushing through the water that he was already backing away.

"This is why we don't talk about our sex lives."

CHAPTER FIFTEEN

blake

I SAT WITH A cup of coffee the next morning, staring out at the hot tub—the place where I nearly lost my goddamn mind.

Last night almost ruined me. The memory of Delaney wearing that tiny bathing suit while groaning my name would forever torture me.

But it wasn't just the hot tub that did me in. It was also the way the waves echoed in my ears all night, taunting me as I tossed and turned on a couch that was about as comfortable as the on-call beds at the hospital. I woke up with muscles that screamed at me.

Rubbing the back of my neck, I experimented with stretching it, tipping my head down.

"Looks like it's your turn for a neck massage."

I stilled at the sound of Delaney's voice. As much as I wanted to beg her to touch me, it was a bad idea. Last night was the first time I'd been certain, absolutely positive, that she recognized we had chemistry. That there was *something* there, something I'd known about for fucking ever. Hell, she checked me out. I'd stepped outside in my shorts, and Delaney had stared. *Stared* at me.

A ridiculous amount of satisfaction burned in my chest as I

remembered the heat in her gaze and the deer-in-the-headlights look she gave me when she realized she'd been caught giving me a once-over. Or twice-over.

It was the reason I was sitting at the kitchen table decidedly *not* wearing a shirt.

Yeah, so what if I wanted to see her look at me like that again? Sue me.

Her reaction was also the reason I'd been more forward with her last night about my own attraction, more than I'd ever been before. Maybe I shouldn't have done that. Maybe I'd revealed too much when I still didn't know what was going on in that pretty head of hers. And maybe until I had a better idea of where she stood on me admitting she made me fucking hard as a rock with those breathy moans of hers, I needed to play things safe. Even if I wanted to take that look she gave me last night and run with it, I knew I had to walk.

Her touching me—for any reason—was not in the category of playing it safe.

"Don't worry about it," I said, my voice scratchy.

"It was the couch, wasn't it?" she asked, walking around the table to make herself a coffee with the tiny Keurig-like machine on the counter. "I told you I should take it. You're too tall."

"You're not *that* much shorter than me."

Delaney was a tall woman. Or maybe it was just that she always stood tall with that ramrod-straight posture of hers.

"I'm at least four inches shorter than you," she said with a roll of her eyes. "Here, let me help."

She padded her way back over to me, wearing these cute little pajama shorts that made it hard to think. Breathe. I definitely couldn't talk. Or protest what she was about to do. And suddenly, Delaney's hands were on me, just resting on my shoulders at first and then massaging them. Lightly, but then...not. Her thumbs pressed into a knot at the base of my neck, and my heart rate spiked. Warmth coated my skin. A groan slipped out of me.

Delaney leaned in. I could feel her, so close to me. So close I could almost taste her. My brain spiraled down into a memory, one where I *had* been tasting her. One where she'd been in my arms wearing a wedding dress, and I felt her everywhere, and when I kissed her, she kissed me back.

I didn't care what we called it aloud; we both knew in the whispered recess of our minds that there had been nothing fake about that kiss.

"Not so easy, is it?" she breathed, making my skin tighten. "To keep quiet?"

I gritted my teeth together, trying to dampen the desire that had flared inside me at hearing her voice sound like that. Seductive. Sensual. Did she even realize what she was doing? "Not when it feels this good," I admitted gruffly.

"Good." She made a humming noise in the back of her throat, and I felt my cock stiffen against the fabric of my shorts. "I don't mind."

"I didn't *mind* it, either, you know." I actually really fucking liked it. Hearing Delaney moan my name? It had been a new form of pleasure I never thought I'd get to experience. "I just wanted you to know what you were doing to me last night."

"And what, exactly, was I doing to you?"

The same thing she was doing to me right now. Making it hard to think and turning me the fuck on.

"Delaney..." I groaned her name, struggling to keep my composure as her hands worked over my bare skin. Fuck me, this was bad. And good—too good. "Why do you want to know?"

"Because I think you might be doing the same thing to me, and I don't..."

Her whispered voice vanished a second before her hands did, and I felt her retreat. Not so unlike I did last night. Was this payback? Or was she just as unsure of what was happening as I was?

All I could do was stare at her as she picked her coffee mug back up.

"So what are the plans for today?" she asked, sounding

completely unaffected by what had just occurred between us. Which meant she was wrong. I *wasn't* doing the same thing to her as she was to me. Because I couldn't turn off my feelings as quickly as she just had. I didn't know how to defeat the all-encompassing arousal as easily. I'd been pretending around Delaney for a hell of a long time, so it wasn't like I didn't have experience. But pretending it didn't affect me when she fucking moaned my name or let her fingers wander my body? I couldn't breathe, let alone carry on a normal conversation about our plans.

Delaney's mug was floating in midair. She'd been about to take a sip of coffee when she froze, realizing I was looking at her, breathless.

"Lane," I rasped.

At the sound of her name, she relapsed into motion again, taking a slow, steady sip of coffee. Her eyes stayed on mine above the rim of the mug, though. And I realized this trip was going to teach me things about desire I never knew before.

What the fuck was happening?

"I think we should get some groceries," she said after putting the coffee back on the counter. Her cheeks were rosy, telling me there might be hope, that she *was* affected. I wondered for a moment what she might look like flushed from an orgasm. God, I'd love nothing more than to give her one. Just one. Just once. She'd make all those sounds for me like she did last night, and instead of telling her to stop, I'd tell her to be louder.

Scream my name, sweetheart. Go on.

"Just to have a few things here for the week," Delaney continued. "For breakfast and...whatever."

She cleared her throat, and I wasn't sure if it was for my benefit or hers, but it worked.

"That sounds good," I finally replied, pulling myself out of a daydream where Delaney was coming on my fingers. "I had the same thoughts, actually." Between thinking about what she'd look like when she fell apart. "We could head into town, grab some groceries, get a bite to eat, explore a little bit."

"Perfect." She cocked her head to the side and pulled out her phone. "How far is it?"

"A mile or two," I answered before she had a chance to look it up. "We could bike—there's a few in the garage. Otherwise, this upgraded rental came with a Vespa we could use. Only one, though." I flashed her a grin that I hoped didn't look too excited. "I might not be an Italian pop star, but I can still do my best to drive you around Europe and do whatever your Lizzie McGuire dreams are made of."

Delaney burst out laughing at that, and the tension broke between us.

For now.

Delaney and I opted to ride the Vespa into town, simply because it had a compartment under the seat where we could put a few groceries.

Not because it meant that we'd be squished together on that seat.

Not because it meant that she had to straddle me from behind.

That had nothing to do with the decision-making at all because I honestly wasn't really looking to be tortured any more today.

I wasn't sure if Delaney had thought of those details or not, but based on her giddy expression as she fit the helmet over her braided hair, I was almost positive her brain was not where mine was. That was for the best because, as I'd learned in the last twenty-four hours, it was considerably easier to pretend when Delaney was oblivious.

"How do I look?" she laughed as I buckled the helmet beneath her chin.

"Perfect," I said automatically, giving her chin a tap to indicate she was all good to go.

She rolled her eyes at my response before looking down at her outfit—a pair of loose jeans and a linen shirt. "Well, considering you're used to seeing me in scrubs or sweats, I probably look better than normal to you."

"You always look good, Delaney," I muttered, not wanting to lie when I didn't absolutely have to. "You're stunning no matter what you wear."

"Stop." She flicked me in the arm. "Just because we're married doesn't mean you need to feed me compliments. Appeasing my ego was not part of the deal."

I hopped on the scooter without looking at her. "I'm not trying to appease your ego."

She inhaled before she followed suit, sliding onto the seat with a more delicate approach. I felt one leg brush against mine and then the other. Luckily, we both wore pants, which helped to avoid that skin-to-skin contact that seemed to mess with both of our heads. But then Delaney's chest grazed my back, messing with my head anyway. Her hands skimmed my sides as she wound herself tightly around my waist, flattening her body to mine.

"Well, then...thank you," she said, breathing in my ear.

I'd forgotten what we were talking about.

I swallowed hard as I fit the key into the ignition. Hopefully, Delaney wouldn't clock my harder-than-normal breathing or the way my pulse likely fluttered in my neck, right by where I could feel her presence. If she did, it would only take her a few moments to deduce what was happening to me, considering my lack of other symptoms that might correlate with tachycardia.

"I think we're doing a very good job at faking this honeymoon," Delaney said with a breathy laugh, and I decided breathy laughs when she was this close to me were almost as bad as breathy moans. "This feels very couple-y."

I wanted to answer, *You think, Lane?* But instead, I nodded and suggested, "Maybe we should take a picture. I suppose this honeymoon is only as convincing as the evidence we bring home about it."

"Good idea." Delaney handed me her phone and then tightened her hold as though how hard she was squeezing me could be conveyed through the picture. "We can send it to Sully. I'm sure he'll approve."

I lifted her phone to snap the photo, and a grin immediately bloomed on my face from seeing Delaney's head hovering over my shoulder, her smile wide, eyes sparkling. She looked happy, and maybe it was fake or forced, but at the moment, I was going to choose to believe it was real. That whatever ended up happening on this trip, regardless of the pretense of why we were on it, was real.

"I'd give you a convincing kiss on the cheek or something, but I can't get that close to you," she chuckled as I snapped a few pictures. Her head bobbed toward mine, and our helmets clinked together, demonstrating her point.

"Maybe another time," I murmured, feeling the adrenaline shoot up in my body at the idea of Delaney's lips anywhere near my body.

"Yeah," she breathed, and her expression morphed into something unfamiliar in the phone screen before I lowered it, handing it back to her.

"Ready?" I prompted.

"Ready," Delaney echoed, giving another squeeze to indicate she was holding on and prepared to take off. I ran my hand over her interlaced fingers on my stomach, wanting a little bit of proof that she was there and I wasn't imagining it. I felt Delaney inch closer, her hips flexing into my ass in a way that had me reeling.

"Lane..." I choked on thin air for a second before getting myself together. "Trying to make it hard for me to breathe is not really the best approach when I'm about to drive us around in a foreign country."

"Do you want me to drive?" she quipped back, loosening her

hold a little as though *that* was the reason I couldn't get air into my lungs.

"No, that's not—"

"Wait, do you even know what you're doing?" she pressed, worry threading through her voice as her grip intensified again.

"I know what I'm doing," I groaned.

But apparently, I wasn't very convincing.

"I should have asked you before we decided on the Vespa if you actually knew how to drive one of these things. Maybe we should switch to the bikes. Just bring our backpacks to put the food in."

"I know how to drive a motorcycle, so I'm pretty sure driving this isn't going to be too difficult in comparison," I argued.

To prove that I was confident and ready to go, I turned the key in the ignition and powered up the engine. It was, of course, a lot more subdued than the sound of a motorcycle revving to life, but subtle vibrations still coursed through my body. A gentle thrum heightened my already piqued senses.

I felt Delaney shift on the seat behind me. "You know how to drive a motorcycle?"

"Yeah, Noah has one," I said over my shoulder.

"Of course he does," Delaney sighed as though that explained everything.

"I don't know what that means," I said bitterly, knocking the kickstand up on the side of the scooter. "But I'm going to choose to ignore it."

"It doesn't mean anything."

"Sure."

"Other than that he seems like the type to have a motorcycle. You know, with the tattoos and everything."

"You into those, Lane?"

"No," she said simply. "Not really. I mean, I'm not *not* into them. Like they don't bother me. Like if *you* were to get some—" She snapped her mouth shut again before ending with, "They're okay, I guess."

I nodded as slight amusement pierced through the haze of jealousy that had momentarily swooped over me.

"Let's get going before they run out of food at the grocery store," Delaney urged, and I realized I'd never been so excited to go shopping for food before.

"Okay," I agreed, feeling lighter than I had in years. "Let's do that."

"So how do I compare to Paolo?"

Delaney and I had made it back to the house about an hour before sunset. The Dutch village closest to us was quaint and whimsical. Breezy, in a literal sense. The gusts of wind off the North Sea were intense but refreshing.

We'd spent the morning stuffing our faces with pannekoeken, which was an even more delicious version of a pancake, and the afternoon shop-hopping. Delaney found an ornament of Delft Blue ballerina slippers that I insisted we get because suddenly, all I could think about was putting up a Christmas tree with her. I'd never really decorated for the holidays before, but I wanted to this year. With Delaney. I wanted to put things under it for her to open. More presents than she ever needed. She'd complain, and I'd do it anyway. Fuck, I wanted that. I wanted to spoil my wife.

"Considering Paolo was a fraud in the end, I'd say you're definitely coming out ahead," Delaney replied, yanking me out of my delusional thoughts. "Although you're your own brand of fraud."

I frowned. "And how am I a fraud?"

Delaney wiggled her left hand at me, her wedding ring sparkling, glinting off the setting sun. We'd whipped up some pasta—it was a carb day, apparently—and had dinner on the back patio. I'd just polished off the last of my food in time for her to deliver a gut punch, making me fight to keep it all down.

"As my faux husband."

I leaned back into the plastic chair, folding my arms across my chest.

God, how I wanted to tell her exactly what I thought about that title. *Faux husband.* Especially considering how *real* that ring she was showing off was.

I raised a brow at her. "Whatever you say, Delaney London," I said under my breath.

She heard me. Her cheeks pinkened. "You know what I meant."

"Uh-huh," I muttered, acknowledging that I understood it even if I hated it.

"Regardless." Delaney folded her hands on the table in front of her. "You're miles above Paolo. I've heard your rendition of 'What Dreams Are Made Of.' You can actually carry a tune, *and* you'd never try to frame me for being talentless."

"I'd never be able to convince anyone you're talentless," I chuckled before adding, "To be honest, I forgot how the movie ended."

Delaney gasped dramatically. "You forgot about the best cinematic climax of all time?"

"You're talking about *Endgame*, right?"

Delaney glared at me. "See, this is why you're a fake, Mr. London."

My lips twisted, trying to restrain myself. "And why's that, *Mrs.* London?"

"Because my real husband would never deny the cultural significance that is *The Lizzie McGuire Movie*."

A laugh slipped out of me. "Maybe your husband just needs a refresher. It's been years since we watched it. Should we see if there's somewhere we can stream it tonight?"

Her eyes lit up with a brilliant, childlike wonder, and my chest ached at seeing her like this. This side of Delaney had always existed, but it got shadowed by everything else in her life, all the responsibility she put on her shoulders.

"Really, you want to watch it?"

I'd never wanted anything more.

"Absolutely." I went to pick up our plates, eager to follow through.

"Yes!" Delaney jumped out of her seat, grabbing the glasses from the table and shooting ahead of me into the house. "Can I shower quick?" she called over her shoulder. "I feel like I have sand stuck to me even though we didn't even go down onto the beach. I swear it's like embedded in the wind or something."

"Of course." I smiled, following behind her. "I'll get it set up."

Delaney raced off to the bathroom in response, practically skipping down the hallway, leaving me to sift through streaming apps in search of *The Lizzie McGuire Movie*. I found it—thank God —by the time I heard Delaney leave the bathroom, pad across the hall, and close the bedroom door behind her. But when nearly twenty minutes went by and she still hadn't emerged to join me, I decided to investigate.

"Lane?" I called, giving a soft knock on the door.

Silence greeted me, which caused my mouth to tug into a frown.

"Delaney?" I tried again, louder this time. "Is everything okay?"

When she still didn't answer, worry washed over me. Morbid scenarios flashed through my mind, and those thoughts caused me to twist the handle without a second thought, pushing my way into the bedroom. I didn't hesitate, didn't pause to think that maybe what I was doing would have consequences. I didn't care about anything that didn't involve Delaney's well-being.

I stopped short when I saw her curled up on the bed, still wearing her towel. It was tucked around her securely, covering every bit of her I had no right seeing. Her damp hair was strewn over her shoulders, tangled on the pillow. She had her phone in her hand, like she'd been looking at something before simply... falling asleep.

Something seized up inside me at the sight.

Taking careful steps, I walked around the bed, wanting to double-check what I was seeing.

"Lane?" I said again, my voice barely a breath.

I didn't really want to wake her up; I just wanted her to stir enough for me to ensure she was okay.

And that was exactly what she did, curling tighter into a ball and wrinkling her nose. She adjusted her head on the pillow. Then she inhaled and exhaled deeply, settling further into a heavy sleep.

A grin slid onto my face, and I folded the other side of the comforter over her, tucking it over like a taco shell. Then I moved her phone to the bedside table, plugging it in before turning to walk back to the living room.

I sank back onto the couch, back to where I was last night.

And then I pressed Play on *The Lizzie McGuire Movie*.

Maybe it would drown out the sounds of the ocean slamming against the shore.

CHAPTER SIXTEEN

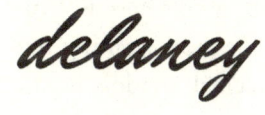

I WOKE WITH A jolt and flung the covers off. My pulse raced as I looked around, taking in my dark, unfamiliar surroundings. Salt air clung to my lungs as I gasped for a breath. Sweat tickled the back of my neck, probably from the heavy comforter I'd been cocooned in. My heart was pounding, but I wasn't sure why. I registered the shape of the window, the moonlight streaming through it, saw the shadowed stretch of beach, heard the lull of the sea.

Honeymoon. I was on a honeymoon. In the Netherlands. With—

A shout from the other room had me springing to my feet. That was the sound. That was the sound that woke me up.

And I knew who it was.

"Blake."

His name burned with worry on the way up my throat, and I shot out of the bedroom to find him. He must be on the couch, but *why* was he on the couch? I was supposed to sleep on the couch tonight. Wasn't I? Right after we watched—*oh*.

The credits of *The Lizzie McGuire Movie* were rolling on the TV screen in the living room. I didn't remember watching it. Confusion seeped through me, but I didn't have time to dissect it. Not when Blake came into view, his body flinching at an invisible attacker, his face screwed up with desperation.

Oh, no, no, no.

"Blake," I breathed, a soft coo as I rushed over to him and reached out to touch his face, wanting to soothe the pain there. The scruff of his five-o'clock shadow bristled against my palm as he panted, eyes squeezed shut. His bare chest rose and fell in quick, rapid breaths, close to hyperventilation. "*Blake*, it's okay."

My touch didn't rouse him from whatever nightmare he was battling, so I lay down beside him on the couch, squeezing myself onto the cushions so I could fit against his body. So I could wrap my arms around him and bring him back to reality with a little shake.

"It's a dream." I said the words into the crook of his neck, hoping they would find their way into his ear. "Wake up, okay?"

"Delaney," he choked—the first audible word I'd heard from him, and I hoped it meant that he was waking. But then he said my name again, and this time, it ripped from his throat in a cry.

"I'm right here," I said, speaking more forcefully, trying to get through to him. I pulled back to look at his face, and it was in that moment that his eyes flicked open. He went still, deadly still in a way that terrified me beyond anything I'd experienced before. His pupils were dilated, dark, and distressed. They darted around my face, and I watched as the pieces flew back together, as his brain returned to reality.

"I'm right here," I repeated before I continued to chant a mantra of things that I thought might help. That I thought might get through to him. "We're on land. No one's hurt. You're okay. Everyone's safe. I'm right here, Blake."

"You're here," he echoed, his lips seeming to move in slow motion. "You're safe."

I nodded and wrapped my arms around his neck, tucking my head in to hug him. Hold him. And in an instant, he decompressed with a shuddering exhale.

"*Fuck*, Lane," he rasped. He buried his head in my neck,

breathing me in. "It was you." I felt his lips brush against where my pulse was hammering. "It was you this time." His tongue lashed out, flicking my skin like he needed to taste my heartbeat to know that it was real, and I couldn't withhold a gasp.

"Everything is okay," I said, but my voice was no longer steady. It shook with emotion I couldn't name.

"Thank fuck," Blake groaned, exploring the column of my throat with his lips. "Lane. Delaney."

My head spun. "Yes?"

"Don't you dare get in that fucking ocean," he growled into the hollow at the base of my neck. Then he nipped at my collarbone, and a shiver erupted up my body. Blake didn't notice. He was too busy dragging his open mouth back up to my ear, pressing hot kisses into my skin. I felt like I was being branded by his desperation. "Do you understand me? I don't want you fucking near it."

"I understand," I whispered, even though I didn't. I didn't fully understand what had happened to him, and I really didn't understand what was happening to me.

My body didn't feel like it was mine anymore. It felt like part of it belonged to Blake and the way he was clutching me, touching me. Part of it ached with whatever he was going through. Felt untamed like the desperation I heard in his voice, like I had so much unexplained emotion coursing through me that I might burst at any moment. And I knew that if he started dragging his lips down my body again, I wouldn't stop him. I didn't want to, even if I probably should, considering he wasn't thinking clearly.

"It was you," he breathed again. This time, I felt his nose graze my skin, following that same trail along my neck. "I wasn't able to save *you*, Lane."

My heart cracked at the agony in his voice. The final pieces of the puzzle snapped together, and I closed my eyes, gripping Blake harder.

"I'm safe," I assured him while trying to ground myself. He was spiraling, and I wanted to be his anchor. But I didn't feel like I could find the floor to stand on at the moment. "You saved me. You always save me, Blake."

He took a deep, quivering breath before letting himself sink into my embrace. His body relaxed, gave in to the reality of this moment. That everything was okay. That I was here, and so was he.

"Please don't leave."

It was his final request before he sighed and his breathing evened out.

"I won't," I promised.

Leaving Blake was not something I ever imagined doing, and I longed to tell him just that.

Never, Blake.

He'd been the one who'd left me. Didn't he remember that? When he'd moved across the country without me?

And then, I'd followed.

So, no, I wasn't going anywhere.

"Sleep," I encouraged. "I'll stay."

Blake fell silent, and I wondered if his subconscious had already dragged him back under.

I hoped it was nice to him.

But since there were no guarantees of that, I fought to stay awake for as long as possible, ready to pull him out of that ocean he fought so hard against. I made it until a pinkish light filled the room before my eyes drifted shut, and I splashed down into my own dreams—ones that I hoped one day I'd understand.

The next time I woke, my senses rolled over me like fog on a dewy morning—nothing like how I'd jolted into awareness last night.

My heart thudded, growing from faint to steady. Light crept

into my vision. I felt warm, a flush rising up my body. But then, at the same time...cold. A shiver abruptly ran down my spine.

I frowned at the sensation of air. Just air. There was nothing on me. Not a blanket.

Not even...a towel.

I gasped.

I was naked.

Naked.

Oh my God, I was naked.

My eyes flew open as the muskiness of man filled my surroundings. The smell of salt air and woody vanilla lingered. Chocolate-brown hair filled my vision. Somewhere in the back of my mind, I registered the feeling of a hand on my bare back, muscular arms wrapped around me. *Blake.* Blake was clutching me to him. His deep breaths caused the rise and fall of his chest. His bare chest. His bare chest that brushed against *my* bare chest.

Oh my God, I wasn't just naked. I was naked in Blake's arms. Squished together on a couch.

Before my brain could run with that information, snapshots of last night replayed across my vision. Blake's nightmare, the way he screamed my name, how his lips had felt on my skin. And now, we were still intertwined. *More* intertwined. My fingers were buried in his hair at the base of his neck. Our legs twisted around each other. His ankles trapped mine. Our bodies flush.

Fuck.

I attempted to toggle my foot out between his, but he shifted at the movement.

Double fuck.

My heartbeat tripled, realizing that Blake was seconds from waking and finding me in his arms, unclothed. It was either wait and let that happen or make a break for it.

I chose the second one.

I yanked my foot free and began to roll toward the edge of the couch, only to be flattened back against his chest as his arm tightened around me.

"You said you wouldn't leave," he mumbled in a sleep-coated voice. "Where's my wife going?"

Considering the state he was in before he fell asleep last night, I was surprised he even remembered me saying that.

"It's morning," I whispered.

"So?"

"Blake." His name came out like a plea.

"Fine," he grunted in my ear.

Giving in, his hold on me loosened. His fingers drifted over my bare back, retreating so I could presumably escape. But then he stilled. His breathing shifted. Quickened. Blake's chest rose, grazing mine. I could identify the exact moment when he felt my hardening nipples—when he realized I wasn't wearing anything.

"Blake," I repeated weakly.

"You're...you're not—" he stuttered and then broke off. "Delaney, you're not—"

He couldn't seem to get the words out.

"The towel," I tried to explain. "I fell asleep in the towel. And then I ran out here in the towel. And then I think the towel must have...fallen off."

"Fallen off?" Blake repeated like he couldn't conjure any words beyond the ones that were already said.

"Fallen off."

This should be the moment that I jumped off the couch. Ran away. Disentangled myself from Blake's body so that we didn't have to do whatever dance we were doing right now. It felt like we were in a supported pirouette, where I was spinning round and round in circles, and Blake was just...holding me. Unmoving.

"I suppose..." He stopped to clear his throat. "I suppose this is why you were trying to leave, huh?"

I nodded, remaining still.

I didn't move, but I suddenly felt...closer to him.

Did Blake's arm tighten on me again?

That didn't make sense.

Nor did how I unlaced my hands from behind his neck, sliding them down his chest. I mean, it would have made sense if I'd done it to push him away. But my hands stayed there, fingers drumming on his collarbone, feeling the way his breathing changed.

"Hey, Lane?"

His breath tickled the curve of my ear, and I wasn't sure why, but it made my head spin. I felt like I was stuck in a never-ending turn sequence.

"Yeah?"

"Do you still get the money if I die after you've married me?"

My lungs deflated. Punctured. Were no longer operational.

"Why the hell would you ask me something like that?" I choked.

He groaned. "Because I swear to God, you're trying to kill me on this trip."

"This trip was *your* idea, Blake."

"Yeah, but I didn't know it would be like this."

My breath hitched. "Like what?" I asked, even though I knew what he meant. Something had shifted in the last forty-eight hours. Something about the way we were together. And even though we kept trying to avoid it, I wasn't sure it would be possible.

"Like..." His attempt at an answer descended into a groan that sounded an awful lot like mortification. And I understood a second later, gasping when I felt him. *Really* felt him. Hard. Against me.

"Just a man," he muttered as a reminder. "I'm sorry, but I'm just a man, Delaney."

"Right," I breathed, unable to move. I knew I should disentangle myself from him. I knew I shouldn't be feeling him this way. But at the same time, all I wanted to do was explore whatever was blooming inside me, caused by having Blake so close to me. So I remained immobile, stuck between what I should do and what I wanted to do, unable to do either. "It's just...biology. Chemistry. Sciencey things."

"Says the medical doctor." His husky chuckle in my ear was not helping my situation.

"Shut up. I'm a cardiologist. Not a..." My eyes rolled back as Blake tried to adjust his position on the couch and ended up brushing his length directly between my legs.

"Sexologist?" Blake offered.

"Sure. That." I released a shuddering breath. "I just know hearts."

"Hearts, hm?" Blake said absently. His fingers were dancing on my back, and I was finding it hard to think. "And what's my heart doing right now, Delaney?"

I closed my eyes, tuning in to the rhythm in his chest. "It's beating...it's beating fast."

"Good." He sounded genuinely relieved. "Wasn't sure if I was still alive or not."

I wiggled my hips, shamelessly wanting to feel him again. And oh, did I. *Holy shit.* How had I gone so many years without realizing that Blake was so...so...

"Delaney?" Blake prompted, like he knew I'd short-circuited inside. "Are you okay?"

A great question, honestly.

"I'm okay," I squeaked out. "I was just going to say that I think you're, uh, very alive."

Blake laughed, and I felt it in every nerve ending in my body. "You know how you know that?"

Yes. Yes, as a matter of fact, I did know how I knew that. Because his giant—

"Because your tits are pressed right up against my chest, Lane."

Oh, yeah. That, too.

I suppose we were experiencing new things about the other person. And I suppose this was my reminder that I shouldn't still be lying here next to him. I should definitely have put an end to this long before this moment.

"Right, I should...move."

I felt Blake nod. "Probably for the best."

But even as he agreed, his arms pulled me closer, hugged me tighter. Like he wanted one last taste of what...this would be like. Whatever this was. He flexed his body toward me, chasing one last feel of me. And then I couldn't help but do the same. I melted into his hard frame, in awe of the desire it sparked in me.

What was going on?

"Tulips," Blake said abruptly, nearly shouting the word into my ear. "Tulips. We're here to see tulips."

"Right, that was our plan today." I gulped, pushing down the full-blown arousal that was now coursing through me. "Can you close your eyes?"

"Of course," he rasped.

His arms finally released me, and I pulled my head back to verify that his eyes were closed before stumbling off the couch. I averted my eyes, too, even though I wanted to sneak a peek back at him. Instead, I focused on snatching the towel off the ground.

"Delaney?" Blake's voice sounded pained.

"Just let me put my towel back on, one sec," I said breathlessly, unsure I was ready for whatever it was he was about to say. "Okay."

"I wanted to apologize for last night," he said hoarsely, and once I had my towel wrapped around me, I turned back around to see him sitting on the edge of the couch. He was leaning forward, bracing his elbows on both of his knees. His hair flopped messily over his forehead, and he peeked at me from beneath the hanging strands, checking to see if I was covered yet. And then when he realized I was, deep brown eyes pierced me, making it hard to function.

"You don't need to apologize, Blake."

"I..." He opened his mouth, but no words came out.

"I didn't realize you were still getting nightmares," I said quietly when he never continued his thought.

"I hadn't been." He shrugged. "Not for a long time. When I

moved to Boston, I had a couple. And here…" He glanced toward the window. "I think it's just being so close to the sea."

"We can relocate," I offered without thinking. "We can find a hotel in Amsterdam. Further inland."

He shook his head. "I don't want to do that."

"Are you—"

"I'm sure."

"I'd like to sleep next to you tonight." I tugged my towel tighter around me. "Wearing clothes, of course."

I smiled, forced a laugh, tried to make this thing, whatever it was that had just happened, a joke.

But Blake didn't laugh. And he didn't smile. He closed his eyes at my words, swallowed hard, and then opened them again.

"Of course."

eight years ago

BLAKE

"Can I have an appletini?"

The bartender at the bar right off campus raised a surprised brow at my order. "For your girl?"

His eyes shot over to Delaney, sitting at a table behind me. I followed his gaze and then ran his words over and over in my head.

Your girl, your girl, your girl.

But what I said aloud was, "She's my best friend."

And yeah, the drink was technically for her. The first time she tried to order an appletini here, a different bartender had given her shit about it, so now she always ordered something else. But I didn't want her to know that I only ordered appletinis so she could "sneak" drinks of it while I "wasn't looking." So I didn't confirm nor deny the rest of his question.

The bartender made a snort of disbelief.

"Could have fooled me."

I nodded, accepting that as truth. Delaney and I could have fooled a lot of people into believing we were together. Pretty much everyone who knew us had asked at some point.

Everyone was fooled into believing we were more.
Everyone but us.
Or maybe everyone but Delaney.

CHAPTER SEVENTEEN
blake

I F WE HADN'T PLANNED to go see the tulips today—the main reason we'd traveled here to begin with—I absolutely would have come up with some kind of excuse to detach myself from Delaney. Fake a stomachache. Say that a new episode of *Knockout News* just dropped. Something.

But I couldn't do that.

So here I was, watching the sinfully sweet sway of my wife's hips in a life-altering sundress as she walked in front of me.

Life-altering.

My life had altered this morning.

Because I would never, ever know a longing like I experienced when I woke up this morning to find not only Delaney in my arms but *naked* in my arms. *Naked.*

And somehow, I'd found the strength to keep my hand on her back. Fuck, to feel her but not be able to touch her was a new kind of torture altogether. My mind had gone blank, hazing over with lust and desire, when I realized her bare breasts were pressed against my chest. Her body was so soft, her weight so luxurious. I was left wanting her more than I ever had, and I hadn't been aware that was even possible.

I also wasn't sure how much longer I'd be able to handle it.

Because while I'd kept my hands to myself, my cock had acted with a mind of its own.

I should probably give more of a fuck about that, but I couldn't. Mostly because Delaney had been chasing the feel of me. Hard, between her fucking legs, wanting her like the world would end if I didn't have her. And maybe she wasn't equally affected by our predicament—there was not a chance in the world that she'd experienced the reaction that I had—but there had been *something* there. Something that made me wonder if she'd walked away from me wet and wanting.

That line of thinking was so fucking distracting.

So distracting that I'd almost been able to pretend that last night—before I'd woken up to find Delaney in my arms—hadn't happened. That the flashes of Delaney drowning weren't real.

Because they *weren't*.

They *couldn't* be.

I'd dreamed of that day before, of the drowning that had fucked me up from the inside out. But in my dreams, the person I pulled out of the water had always been faceless. Even though I knew what she looked like, the poor woman I'd failed that day. I wouldn't be able to forget her face if I tried. I never had tried, though, despite desperately wanting to. I wanted to forget everything about that day.

But that seemed selfish.

So I remembered all of it.

In my dreams, though, the details never fully translated to my brain. There was never a face, which made it worse. It felt like my mind's way of convincing me that there were more, that the number of people I could let slip through my fingers during my career was endless. That the dreams were just a representation of my failure as a person, as a doctor, as a brother, as a best friend, and not the reminder of a singular event. That taking risks might not pay off. That there was always more than one outcome, and I should never forget that.

But last night was worse than anything I could ever imagine. I never wanted to see a face in my dreams again. Because now, the images burned into the walls of my brain were all Delaney. Her blonde hair plastered to my chest as I pulled her out of the water. Turning her lifeless form over to find her pretty face looking detached. The void in her eyes. But then her voice cut through to me, pulling me away. I hadn't wanted to go, hadn't wanted to leave her.

When I woke to find her there, I'd lost it. Right there, arms around me, body pressed close. She was okay, safe, saved. The relief was unexplainable. Unparalleled. So heavy it carried me off to sleep again.

Suffice it to say, the last twelve hours of my existence had crashed in tidal waves of emotions, all surrounding this woman who was my *wife*, and I wasn't sure if I was surfing them very well. It felt more like I was being pommeled.

To make it worse, a new swell of feelings smacked me right in the face as Delaney squealed with delight as we approached an endless sea of bright flowers.

"It looks just like the puzzle!" she gushed, looking back at me over her shoulder with a radiance that blew me the fuck away. I gave her an encouraging smile, and then she kept walking, giving a little spin of happiness as she followed a path between two colorful rows of tulips. On one side, they blazed orange, and on the other, they were deep pink, like the lining of my heart, which beat wildly in my chest as I watched the most beautiful woman in the world just...enjoy the moment.

Yep, this was worth it. This, right here, was worth everything. Every bit of torture, all of it.

Delaney stopped, planting her feet in the earth and tipping her head toward the sky. The sun peeked through the clouds, streaming over her face. We were here really early, since both of us had woken up on that couch at the crack of dawn. Not very many people were around. Just me, Delaney, and the tulips. Her blonde hair whipped in the wind. She pulled her jean jacket tighter around her but smiled nonetheless, eyes closed.

I pulled out my phone, not willing to let this moment expire without documenting it. I wanted this, right here, forever.

"Lane."

She glanced over her shoulder, and I snapped a picture just as she grinned in response to seeing me there with my phone out.

"Best picture ever," I declared.

Her lips thinned into a suppressed smile. "It's hard to go wrong with such stunning scenery."

"Yeah," I hummed. "The scenery."

"I know you probably don't like it." She gave me a sideways glance, her lips twisting. "What with all the color and everything."

"I *like* color," I said defensively.

"Blake, look at your outfit."

I stared down at my black shirt and the black jacket hanging open over it.

"Black is a universally flattering color," I argued.

"Is that why you like my graduation dress so much?" Delaney raised a brow. "Because it's black and therefore my only flattering dress?"

"No," I sputtered, thrown off that she'd brought up that dress. And that she knew I liked it so fucking much. "I didn't say black was the *only* flattering option. Just *a* flattering option. You do remember what I thought about that red dress you tried on for me, right? Case in point."

"Oh, yeah. That dress." She tapped her chin thoughtfully, and I immediately regretted bringing up any mention of that dress. Or how I'd reacted to it. How I'd come dangerously close to throwing it all away and telling her exactly what I thought about her in that dress. Most specifically, how I'd do anything to strip it off her. "We have dinner reservations at a place in Amsterdam tomorrow, right? I think I'm going to wear that."

It was possible I stopped breathing.

Or maybe my heart stopped beating.

If it hadn't already, it would soon.

Because Delaney was trying to *kill* me.

"You...packed it?"

She nodded sweetly, but I had a feeling that whatever thoughts were dancing through Delaney's brain were not entirely sweet. And I had no idea what to do about that.

She flashed me a smirk. "I think it will pair nicely with the all-black ensemble I'm sure you have lined up."

"I like color," I ground out. "Just not on me."

"If black isn't your favorite color, then I have no clue what is," Delaney laughed.

"Blue," I said automatically.

"Blue?"

I cleared my throat. "Like a sapphire blue."

That seemed to catch Delaney off guard. She cocked her head to the side, considering my answer. But I didn't really want her to dive too far into it. Delaney was smart, too smart, and if she thought about it for just two more seconds...

"Here, let me take some more pictures of you." I lifted my phone again. "We can turn them into a new puzzle. One you don't already have memorized."

"I don't want my puzzles to have pictures of *me* on them." Delaney rolled her eyes but smiled as she backed up so I could snap a few more photos of her between the rows of tulips.

"Should we take one together?" she asked after I'd taken more pictures than was truly logical. I wondered if she would notice if I changed one to my lock screen. Probably. *Damn.*

"Sure," I agreed, striding to stand beside her. She slipped her arm behind my back, and I took a steady breath as she inched closer to me. So close, so very close. Not as close as this morning, but still. She smelled sweet, like spring. And that, combined with the brush of her fingers on my back, was enough to suffocate me with desire.

I held up my phone and smiled. She did the same. I took the picture, and she tilted her head to the side, resting it on my shoulder. So I took another picture. She turned to look at me, and on instinct, I turned to look back. Her eyes sparkled as they blinked up at me, and in that moment, everything in the world ceased to exist except her.

I was so fucked.

"This was the whole reason you told your family that we were coming here," she said quietly.

"Yeah, it is."

She licked her lips. My gaze shamelessly dropped to her mouth. My arm fell, my phone forgotten. I watched as she tried to find the courage or the words to say something.

"I suppose these pictures should be...really convincing," she breathed, all while I was tracing the shape of her lips with my eyes.

"Would definitely help me save my ego."

"And we certainly wouldn't want anything to happen to your ego," she said, and then, unless I was imagining things—which was completely possible at this point—Delaney's gaze flicked to my mouth. But not in a way that she was trying to hide. More in a way that she was trying to imply something. "I think the occasion calls for it, Blake."

"I think you might be right," I agreed because *like hell* was I going to pass up the opportunity to kiss Delaney. I'd narrowly missed out on the chance that night at the fundraiser, interrupted by her dad and distraught by trying to figure out how to give her *just a peck*. I hadn't known how to do that.

But Delaney gave no such instructions this time. So I cupped her cheek, tilting her head back and lowering mine so we were inches apart. "Does this make you feel uncomfortable?"

She made a breathy, incredulous noise that went straight to my dick. "Blake, this morning you were holding me while I was shirtless."

That reminder was not helping the situation with my dick.

"Shirtless?" I repeated. The tip of my nose grazed hers. "Were you wearing pants?"

"No." I watched, amused, as her pale skin turned a pretty

pink. "Fine. You were holding me while I was naked," she amended.

Jesus Christ, why did I push that point?

"You did try to run away at one point, though," I pointed out.

She tried to run away, and I'd been reluctant to let her go. My arms had kept tightening around her, acting on an instinct I was helpless to stop.

"Not very fast."

"No," I said softly. "Not very fast."

"I'd say I'm comfortable." Her lips parted, and I just stared. Stared at them and imagined what they were going to feel like. "And I think the occasion calls for it, Blake," she reinforced.

"Yeah?"

She nodded, but she was so close that our mouths brushed when she moved.

"Yeah..."

"Just for clarification, that means you think we should kiss for the camera, ri—"

"Oh my God, just take the picture," she groaned, and then Delaney yanked me by the shirt, pulling me down until our lips met.

The amount of restraint it took for me to *not* crush my mouth to hers was unbelievable. Just a *touch* of her lips had me losing control. She tasted so fucking sweet, and all I could think about was how I wanted to make this woman mine. How she *was* mine. My wife. My best friend. My everything.

But somehow, I restrained myself. I swept my lips over Delaney's instead, taking my time tasting her, seeing how she'd react, judging what she wanted. All while an uncontrollable heat coursed through my body, taking hold.

She pulled me closer, intensifying the kiss, and everything inside me cheered. At least until a moment later when she broke away.

"Are you even taking a picture?" she breathed against my lips before diving back in again, not even waiting for an answer.

Oh, right. Yes. A picture.

That was why we were kissing.

To take a picture.

For my fucking family.

"Right," I muttered, swiping up on my phone screen before lifting it in front of us. Then I pressed my lips to Delaney's, luxuriating in the simple feel of her as I snapped the photo.

"Thanks," she said, sounding dazed. Her lips brushed over mine once more, kissing me one more time for good measure before releasing the grip she had on my shirt.

Releasing *me*.

I had no idea how she did it because I was hungry for so much more of her. If I had the choice, I'd never let her go.

But Delaney took a step back, straightening her dress unnecessarily before she pointed at my phone. "Does it look okay?"

Since I wasn't sure if I'd survive looking at the picture in my current state, I handed my phone to her so she could have a look. Her cheeks reddened as soon as she saw it, filling me with a curiosity that would likely destroy me if I followed it. So when she handed it back to me, I immediately pocketed it.

"Maybe they have some, um, sapphire-blue tulips around here for you," she said before I could ask her if the picture was good enough. Hell, I wouldn't mind taking another.

I chuckled. "I don't think that's a thing, Lane."

She grabbed at my hand, quickly leading me away. Almost like if she left this spot, she could run away from whatever just happened.

"Let's look anyway," Delaney insisted, and I followed her as we strolled through the fields for another half an hour, pretending that we hadn't just kissed. Pretending that it had been for a photo. Pretending we were just two best friends who happened to be married and nothing more.

In the end, we didn't find any.

No sapphire-blue tulips.

Only sapphire-blue eyes.

And a shiny sapphire ring that kept sparkling in the spring-time sun.

After we finished at the gardens, we took a bus back to the train and rode it to the city of Alkmaar in time to catch the last of the weekly cheese market they put on in the city square. It also meant that it was jam-packed with other people here to do the same thing.

Delaney reached for my hand as we shimmied and slipped through the crowd, following the voice of the announcer and the flashes of men and women in traditional Dutch attire, carrying around wheels of cheese on so me kind of wooden sling between them.

"This is amazing," Delaney laughed as she snagged a spot at the rope that surrounded the live market. "I've never seen so much cheese in my life."

It really was *a lot* of cheese.

I stood behind her, watching as the man to her left glanced over at the sound of her voice and then did a double take. I couldn't blame him; Delaney was so fucking beautiful it hurt to look at her sometimes.

I was so busy glowering at the gawker that I didn't notice the guy trying to budge his way in front of Delaney until she stumbled back into me from the force of the man's intrusion. I wrapped an arm around her waist, tugging her back into my chest and bracing her from behind. Glaring at the back of the man's head, I wondered if I should say something, but then he turned around and made up my mind for me.

"Move the fuck over, will ya? We're all trying to see here."

His voice dripped with irritation, and while I couldn't place his accent, I knew it wasn't Dutch, telling me he was likely a tourist like us. His brows furrowed as he looked straight at Delaney like *she'd* done something wrong.

"Oh, I—" she started, stumbling over her words with noticeable shock at his anger. I waited for a second to see if she was going to continue, but when she didn't, the man mocked her. Fucking *mocked* her.

"Oh, I—" he mimicked before rolling his eyes, and my vision blurred, a hazy red overtaking my senses.

"Leave my wife the fuck alone, or the only thing you'll be seeing is stars," I threatened.

The man's beady eyes flicked up to me for the first time, and I could tell he hadn't registered that I was standing there behind her. Or maybe he just hadn't registered that we were together. Whatever it was, he was just a pathetic asshole who clearly preyed on women that he thought he could push around. Literally.

"Get the fuck out of here," I pushed out through gritted teeth, in case he hadn't gotten the picture yet. Delaney tensed in my arms, and I squeezed her tighter, holding her firm to my chest.

To my surprise, the man took a few moments to glare at me and then turned on his heel, muttering something about how this shit wasn't worth it. I watched him go, keeping my eyes on the back of his head until I could be sure he was gone. Meanwhile, I didn't let go of Delaney, and she didn't protest. Her attention had drifted back toward the market, observing how they weighed and sorted the wheels of cheese.

A moment or two passed before she muttered over her shoulder, "You can't just threaten people who are rude to me, Blake."

"Why not?" I grunted. Did she seriously think I would just let people talk like that to her and stand by, doing nothing?

"Because you're going to get hurt."

"*I'm* going to get hurt? Ouch, Lane."

"What? I was worried he was going to punch you for a second."

"You've wounded my very important ego." I leaned forward,

letting my lips graze the shell of her ear as I reminded her, "You do remember that dodging punches and punching things back is, like, my only hobby."

"I bet people's faces are harder than a punching bag," she reasoned, although I couldn't help but note how her voice sounded threadbare. "We wouldn't want you bruising your knuckles."

"I would happily bruise my knuckles for you, Delaney."

I'd do a whole lot more than that, but she didn't need to know everything. Not yet.

She shook her head, and though I couldn't see her face, I could imagine it was exasperated. She thought I was joking, but I wasn't. Not even fucking close.

"All this cheese is making me hungry."

I smiled against the top of her head, enjoying the position we were in right now far too much. Delaney leaned back slightly, resting against my chest.

"Want to get food after this?" I offered.

She nodded happily, and we watched the rest of the cheese market, not moving from our spot. Or our position. And I felt like the luckiest man in the whole goddamn universe.

It was a feeling that continued for the rest of the day. From lunch in Alkmaar to a walk along the canals, watching Delaney marvel over all the flowers that lined the streets—all of it was perfect. And real. And not at all like something that was fake or just for show.

It made me realize that I had a few more days here with Delaney to make her understand the same thing.

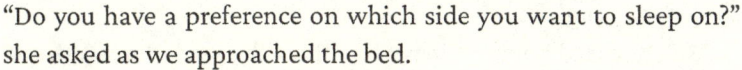

"Do you have a preference on which side you want to sleep on?" she asked as we approached the bed.

That we would both be sleeping in.

Both of us.

In one bed.

It shouldn't feel like a big deal. Not considering how we'd woken up this morning, smashed together on the same couch. Me, half-naked. Her, completely naked. We couldn't get ourselves in a more precarious situation than that, could we?

But it *was* a big deal. Because I had to pretend that I hadn't experienced how good she felt in my arms. How perfect her body was. How precisely we fit together.

"I'd rather not sleep by the window," I said, not wanting the vision of the sea to taunt me even when my eyes were closed. But then I thought about it for another second, thought about Delaney lying there instead, and immediately changed my mind. "Actually, I'll sleep by the window, that's fine."

Delaney stood next to the bed with a wrinkle between her brows as she considered me, trying to puzzle me out.

She was always trying to puzzle everything out.

I wasn't sure how she hadn't completely put all my pieces together yet, how she hadn't figured out they all added up to equal her.

"You know if I sleep next to the window," she said slowly, "I'm not going to roll off the bed and into the sea in the middle of the night, right?"

Or maybe she had figured me out more than I realized.

"You never know," I muttered, looking down as I walked to the window side of the bed and pulled back the covers on it. "I'd like to keep you as far away from that water as possible, thank you very much."

"Blake," she sighed as she collapsed on the opposite side of the mattress. "I wish I could just take away all of your worries. I'd shoulder them for you if I could."

I shook my head and slipped into bed beside her. "You shoulder enough."

She released another heavy breath as she settled beneath the covers. She turned on her side, facing the interior of the home, and I did the same. We were in the same position, but it felt like there was a whole ocean between us. And as much as our closeness tortured me, the distance did, too. I needed to *feel* her to ground myself, especially as the sound of the sea kept crashing into my ears.

I extended my leg until I found Delaney beneath the covers, brushing my foot against hers and letting the littlest connection and that slight sizzling of awareness soothe me.

Delaney gave me a cursory glance over her shoulder. "I know that we've established that we're not the kind of friends who talk about our kinks, but do you have a thing about feet I should be aware of? I don't think you're going to like mine."

A tight laugh fell from my lips. Mostly because hearing Delaney say the word *kinks* made my lungs feel like they were being squeezed.

"Are you saying you want to be the kind of friends who talk about their kinks, Lane?" I asked, doing my best to sound like I was teasing. "Because if you want to change things up, I can give you a full rundown."

The light of the moon revealed Delaney's cheeks tinting a vibrant pink, and God, it was so incredibly tempting to keep going, just to see how brightly I could get her to blush. But I didn't want to push the envelope if she wasn't ready.

I could probably also ease into things a little bit more instead of just offering up my sexual fantasies on a silver platter.

Yeah, that would probably be for the best.

To my surprise, Delaney twisted around, turning to fully face me. Her cheeks were still a delicious rosy color, but her stare was direct. "Maybe," she said, and I momentarily stopped breathing. Delaney continued to stare at me, leaving me to wonder exactly what that *maybe* meant. "But for tonight, can I just get a yes or no on the feet?"

I chuckled, trying to ignore the way my heart raced.

"I don't have a thing for feet," I answered. "I just wanted to…"

I flicked my eyes up to the ceiling because I wasn't sure I could look at her while I admitted this. "I slept better last night on that couch with you next to me than I have in a long, long time. And I just wonder if...touching you will help keep my reality grounded."

The room was quiet in the wake of my admission, and when I chanced looking back at Delaney, her eyes were glistening. She didn't say anything for a long moment, and then she abruptly rolled toward me beneath the covers, scooting closer until the length of her body pressed against the length of mine. She faced the opposite way again, tucking her head just beneath mine on the pillow, her back pressed to my chest. Then she grabbed my arm from where it had been resting against my side and wrapped it around her torso.

"How's that?" she breathed once we were settled in our new position, her voice wispy and dry.

"It's perfect," I said hoarsely. I buried my nose in her hair, breathing in deeply. "You're okay with this? You're comfortable?"

"Yeah." She nestled closer to me, and my heart lurched in my chest. "I'm comfortable, Blake."

Fuck me, this woman was perfect.

Perfect on her own.

Perfect for me.

And I was starting to think it was about damn time I made her aware of that.

CHAPTER EIGHTEEN

B LAKE WASN'T IN THE bed when I woke the next day, and I found myself feeling somewhat disappointed.

Actually, it was more than disappointment, but I couldn't name the other feelings that had been plaguing me for the last twenty-four hours—since yesterday morning. It didn't just have to do with the way we'd been smashed together on that couch or how it made my body heat from the inside out when he touched me. It also had a lot to do with the emotions I felt when he simply *looked* at me. It was *everything* about yesterday. It was the picture, the kiss, his arms curled protectively around me at the market. Everything.

I was trying really hard not to read too much into it. After all, *I* had initiated the kiss. *I* had reached for his hand in the market. *I* had insisted we sleep together last night. And Blake *was* Blake. He'd always had a thing about watching over me and keeping me safe. He'd been my silent sentry at every party and bar I'd been to for the past ten years.

But he didn't usually touch me.

Actually, he *never* touched me.

And I was terrified at how much I was enjoying his switch-up.

Rolling over, I picked up my phone to check the time and found a text from Ophelia.

> FI: Bryan showed me that picture of you and that guy on the plane. Is that your doctor friend??

I sighed, wishing Bryan hadn't done that but knowing it was my fault for sending it to him.

> Yeah, that's him. Blake. We're on a trip right now.

Ophelia responded immediately despite the fact that it must be like one in the morning for her.

> FI: When did he get so hot???

My stomach coiled with irritation, and I responded before I really had a chance to think through what I was saying.

> He's always been hot, Fi.

> FI: I mean, yeah. But now he's, like, really hot.

> Aren't you married?

> FI: Yes, very much married. But I have like three friends who would totally take his number. Is he single?

> No, he's definitely not single.

Not single. And he wouldn't be for the next year, thank God.

> FI: And his girl/guy/partner let you go jetsetting with him? Wow, they must be chill.

I ground my teeth together, for some reason annoyed that the obvious answer didn't occur to her.

> I am very chill, thank you very much.

FI: WHAT, since when??

FI: You started dating hot doctor guy friend without telling me? Delaney Delacroix, shame on you!

> Don't hate me, but it's actually Delaney London.

For some reason, I found that oddly satisfying to type.

FI: SHUT. UP.

FI: LANEY

FI: OMG?? CONGRATULATIONS????

FI: Wait, is this a HONEYMOON?

> Yes, and I promise I'll call you when I get back!

With that, I put my phone down and decided to go find my husband. My very hot husband, who was very much taken and whose number I would not be giving out to Ophelia's friends.

"What's wrong?" Blake asked as soon as I walked out into the kitchen, and I realized that my facial expression was all twisted from the conversation with Ophelia. He stood at the kitchen counter, a spread of fruits and pastries on the cutting board beside him and a knife in one hand.

"Nothing." I shook my head, giving him a small smile. "Just... Ophelia texted me."

Blake furrowed his brows. "Did something happen? Everything okay with Bryan?"

"Bryan's fine," I assured him. "Just showing off that picture of us to people, and now Ophelia wants your number."

"My number?" he laughed.

I glowered at him and how happy he seemed about that fact. "She wanted to know if you were still single so she could hook you up with her friends."

Blake pressed his lips together like he was trying not to smile. "And what did you tell her?"

"That you're not," I said with a sniff, walking around him to get a glass of water. "Because you aren't."

Blake followed me with his eyes. "Did you tell her that we got married?"

"Yes," I sighed. "Which I probably shouldn't have because she's bound to say something to the rest of my family, but..."

I decided to focus on drinking my water instead of finishing that sentence.

"But you wanted to stake your claim, huh?" Blake supplied for me, leaning his hip against the counter and watching me closely. His mouth cocked to the side in a smirk that made my stomach flip.

Goddamn him.

"It's okay, Lane." He stepped toward me, tucking a limp piece of hair behind my ear. I felt his closeness, his presence so acutely, and I just didn't know what to do about that. "You can stake your claim on me whenever the fuck you want," he muttered before leaning back and gesturing to the food on the counter. "I was thinking we could take a morning walk on the beach. It might be a little chilly, but if it's nice enough, I was going to pack this to eat down there."

"You want to take a walk on the beach?" I repeated, both distracted by the flutters his words and proximity had set off inside me and confused by what it all meant. Not to mention, surprised about Blake's suggestion of going to the beach, considering he'd had that nightmare two nights ago.

"If you want to." He shrugged. "And if you promise not to be upset with me when I act like a helicopter parent."

My lips quirked. "If you wanted me to call you daddy, you could have just said so, Blake."

Blake raised a brow, and the glint in his smokey gaze cut right through me. His smirk grew, giving him a devilish look that was so unfamiliar to my perception of this man. But fuck if it didn't set off a buzzing sensation in my veins.

"Careful what you joke about, Delaney," he said, his gaze searching my face, seemingly trying to figure out if I was being serious, before dropping to my mouth and lingering there. "I just might take you seriously one of these times."

My breath caught in my throat. I licked my dry lips as I pieced out what to say, but that only made Blake's pupils dilate and my heart pound in my chest.

Suddenly, I was wishing that I'd taken Blake up on his offer last night about the kink conversation. I'd never been curious before about what made this man's pulse race in the bedroom, but now I couldn't stop thinking about it. What would he be like? What was he into? These were thoughts that I absolutely should *not* be having about my best friend who just happened to be my husband, but curiosity had won over logic, and now I was dying to know.

"Is that so?"

He nodded and then switched the topic back again without so much as a blink of an eye.

"I think going down to the beach will be good for me. There's no one in the water here, you know? Too cold. I won't have to be on such high alert. Maybe I can try to just...enjoy it. Push past the other thoughts."

His words brought me back down to Earth. This was an important conversation, one I should be giving my full concentration. Not thinking about what Blake's sexual fantasies might be.

"I'd like for you to experience that if you think it's possible," I said. "But there's absolutely no pressure if you're not comfortable with it."

Blake's gaze cut to the window and the waves beyond before

finding its way back to me. "I think it's possible. If you come with me."

"Of course I'll come with you."

Like hell would I leave Blake to navigate through that experience on his own.

"Thank you." Blake stepped in and pressed a quick kiss to the top of my head before walking over to the refrigerator, opening it and pretending like it was completely normal for us to show that kind of casual affection. "Why don't you go get dressed?" he asked over his shoulder. "I'll finish packing things up here."

With my heart in my throat, I nodded. And then I scurried back to the bedroom before he could see all my emotions play out on my face.

I grabbed Blake's hand as soon as we walked out the door toward the beach, and this time, my desire to touch him had nothing to do with the weird feelings that had been creeping over me lately. This was just me wanting my best friend to know that I'd stay by his side, no matter what.

Blake gripped my hand back, reassuring me that this was exactly what he wanted or maybe needed. I let him set the pace as he directed us down the sloping sand dunes toward the open beachfront. When we got to sea level, Blake switched to my other side, putting himself between me and the water. I gave him an encouraging smile, and he slipped his hand into mine again before we kept walking.

The tide was low, exposing big stretches of sand and allowing us to walk far from where the water met the land. Blake stayed silent as we crossed the beach, his eyes shifting along the shoreline, which was mostly vacant, and then back to me every few minutes. I let that go on without interruptions for a few minutes before I asked if he wanted to talk about what he was thinking. When he declined, I let it go and simply held his hand tighter.

We strode along the beachfront for about ten minutes before Blake stopped, assessed the area, and then spread a blanket on the sand. I sat on it quickly to keep it from blowing away and pulled my sweater tighter around me. Despite the whipping wind, the late-spring sun shone bright, glinting across the water and piercing through the chill. Blake settled in next to me and immediately focused his attention on pulling out the assortments of food he'd packed. And then once that was done, he scanned the shoreline again as he took a deep breath and let it out slowly.

We sat mostly in silence, picking at the pastries and fruit. I scooted closer to Blake, feeling this instinct of needing to be near him, and as soon as I got within arm's reach, he wrapped himself around me, hauling me into his chest. I felt his heart pounding against my back, his ragged breathing against my neck. I inhaled deeply and exhaled slowly until Blake managed to match it, his body calming against mine.

"This is what I needed," he whispered, so soft it might have gotten lost in the wind if we weren't so wrapped up in each other. "To hold you and see that nothing can touch you."

"Only you," I breathed because in this moment on the quiet coastline of the North Sea, it felt like we were the only two people in the universe.

This felt so distinctly right, so distinctly us. And I knew that if someone passed us by, they might view this as a romantic moment, but I knew better than to get any part of this confused. Blake's soul had been damaged by that drowning, and the hurt continued to cut deeper by the way it still haunted him. And him protecting me, saving me, saving the *world* one patient at a time, was his way of trying to heal it—heal himself. This moment was nothing more than that.

"Maybe now when I see the waves, I can think of this instead," he added.

"I hope you can." I really hoped that for him. More than

221

anything. "It wasn't your fault, Blake," I added gently. I'd said those words to him before, but I needed to say them again now. Needed him to know. "It wasn't your fault that you were a teenager who wasn't experienced in CPR."

His breathing stuttered as his body tensed, and I hoped I didn't push him too much. I hoped I didn't ruin everything.

"I still think it's important for people to know, for people to be trained in it," he replied after a moment of silence.

"I agree, and I want to help." I waited a beat for his breathing to even out. "But I also need you to know that you have nothing to atone for."

Blake dropped his head to my shoulder, and I felt his slow, drawn-out nod. I remained quiet as he absorbed those words and their truth, slowly burying himself further into the crook of my neck. A full-body shudder worked through him, and I reached back to thread my fingers into his hair, needing to soothe him, needing to just...hold him. He let me, and we sat there, letting time slip away.

Blake didn't say much else, and I didn't push him. Eventually, he lifted his head and went back to holding me against his chest, seeming somewhat at peace. At least, I hoped he was.

I waited for his cue to pack up again, and then we walked back along the shore to the house, hand in hand once more.

"Thank you for humoring me, Lane." He glanced back over his shoulder toward the sea, like he was making sure it had stayed in place as we turned our back on it. "I...I needed that."

"I'm here for whatever you need, Blake," I said with sincerity. "And you don't ever have to thank *me* for humoring *you*."

"Why do you say that?" he asked with a frown.

"You agreed to marry me on a whim," I laughed.

He scrunched his nose. "That's not how I remember it."

"No?"

"*I* popped the question." He stopped, his eyes glowing as warm as the sun as he looked down at me. "*You* were the one who only agreed after a lot of convincing. Same thing with this honeymoon. Despite what you might think about this arrangement, you've been humoring me this whole time." His lips tilted, and then he tore his gaze away and continued on up the hill while I stayed stuck, attempting to process what he'd said. "Come on, Lane," he called when I remained paralyzed. "We've got a reservation I don't want to miss."

Propelling my body to move, I followed Blake back to the house. His words played on repeat in my head while I spent the next hour or so getting ready for our evening out in Amsterdam. We planned to take the train into the city, hit a few sights on our way to the reservation, and then see where the night took us from there.

A wild sort of anticipation grew in my chest as I considered the possibilities of what may lay ahead. I wasn't used to possibilities. I was used to planning and executing, not living and experiencing. But I found it to be beyond exhilarating, and one look at the clothes spilling out of my suitcase and I knew which dress I'd be wearing tonight.

I wiggled into the red contraption from Ophelia's bachelorette party that I never got to wear before assessing myself in the mirror one more time and taking a deep breath. I had no idea what would happen on the last night of this trip, but I was determined not to take the unknowns for granted.

Walking out to the living room, I stopped short at the sight of Blake. He'd showered and changed in the other bathroom, and while I assumed he'd be ready before me, I hadn't expected him to be standing in the living room expectantly. I also hadn't expected him to be looking so...good.

He froze when he saw me, mid-bite of an apple. His eyes darkened, watching my movements in a way that made my palms sweaty, and when I stopped in front of him, his gaze swept over me. *Blatantly.*

The way he stared so openly caused a surge of heat to blast through me. He took his time, making sure to appreciate every inch of my body in this red dress before he finished taking his bite of apple, lowering the fruit so I could see the way his lips tilted.

"*Fuck*, Lane," he husked.

"Did you just check me out?" I asked, the question slipping out of me from shock.

Sure, there had been some developments of sorts between me and Blake since we'd tied the knot a couple of weeks ago, but I'd never, ever experienced the look he'd just given me. Never seen him be so forward. Never thought I'd see the day where Blake London studied me with such apparent interest.

"I don't know why you sound surprised," he replied, lifting a single brow and taking another bite of his apple. He chewed it for a second before continuing. "I've already told you my thoughts about that dress."

He wasn't wrong, but I'd had to drag that opinion out of him.

And now, here he was just...giving it freely.

"Is this just another one of those things you can't help because you're *just a man*?" I asked when I found my voice, trying to tease.

"No, Delaney," Blake replied, not a single note of humor in his tone. He stepped toward me, one hand in the pocket of his trouser pants. "I can control my actions, and I work very, very hard to do just that when I'm around you. What I can't do is control how my cock reacts to feeling you naked or hearing you moan my name. I couldn't control that if I tried. But this?" He trailed his gaze over me again, and I barely repressed a hot shiver. "I can control that. Which also means I'll never, ever do it again if you ask me to stop."

My jaw all but dropped. He'd not only checked me out, but he was admitting to it. To doing it on purpose. I stared at him, the clench of his sharp jaw, the scruff of his five-o'clock shadow, the wave of his goddamn McDreamy hair. And then I trailed my gaze lower, appreciating the way his shirt was unbuttoned at the collar, exposing his chest, and the way his arms were corded with muscle, which flexed as he clenched the fist that was in his pocket.

And it was in that moment that I came to the full-blown realization that I'd been skirting around for a long, long time.

I wanted Blake London. I wanted my best friend. My husband, the man I was married to. At least for now.

But right now was all that mattered to me at the moment, and what a gift that was.

Pushing past the overwhelming desire, I strode toward Blake. He watched me closely, making it feel like a part of me was trapped in his gaze. When I was within reach, I snatched his apple out of his hand and took a bite, enjoying the way Blake's attention zeroed in on my mouth.

I didn't know what was happening between us, but I'd be lying if I said I didn't like it. Way more than I should.

"I hear an apple a day keeps the doctor away," I murmured, licking my lips before letting them curve into a tilted grin.

Blake's entire body locked up for a moment before he seemed to figure out how to speak again. "If you're trying to keep me away, you're doing a really poor job of convincing me right now, Delaney."

"Mm." I took another bite. "Good."

"You didn't ask me to stop," he commented, his voice strained.

"No." I swallowed slowly. "I didn't."

"You like it when I look at you, Lane?" His phone dinged before I could reply, but his eyes didn't stray from my mouth when he said, "The Uber must be almost here."

"Let's go, then." I put the apple back in his open hand, which hadn't moved since I took it from him. Then I smacked my lips and smiled.

"Grab a jacket." Blake cleared his throat. "I don't want you getting sick from all that...exposed skin."

I turned to do as he said but not before catching how his eyes shimmered with something dangerous.

And I wondered if I was ready to figure out what exactly it was.

nine years ago

DELANEY

"Do you think the library would notice if I stole one of their big whiteboards on wheels?"

"I think you might draw some attention pushing a huge white-board out of the library, yeah," Blake replied calmly as he typed on his laptop.

"Ugh," I groaned. "This tiny-ass diagram is way too small for me to study off of." I waved the piece of paper in front of him, which had a drawing of the human body that needed to be correctly labeled for anatomy dissection. "And I just need something more, I don't know, hands-on or something big to scribble all over, but I can't focus in a setting where I'm not in control of the environment, and I—"

"Hate to break it to you, Lane, but that might be something you need to work on. Pretty sure hospitals are not exactly environments you can control completely, but you'll still have to bring your A game every day."

Blake looked up at me from his screen, his expression empathetic despite his words—the ones that had sent a shock wave of reality through me. I breathed in through my nose to temper my reaction as I nodded silently.

"You're right," I croaked after a second.

A feeling of defeat coursed through my veins, and I could tell the second that Blake realized.

"But one thing at a time." He popped out of his seat and grabbed a marker from the table. "If you need a life-sized diagram, I can help you out with that."

And then Blake did the last thing I expected and whipped off his shirt.

My lips parted, my words stuck in my throat.

Blake London was... I shook my head, refusing to finish that thought.

He was my friend; that was all.

And the only thing I should be thinking about was how he was willing to help me.

By lying on the floor half-naked so I could write all over him.

CHAPTER NINETEEN

ELANEY AND I HAD had meals together on countless occasions. Takeout pizza on the floor of our crappy med school apartments, sandwiches on the lawn between classes, drunken late-night Taco Bell cravings, and even nice dinners, like our graduation night or when I took her to Giovanni's in Boston.

But tonight was different.

Nothing about tonight felt like two longtime friends sharing a meal.

A charge existed in the air between us, and I was having a hell of a time convincing myself that this wasn't a date. Or, at the very least, some kind of torturous foreplay. Because watching Delaney lick her spoon clean as she polished off her soup was turning me on in undeniable ways. And she seemed to know it, her sparkling gaze lifting to mine in a coy glance.

"How has your experience at Boston Medical been compared to Mayo?" she asked, but I was too busy watching her mouth to register her words. It was only when her lips stretched into an amused smile that I realized she was waiting on me to reply.

It took everything in me not to raise a brow. Because *really*? She wanted to look at me like that and then talk about work?

She was still unsure; that was what this was. She didn't quite know how to exist in our new reality yet, the one where we acknowledged that our chemistry was not just friendly. She was holding on to the things that tied our friendship together instead.

But I didn't want to talk about medicine tonight. I wanted to talk about her.

"Well, I'm no longer working with my favorite person, so there's that."

She pursed her lips like she knew what I was doing.

"Do you wish we were both still working at Mayo?"

I considered that before realizing that I wouldn't choose to go back in time if I could. As much as I loved the learning experiences I'd had with Delaney, I'd rather have her living in my home as my wife than have her as my coworker.

"I wish we were still working together, but no. I think I like our arrangement in Boston better."

A slight flush worked up her neck as she nodded. "It's been nice for you to spend time with Natalie, Noah, and their kids, hasn't it?"

A couple of weeks ago, I would have let her believe that was the only reason. But not today. Not anymore.

"It really has," I admitted. "But Lane—"

"Speaking of your family, I need to tell Sully about this dinner so he knows you pulled out all the stops on this honeymoon. That was an amazing meal," she gushed.

Goddamn, she was making this difficult.

"You know, it's funny because I thought about sending him a photo of you sitting there with your wine for that exact reason. But then I realized Sully would permanently have a picture of you in that dress, and I'd probably have to destroy his phone."

"Oh, shut up," she laughed, her cheeks tinting pink enough that I could see her blush despite the low lighting in the restaurant.

I shook my head. "Why do you always think I'm joking?"

"Because that's what we do," she said dismissively, looking down at her glass of wine. "We tease each other."

"Mmm." I waited until she glanced up again to add, "I think it's called flirting, Delaney. You've just been in denial."

Delaney blinked, her red-stained lips parting. She looked at me, staring hard—like pieces were starting to come together, similar to the ones in those damn puzzles she loved so much.

Watching her come to terms with reality was all I'd ever wanted. This was just the start, but still.

"Yeah, Blake?" Her breaths were coming quicker, the rising and falling of her chest so fucking distracting because of that dress and everything it was showing off.

"Yeah, Lane."

I said it without a hint of levity.

"And what else have I not realized?"

Everything, baby.

Her brows furrowed before I could reply aloud. "Are we on a date right now?"

A question I'd love to know the answer to myself.

"Do you want it to be a date?" I countered and begged her to say yes with my eyes.

Her gaze wandered the table for two, lit by candlelight, before it strayed to the rest of the small restaurant, from the waitstaff dressed in black and white to the wall stacked with hundreds of bottles of wine to the gentle, romantic music playing overhead, weaving through the soft murmuring of other diners.

"It feels like a date," she answered finally.

That wasn't quite the answer I was looking for, but I could make it work.

"Is that good or bad, Lane?" I leaned forward, meeting her gaze and noting how dilated her pupils were. "That this feels like a date."

"Good, I think." She licked her lips, and my eyes dropped to her mouth because my self-control was bleeding out. "I'm feeling really good right now," she added, more confident. Then, her eyes skimmed over to the glass of wine in her hand. "But that might just be the wine talking."

I waited until her eyes landed back on me to lower my voice and reply, "I don't think it's the wine."

"No." She swallowed, and I watched the way her throat worked, wondering which parts of her neck were sensitive. I wanted to find all of the places on her body that made her tick, that made her gasp and groan. *Fuck.* "I don't think it's the wine," Delaney agreed breathlessly.

The fact that she felt it, too, that she recognized whatever was happening between us, that she was just as lost to the pull between us—it was doing me in.

"What else do you want to do tonight?" I asked, taking a slow sip of my own wine and watching her over the rim of the glass. "I want you to keep feeling...good."

I wanted her to let *me* make her feel good, too.

"Hmm, dancing." She gave me a reserved smile that did things to my insides. "Dancing would make me feel good. It's been so long. I never dance anymore, but I think tonight feels different."

It sure did.

"I'm not sure if there's any ballet studios we can simply barge into around here, but I can see what I can find."

If I had to beg a dance studio to let us in for the night, I would.

"You know, I *was* trained in other types of dance besides ballet. Becoming a ballerina was just the only acceptable option for my parents."

A tight laugh left my lips, mostly because imagining Delaney dancing in any way or capacity made my cock twitch in my pants. "Okay, so what kind of dancing do you want to do tonight?"

"All I want is to move my body to a beat." She tilted her head to the side, watching me closely. "Would you dance with me, Blake?"

My breathing faltered. *Oh fuck me, this woman.*

"You know I would, Delaney," I answered, holding her gaze. The look in her eyes was electrified, like the thick feeling of the air before lightning struck. Tonight felt like that, like the moments ahead of a perfect storm. When all the conditions were right for something either terrible or exciting to happen, and you just weren't sure which it was going to be.

Delaney's throat bobbed, and I watched her gradually become more unsteady before she took a quick exit off the road we were on. I already knew her next words were about to be dismissive, braced myself for them.

"You're a great guy, Blake," she commented, sucking in a breath. "Your future wife is going to be very lucky to have you."

Oh, fuck that.

"Are you *trying* to piss me off?"

"What?"

But she wasn't looking at me when she said it, and I suspected we both knew why.

"How was your meal this evening?" Our waiter interrupted before I got a chance to tell Delaney that the only wife I planned on having was the one sitting in front of me. And that everything I did that made her think I was a great guy was because my world fucking revolved around her.

It was probably for the best that we got interrupted.

"It was amazing," Delaney answered because I was still too busy clenching and unclenching my jaw. "Thank you."

He smiled politely. "Anything else I can get for you?"

"I don't think so," I said, forcing a smile. "But can you recommend a good place for an after-dinner drink, maybe somewhere with a dance floor?"

"Of course." His eyes lit up, clearly eager for the opportunity to provide a recommendation. "I can tell you my personal favorite, but it's the heart of the red-light district. If you're okay with something a little more...free-spirited, yeah?" He tilted his chin toward Delaney, a tiny, knowing smirk playing on his lips. "They will love her there. She won't have to pay for a single drink."

"I'll be paying for all my wife's drinks." I narrowed my eyes but pulled out my phone anyway so I could look up his recommendation, glancing sideways at Delaney while doing so. Her hands had been in her lap, but she pulled her left one out at the insinuation that she wasn't taken, resting her chin in her palm so the waiter could have a good look at her wedding ring, glittering against the blush on her cheeks. The man gave a little brow raise with a nod and a wink to say he got the message and then turned to me to spell out the name of the bar.

A few minutes later, we were out the door.

Amsterdam glittered with nightlife. The streets were packed with people out and about, enjoying the crisp spring evening. A mix of languages swirled through the air, giving me an appreciation for this experience. But mostly, I was thankful that I got to hold Delaney's hand as we crossed a tulip-lined bridge, bikes locked to the railing every few steps and the canal flowing beneath us.

The red-light district surprised me...at first. It wasn't immediately obvious when we entered the area like I assumed it would be. Cute restaurants and bars still lined the streets; the only difference was that included among them were clearly X-rated establishments. But then, following the directions my phone fed me, we turned down a street that was most definitely the heart of the district, with windows lining the alley and people in those windows who were *not* wearing a whole lot of clothes, and I found myself staring at my feet as we walked.

Delaney giggled—at my reaction, I suspected, and I shook my head, resisting the urge to lean down and let her know there was only one woman in this whole city, the whole world, I wanted to see dressed like that. Or not dressed at all. But instead, I simply gripped her hand tighter until we popped out onto another street to find the bar the waiter had recommended. I gave it a once-over before glancing at Delaney with uncertainty.

"I can't quite tell if this is just a bar or a sex club, Lane. Or something in between."

She considered the dark-painted entry of the building. "I've never been somewhere like that before."

"Do you want to check it out?"

"Can't deny I'm a little curious." She shrugged, her eyes still on the door. "They're certainly playing good music. Dancing music." Her body started to sway and bounce adorably, and I bit down on a smile.

"Okay," I said, nodding in acknowledgment of the thrumming beat coming from the bar. "We can check it out. And if you want to leave, we'll leave. Just squeeze my hand twice if it's too loud to talk."

"Sounds good," Delaney agreed before trying to pull me toward the door, but I tugged her back. A little too hard, apparently, because she gasped as she flew back into my arms. And then gasped again when I spun her around and pinned her against the canal railing, wanting—no, needing—to make something clear to her before she escaped to follow the music.

"Hey, Lane?" I murmured, dropping one hand to grip the railing and the other to curve around her back so she wouldn't fall into the water.

"Hm?" She blinked up at me with those big, blue eyes. They shone with a mix of excitement and wonder, like she liked the idea that she didn't know where the night would lead.

"Remember when you wanted to know if I would ask for your number if I saw you in this dress?" I dragged my gaze over her, making it clear once again how I felt about it.

"I remember," she whispered.

"And you remember how I answered?"

"I remember that, too."

"If we go in there, that's going to be me," I said, wanting badly to set things straight. "Unless you explicitly tell me to back off, I'm not letting you out of my goddamn sight. I *will* chase other guys off and be stuck to your side like glue, okay? Because there's no way in fucking hell I'm going to let anyone else touch my wife."

"Blake..." she breathed, her chest once again rising and falling with a quickness that caught my attention. And fuck me for being tempted to look and failing not to. Because with the way we were

235

positioned and how her leather jacket hung open, her cleavage was practically right in my face, and all it did was remind me of the other morning when she was pressed against me, skin to skin.

"You don't—" She sucked in abruptly when her voice pulled my gaze back to her face, and she must have seen the hunger in my eyes. "You don't have to protect me like I'm your real wife, Blake," she finished, but it was the weakest sentence I'd ever heard fall from her lips. "That's not your responsibility."

I stepped in, locking her against the railing with my hips. "First of all, Delaney London, you *are* my real wife. And you *are* my responsibility. I can't even begin to imagine a scenario where I would let anything happen to you. Absolutely *no one* will be touching you without your permission. Understood?"

Her breath hitched, but she nodded slowly, indicating she understood. Her eyes were glazed, coated with something I thought I recognized. She didn't speak for a long moment, and a sinking feeling set in, one that had me worrying that I'd taken it a step too far, too fast. But I couldn't regret saying words that were fucking true.

"You're the only person who has permission to touch me, Blake," she finally rasped, and my pulse took off like a bullet train, unstoppable.

"Then you want to go in?" I asked, pulling back and holding out my hand.

She took it with a firm nod, and we followed the sound of the bass, pumping almost as loudly as our hearts.

CHAPTER TWENTY

blake

THE CLUB BUZZED WITH an undeniable sexual energy that went beyond whatever was happening between Delaney and me.

With each step we took inside, I felt it build inside me. The music infused my bones, driving toward some kind of peak. My body ached more and more with every second that passed, with every person who danced around us, some out in the open, others half-hidden amongst the red velvet curtains that fell thick and heavy along the walls. Lips sought lips, bodies sought bodies, all with a carnality I felt intensify as we drifted further into the club.

For the most part, we went unnoticed as we entered, but once we passed through an interior velvet-adorned doorway, I felt eyes following us, hot on my neck. I pulled Delaney in front of me, wanting to be able to scan the room and keep her within my eyesight at the same time. A quick survey of the club led me to a few young guys chatting amongst themselves in the corner, beers in each of their hands. But their eyes kept flicking to us. Or, more accurately, to Delaney.

My grip on her tightened as she led us toward the bar, squeezing into an open spot along the counter. As soon as she stopped, I wrapped my arm possessively around her.

Not a single word I'd said to her outside was exaggerated. There was no way in hell I'd be letting go of her in a place like this. The waiter's remarks at dinner had injected concern into my veins, the way he'd promised they would *love* Delaney here. I couldn't blame anyone for loving Delaney, but if they dared to touch her, I'd probably lose my fucking mind. No, I *would* lose my mind. No doubt about it.

Delaney shouted at the bartender, holding up two fingers, telling me she'd ordered for me, too. When she leaned back into my arms again, waiting for our drinks, her head brushed against my nose. The smell of her sweet hair temporarily over-powered the sex haze in the air, and I pressed a kiss to her head. Delaney glanced back at me over her shoulder, giving me a soft smile.

There were a million words in that soft smile, and fuck if I didn't hear all of them loud and clear.

I kissed her again and then dropped to brush my lips against the shell of her ear.

"What'd you order me?"

"Your favorite," she said over her shoulder.

I frowned because I wasn't aware that I *had* a favorite drink.

"An appletini," she laughed, and my lips cracked into a grin.

Thank fuck Delaney hadn't let that cranky bartender ruin her love for appletinis forever and that she'd walked up to the bar tonight and ordered two without a second thought.

Tonight's bartender—a man with suspenders, a grizzled beard, and a shiny, bald head—slid our drinks across the counter a few minutes later. They didn't look like appletinis since they were in regular glasses instead of martini ones, but I reached over Delaney to pay for them anyway, slapping the euros on the bar top and letting the guy know I didn't need change. He thanked me and rushed to help the next person waiting along the cramped bar.

Delaney turned in my arms to face me, but we were so close that I had to suck in a breath to keep my shit together. I could see the dark blue outline around her irises and the equally dark twinkle in them.

"Here you go," she said, offering me the drink.

"Thanks, Lane." I took it, debating if I should tell her the truth about the drink. That it was, honest to God, one of my least favorite drinks in the world, but decided against it. It didn't fucking matter. Right now, the only thing that mattered was how proud Delaney seemed of herself when she handed it over.

"You're welcome," she said. Her eyes stayed glued on me as she slipped her straw into her mouth and sucked, making me choke on air. By the time she lowered her drink, my cock had stiffened in my pants. "I loved that bar we used to go to off of Madison Street."

"It was a good bar," I muttered because I didn't have any other words in my brain. All of my thoughts at the moment were geared toward Delaney's mouth and how she'd returned to toying with the straw, biting on the end of it. "Yeah. Good bar."

She smiled at me like she knew I was struggling.

Fuck if I cared.

What I did care about was the movement behind her, the eyes following her. They were the same eyes that had been watching us when we'd walked in. Watching her.

"Do you want to dance?" I offered, wanting to get her away from them.

She nodded. "That's why we're here, isn't it?"

Right. Because we *weren't* here just for me to sit and stare at Delaney's mouth.

Without another word, I whisked her toward the dance floor. When we reached it, she spun around in front of me and took the lead, which was for the best, considering I didn't have a rhythmic bone in my body.

Well, maybe one.

But that one wasn't the one I needed to come out to play at the moment.

Delaney shimmied backward, her body loosening with every

step until I could almost see how the music flowed through her. She beckoned me with a curl of her finger, walking me like a dog as I followed her.

But then she got distracted, forgetting about me as the song switched to something with a quicker beat, something synth-filled and intoxicating. Delaney threw a hand up while clinging to her drink with the other, giving a joyful shout. And then she let the music sweep her away, her eyes closing and body melting into the sensual rhythm. Her hips rolled and dropped like they had a mind of their own, and shit, my mouth ran dry at the sight.

I could get drunk just by watching her. What a fucking vision. I couldn't remember the last time I'd seen Delaney this carefree, this alive, and it was beautiful. *She* was beautiful. And Christ, did I want her.

She danced. I watched. She peeled her jacket off. I took it from her. She nearly spilled her drink all over herself. I plucked it from her hands and set both our drinks on a nearby table, throwing her jacket there, too.

Delaney didn't seem to notice. Her eyes remained closed. They didn't flick open again until about halfway through the song, like she'd suddenly remembered I existed. Her gaze immediately searched for me, and when she found me standing still nearly a foot away, she pouted.

"You said you were going to dance with me."

"Sorry." I cleared my throat as I stepped forward, happily slipping my hands onto her hips and tugging her toward me. Delaney gave a little shriek of delight as our bodies collided. "I was too busy watching you," I breathed in her ear.

Even with the music blaring, I heard—or maybe felt—her breath hitch. And then she admitted, "I'd rather have you touching me."

"*Fuck*, Delaney."

Hearing her say words like that aloud after so many torturous years of being her best friend who kept his distance was just unbelievable. I didn't have a way to describe how it made me feel, but I knew it was like nothing I'd ever felt before.

"Mm," she hummed in her throat. She pressed her hips tighter to mine, urging my body to mimic hers as if she wanted to teach me how to move like she did. And because we seemed to be stuck in some sort of magnetic field, I found it impossible not to follow her lead, not to move my body at the same tempo as her, with the same sway, following the same pulse.

Delaney wound her arms around my neck, and I took that cue and ran with it, wrapping myself around her and locking my hands on the small of her back. Locking her against me.

Her gaze tracked upward, looking at me from beneath long lashes. Her expression was inviting, urging me to move with her. Which was good because I didn't know how to turn back now. I rocked against her, following the rhythmic beat reverberating through the club like a pulse. Time seemed to slow, our electrical impulses delayed. Arrhythmic.

Because nothing about this moment was normal. But every bit of it felt right.

I didn't take my eyes off Delaney. A pretty flush reflected on her face, either from the heat swirling around us or maybe a reflection from that devastating red dress. God, the feel of her in that goddamn thing while pressed so close to me—*fuck*. She toyed with her bottom lip, also red, also devastating. Plump and kissable. She bit down on it like she was holding in a moan before tilting her head back, presenting me with the column of her throat. She was letting herself feel the music, letting the bright hues from the strobe lights dance across her face.

Once again, I was overwhelmed with the desire to taste her, to press my lips to her skin, and to learn things I didn't know about Delaney London—the only things I didn't know about her. Expose the secrets we'd been holding in our chests. Become the kind of friends who *did* talk about their sex lives. And their kinks. And then fucking explored them together. I wanted to know *everything* about what Delaney wanted, and then I wanted to give it to her.

I was about to lean forward and whisper precisely those words in her ear when I caught a glimpse of that same group of men from when we walked in. They stood along the edges of the dance floor, circled with their beers once more. But I couldn't help but notice the glinting interest when one of their gazes passed over us again, or rather Delaney, and felt my blood boil hotter.

"What?" Delaney asked over the roar of the music, and I realized she'd straightened in my arms, looking funnily at me. Probably because I'd instinctively clenched my jaw so hard that my teeth might be bleeding.

I leaned in to explain in a low voice. "The guys over there haven't taken their eyes off you since we walked in."

Keeping one arm around her, I splayed a hand on her back possessively while using my free palm to cup her cheek. I didn't want her to look around to try to find them. Didn't want them to notice her awareness. And I also *did* want to feel the flush beneath her skin, experience the heat radiating from inside her.

"And you haven't taken your hands off me," she pointed out, her lips twisting with an amusement that told me she didn't mind that I'd been all over her. Good. "I'm clearly not available."

"I don't think it's clear enough," I rasped, shaking my head. Then, I used my hand on her back to press her closer to me. "I don't think it's clear enough that you're my wife, Lane."

"No?" Delaney responded by dragging her palms over my shoulders and onto my chest, as if she wanted to *make* it clear. And her wanting other guys to know that she was unavailable, that she belonged to me, was making the possessive side of me roar to life. *God*, yes.

Delaney watched me for a reaction as one of her hands flattened over my heart, probably feeling how erratic it was because of the way she was touching me. Probably wishing she had a stethoscope to hear how wild she drove me for herself. Her gaze shone with mirth as she rolled her bottom lip between her teeth, pulling all my attention to her mouth. *Fuck*, that mouth. How I wanted it on mine again.

"No, it's not clear enough." I trailed my fingers over the gorgeous contours of her face, slipping them beneath her chin, ready to lift it. "So I need you to tell me, Delaney."

She pressed up toward me, lifting onto her toes. Instinctively, I leaned to meet her, stopping only when I could feel her breath on my lips. "Tell you what?"

"Tell me the occasion calls for it," I begged, brushing my thumb over her luscious mouth, hating and loving how it tempted me. My lips grazed hers, barely a taste, but it kept me alive while I waited for her reply.

"The occasion calls for it," she whispered, just as I realized I couldn't wait to get my lips on her again and dragged them along her jawline, eager to explore more of her, all of her.

"Good girl," I murmured. My mouth lowered further, finding the pulse point on her neck, sucking gently. "Tell me this is okay."

"*Yes*." She gasped softly, winding her arms back around my neck, her fingers tangling in my hair at the base of it. She tugged slightly, making my vision haze over temporarily.

"Yes, it's okay?" I probed huskily. "Be clear for me, sweetheart."

"It's okay." I felt her lips flirt with my ear, and I swallowed a groan. Especially when her wondrously breathy voice started speaking aloud my fantasies. "You gave me permission to claim you whenever the fuck I want, Blake. This is me giving that back to you."

"*Fuck*, Delaney," I cursed roughly, and my restraint snapped.

I pulled back, found her lips waiting for me, and then crashed mine onto them.

Claiming her just like she gave me permission to do.

And holy *hell*, did she taste good.

Delaney tasted like the sugary sweetness of her appletini, and suddenly, it was my favorite drink in the world. I'd drink it day in and day out. *Nothing* was better—absolutely nothing. An apple-tini a day would never, ever keep this doctor away.

"*Mine*," I declared, nipping at her bottom lip as I wound my hands into her hair, fisting her silky strands. She gasped between kisses, and that either of us had time to come up for air told me that I wasn't kissing her good enough, deep enough, thoroughly enough. I covered her mouth with mine, drinking in her groans and dragging my tongue along the seam of her lips, begging her for entry. And when she allowed it, I swore I understood heaven for the very first time.

Control began to slip away as I slanted my mouth over hers, deepening the kiss until Delaney's tongue was exploring my mouth and my hands were dragging down her body. And just when my palms were about to slide over the curve of her ass, someone bumped into me from the side, knocking awareness back into my brain and forcing me to step back.

Fuck, I was losing it. From the second my lips touched her, the force of just how badly I wanted her had knocked through the well-built dam I'd constructed years ago, and now, nothing was holding me back.

"Blake," Delaney breathed, and I realized she was staring at me, her chest heaving from the pure adrenaline of the moment. She lifted her hand to her mouth, tracing her lips lightly as though she couldn't believe a kiss like that existed in this universe.

Same, baby. Same.

"I..." Bewildered, she looked around. "What was... Wait, where did my drink go?"

I might have kissed the fucking sense out of her, but I was okay with that.

I shook my head with a soft laugh, stepping back to take my place—arms around her, bodies locked together. "Doesn't matter. I need you to stop drinking anyway."

She looked confused. It was adorable. "Why?"

Leaning down, I brushed my lips gently over hers, forcing

restraint on myself. At least while we were in public, even though the other people in this room sure didn't care about that. Right behind Delaney, two men were feasting on a woman's neck.

"Because it's either you stop drinking, or I stop kissing you, and I don't know if I'll be able to do the latter."

"Ah." Her lips stretched into a smile that I felt. "My husband, the gentleman."

I moved my mouth to her ear, nibbling on it before whispering a promise. "Your husband is not the fucking gentleman that you think he is."

God, it felt good to say that aloud.

"Oh?"

The single syllable released from her lips on an upward hiccup. I pulled back to see the burning wonder in her gaze. But instead of answering all the questions in her expression, I kissed her again. Simply because she was tempting me, and I *could*.

"More dancing?" I asked, ripping my mouth from hers before I got too carried away.

Delaney cocked her head to the side, and all I could do was stare at her swollen lips. "I thought you wanted to kiss me."

Yes. *God*, yes, that was what I wanted to do. But I also wanted to do so much more than that—a problem considering we were standing in a packed club in the middle of the red-light district.

"I think I can do both," I said, gripping her hips and then spinning her so her back collided with my front. It might be safer this way. I couldn't see her lips, those ridiculously kissable lips. Or her eyes as they begged me for more. Bending my head, I dragged my mouth to a spot just below her ear and asked, "Where else do you like to be kissed, Delaney?"

"I—" She broke off with a moan when I traced a line down her neck with my tongue. "I don't know."

Fuck, did I both love and hate that answer. Delaney deserved all the kisses. She deserved to have someone to make her feel confident in what made her feel good. But if I got to be the one to help her understand that? Help her learn what she liked? Well, I sure as hell didn't mind that.

"Mm," I murmured in her ear, and she dropped her weight back into me, letting us mold together. "We can work on that."

Delaney sighed her approval, letting her head fall onto my shoulder as she danced in my arms. She felt so fucking good that I couldn't help but grind against her, and her reaction was instantaneous, her realization that I was hard as a goddamn rock for her.

Delaney's lips curved into a tilted grin as she looked back at me. "Just a man, right?"

I matched her expression. "Something like that."

"Is it the dress?" she asked, a teasing note in her voice because she fucking knew it wasn't the dress.

"Yes, but no." I let my fingers wander over her hips and down her thigh, finding where the fabric stopped and her smooth, bare skin began. "It's what I know is underneath the dress."

Delaney pushed her ass into my crotch as she danced, seemingly determined to end my life. "Kind of like how I know what's in your pants, right?"

Bursts of heat exploded inside me, brighter and hotter each time she rubbed against me. I gripped her thigh, fingers digging into her flesh, on the edge of losing it. "Delaney, if you keep doing that—*fuck*."

"Do you want me to stop?"

"No," I croaked, "but you have to."

She was going to have me coming in my pants like a fucking teenager.

Delaney straightened immediately, and I dropped my forehead to her shoulder, taking deep breaths to steady myself.

"Why?" she murmured in my ear.

"Because," I muttered, kissing the curve of her collarbone, "I want you too fucking bad to be teased right now."

I glanced over to find her gaze on me. It reflected the flashing lights in the club, giving it a luminous quality, especially when strokes of blue light crossed her face, deepening the color of her eyes. "Who said I was teasing?" she challenged, and suddenly, I felt a finger trail up the length of my erection, making me shiver with nearly unbearable desire.

Gritting my teeth to hold back a stream of expletives, I grabbed Delaney's wrist to stop her torture with one hand and used the other to wrap around her throat, drawing her back until she was looking up at me with those gorgeous sapphires. When I spoke, my breathing was uneven, and my voice wavered, threaded with need. "Delaney Rose London, if you touch my cock one more time, I'm going to have to find something to bend you over."

Delaney's lips stretched in a slow smile at my threat.

A fucking *smile*.

And then she dared to toy with me even more and ask, "What are you going to do with me once you've got me bent over?"

"Fuck the little tease right out of you," I grunted, lifting my hips just enough that she'd feel how ready I was to do that. "And then I'd fuck that smart mouth of yours while I'm at it."

Delaney's lips parted, and she grew speechless for the first time. It was as though she couldn't talk because she was too busy imagining what it would be like to have my cock in her mouth. Or her pussy.

"You like the sound of that, don't you?" I worked my thumb over her jawline to her mouth, brushing over it. And when her lips parted just a bit further, I popped it in, letting Delaney suck on the tip of my thumb. God, her wet, hot mouth was so fucking exquisite. And when her cheeks tucked in, I nearly expired on the spot.

"Mhm," she moaned.

"Yeah?" I asked, my ability to breathe declining by the second as Delaney swirled her tongue over the pad of my thumb. "Does thinking about having your lips around me make you wet, Lane?"

I pulled my thumb from her mouth so I could hear her response.

"You can find out for yourself," she said breathlessly, and it took me a second to realize that she really wasn't teasing. There was no tilt of her lips, no glint in her eyes; the only thing filling her expression was a need, thick and heavy. "No one will notice. And if they do, they won't care."

"*Fuck*, sweetheart." I closed my eyes to try to temper this new level of desire coursing through me, a level that I didn't think existed before this moment. "It's unbelievable how badly I want to touch you. But—" I broke off with a groan. "God, you're making me lose my goddamn mind. What the—"

"Should I find out for you, then?" she cut in, clearly seeing me lose my mind with indecision. "If you're not going to?"

"Jesus Christ, Lane," I cursed, and I might have fallen to my knees if I didn't have her in my arms to hold up. "You have no idea what the thought of you touching yourself does to me, but that's a show I want all to myself. Like *hell* do I want anyone else seeing you like that."

"Okay, Blake." She nodded, but I could nearly *taste* the desperation in her expression.

She would just have to wait, though. I knew people were watching her, including those guys from earlier. I caught them circling closer out of the corner of my eye, and fuck if I'd let them see Delaney like that. I was a greedy bastard who had absolutely no plans of sharing my wife. And I felt more and more unhinged about that fact as it became clear that other interested parties were closing in on us.

Which was why I couldn't be more grateful when Delaney said, "Then I think we should go."

We were out the door in a matter of seconds.

nine years ago

BLAKE

"I can't just...just use you as my study guide."

"You can use me however you want, Delaney." As soon as the words came out of my mouth, I cleared my throat, aware of how they sounded. Then I added, "Honestly, this is a lot less work than stealing a whiteboard from the library."

Delaney kneeled next to me with the marker in hand. Her brows drew together as she studied my body, her gaze drifting over the planes of my stomach. Rationally, I knew she was just considering me as a study canvas, but the way her eyes trailed up my chest made me feel hot and clammy all the same.

Fuck, maybe this was a bad idea after all.

Tentatively, Delaney reached out, bracing one palm on my chest as she brought the marker to my skin with her other hand.

Her touch made me shiver.

I tried to suppress it, but I couldn't.

Suppressing my body's reaction to Delaney was a hell of a lot harder than suppressing my thoughts. I had far less control, and considering I'd just offered up my body for her to touch and write all over, that might be a problem.

249

She released an airy laugh. "Does that tickle?"

"Yeah." I coughed through the tension coiled up inside me. "Tickles."

Her eyes darted to mine, and the spark I saw caught me by surprise.

But then I lost sight of it when she looked back down.

I might not have been able to see it anymore, but I could feel it.

The marker dragged over my skin for the next hour.

And Delaney's touch imprinted on my being.

As if I needed any more reasons to be attached to my best friend.

CHAPTER TWENTY-ONE

ORDES OF PEOPLE SWARMED into the train station at the same time we did. I wasn't sure why and wasn't sure I cared why, either. But I did care that the result was a packed train out of Amsterdam. Meaning Blake and I ended up sharing a seat. Or rather, Blake sat in the seat.

And I sat in his lap.

It was a new, special kind of torture. For both of us.

When I repositioned for the third time, trying to find a comfortable position despite people pressing us against the window, Blake's fingers dug into my thigh, and he grunted my name in my ear.

"Delaney." He paused, taking a ragged breath. "If you move one more fucking time, I'm not going to make it. We'll be getting off at the next stop regardless of if it's the right one."

I sucked in a breath, my eyes fluttering shut as hot desire washed over me. It had been like this all night. Ever since I walked out in my dress and Blake had given me that look. And then *kept* giving me that look. Not to mention the things he had said, things I *never* imagined would come out of his mouth. It caused wave after wave of arousal to swallow me whole, growing harder and harder to ignore.

Based on Blake's words and the erection sitting between my asscheeks, he was struggling just as much as me.

I wasn't sure how we'd gotten to this level of desperation, but I was too drugged by it to care.

"Do you want to sit on *my* lap?" I offered over my shoulder, catching a glimpse of Blake's darkened gaze. The train rattled as it approached the next stop, causing me to throw a hand against the window to catch myself from falling. Blake's arm tightened around me, and I shot my ass back, steadying my balance.

Blake used the curve of my neck to stifle his low groan, the vibrations carrying from his body to mine. His lips sucked at my skin, and then his teeth scraped at it.

"Delaney." He breathed my name again, like it was the only word he had in his mind.

"I know," I panted, feeling my heart rate spike as one of his hands began to wander. "I know, Blake."

I felt him shake his head. "I don't think you do."

"We're almost there," I assured him.

In other words, alone. We were almost *alone*.

What would happen once we were alone?

I'd never thought twice about being alone with Blake before.

It hadn't been something I'd needed to think twice about.

But now, it was *all* I could think about.

Getting Blake alone and doing, well, I didn't know what, but *something*. Something to ease the overwhelming ache pulsing in my body, the throbbing between my legs. Something that let me experience more of the Blake I had in that club. Something that gave me the chance to *feel* him again. Feel him more than I did right now, even though he was all over me, all around me. But it wasn't enough. Not even close to being enough. *God*, did I want more.

"Lane," he rasped in my ear. "What I wouldn't give to know what you're thinking right now."

I cleared my throat. "Nothing. I'm thinking about...nothing."

"Don't lie, sweetheart." He dropped his voice, ensuring no one would hear him except me. "I can feel the way your pussy is pulsing for me, you know that, right?"

I gasped at the revelation of his words, and the throbbing—that he could apparently feel—only intensified. Meanwhile, Blake's soft chuckle tickled my nerve endings.

"We're almost there," he soothed, echoing my words from earlier.

Luckily, he was right. Another five minutes on the train, and we were squeezing through the crowds to hop off. Just like the first time we'd arrived at this station after our flight, Blake had an Uber waiting for us.

This time, the car ride to the rental house stayed silent, filled only with a heavy, nearly unbearable tension. It stretched between us in the back seat despite Blake keeping his eyes firmly out the window the entire ride. His touch, on the other hand, strayed, finding my leg...and then the hem of my dress. He slid his fingers beneath the fabric to palm my inner thigh, squeezing lightly. His thumb traced semicircles, trailing so close to the edge of my underwear that I had to grab onto the door handle and hold my breath.

While I couldn't see his expression, I could practically *feel* Blake's satisfaction with my response to his touch. To his teasing.

He was right. We'd always teased each other, always played this game. I just hadn't seen it for what it was: flirting. And now, seduction. Had he known? Had I been the only one in denial this whole time?

I didn't really care at the moment; all I cared about was appreciating it for what it was in the present. Because it was definitely something. And I refused to leave this trip without experiencing whatever I'd previewed in the club. Who knew what would happen when we got back to Boston, when we returned to a life that felt more real and not make-believe. All I knew was tonight and the time I had until we touched back down at Logan International.

Neither of us could seem to stumble out of the car fast

enough. When we made it to the house, Blake unlocked the door and threw it open, and I dashed inside. I walked a few paces into the living room before turning to find Blake hot on my heels, watching me with an animalistic hunger that took my breath away.

But as soon as I stopped, he stopped, too. His chest rose and fell in quick successions. His gaze trailed over me, lingering in a way that made me instinctively raise a hand to my face, wiping under my eyes and the mascara that had probably smudged, and my hair, making sure it wasn't in disarray.

"You're fucking beautiful, Delaney," Blake cut in, looking almost pained to say it. "Your hair is perfect, your face is perfect, everything about you is so goddamn perfect. It's infuriating."

"Infuriating?"

"Yes, because I—" He clamped down on his words, pressing his lips together and raking a hand through his hair. "When you first walked out wearing that dress at our apartment, you thought I didn't like it. But I was just too busy trying not to undress you in my mind to be able to form a single coherent thought."

I stared, shocked by his admission, struggling to wrap my head around the reality of that moment. And once I got my shit together, I swallowed past the emotion in my throat and raised a brow. "Were you successful?"

"What?"

"Were you successful when you *tried* not to undress me in your mind."

"Yes," he said without hesitation. "My respect for you as my friend runs so fucking deep, Lane."

My heart pounded so loud I wondered if he could hear it. Blake meant the world to me. I'd realized the extent of that when he'd left me behind in Minnesota a few months ago, making me wonder when our friendship had run so deep that it left such a gaping hole in my chest when he was gone.

The question on the tip of my tongue might risk that

happening again. That maybe we were about to cross a line that would ruin us in the long run.

Or maybe we weren't crossing a line at all. Maybe we were just redrawing it.

"Are you going to respect me as your friend tonight?" I pushed myself to ask.

"No." Once again, no hesitation. Just a blazing confidence that made my heart flip into my throat. "I'm going to fuck you like my wife."

My jaw dropped, but Blake didn't waste time stepping toward me.

"Tell me you're sober, Delaney."

Once I figured out how to breathe again, I replied, "I'm sober."

That train ride of torture had ensured that. Plus, I'd only had one glass of wine with dinner and just a taste of that appletini before Blake got rid of it. And now I knew why.

"Good girl." Blake planted one foot in front of the other, walking slowly toward me. "Now, tell me I can strip that dress off you." Another step. "I'll get on my knees and beg if you want me to."

The intensity of his stare made goose bumps erupt across my skin. "You can strip the dress off me."

Blake smirked as he closed the distance between us. "So compliant. You must want it bad, Lane."

I nodded, my eyes fluttering shut as Blake bent his head, leaving a chaste kiss on my collarbone. Then, his finger traced the bone to my shoulder, slipping beneath the dress's strap and flicking it off.

"Bad," I repeated, barely a murmur.

"I know, sweetheart," Blake breathed, and I felt his lips on my other shoulder before that strap fell off, too. "But you're being such a good wife, and good little wives get to come. Don't worry."

I squirmed on my feet, desperate for him to make good on those words. Blake laughed, husky and soft, and I felt it in my very bones.

"Oh, now you're laughing, huh?" I muttered while Blake pressed against me, reaching around to undo the laces of my dress. "Wasn't so funny when we were in the club."

"There's nothing funny about what's happening right now." Blake began peeling my dress off, inch by inch. He straightened once it was bunched around my waist, and his heated gaze met mine, an odd mixture of humor and arousal swirling in its depths. "But I can't deny that watching you squirm isn't satisfying."

I licked my lips, and Blake's attention dropped to my mouth, his jaw clenching. I put a hand on his chest, feeling the hard wall of muscle against my fingertips. And even that simple touch had Blake breathing faster. Leaning in, I murmured in his ear, "I bet I can satisfy you in other ways, too."

"Jesus *fuck*," Blake swore, his entire body tensing momentarily before he recovered and stripped the rest of my dress off me, dropping to the ground with it. Then, he stilled. And so did I. Everything stayed still—except his eyes. They wandered in a slow, hot perusal up my body. And when they got to my face, he rasped, "You're exquisite."

Fire licked my insides, pooling in my cheeks and between my legs as I looked down at him. My entire body felt flushed, and it only grew worse as Blake, without moving his gaze from mine, reached out and cupped my calf, caressing it as he smoothed his hand down to my ankle. He lifted it gently, placing my foot on his knee. Only then did his eyes lower, dropping to focus on the buckle of my shoe as he undid it. Once he was done, he slipped it off my foot, cupping my heel in his palm.

I cringed and tried to pull back, but his grip tightened. "You don't want to touch my feet," I said breathlessly. "They've never been the same since I started dancing years ago."

I'd never been the same.

Blake flicked his attention up to my face, his expression smoldering and hard. "I want to touch every fucking inch of you, Delaney."

It felt like he was talking about a lot more than my body, and that thought made it hard to breathe while Blake continued. He held my gaze while moving to the next foot, repeating the same sinfully slow motions.

When he was done, I stood there, in the living room of our rental house, wearing nothing but my underwear and bra in front of my husband. Meanwhile, he still wore his black shirt and slacks, tented by his erection. He was shameless about it, not bothering to hide how much he wanted me as he stood again.

It was time for me to be shameless, too.

"My turn," I said.

He cocked a brow. "You want to undress me?"

"Yes."

He spread his arms out in a welcoming gesture. "I'm yours to undress."

With his permission, I closed the distance between us again and began fumbling with the buttons on Blake's shirt. His chest heaved against my touch, quickening the lower my hands traveled. I did it slowly, wanting to repay him for what he'd just done to my nervous system a few moments ago. And it seemed to be working. By the time I pushed his shirt over his shoulders and dropped to unbuckle his pants, Blake's breathing was ragged, his impatience showing. He kissed the top of my head while I focused on what my hands were doing—shoving his slacks to the ground.

Blake kicked his shoes off and then stepped out of his pants. His socks were the last to go.

And then we stood there.

Both naked except for our underwear.

Both breathing heavily but unable to move.

Blake looked exhausted and invigorated all at once. His thirsty eyes stared at me like he'd been stuck in a desert and couldn't decide whether I was a mirage. Whether I was real.

I wanted to show him that I was.

I just wanted to *show* him.

And I wanted to do it where all of this had started a few nights ago.

"Will you come outside with me?" I asked.

"I'll go anywhere with you," he replied without missing a beat.

I studied him for a moment, looking for any signs that he might not be telling the whole truth. Maybe he'd rather not hear the crash of the waves.

"You sure?" I checked.

He held out his hand. "Absolutely."

With that reassurance, I slid my hand into his and led us outside to the edge of the hot tub. Blake gave me a prolonged, heated look before sliding into the water first. He settled in a seat on the opposite side of the tub, turning to face me. To watch me. Just like I wanted.

Draping both arms up on the edge of the tub, he appeared relaxed despite studying each movement I made carefully, noting how I dipped one foot after the other into the still, steamy water and then perched on the side of the hot tub.

"Is this private enough for you?" I asked, and Blake's attention snapped to my face.

We were shrouded in darkness, but faint light from the house angled over Blake, exposing the sharp lines of his expression.

"Why?"

I answered his question by spreading my legs and running my fingertips along the seam of my underwear, and Blake's gaze darkened to a new degree. I heard him emit a soft curse beneath his breath before saying, "Are you going to touch yourself for me, Lane?"

"You seemed to like that idea before," I said and then sheepishly added, "And I like the way you watch me."

"Delaney." He gaped, seeming momentarily speechless. I'd never seen Blake look like this before, so equally tortured and eager. "I could watch you all night and day. You have no idea."

I was starting to have a little bit of an idea, and God, I *really* liked it. So much so that I could feel my heartbeat in every inch of my body. All the way to my toes.

But mostly between my legs.

"I might explode if I don't do something," I said honestly as I tried to catch a breath through the thick steam rising around me. "I don't know how you're so calm."

"You know I'm not calm." Blake's hooded eyes caught on my chest, seeming to study my breasts and how they nearly spilled over the top of my bra with every deep breath. "Not on the inside. I know you can see that."

That was true. I did know. The tightness of his body and the intensity in his eyes told me he was restraining something wild. But he also didn't seem in a rush to let go, unlike me.

"I'm on the edge of falling the fuck apart," he reinforced, leaning forward and pinning me with a look of desperation. "Let me see you. Please."

Not taking my eyes off his, I stood, letting the hot water swirl around my ankles. I hooked a finger into either side of my panties, shimmying out of them while enjoying how a muscle in Blake's jaw ticked. Then I threw the discarded underwear to the side and sat back on the edge of the hot tub.

The night air was cool. Cold, even. The glass wall around the patio helped break the wind, but still. In the back of my brain, I knew being nearly naked on a spring night along the coast should set a deep chill into my bones. I knew I should be freezing. Shivering. Shaking. And I was, but from the *heat*. Of Blake's gaze, of the water, of the pent-up need inside of me. My hands were clammy, my body feverish, and then Blake commanded, "Legs open," and I nearly blacked out.

"You want that?" I asked, lips drawing into a smirk because I couldn't help it.

"Don't fucking toy with me now, Delaney." Blake's voice was harsh, but there was also a tremor in it as he spoke. "I thought you were being good for me tonight so I could reward that pretty pussy of yours. But first, I want to see it."

I rolled my eyes despite the undeniable thrill that coursed through me and the corresponding decision to do exactly what he

259

asked of me. Keeping my focus on Blake's face, I spread my legs for him. The steam rose between us, slightly distorting my view of him, but there was no mistaking the burning hunger in the way he watched me. That look was the only reason I didn't feel self-conscious.

"So pretty," he murmured, barely audible beneath his breath. "So fucking pretty."

I slipped my hand between my legs, releasing a moan when my finger skimmed over my clit. God, I'd been aching for that, for some kind of friction, some kind of touch.

"Shit, Lane," Blake cursed. "You make the hottest goddamn noises."

A breathy laugh slipped out of me. "Can't help but notice you're not asking me to stop this time."

I dragged my finger lower before pushing it inside me slowly, letting Blake see how it disappeared and watching his jaw drop.

"Never asked you to stop," he countered, sounding dazed as he kept his focus on my hand. "Just wanted you to know what it did to me."

I pulled my finger out and ran it over my clit again. Another moan flew from my lips, but I was more interested in what Blake had just said.

"Can I see?"

I wasn't sure if Blake heard me at first. It wasn't until I removed my hand from between my legs that Blake yanked his gaze up to my face. "What?"

"Can I see what it does to you?"

Raising a brow, he wordlessly pushed himself up on the side of the hot tub, perching on the edge across from me. The wet fabric of his underwear molded to his legs and his *holy hell*—

"This?" he asked, wrapping his hand around his erection without looking away from me. "Is this what you wanted to see?"

"Yeah." I nodded, my mouth running dry. "That's what I wanted to see."

"It doesn't make you uncomfortable, Lane?" he asked, looking at me like he badly needed the answer. "That all I can do is think about you?"

"Think about me, how?" I countered, asking the thing *I* wanted to know.

"Answer the question first, Delaney," he urged, and I could tell he wasn't going to let it go. "Does it make you feel uncomfortable that I'm thinking of you while I have my hand around my cock?"

"No." I licked my lips without even realizing what I was doing. Blake's eyes blazed. "It doesn't make me uncomfortable."

"You like watching me stroke myself while I imagine how fucking good it would feel to be inside you? I bet it's un-fucking-believable."

I nodded wordlessly, too distracted by the thoughts Blake was voicing aloud and how he was touching himself.

"I've been hard for you all fucking night, Delaney," he groaned, twisting his hand slowly. "Do you know how agonizing that is?"

"I can help with that." I slipped into the water and waded toward him, suddenly wanting nothing more than to watch Blake lose the rest of his careful control. Ever since he threatened to fuck my mouth in the club, I'd had an image of that burned into my mind. I wanted to bring him back to that point where he seemed ready to risk it all. Because that's where I was.

Blake seemed to stop breathing as I approached, his body going still. Only his eyes moved, watching my every movement. When I dipped lower in the water, dropping so I was eye level with his waist—and his dick—he rolled his bottom lip between his teeth.

"Can I?" I asked, kneeling on the seat by where his feet were planted and reaching for the waistband of his underwear.

"I told you," Blake said solemnly. "You can do anything. Anything to me, Delaney."

"Had to check." I gave him a sly smile as I pulled down his briefs. "When you said that, I doubt you were referring to letting me suck you off."

"*Fuck*, Lane," Blake growled, but I wasn't sure if it had to do with what I'd said or with how I'd stroked a hand down his now exposed erection. Which was...big. So big I wasn't sure how it would fit in my mouth. But that didn't mean I didn't want to try. "Anything," he reemphasized through gritted teeth. "I meant anything then, and I mean it now, too. You can do anything to me. But you don't have to."

"I want to," I breathed, fisting the base of his cock and loving how Blake dropped his head back with a moan. "Because you threatened to fuck my mouth earlier, and I'd really like for that to happen."

"I knew it." Blake spoke up to the sky, and I watched the way his throat worked as he swallowed hard. "I knew you wanted my cock in that pretty mouth of yours."

"Mhm," I murmured and then lowered my head, letting my lips brush his tip. Blake squeezed his eyes shut in response, and I licked at his precum, trying to get his attention. His jaw clenched while he continued to look at the stars. So I sucked the head of his cock into my mouth. But he still didn't look at me.

"Aren't you going to watch?" I finally asked.

"I want to. *Fuck*, I do." He dragged a hand through his hair, pulling at the strands. "But I also want this to last. And if I watch you suck my cock and play with it like you're doing right now, it's gonna be all over. I already feel so fucking close to the edge."

Blake always remained incredibly measured and calm, no matter what he was doing, what circumstances he'd been thrown in. And watching him get so wound up, about to lose it because of something *I* was doing? Nothing compared.

I'd always wondered what might sever his control. I never considered that it might be me.

"You're strung so tight," I cooed before taking him deeper into my throat. "I think you might need someone to suck you off more often, Dr. London."

"Someone?" he scoffed. "I'm married, sweetheart. The only one allowed to touch me is my wife."

My stomach flipped. "Guess I'll have to be the one to do it, then."

"You're so fucking good at it." He gave in, looking down at me. I was ready, my eyes on his as he watched with a ferality that should have set off alarm bells in my head but aroused me instead. He brushed my hair out of my face and then kept his hand on my head, fingers tangling in my hair. "Such a good little wife, taking me into your mouth like that."

I smiled up at him, his cock still in my mouth, and Blake's lips parted with an awe I felt in my bones. The heat radiating from the water had nothing to do with the heat that radiated from this man. My husband. My best friend.

"Holy *fucking shit*, Delaney."

The grip on my hair tightened, and he started thrusting upward into my mouth. I relinquished control, letting him take what he wanted.

"Are you going to let me come down your throat?" he choked, and I could tell he was almost at his breaking point. His movements were frantic, his hold on me nearly crushing, like he was hanging on as long as he fucking could.

I nodded, refusing to pause what I was doing to say anything.

"Unreal," Blake muttered, strands of his dark hair hanging over his forehead as he looked down at me. "You're fucking unreal."

The praise lit me up inside, and I hollowed my cheeks, taking more of him. Blake responded with a hoarse cry before groaning, "No one fucks this sweet mouth except for me. Understood, Delaney?" He lowered his voice further, and I could hear the grit and promise in it. "It's *mine*."

I nodded again. Yes, his. He was the only one I wanted to be doing this with. And my confirmation seemed to be what sent Blake over the edge. "Lane, I'm going to—" he began frantically, but then I sucked harder, and any hope of coherent words was lost as he came with a string of curses.

Swallowing, I licked my lips and stood, grinning at Blake as he tried to regain control of his breathing. I was panting, too. My pulse raced, the mix of adrenaline and heat sending my body into overdrive.

The world seemed to tilt a little, like I'd stood up too quickly, and I turned to go back to my perch on the side of the tub, needing a break from the hot water. But then my vision blurred, and I swayed for a second time, and in an instant, Blake's arms were around me.

"Delaney?"

His voice was husky but panicked in my ear.

"Hi," I whispered, reveling in the feel of being in his arms and simultaneously wanting more. It was overwhelming, it was...it was *all-consuming*. I couldn't think; I couldn't breathe.

"Hi, Lane." Lips brushed my skin. "Are you okay?"

"Hot," I croaked, leaning back into him even though the furnace that was Blake's body was not going to help my situation. I couldn't help it; he was all I wanted right now. "Just really...burning."

The next thing I knew, I was in the air, a shriek flying from my lips. Blake wordlessly swept me into his arms, carrying me into the house. My surroundings passed by in a blur. Chilly air replaced the warmth of the water, and then that left, too, and I knew we were inside. Blake wrapped a towel around me, and I felt the softness of a bed. I sank into it, but the comfort of the mattress did nothing to make me feel better.

All I could do was struggle to suck in air as desire continued to constrict my lungs.

"Do you need some water?" Blake voiced, and I blinked to find him hovering over me. His soft, worried eyes scoured over me. He touched my cheek and then my forehead, but then he pulled away, and my body continued to seek it. His touch, I needed more of his touch. I needed something to soothe the burning. "Here, let me go get you a cool washcloth."

"No." I grabbed at his arm, and he dropped lower obediently, his body flattening over mine. "I don't need anything, I just need..." I struggled to explain myself because I'd never felt this *needy* before. I knew I needed something, and I knew nothing felt right, but water wasn't going to help. A cool washcloth wasn't going to help. Only...

"Delaney, you're shaking," Blake said, sounding stricken as he began to pull away again.

My grip on his arm tightened, stopping him. "Not from the hot tub."

"Are you sure?" Blake's brows pulled together as he looked down at me. "I think you overheated."

"Maybe a little. But it's not that. It's..." My words descended into a shameless groan as I tilted my hips up until they came in contact with some part of his body. I felt so delusional with how I needed him that I didn't even care how desperate I was acting.

"Oh, baby," Blake sighed, finally understanding. "I can fix it. I can make it better. Is that what you want?"

"Yes, please."

"Of course," his husky voice reassured. He peeled the towel back from my body, exposing me again. "I told you good little wives get to come, didn't I? And you've been *such* a good girl, Lane."

He lowered his head, finding my neck with his mouth, and I arched back, giving him better access. Little mewling sounds left my lips that I didn't recognize, but I couldn't stop, didn't know how to.

"I know how much it aches." Blake's lips trailed down my throat, skimming over my skin and making me shiver despite the fire in my veins. "I know, sweetheart. It's so overwhelming, isn't it?"

"I don't know what's happening," I gasped. "I've never... I've—"

"It's okay." His lips caressed the swell of my breasts, nipping at the edge of my bra before disappearing again. "I know. I know it's new for you."

My brain was too addled to understand the heavy undercurrent of his words. All I wanted was for him to hurry the fuck up with whatever he was doing.

"*Please.*"

I felt Blake's soft chuckle against my inner thighs and parted them further, wanting him to have better access. He grabbed my hips at the same moment, abruptly yanking me to the edge of the bed. A squeal slipped out of me and then a moan when I felt Blake's mouth tease my inner thigh.

"Does this make you feel uncomfortable?" he breathed, lips tilted to the side because he knew the answer, and he seemed *proud* of it.

"No," I confirmed, lifting my hips, anxious for more.

"Good," he grunted. "I'm going to eat your pretty pussy now, Delaney. Been dying for it, and I think we both deserve this. *God*, yes."

"*Blake*," I whined because it was the only word left in my brain.

"Yeah?" His dark eyes flicked up to mine, strands of hair dangling over them. He pushed a hand through his hair getting it out of his line of sight as he waited for me to reply.

"Just...please," I begged.

"Anything for you."

And then Blake lowered further, grazing his tongue over my clit, and I barely swallowed a scream while Blake made a deep, throaty noise, like he was equally satisfied by just that little taste. I grabbed at his head, twisting my fingers into his hair, hoping he understood that it meant I wanted more. And he did, swiping his tongue deeper between my legs and then finding a steady pace where each stroke hit my clit perfectly each time.

"You taste so *fucking* good, baby," he rasped before readjusting his body and adding, "God, I want to touch you, too."

"*Yes.*" It was all I could say as I bucked my hips up for him. "Yes, Blake."

Blake dragged a finger through my pussy before thrusting it

inside me, and I moaned with unparalleled pleasure as he muttered to himself about how wet I was.

"Is that what my girl wants?" he checked, and when I looked down at him, his lips were screwed in a crooked smile while his eyes glowed.

"Yes. More," I breathed, and Blake gave it to me, pulling his finger back and driving another one inside me, hitting deep at the same time he licked at my clit. And then he continued, doing that again and again until I was writhing on the bed beneath him. His pace was relentless, pushing me all the way to the edge until I was dancing on top of it and then dangling over it, so close to falling.

And then Blake murmured, "Come for me, Mrs. London," and I lost it.

My orgasm crashed down over me, causing a cry to rip from my throat. It was relentless, taking and giving until I was slumped on the bed, feeling boneless and sated. The world blurred around me. It was only Blake and his husky murmurs as he climbed back up my body, saying things like, "I knew you'd be even more gorgeous after you came," and, "Let me clean you up, sweetheart."

I'd never felt more relaxed in my entire life. More perfect. I let Blake care for me, only half-aware, my eyelids fluttering shut with a drowsiness that went beyond anything I'd experienced before. Then I curled onto my side, snuggling into the bed as a thought occurred to me.

"I thought you were going to fuck me tonight," I muttered, even as my eyes were closed.

I heard Blake's distant chuckle. "Funnily enough, I like my women to be conscious when I fuck them. And I think I just ate you into oblivion."

"Mm." It took a second for his words to register, and then I frowned. "Women?"

"Woman," he corrected. There was a smile in his voice. "Just one woman. Just you. No need to be jealous."

"I'm not jealous," I mumbled, but my bones melted with relief.

"Okay, Lane." I felt a kiss brush my forehead. "I don't want to rush this," he whispered. "I don't want to rush anything with you. You're tired, and that's okay. We have a long day of travel tomorrow that you should be well rested for, and if we keep going —" His words morphed into a soft groan.

I forced my eyes open to see his twinkling brown gaze cutting through the semi-darkness. "But—"

"Delaney. It's okay." He pressed a finger to my lips. My body tingled from his touch, and even though I was exhausted and my limbs felt like jelly, I couldn't ignore the disappointment that tonight was ending.

Still, my eyelids drifted shut.

Blake's lips brushed against my ear as I clung to semi-consciousness.

"We wouldn't want you to not be able to walk through the airport tomorrow, now would we?" His words were like a promise. I felt him tuck a piece of hair behind my ear, tender and soft like he hadn't just threatened to fuck me until I couldn't walk straight. "Just sleep right now, sweetheart."

I gave in despite my reservations, curling into a tighter ball in our shared bed.

"Just sleep," he murmured, and I couldn't fight it anymore.

eight years ago

DELANEY

Blake watched as I piled spaghetti noodles onto his plate, his lips twisting in a way that made it easy to tell he was holding in something.

"What?"

"Nothing." He struggled even more to withhold his grin. "Thanks for making dinner, Lane."

I began to reach for the pot of sauce before pausing with a frown. "Is there something wrong with it?"

He shook his head with a laugh that finally escaped. "No, not at all. This is just enough pasta to feed an entire army. We have an Echo practical tomorrow, not a cross-country meet."

I rolled my eyes and continued what I was doing, ladling a red meat sauce onto Blake's spaghetti. "I'm not convinced you're getting enough to eat. I looked in your fridge just now, and all I found was beer."

"Helps me study," Blake grunted, his amused expression falling.

"It does not," I scoffed. "If you want to fuel your brain, you have to fuel your body."

"I think after I eat this, I'll be fueled enough to study and do a 5K."

I snorted. "I didn't realize you were a cross-country runner."

"I'm not, and I never have been." Blake raised a brow. "Do I look like a runner?"

I flicked my gaze over him in a way that should be forbidden, and yet, I felt like I could because he invited it. No, Blake didn't look like a runner. He looked more like a contact sports athlete, more brawny and sinewy than a runner would be. He looked—

Blake cleared his throat to get my attention when I still hadn't answered, and I jolted, causing the ladle to slip out of my hands, clanging to the counter. Red sauce splattered onto my white shirt, and I groaned, looking down at what I knew would be stains.

I swore beneath my breath before grabbing a towel to wipe off the sauce. Meanwhile, Blake stood, striding across the room. "I'll go find you a new shirt so you can soak that one."

Before I could protest, he was gone. And a few moments later, he returned with a U of M alumni shirt in his hands.

"Here," he said, handing it over. "Now you can pretend you went to the U for undergrad, too."

I bit down on a teasing retort about how I had no desire to claim a different undergrad, considering mine was already the best, and took his shirt with a sigh, retreating to the bathroom to swap tops. I put my stained one in the sink and threw Blake's on. It was soft and smelled like him, like a musky, woody vanilla. Despite the U of M connections, I felt upgraded from the shirt I'd been wearing.

"Thanks," I said, walking back out to the kitchen. "Hopefully my shirt is salvageable, but I think I might like yours better."

Blake blinked up at me. His eyes grew round before they lowered to his plate of spaghetti.

"Looks good." He cleared his throat. "Glad you like it."

Blake barely looked at me for the rest of the meal.

CHAPTER TWENTY-TWO

delaney

WALKING ONTO OUR FLIGHT this time around felt completely different. We were immediately directed to the first-class cabin, which was even more luxurious than our other flight. We settled into our seats, which had curved walls on the outside for privacy and a collapsible divider between us that Blake immediately took down.

The seats weren't what felt different. It was Blake. It was us. It was the way he held my hand through the airport and let his gaze drift to my mouth every time he looked at me. It caused heat to simmer just beneath my skin. A want like I'd never known before burned inside me. All I could think about was last night. All I could picture was Blake between my legs, watching me with molten desire in his gaze. All I could hear was Blake rasping my name. All I could feel was the brush of his lips across my skin.

I could still feel it, a ghostly touch, taunting me. Reigniting my need for more. But there hadn't been time for more this morning, and now, I wasn't sure what was going to happen.

There hadn't even been time to talk. I'd been tangled in Blake when I woke up, his warm body encompassing mine, making me feel things I didn't understand. But then he quickly extracted himself and shuffled out of bed, returning a moment later with a cup of coffee. He placed it next to the bed for me and leaned down to press a kiss on my temple. And then he'd gotten busy—packing, arranging transportation to the train station, tidying the rental home.

We didn't talk about what happened. The things we'd said. The things we did.

I wasn't sure how I *should* feel about everything that transpired, but I knew the entire night made me feel shamelessly good. I'd never in my thirty-three years had a sexual experience like what I'd just experienced, and knowing that, of all people, it was with *Blake*? It was both shocking and weirdly sensical. We'd always understood each other in a way that no one else had; why wouldn't that extend to the bedroom?

This trip had been our catalyst. We'd left for this honeymoon as friends and returned as something entirely new. Blake didn't mean more to me than when we'd left, and I doubted I meant more to him. He'd always occupied such a big space in my life, but the way he occupied it now had *changed*.

That fact was exhilarating. But also terrifying. Because despite the stint of time when he'd moved to Boston without me, Blake had been the one constant in my life for so many years now. And what happened when something so solid suddenly morphed in front of your eyes, became something different, something you didn't quite understand yet? Even if I *really* liked this new version of him—of us—it still made my stomach flip when I thought about the uncertainty that accompanied it.

"You're wearing your compression socks, right?" Blake asked, his eyes sweeping down to my feet as though he could see through my sweatpants.

"Yes, I am," I answered, and Blake gave the kind of perfunctory nod he would at the hospital.

"That's my girl," he muttered—something he absolutely would *not* have said at the hospital—before tugging my seat belt tighter.

My chest ached as I wondered if Blake had always been this attentive and I'd just missed it or if this was new.

It felt new.

But it also felt comforting.

Like it was just Blake.

And Blake was a form of home I'd always relied on. And maybe just the understanding of how deep that ran was new.

After all the passengers boarded, the plane took off, and I curled up in my plushy seat, pulling one of the blankets they provided over me. Blake tugged on the corner of it like he wanted to be included in my cozy setup, and I draped the blanket over him, too.

For some reason, it made me excited to get back to Boston. I liked imagining this same scenario on the couch in Blake's apartment. I wanted to spend my weekends like this, watching movies and cuddling under blankets. I had no idea if that was what *Blake* wanted, though. We might have shared a bed the past couple of nights and done other unspeakable things, but maybe that wasn't the direction he wanted to go with this. Did *I* want to go in this direction?

A flight attendant came down the aisle as soon as we got to cruising altitude, taking our drink orders and giving us a rundown of the menu options for the flight. She didn't give an indication that she knew who we were until she came back with our beverages a bit later and smiled.

"Tell your brother good luck at training camps for us," she said and then continued to sweep her gaze over Blake as if to quickly compare him to his brother. And when she apparently decided she liked what she saw, she did it a second time, this time so blatant that I acted without thinking, slipping the hand with my wedding ring onto Blake's thigh possessively.

"We'll be sure to tell him," I said with a tight-lipped smile. "We're all really excited for this upcoming season. I was just making plans with Noah's girlfriend to go to his first preseason game together. It should be so much fun."

273

Blake stayed silent. Or nearly silent. Just as the attendant gave a placating grin and walked back down the aisle, I heard him swallow a throaty noise.

"Jesus fuck, Delaney," he groaned before shifting in his seat.

"What?" I glanced over at him, noting the way his jaw flexed. "You've never cared before when I scare off the women who try to use you because of Noah."

"No." He gave me a steady look that flared when I slipped my hand beneath the blanket and started trailing my hand up his inner thigh, tracing the seam of his pants. "I've never cared about that."

No, he hadn't.

I'd interrupted women who were hitting on him a number of times, and he'd never cared, had he? He let them walk away without so much as a glance their way and then turned to me with a knowing grin.

Like he'd known what I'd done.

Even if I hadn't.

Oh my God, had I *always* been so—

"Jealousy looks really fucking good on you, though, Lane," Blake murmured in my ear, suddenly so close to me that I could feel his breath on my skin. "And it feels good, too."

He found my wrist beneath the blanket and wrapped his fingers around it, stopping my movements.

"*Too* good," he rasped, leaning back and squeezing his eyes shut. "Also, Gemma's going to love you when I tell her what you just did. I hope you're ready to actually go to that game with her because you're definitely getting an invite now."

"Of course. Happy to help out my new sister-in-law."

"And Noah's going to love that you just called her that. Fuck, I do, too." His breathing grew more labored as I traced circles on his thigh despite not being able to move my wrist. "*Shit*, Delaney."

My heartbeat was so loud I heard it pounding in my ears. "Something wrong?" I asked, half-teasing, half-serious.

Maybe I was being too forward. Maybe he didn't want to continue whatever had happened between us on this honeymoon.

"Wrong?" He shook his head, eyes still closed. "God, you have no idea."

Nerves tightened in my stomach as my brain rushed through the possibilities of what that might mean. I hesitated for a moment, debating, before I leaned over the space between our seats and lowered my voice, finding his ear. "Give me an idea, Blake. Please."

He opened his eyes and dipped his head, facing me. Our mouths were only an inch apart, and after getting to taste him yesterday, I badly wanted to kiss him again. How many days had we been married? Was it more than twenty-one? Was that why kissing him and touching him already felt like a habit? Or why was I already so addicted to this, whatever *this* was?

Maybe this wasn't new. Maybe *I* was.

The cabin grew dark a second later, the lights dimming to allow for sleep on our trip across the Atlantic. Too bad I wasn't tired. I was more awake than ever. Passengers' screens cast the only soft glow in the plane. That, and Blake's eyes. They shone through the darkness.

"You want to know what's wrong?" he breathed.

I nodded.

Desperately. I desperately wanted to know. I didn't want anything to be wrong. I wanted everything to be right. I wanted last night to be right. I wanted *this* to be right.

"I'm not okay, Delaney," he confessed. "Your hands are on me, and now all I can think of, all I can see, is you kneeling in front of me in that hot tub last night. How your mouth—" His husky words broke off momentarily as he got a grip on himself. Or tried to. "Fuck, Lane. And the way you just got possessive, I—" He swallowed. I watched his corded throat work. "How the fuck am I supposed to make it through this plane ride?"

I stared at him, stunned in a way. So he was right where I was, then. We were here, together.

"I shouldn't even be saying these things to you," he went on. "Not before we have a chance to talk about what happened. Not when I'm still not sure how you feel or what you want. I'm not trying to shy away from that conversation or what happened, but I wanted to give you time to process everything."

"Do you need time?" I asked, wondering if that was what he was really trying to tell me. Because I didn't feel like I needed time. My body didn't feel like it wanted anything but him. More of him.

I held my breath while waiting for his response.

"No, Delaney," he said slowly after a beat of silence. "I don't need time. But it's d—" He cut himself off, pressing his lips together. "I don't need time," he repeated instead, eyes wandering my face.

My eyes, on the other hand, lowered to his lips. They were close, with so many memories of last night attached to them.

I released a shaky breath, relieved by his response. And ignited by it.

"Then maybe you can do something for me," I said.

"Anything," Blake murmured, and my gaze flicked back to his eager one.

I had to swallow past the nerves threatening to choke me before answering. "Tell me the occasion calls for it."

His brows shot up. "And what, exactly, is the occasion?"

"To say thank you," I answered because it was all I could think of. "For this trip. For last night."

Blake's gaze heated at the mention of last night, lingering on my lips before sweeping around the rest of my face. I watched with bated breath as his lips twisted in barely concealed amusement. "You don't have to kiss me to say thank you, Delaney. You can just say it."

Damn him.

"I know, but—"

"Just tell me what you really want," he cut in. "No more games."

I narrowed my gaze at him. "That's not fair, considering how in the club you—"

"I know. I'll start, then. Would that be fair?"

I gave a slow nod, feeling more jittery than my first day of med school.

Probably because I met Blake within the first five minutes, and then everything was okay.

"Yes," I breathed.

"I want to kiss you," Blake said simply, making my head spin. He tucked a piece of hair behind my ear and then left his hand there, cupping my cheek. "Badly. I don't know what's going on in your head, but I've been thinking about it all morning, wondering if I'd get a chance to do it again. I want to kiss you, Delaney. And the next time I get a chance, I'm going to."

I stared at him in awe before finding the courage to whisper, "I think you have a chance right now." And when Blake still hesitated, I added, "It's all I've been thinking about, too."

"Delaney." His gaze smoldered as he took in my words. "While I'm so fucking happy to hear that, you clearly don't understand what the feel of your lips do to me if you think I can kiss you right now and still survive this plane ride back to Boston."

"I could help you survive," I offered, only half-aware of our surroundings at this point, my brain hazing over with an undeniable level of lust. I tried moving my fingers again, wanting to feel him, to *help* him, but Blake's grip tightened on my wrist as he swore under his breath.

"Lane. Baby." A rumble came from deep in his chest as he closed his eyes. "You don't understand," he croaked.

He was right about that. I didn't understand a lot of this. But I did understand the way he made me feel and that I wanted more of it.

"I think I understand a little bit." I smiled, enjoying his tortured look, enjoying the knowledge of what I could do to him.

"I don't think you do." He shook his head, leaning back, distancing himself from me. "Because just the thought of your lips, your mouth, your touch fucks me up so bad that I need to pretend you don't exist for a few minutes."

I thought at first that maybe he was exaggerating, but the way he tipped his head back and refused to look at me told a different story.

"Just picture me wearing that ridiculous helmet from the Vespa ride," I offered with a light laugh.

To my surprise, that made Blake squeeze his eyes shut and grunt, "I don't think that's going to help."

"Really?"

"Your hair was in braids that day. In a way that really made me want to tug on them and see how you'd respond."

"Oh," I said breathily, feeling that tug he'd described between my legs. "I...I guess I know how I'm doing my hair from now on."

Blake groaned. "Not helping, Lane."

I bit down on my lip, thinking for a second before offering, "What about the time in med school when—"

"Also not going to help."

"Wow, you didn't even let me finish."

"Delaney." His free hand gripped his armrest, fingers curling over the ends. "I can't pretend you don't exist if you keep talking."

"Right." My lips curved. "Sorry."

"I can hear you smiling."

A full-out grin broke onto my face. "It's just not every day I get to see you, you know, struggle."

"I usually hide it better."

"What do you mean?"

"Never mind." He squeezed his eyes closed tighter. "Just shut up."

"You're the one who started talking to me again."

He blew a breath out between his lips. "This is why we can't sit together."

"Never could."

"Never for reasons like *this*, though."

"You never thought about me touching you while sitting in lecture?"

"Delaney..."

The way he said my name sounded like a warning, and I wasn't entirely sure why. Out of all the things I had said and done in the last few minutes, I wasn't sure why bringing up med school lectures was the one thing that had pushed it too far.

"What?"

He sighed, his eyes blinking open again. They took a second to find me, and when they did, I realized there was nothing teasing in them. His lips were set in a firm line. "First of all, I've already told you how seriously I take our friendship and how much I respect you as a person."

I cocked my head to the side, my lips tilting. "Is that a no, then?" I asked, trying to bring back the Blake who didn't respect me quite so much.

"Second of all," he continued, only acknowledging my question with the little twinkle that appeared in his eyes. He leaned forward, his lips flirting with my ear. "It's pretty bold of you to be sitting over there laughing about what you do to me when you were *begging* me to touch you in front of everyone in that club last night."

There he was. And he punctuated that statement by nipping at my earlobe, causing me to let out a tiny whimper as heat enveloped me.

The gravel in his voice, the reminder of the club, of what happened when we got home from it, the feel of his lips grazing my skin, giving me goose bumps.

Fuck.

"Ah, goddamn, Lane," he moaned into my neck.

"What?"

I didn't even do anything that time.

"You made the noise," he breathed. "That little whimpering you do that drives me absolutely wild."

"It's your own fault," I argued weakly. "You brought up last night. Again."

"That was a bad idea." Blake released his grip on my wrist and slipped his hand beneath the blanket, too. I felt the moment his fingers found my thigh, tickling over the top of it. "So is this, but I..."

"But you what?"

I had to hold in a sigh when his touch brushed between my legs.

"Need to hear you make that sound again," he murmured, sounding dazed and barely audible above the hum of the plane. "God, the way I wanted to reach beneath your dress and touch you in that club."

My eyelids fluttered shut as his fingers pressed harder. "Blake..."

"Fuck," he hissed. "This is bad. This is so bad."

"So bad," I echoed, tilting my hips because it wasn't enough. I couldn't feel *enough* of him. There were too many layers of clothes for me to feel him the way I wanted to. *Needed* to.

Blake's breathing hitched as I began to move my own fingers again, drawing a line up his rock-hard cock. "How much longer is this flight?"

"Hours," I groaned. "So many hours."

"I can't do this."

He abruptly yanked his hand away, and I thought he was going to put a stop to whatever we'd started until he leaned back in, issuing a gruff demand in my ear.

"Bathroom. Follow me in two minutes."

It was the longest two minutes of my life.

A different version of me might spend those two minutes trying to decide if this was really something I should be doing, but no. I didn't have any doubt when I got up and followed Blake through the first-class cabin to the bathroom, and the only anxiety I felt was in the form of pure anticipation.

As soon as I slipped into the bathroom, Blake grabbed my hand, pulling me to the side, into him. With his other hand, he simultaneously shut and locked the door. And then his lips were on mine, and I was reeling, lost to the desperate way he was kissing me. A hot rush of desire flooded my body—an instantaneous reaction to the feeling of his mouth ruthlessly taking mine.

"This is what I wanted," he groaned before slanting his mouth over mine and deepening the kiss further. His tongue sought mine, not even letting me respond as he stroked into my mouth, reigniting a familiar fire within me. "Your lips on mine again. You wanted it, too, didn't you?"

"Yes," I gasped, drowning in the reality of what he'd just said.

"No more games, Delaney," he said brusquely—almost like a demand.

"No more games," I agreed, sounding breathless.

"There doesn't need to be an occasion to call for this. It's yours whenever you want. Got it?"

I nodded, eager and ready for these new rules. "Got it."

"*God*, Lane," he moaned in response, canting his hips so I felt how aroused he was. His hard length rubbed between my legs, causing a whimper to fly out of me—just like the one he'd wanted to hear. "Yes," he hissed. "Fuck yes. Just like that. Just want to hear you make more of those sounds. Want to touch you. Feel you. Slip my fingers into your underwear like I was itching to last night. Can I? Please say yes."

"Yes," I consented, and within seconds, Blake had flipped me around, pressing my back against the tiny counter in the bathroom and sliding his hand into the waistband of my sweatpants. And then when he found the seam of my underwear, he slipped his fingers beneath that, too. His fingertip flirted with my clit and then dove deeper between my legs, making me gasp against his lips and grind against his hand, seeking more.

"That's it, baby," he praised while sinking his fingers inside me and pressing the heel of his palm against my clit. My mouth opened and closed in shock of the sensation—the immediate high. "Ride my hand and take what you want. Just let me hear you."

"We need to be quiet," I argued, all while I continued to rock against him like he wanted, chasing the buildup of pleasure his touch caused.

"I don't fucking care." Blake's voice was hoarse, like he was hanging on by a thread. "I only care about you, Lane. Have only ever cared about you."

He angled his hand in a way that created more pressure directly against my clit and pushed his fingers deeper inside me, and a silent scream slipped through my lips.

"*Delaney.*" He pushed my name out through his gritted teeth, a reprimand for keeping my sounds to myself.

"Blake," I moaned in response, giving him what he wanted. "Oh my *God.*"

"Fuck, you have no idea what it does to me to hear you say my name like that." He licked the seam of my lips before diving into my mouth, tangling his tongue with mine for a breathless second. And then he was back to murmuring against my lips with a gritty, sinful voice. "You feel so fucking good, Lane. So wet for me. God, I want to strip you down and worship your sweet body until you're chanting my name, begging me to let you come. But we don't have that kind of time right now."

"I'm already so close," I assured him, meeting his hand with little thrusts of my hips, uncontrollably seeking more.

"I know you are." I could feel his smile against my mouth. "Your tight little pussy is clenching around my fingers. And I love it. Love this pussy. Love when it comes for me."

He punctuated that by curling his fingers deeper, rubbing them against a spot that made me see stars, succumbing to a feverish explosion. I clutched onto his broad shoulders and chased after that high, grinding harder against his hand.

"Yes," he encouraged, a low growl that shot a thrill through me. "Come all over my hand. Soak my fucking fingers, baby. I want to taste you on them for the rest of the goddamn day. Until the next time they get to be inside you like this."

The combination of his crude, gruff words—ones I never imagined Blake, *my* Blake saying—and his insistent, demanding touch pushed me over the edge, and I climaxed within seconds. It was fast and intense, and I crumbled into Blake, my legs shaking and my cries soft against his chest, repeating his name over and over again.

"Good girl." Blake kissed the top of my head as the aftershocks rippled through me. "You're such a good girl for me, Lane."

He pulled his hand from my pants, and I looked up to see him licking his fingers, sucking them into his mouth with an expression of pure enjoyment. Like I was a delicacy he'd been waiting years to taste. His cock twitched against my stomach, and I squirmed in response. Feeling and seeing how much he wanted me quickly reignited something that I had no idea could burn so bright. So hot.

So *incredibly* hot.

"You," I panted, struggling to say any more words than that.

Blake shook his head as he looked down at me. "Delaney, if you wrap that pretty little hand around my cock, I'm going to make an absolute mess of you."

I wanted that. Badly. But I also had enough reason to know that it wasn't the best way to go about this.

Because we *were* going to go about this. I wasn't going to let Blake suffer through the rest of this flight without getting his own relief.

"I told you I was going to help you survive, and I'm going to," I insisted. "Come inside me, Blake."

He lifted his brows, but I saw the flash in his eyes. Pure electricity, like a bolt of lightning. But still, he choked out, "Delaney, no."

"Yes." I nodded, pulling my sweatpants down over my hips and kicking them off. Then, I unzipped Blake's pants and pushed them down. Blake watched me, seemingly dumbfounded, but as soon as I wrapped my fingers around his cock, he grabbed my wrist to stop me.

"I am *not* fucking you in an airplane bathroom, Delaney," he said, his voice harsh but unraveling at the same time.

"But—"

"No," he asserted through gritted teeth, but at the same time, he moved us closer together. Like he couldn't help it. Like we were magnets, and words did nothing to resist the pull that anchored us together. The tip of his cock brushed between my legs, and I widened my stance, wanting more. "I'm not rushing this with you, Lane. Not after so—" He broke off with a groan. Most likely because I pressed my hips closer to his, letting him slide further between my thighs, hitting the apex of them. I knew I was soaking his cock, knew he could feel how wet I was for him. How hot I ran for him. How badly I wanted him to just say, "*Fuck it.*"

"Oh my—oh, *shit*—" Blake choked off his words, tipping his head back and squeezing his eyes shut. I watched the muscles in his throat work, his Adam's apple bobbing as he swallowed down whatever else he was going to say. Grabbing both of his shoulders to steady myself, I swallowed a groan.

But staying quiet was useless because a second later, Blake glanced back down at me with a piercing look, gripped my ass with both hands, and lifted me up into his arms, making me gasp—probably too loud. Then he lowered me down slowly, allowing his cock, which was erect against his abdomen, to glide through my pussy. His tip grazed my clit as he moved both his hips and me up and down, exploring feeling me like this. "You're so—" he choked, but that seemed to be all he could say.

"Blake, please," I whimpered, tightening my grip on his shoulders. I wanted him so badly. He was so hard between my legs, but it wasn't enough.

"If you still want this when we get home, I'll give it to you," he rasped. "I promise I will. I'll give you so much more, too. Everything. But right now, I'm not going to last." His breathing sounded stilted in my ear, proof of his words. "This is all it's going to take for me. Just feeling you like this. Hearing you. Just *you*, Lane."

"That's okay," I whispered in his ear, struggling to speak when I had his dick between my legs. But I understood what he was saying, and I could wait for him. I could wait until we got home. "That's perfect. Just come for me, Blake."

"Is that what you want? You want my cum all over that pretty pussy of yours, baby?"

I nodded.

"Need to hear you say it."

"Come all over me, Blake," I panted.

"Oh, *hell*," he groaned, and true to his words, that was all it took. He moved me up and down once more, and then I felt his climax tear through him, felt his release coat my skin. All I could do was watch him—the way his eyes fluttered shut and his throat rippled and his jaw clenched, trying to keep in the roar of pleasure as it coursed through. We were making a mess anyway, but I didn't care. I didn't care about anything except the expression on Blake's face and how it felt like he was seeing right through me when he opened his eyes again.

Neither of us spoke at first. I wasn't sure either of us knew what to say. Wordlessly, Blake reached between us and swiped his fingers through my pussy, causing my breath to hitch. His gaze grew steely.

"You wanted it inside you," he said, sounding strangled. His fingers swirled around between my legs, and I realized he was catching his dripping release. "You wanted me to come inside you."

I whimpered, nodding, and Blake thrust his cum-soaked fingers back into my pussy without another warning. Then he leaned closer, breathing in my ear. "There you go, baby."

"*Blake*," I breathed, unable to believe the sparks he just ignited inside me by doing that. What the hell was he doing to me? What the hell was happening? Instinct told me to laugh it off, so I tried.

"When I said that thing about coming home with a baby on the way, I swear I wasn't serious. You know that, right?"

"Yeah, I know," he said solemnly, not laughing even a little bit. He lowered his voice. "But I was when I said it wouldn't scare me."

My throat constricted. My chest tightened. My pulse soared.

But he didn't mean it like *that*.

"No, you've always wanted kids," I said as Blake let me slide back down to the floor. Because it was true. He had, hadn't he?

Blake only responded with a soft hum, focusing instead on fixing our clothes so we could escape the bathroom before we were detected.

I never would have guessed we'd be ending this trip by nearly fucking in the plane bathroom, but I had absolutely no regrets.

Especially because this new era of our relationship meant that when we both had righted our clothes and snuck back to our seats, Blake immediately pulled me into his arms. And while I couldn't decide if that meant cuddling *was* on the table or if this was just an extension of fooling around, an aftercare moment, I was enjoying myself too much to think about it for more than a few minutes.

It was the most comfortable I'd ever been on a flight and certainly the happiest. It might have been the happiest I'd been...ever.

I turned on a movie, and Blake's lips grazed my neck before he sighed in my ear, sounding almost regretful and setting alarm bells ringing in my head.

"Everything okay?" I asked, glancing back at him.

"Everything is more than okay. Everything is amazing." Despite his words, his voice sounded strained. "But also, no."

"No?"

He sighed again, his eyes rolling up for a moment. The plane could have fallen from the sky, and I probably wouldn't have noticed, too busy waiting for whatever Blake was about to say. And when he spoke, it was with such a hushed reverence it felt like the world stopped spinning for a second, and we were just floating in the air.

"I'm just constantly tortured by you, Delaney."

I laughed, but it was forced. Because there was simply nothing funny about this moment. "Tortured?"

He lowered his voice, leaning closer. As close as he could get. I reveled in his nearness in a way I never suspected I would. I knew it wasn't scientifically possible for a heart to vibrate, but that was what it felt like when Blake's skin kissed mine.

"Tortured, baby." He sucked my neck like he wanted to mark me there. "You're sitting there like nothing happened, and meanwhile, all I can think about is how my cum is between your pretty thighs. I still don't know how the hell I'm going to make it to Boston in these conditions."

I sucked in, reeling from his words and crossing one leg over the other, trying to tame the pulse between my legs before it grew unbearable again. And once I thought I could speak coherently, I muttered, "I am not sitting here like nothing happened, Blake."

"You could have fooled me."

I shook my head, looking at him. "I was actually just thinking about how happy I am."

Blake's gaze bored into me, studying my face. His breathing seemed stilted, and his lips parted before he licked them slowly. "Really?"

I nodded. "Really. I'm very...happy about what just happened. And I'm going to be thinking about it the entire way home. Likely longer than that."

"Mm," Blake murmured. "I think maybe this is a sign that we should travel more often. I can book the next flight as soon as we get home."

"I'd like that," I whispered. "We should see how many plane rides we can squeeze in over the next year."

I'd never been much of a traveler before, but I'd learned I really liked traveling with Blake.

"Yeah." Blake's voice suddenly sounded duller. "I bet we can fit in a lot...in a year."

In a year.

Was that when this—whatever this was—ended?

I wasn't sure.

But I was starting to feel sure I didn't want it to.

Maybe that thought was rushing it.

Or maybe that thought was way past due.

CHAPTER TWENTY-THREE

blake

W E'D ARRIVED HOME ABOUT an hour ago, and I was already lying in my bed, alone, missing Delaney. She'd gone into her room to unpack right away, so I showered and then collapsed into my bed, expecting to fall right asleep immediately. But then I heard her turn the water on in the bathroom, and all I could do was lie there thinking about how badly I wanted to be in that shower with her.

Exhaustion had nothing on the way I wanted this woman.

I closed my eyes, trying not to spiral about Delaney and the honeymoon and the plane and what the fuck would happen now that we were back, and when I opened them, she was standing in my doorway. She had her arms wrapped around a pillow that was tucked to her chest. Her damp hair fell loose around her shoulders, and all she wore was an oversized T-shirt.

That was it.

I grinned. "Are you coming for a sleepover?"

"It's just, we haven't slept apart since..." She bit down on her lip, bouncing on her toes adorably.

"I know," I said so she didn't have to spell it out.

We hadn't slept apart since the night she'd jolted me out of the worst nightmare I'd ever had—one I never, ever wanted to repeat.

"I wasn't sure if you'd still want company now that we're home." She glanced down at her feet. "I don't care either way, but I..." Her gaze lifted slowly, finding me. She lowered her voice. "I don't want that to happen again. I really hated that, Blake."

Pain swirled in her eyes—pain that she felt on my behalf.

I should have been disappointed that she was standing in my bedroom doorway because she thought I was too fragile to sleep by myself and not because she wanted me to fuck her the way I'd promised to when we got home, but I wasn't. As much as I was tortured by the way I longed for her, by the tension that simmered in my veins every time I thought about the things that had transpired between us in the last twenty-four hours...the way she cared for me meant so much more.

It gave me hope that maybe our friendship could withstand this change in our relationship. That being physically intimate wouldn't destroy our other connections but make them stronger.

I had to clear the emotion from my throat before I was able to talk.

"I really hated that, too." She had no idea just how much. I hated everything except what happened afterward, when I got to sleep with my arms around her for the first time ever. "I don't think it will happen again, but I always want your company."

I hadn't had a single nightmare since that night on the couch. Not since I had Delaney tucked against my chest when I slept. Safe, in my arms. Her breath against my skin. Her heart beating steadily, her pulse echoing inside me.

Not even the sound of the sea outside our rental house had been able to detach me from reality and bring me back to that moment that changed so many things for me.

Delaney kept me grounded, attached.

To her, always to her.

She smiled but then tried to hide it, looking back at her feet as she walked over to the bed and dropped her pillow on top of mine. She was about to slip beneath the covers when I realized what she was wearing: a maroon-and-gold U of M alumni shirt. The same one I'd been missing for God knows how many years.

"You kept it?"

Delaney glanced down at her shirt as though she'd forgotten what she had on. As soon as she realized, a pretty blush spread across the apples of her cheeks.

"You never asked for it back, so I just figured that meant I got to keep it." She pulled the covers over her, twisting onto her side to face me and then tugging the blankets all the way up to her shoulders as if to hide the fact that she was wearing my stolen shirt. "I'm sorry. I'll return it if you want."

"Delaney." I released a hoarse laugh, turning to lie on my side, too. Then I dropped my voice and said, "Trust me, you do not need to apologize for coming to bed wearing one of my shirts. Even if it is one that I haven't seen in years. I'm only upset that you didn't give me the chance to properly appreciate it."

Delaney's voice was thick when she spoke, her eyes blazing to life. "Appreciate it?"

My lips split in a crooked smile.

"Appreciate *you* in it," I clarified. "Can I see you, Lane?"

If I thought Delaney's cheeks were pink before, they were especially rosy now as she dragged the covers back down her body, exposing her in my shirt. A shirt I let her borrow years ago. A shirt she kept. A shirt she wore to bed. Jesus, I thought it had long disappeared, but she'd had it all this time.

Delaney got back out of bed, the shirt lifting as she stood, bearing the curve of her ass beneath that maroon-and-gold fabric. Nothing else. Not a single other thing was on her body except that shirt. *Fuck me.*

She spun, giving me a proper show to take her in, to appreciate her. And shit, was I appreciating her—her bare thighs that I'd been between and knew how good they felt, her bra-free breasts curving beneath my shirt, her sweet lips pulling into a smile. My cock twitched, coming to life with a desire that was even more intense than on the plane, than our night in the club, than anything that happened on the honeymoon.

Because this was it. We were back in Boston, and Delaney was in *my* bed, wearing *my* shirt, biting down on *my* smile as she watched my reaction, and fuck if I didn't want to do the same thing. Just a little nibble on those kissable, plump—

"Blake?"

I jerked my gaze up, staring straight into those sparkling, sapphire eyes. My heart lurched. The chokehold this woman had on me was so unbelievable that I honestly wondered if I would survive tonight.

"Yeah?"

"Nothing." Her lips curved higher. "You're just staring."

Damn right I was staring.

I flashed her a wicked grin, unable to help myself. "Appreciating, remember?"

She bit down harder on her bottom lip, and I was *so* painfully hard. It was *painful* the way I wanted her. "Want to appreciate with your hands?" she asked.

I gaped at her for a moment, stunned. And then I got my shit together and took her straight up on that invitation.

"How did you know?" I rasped, leaning over to cup my hands on the back of her thighs and urge her closer to the side of the bed. Closer to me. Then I ran my palms up her smooth legs, shifting my eyes to hers when I reached the hem of the shirt. "How did you know that's what I wanted?"

"Something about the look in your eyes." After those sinfully soft words, she held my gaze, almost to prove a point. That there was something there. Something rare. Something that explained everything that was happening in this moment. Something that tugged on my heartstrings and then tied them all up into a knot.

Then Delaney nodded, a tiny indicator of consent that spurred me into action.

I slipped my hands beneath the shirt, skimming my palms over the curve of her bare ass and then her lower back before rounding to her hips, settling them there. Delaney didn't look away from me as I touched her, as I experimented with how her body felt when the only thing on it was something that belonged to me. Her chest was the only part of her body that moved, heaving with labored breaths that looked a lot like the ones filling my lungs.

My bed, my shirt, my hands, my wife.

"You sleep in this shirt a lot, Lane?" I asked, needing to know.

She gave a sheepish shrug—not quite an admittance, but not a denial either. And I'd take it. Fuck, the knowledge that Delaney had been wearing this shirt to bed for years had my chest tightening. I didn't even care if the only reason she wore it was because it was oversized and comfortable. I'd pretend otherwise, feed my delusions where she was concerned.

I didn't press her for clarification, either. Maybe I was afraid of the truth, that it wouldn't be what I wanted to hear. Or maybe I just had other things on my mind.

I cleared my throat. "Delaney, can I ask you something?"

She nodded, more confident this time. "You can ask me anything, Blake," she whispered, her voice a low sort of hum. A frequency that my body hadn't heard coming from her before. It made me absolutely vibrate with need.

I squeezed her hips as an experiment, and she released the tiniest moan.

Eagerness appeared as a glaze covering her eyes.

There would be no going back now.

"When's the last time you had sex?" I asked softly, urging Delaney back into bed. But this time, I rolled onto my back and pulled her on top of me, one leg on either side of my hips.

Fuck, Delaney straddling me might be the hottest thing I'd ever seen. I gripped her thighs, keeping her there, not wanting her to ever move.

"Are we friends who talk about our sex lives now, Blake?" she countered, her voice just as quiet, just as gentle, even though having this conversation was rocking both of our worlds—I knew it was.

I traced the outline of her face with my eyes. "I think we are. I think we need to be if we're going to do this."

And I *really* wanted to do this.

"We're going to do this," she confirmed, making my blood run hot. And then she confessed shyly, "It's been years."

"That's okay," I said.

She had no fucking idea how *okay* with that I was. I would have survived if she'd told me something different, like that maybe her fake relationship with Austin had come with benefits, too. But I might have also spiraled a little bit at hearing it.

"You dragged me out to a party," she said with a sigh. "And I—"

"*I* dragged you to a party? Fuck, I don't need to hear the details," I interrupted. Because Christ, I didn't think I would make it through a retelling that involved other men touching my wife. "I don't like thinking about assholes having their hands on you."

"Well, I'm pretty sure *you* had your hands on another girl you disappeared with. And I don't know. I think I might have been—" She choked on the last word, and I wanted to beg her to continue. And then she did, and my jaw nearly dropped. "Jealous," she admitted.

"No." I tipped my head back with a groan. "Jealous, Lane?"

She'd been jealous? She thought I'd been with another woman, and *she'd* been jealous? I wasn't sure I could stomach the fact that Delaney had slept with someone else because she'd been jealous of someone being with me. I didn't know how to wrap my head around the truth of that.

"Yeah." She grimaced. "I'm not proud of it, but...I don't know. I guess even though I've always understood what our relationship is, I never really liked, um, sharing you with other girls."

Fuck everything.

"You didn't need to be—*shit*." I broke off with a sigh.

"Well, did you?" she pushed after a slight pause.

"What?"

My brain was too busy spinning to keep up with this conversation.

"Were you—" She bit down on her lip before shaking her head. "Never mind."

But now that I'd taken a second to work through things, I was pretty sure I understood what she was asking.

"Are you wondering if I slept with someone that night? Because the answer is no."

"Do you even know the night I'm talking about?"

"Doesn't matter, Delaney." She really had no idea. "I haven't had sex since before grad school. Since before..." *Since before I met you.* "It's been a long time."

"What?" Delaney's lips parted in surprise. "What about all your other dates, dating apps, everything?"

All I could do was shrug, looking up at the ceiling. "It just... never progressed that far."

Delaney stared at me. I could see her out of the corner of my eye. "I don't understand."

I glanced over at her, partly wishing I could just lay it all out on the table right now. But our relationship had already gone through a massive restructuring in the last twenty-four hours, and I hadn't played the long game with Delaney just to fuck it up when I finally got close to the end. I might want to sprint to the finish line, but she'd only just joined the race. I needed to give her a little time to catch up.

"I went on all those dates to find someone to marry, but I was never going to marry any of them, Lane."

There was only one woman in this world that I imagined myself married to, and she currently had my ring on her finger. Dream come fucking true, even if it might all come crumbling down in less than a year.

"What?" she breathed, her brows drawing together. "Why?"

Because they weren't you.

I looked back to the ceiling before answering. "Just wasn't

right. And sleeping with them when I knew that I wasn't going to marry them..." It didn't feel right.

"But it's okay to sleep with...well, I guess we *are* married, aren't we?" A humorless chuckle fell out of her lips, and I understood the laughter. Everything felt a little bit funny right now.

My eyes found hers again, and I cupped her cheek, our eyes meeting. Heat spiraled through me from that simple touch. That simple look. "Yeah, Lane." I brushed my thumb along her jawline, and her breathing picked up. Mine did, too. "We are."

Married. We were married. And I'd never really get over that.

She leaned down, her body seeking mine, on a single mission to be closer together. And fuck, did I love that. Even while her brain was trying to comprehend what was happening, her body knew what it wanted. "But it's..." she started but didn't finish.

Fake.

It was fake.

We both knew it, but neither of us felt like saying it.

"I know," I murmured against her lips. "I know. But still, Lane. It's—" *It's real to me,* I wanted to say. But I couldn't, so I tipped my hips into hers, moaning when she writhed back against me. "Fuck, you just feel so goddamn good."

"*Yes.*"

So good.

So *goddamn* good.

"For the record, I don't like sharing you, either. Never have," I clarified because I needed to say something that made her understand what she meant to me. I couldn't fuck Delaney without her knowing that she was mine. She'd always been mine. Maybe she didn't understand the full extent of that yet, but hopefully, one day, she would. And for now, I'd claim what I could. "Never will. In case that wasn't clear enough last night when I was fucking this sweet mouth."

"It was clear," she said without hesitating. Without seeming bothered by it, too.

"Good."

I kneaded her hips like a reminder.

Mine.

Delaney squirmed beneath my touch, rocking forward into it, seeking more.

And fuck did I want to give it to her.

"Blake, I want you," she confessed breathily, and my heart flew into my throat.

Blake, I want you. Want you. Want. You.

It echoed through my bones as I used my grip on her hips to align us perfectly so she could feel how hard I was for her through my shorts. Then I thrust upward, giving her a taste. I wanted this, right now, right here. Just like she did.

Delaney gasped, her hands flattened on my heaving chest, her eyes rolling back and then seeking mine, waiting for me to say something. As if the position I'd just put us into wasn't an explanation enough.

But I'd happily clarify it for her.

"Then put me out of my goddamn misery and take me," I demanded.

blake

"DO YOU WANT ME to keep the shirt on?"

Delaney's fingers toyed with the hem of the U of M shirt, ready to take it off at my command.

I felt like I had the whole universe in my hands.

This was too much power, more than any man should have.

But if any man was going to have the ability to strip Delaney down with his words alone, better fucking believe it was going to me.

Still, that didn't mean I knew how to answer the question. The possession that ripped through me when I saw her in my shirt was undeniable. But on the other hand, I was dying to see her bare, with nothing to cover the flush I planned on spreading across her entire body.

I shook my head, realizing she was waiting on my answer. "That's an impossible decision."

Delaney's lips curved. "Then I'll just keep it o—"

"No."

As soon as she suggested it, my whole being vetoed the idea of her keeping any bit of clothing on.

I needed to see her. I'd never forgive myself if this was my one opportunity to see Delaney stripped naked and I'd let it go.

"Take it off," I grunted.

I studied the curve of Delaney's lips as she said, "Okay, Blake." So soft, so gentle, but so fucking seductive when combined with the way she looked down at me, lifting the hem of the shirt an inch at a time. Her long, blonde hair framed her face, still damp from her shower. I'd never in my life seen anything sexier, and when the shirt lifted higher, I swore I felt my heart palpitate. The curves of her breasts were exposed little by little, sending me into orbit with anticipation.

"Delaney." I dug my fingers into her hips, desperate. "I can't do this."

"What?"

She stilled, and I took advantage of her momentary confusion, stealing the shirt from her hands and ripping it up and over her head. I threw it to the ground.

Delaney blinked at me, and then her lips parted into a slow smile.

"Someone's impatient."

"You have no fucking idea, Lane. I—" I stopped my words, gritting my teeth. I'd confessed far too many things recently. I didn't need her to know the extent of how long I'd been wanting this—wanting *her*.

And now she was sitting here, straddling my lap, naked.

It didn't feel like my heart was pumping enough blood to keep my body alive, and my breaths started coming in short spurts. I knew, in the back of my head, that I was experiencing symptoms of some kind of cardiac catastrophe, but I couldn't get myself to give a shit. I'd die a happy fucking man after seeing Delaney like this.

My hands started drifting up her sides, uncontrolled, needing, wanting.

"Can I touch you?" I breathed.

Needed to touch her.

Needed to taste her.

My brain felt like it was short-circuiting, and I wondered if I was having a neurological malfunction, too. My thoughts were incoherent, a jumbling mess that consisted only of experiencing more of this woman in the way I'd always dreamed of.

Fuck, that wasn't even true.

I'd never dared to dream that this would happen.

So pretty. So perfect. So pink, her nipples were so pink. And hard, begging to be pinched.

"Please," she whispered, and my hands were all over her, palms cupping her breasts, thumbs drifting over her nipples. Her body molded to my touch like an artist had sculpted us with each other in mind. Meant to be. I knew I shouldn't get ahead of myself, but fuck if it didn't feel like this was meant to be.

"Lane..." Finding the words I needed was so hard. "Dear God, Lane, let me taste you."

There, yes, that was what I wanted.

"Take your shorts off, and I'll consider it."

Christ, Delaney.

The way she was so confident about this, about what was happening, gave me hope. And drove me fucking wild, too.

I'd never stripped down so quickly. Delaney helped, shucking my shorts off as fast as she could, and as soon as they were tossed to the ground with my underwear, I was leaning forward, my lips finding her. First her shoulder, then her collarbone, and eventually, the swell of her breasts. Delaney arched forward, begging for more, urging my mouth to finally wrap around her nipple, sucking and licking, and *shit*, the sounds she was making caused my dick to stiffen that much more. It was painful and glorious all at once.

Delaney leaned into me, letting me switch from one nipple to the other, lavishing my mouth over her breasts while my hands wandered her body. She squirmed beneath my touch, and every slight move she made caused her bare pussy to graze my cock. I watched her touch that pussy last night, and then I got to bury my face in it afterward, and while all of that was earth-shattering, it was nothing compared to feeling her like this.

"Inside you," I panted, forcing myself to lie back down so I stopped distracting her. "Need to be inside you. I can't wait any longer, but I promise I'll be so fucking good to you, Delaney."

"Yes, need you," she agreed, looking dazed as she slid forward over my cock, coating it with arousal.

I broke out in a sweat.

I'd never known hunger and desire like this before in my goddamn life.

Christ, I wasn't going to make it.

Especially when she bit down on her lip, moaning when we connected just right. Still, I tried. Tried to keep it together. I kept my eyes on her gorgeous face and those brilliant blue eyes even as I felt her hand wrap around my shaft, repositioning us.

Somewhere in my spellbound brain, reality made a brief appearance.

"Condom, Delaney," I rasped. "Fuck, I don't even know if I have one, but I can look."

"We don't have to." She shook her head, looking baffled upon having her exploration of my cock interrupted. "It's up to you. I'm clean."

"Same." I exhaled with relief. Until she dragged my tip between her legs, and liquid heat erupted inside me. She was so... so, *fuck*. "Do you have any idea," I choked out, "how fucking wet your pussy is for me right now?"

"Yes, I do," she admitted breathlessly. She blinked down at me with eyes that were anything but innocent. "I told you I wanted you."

She could repeat that a million times, and I'd never get sick of hearing it.

I had to clear my throat before I could speak, and even then, it came out low, gravelly. "And I told you to take me."

Delaney's body vibrated with tension as she stroked my length from top to bottom, eyes growing wide. I hissed through my teeth, not wanting her to stop because I knew she was familiarizing herself with my body, preparing herself for what was about to happen. But waiting was so fucking hard.

Literally.

"Blake." I nearly fainted from how she said my name. "You're so...will you fit?"

"Yeah, baby," I reassured. "I will. You can take it."

Her breathing picked up, and I couldn't tell if she was anxious or eager. So I added, "I promise, Lane. Just...go slow if you need to."

I wasn't sure why I was encouraging her to torture me more.

Actually, that was a lie.

I knew why.

Delaney's well-being and comfort would always come before mine. Even if it drove me to my goddamn wit's end.

Her bright gaze found mine, our eyes locked as she did exactly as I told her. She took me, slow and measured, her lips parting with a gasp as she sank onto me, letting me slide deeper and deeper. *Shit.* It was agonizing and amazing, the first taste of friction and my first dip into unprecedented bliss.

There was nothing before her and nothing after her that would ever feel as perfect as this. She was the end-all and be-all of everything I had ever wanted.

"Good girl," I praised, my voice a husky mess. "You're doing so good. You know that, right?"

Delaney nodded, emitting a tiny whimpering noise as she concentrated on what she was doing, hands braced on my chest, tits pushed together.

Fuck, she was so hot. So gorgeous. How was I supposed to do this?

Clearly, I was a glutton for torture because the next murmured words out of my mouth were, "I'm not all the way in yet. Just a little more, baby. You can do it."

With one final movement, she sank all the way down. *Fuck.* Bottomed out inside her, I took a deep breath and looked up at the ceiling. It was all I could do. Watch the ceiling fan go round and round, trying to count the number of times it turned. But it was impossible.

"Blake?"

"Same problem as last night," I managed to get out, hardly able to talk with how paralyzed by pleasure I felt. "Watching you is too...Lane, the way you look seated on my cock is..." I shook my head. I didn't have words for it.

"What do you want me to do?" Her voice came through as strained as mine. Like it could be plucked and played like a fiddle.

"Nothing. Everything. *Fuck*."

"Can I move?" She sounded like she was begging, and *holy shit*. Delaney begging to fuck me was the pinnacle of my existence —nothing could ever top it. "I think I need to move. You feel..."

"Please say good."

"*So* good."

"Thank God. Ride me, sweetheart," I begged. My turn. "Please. Use me however you want."

"But I want you to feel good, too."

"I'm inside you, Delaney. I'm in fucking heaven."

Delaney relented, experimenting with sliding up and down my erection, and a moan broke through my lips. More heat unraveled in my gut, taking over. More sweat broke out across my skin, a feverish need. And she'd barely even moved.

"Can you look at me?" she asked, her breathing erratic. And then more steadily, "I want you to watch me."

Delaney being bold enough to ask for something that she wanted—and in the bedroom, no less—was something I could never deny.

I took a few seconds to even my breathing, bring my body back down to a point where I knew I could hold out, make this last, make it good. Give her everything she wanted. Which, right now, was to look at her. So I did, flashing a wicked grin while taking in her gorgeous face. "Between last night and now, I think I've figured out what one of your kinks is."

She blushed. "Well, I..."

I shook my head. She didn't need to be embarrassed. I wanted to hear more about what she wanted. I wanted to hear everything. *Needed* to hear it. "It's okay, Lane."

"I also just like to see your expression," she said with a shrug and then came down on my cock even harder, throwing her head back with a groan before peering down at me, a smirk on her lips when she saw the way my jaw had dropped. "I like to see how you're feeling."

"I promise you, Delaney London..." *Delaney London, Delaney London, Delaney London.* "Being inside you feels better than anything I can ever remember. You've barely even moved yet, and this is the most erotic experience of my life."

Her lips parted, and fuck, I wanted to kiss them. "That can't be true."

I couldn't reach her lips with mine, so I ran my hands up her body and brushed my fingers over her mouth instead. She trapped my ring finger between her lips, sucking slightly, and I couldn't help it; I canted my hips upward, needing to sink further into her. Delaney released my finger on a gasp, her eyes growing bright in a way that told me I'd found the spot that would end her when she was ready.

"You can believe whatever you want to believe," I said shakily. "I don't care. But I need you to just stop thinking and fuck me, Lane."

I needed Delaney to fuck me because I knew I couldn't fuck her. I didn't trust that I could stay controlled enough without completely unraveling. Without baring my entire fucking soul while I got lost in her.

I needed her to get lost in me instead.

"I can do that," she breathed, and then Delaney rolled her hips back and forth with a sensual rhythm, proving what I'd suspected: all those years of dance had given her the skills that I wanted to spend a long time exploring. And then she paused that movement, switching to riding my cock up and down, and I clenched my jaw to keep from sputtering out unintelligible words.

"*Blake*," she moaned.

She moaned my name while fucking me, and I would forever know satisfaction.

"Just like that," I panted.

"Yeah?" Her eyes lit up, and I realized how much she liked the praise, craved the feedback, the reassurance. I'd happily give her more of that.

I grabbed her hips, helping her keep the pace. "Yeah, that's perfect, baby."

Delaney rode harder, and I encouraged her, my grip tightening, urging her thrusts on.

"So good," she muttered, her eyelids fluttering shut. "Oh my *God*, Blake, it's so..."

Her words trailed into a moan, and she picked up the pace even more, her perky, perfect breasts bouncing as she clenched around my dick. *Holy hell.*

"I know," I groaned. "I know exactly what it is, Lane."

I drove my hips upward to meet her, and when a sharp gasp flew from her lips, I knew I'd found that spot again. And I knew she was close. Trailing one of my hands from her hip to where we were joined, I slid a finger between her legs, finding her clit and teasing it with consistent, soft flicks.

"*Oh*—" Delaney leaned forward, pressing closer to my chest. She flexed her hips repeatedly, keeping a steady beat with her body as she sought more from me. "Oh, yes."

Her breathy whimpers were doing things to me I couldn't even comprehend, but I also knew what they meant, and I knew I couldn't stop. I knew I had to keep going, take her all the way.

"Blake, *please*."

Her face contorted as I watched her soar toward her peak. She kept saying my name, over and over again, and I kept cataloging the sound in my brain to remember forever. Her lashes fluttered shut, her lips pressing together. There was a look of concentration that I knew I shouldn't interrupt, but fuck, I had to. Because now I understood where she'd been coming from earlier.

"Look at me when you come, Delaney," I commanded.

She immediately opened her eyes at my tone.

"You wanted me to watch you, so let me watch you. All of you. I don't want to miss a single thing when you come on my cock."

Delaney gave a tight little nod as she bit down on her lip. One of her hands found my hair, dragging her fingers through it and then *tugging*.

"God, I *love* your hair," she panted unexpectedly, and I reveled in the desperation in her voice, grinning.

"You can hold on to my hair while fucking me like this any goddamn day, baby."

A throaty sigh left her, and I felt the way her tight walls fluttered around me. Oh, fuck yeah. I kept steady, rubbing her clit as she rode me harder.

"Blake, I'm going to—"

Yes, yes, yes.

Delaney broke off before she could finish the sentence, but that was okay.

"I know," I whispered, leaning forward to press my lips to her throat. I wanted to feel the vibrations of her cries when she came for me.

I felt her body seize up a second before she even made a sound. Her pussy pulsed in waves, strangling my cock in the most beautiful way. And then Delaney fell apart with a gasping cry, my name on her lips. *My* name. *Her* lips. I could feel the orgasm ripping through her as she shook on top of me, and only once she began to slump, sated and satisfied, did I pull my fingers from between her legs.

And then promptly sucked them into my mouth.

Tasting her when I was this fucking desperate probably wasn't a good idea.

"Holy shit, Delaney. I'm gonna—" My words descended into a growl when Delaney fell forward onto me. I could feel the brush of her nipples on my chest and the tickle of her damp hair like a halo around my head. And then she continued to pump her hips, causing stars to fill my vision.

She leaned down and whispered in my ear. "I know."

"Can I?" I asked, teetering on the edge of unleashing a different side of me. I started driving my hips up, thrusting into her as I chased my release. "Are you gonna let me fill this pussy up?"

She sucked at a sensitive spot on my neck. "Yes. I wanted it on the plane, and I still want it now."

"Yes, Lane?" Her consent made me dizzy. "You want me to fill your tight cunt with my cum?"

"Mhm," she hummed. "I want you to let go, Blake. I want you to fuck me like your wife."

That was it.

I flipped us over, flung Delaney's legs over my shoulders, and drove home.

"You *are* my wife." I snapped my hips against hers again and buried myself as deeply as I could.

A pleasure-soaked cry sprang from Delaney's lips, her eyes sparkling with a familiar look, and the realization that Delaney liked it a little rough was all I needed to relinquish some of my control.

"*Yes*," Delaney said, a breathy agreement that meant the goddamn world to me.

My wife.

"Friends don't fuck like this, Delaney," I reminded her, thrusting again. And then again, until she got that idea lodged in that big, beautiful brain of hers.

She nodded while gasping for air, and even that tiny acknowledgment of the truth overwhelmed me, yanking on my heartstrings in new ways, ones that went beyond my understanding.

I thought I knew everything there was to know about hearts and Delaney. And the intersection of the two.

Delaney grabbed at my shoulders, her nails digging in as she urged me for more, and I gave it to her. I gave *everything* to her while taking at the same time, getting lost in her again and again and again until I could feel the beads of sweat rolling down my back and the only sounds in the room were our rough gasps, Delaney's repeated soft pleading, and our skin slapping together.

"You're doing so good, baby," I praised, smacking my hips so hard against hers that Delaney's jaw dropped and one hand grabbed the headboard above her, holding on as I delivered another thrust. "You take me so *fucking* good."

"Don't stop," she begged, as if I even knew how.

"Never," I promised. "Is this how my girl likes it? She likes it when her husband fucks her hard?"

"*Yes.*"

"Is her husband going to make her come again?" Even harder thrusts separated each one of my words because I'd lost it. I'd lost almost every shred of control I had. Fuck, this woman. "*Please* come, Lane. I need to feel it again. God, you have no idea what you fucking do to me."

I watched Delaney's lips part, but no sound came out. A silent scream that I took to mean another *yes*. So I kissed those lips hard before moving to her neck and the sweet curve of it, breathing in the scent of her. *Her.* I was so utterly obsessed with her, and in this moment, when I was on the brink of losing it all, she was the only thing I knew. All my brain could scream was *mine*.

"*Yes*, Delaney," I gasped. Because she was all I could think about. "*God*, I l—"

I forced back words I absolutely should not be saying, not yet, instead biting the curve of Delaney's neck as I reached my climax. The heat running wild in my body finally crested, and I was left to surf the fiery waves. I came hard, with an intensity I'd expected but took my breath away all the same, and then Delaney surprised me by crying out a beat later, her body shaking beneath mine from a second orgasm, one that seemed even stronger than the first.

Our chests heaved against each other as we both tried to slow our breathing. But then our eyes caught, and I wasn't sure how that would ever be possible. When she looked at me like that—like she could see me, *all* of me, the only one who really could—how was I ever supposed to move on?

Delaney started roaming my back with her hands, almost like she was trying to soothe me, and all I wanted to do was melt into her. But I also didn't want to crush her beneath my weight. So I gently moved her legs from my shoulders and lifted myself off her, letting my cock slowly slide from her filled pussy. Delaney whimpered, her body twitching, oversensitive.

I sat back on my knees, looking down at her in awe. More specifically, looking down at my cum dripping from between her legs. Wordlessly, I used two fingers to swipe it back up her inner thighs and push it back into her pussy, where it belonged.

Where I knew she wanted it.

She hummed her satisfaction, proving that point.

When I did this on the plane, Delaney joked about babies and then brushed off my comment about how it would never scare me to see her pregnant. But that was okay. She could pretend I said that because I'd always wanted kids and not because it was *her* having my kids. It wasn't reality, but maybe one day, I'd tell her the truth of it: that watching my cum drip out of her was making me feral.

"I'm a little scared," Delaney whispered.

I stilled in my thoughts on pregnancy. "Why? Delaney, I—you *are* on birth control, right? I'd never—without your—"

"No." She shook her head and pulled at my arm, leading me back down onto the bed. Our heads hit the pillows, facing each other. "I'm on birth control, Blake. That's not what I meant."

"What did you mean?"

She bit down on her lip like she was debating whether or not to tell me. And I was about ready to plead with her when she admitted, "It was too...good. That was the best sex I've ever had."

An understatement, in my opinion. But her saying that had me floating on cloud nine all the same.

I thought about what to reply while I threaded my fingers through her hair. It was messy and wild and perfect.

"That's because I know you. I know how to read you. And you can trust me. You can let yourself go and ask for what you want."

And because we fit together—a perfect, two-piece puzzle.

One that made all the sense in the world.

Delaney pursed her lips. Her swollen, puffy, gorgeous lips. They momentarily distracted me until she spoke again.

"Yeah," she agreed softly. "I think it's more than that, though. I think there's...something else, too."

The world around me momentarily ceased to exist. Somewhere in the far distance, the sea stilled along the shore, and everything was silent. Everything but Delaney's stilted breathing and the shuffling of linen as she pulled the covers over her body, snuggling into the bed as though she hadn't just altered my existence.

"Glad you're finally catching up," I muttered, but Delaney's eyes were already closed.

And I wasn't sure if she heard me.

CHAPTER TWENTY-FIVE

I COULDN'T REMEMBER THE last time I slept so soundly.

And I also couldn't remember the last time I woke with such a profound ache between my legs.

An ache for Blake and an ache *from* Blake.

I winced when I turned over, looking for the man responsible. But I found Blake standing at the foot of the bed, a slight smirk skewed on his handsome face as though he knew why I was wincing, and he liked that it was because of him.

I liked it, too.

"Good morning," he said, his voice deep and husky—toe-curling in how attractive it was. His brown eyes flicked from me to the belt he was adjusting around his waist, already wearing his black slacks and a crisp, white shirt. He moved slowly, like he knew I was watching him.

He reinforced that idea when he lifted a brow at me.

I cleared my throat before responding. "Good morning."

It was *definitely* a good morning.

Blake's lips curved in a knowing grin as he slotted his belt into place. And I continued to watch, eating up every moment of my morning show. I certainly wouldn't mind waking up to see this every day.

"I have to leave soon," he said, sounding regretful. "I have a few early appointments scheduled this morning."

"Okay, Dr. London." I smiled as I stretched my arms over my head, luxuriating in the feel of his sheets against my bare skin. The covers shifted as I moved, slipping down my body and exposing my breasts. Blake's gaze darkened, wandering over me, while the rest of his body stilled. He took an unsteady breath.

"Delaney." He said my name like a warning. But then he walked to the side of the bed, leaned over it, and pressed a kiss to my cheek. "Go back to sleep, sweetheart. You were the smart one between the two of us and took today off."

I hadn't really wanted to take an extra day, but I'd wanted even less to show up to my new position and not be on my A game. So I'd planned an extra day to recover from jet lag and our travels. Of course, I'd had no idea that I'd also need today to recover from *Blake*.

I turned my head so our lips brushed and whispered, "But I was appreciating you."

Blake dragged his lips across mine, a reverent sort of kiss before he swore beneath his breath and pulled away, walking with stiff movements back across the room.

"Lane, I—" He shook his head, struggling to figure out what to say. Instead, he focused on grabbing a tie, throwing it around his neck.

I just grinned, happy to sit back and observe. Somewhere in the back of my mind, I knew I should be freaking out. Blake and I had slept together. We'd redrawn a line that was impossible to erase.

The minute we walked into that club in Amsterdam, I knew that something was changing, and it would never be the same between us again. And now, here we were. That should terrify me, considering there was just so much on the line—on the very line we'd redrawn. But I'd never felt lighter.

"It's only fair," I reminded him. "That I should get to appreciate you, too." My smile grew as Blake glanced over at me again, only to dart his gaze away like he could only handle tiny glimpses of me naked in his bed. "You know, I didn't realize that getting married would come with so many perks. Maybe we should have done it a long time ago."

"Perks, huh?" Blake's lips quirked, and then something tensed in his jaw. "Is that what last night was?"

Hearing him repeat that back to me made something feel off. Wrong. Phrasing last night as though it was some kind of simple benefit of marriage cheapened the reality of what happened. But I couldn't really explain why.

"You tell me," I said after a minute.

Was that what last night was?

But Blake refused to answer, shaking his head again. "I don't think I can."

I frowned, and Blake seemed to catch my reaction out of the corner of his eye. After a quick, final adjustment of his tie, he swooped back to my side, sitting on the edge of the bed. My name came out of his lips on a sigh I didn't quite understand.

"I just—" I started before pausing. The words we shared this morning were important, and I didn't have any prepared. "What happens now?"

Blake answered me with another kiss, pressing his lips to mine. And as much as I liked this newfound freedom we had to kiss each other for no other reason except that we wanted to, this kiss confused me.

"Are you trying to distract me?" I breathed against his lips— his soft, warm lips that were, admittedly, very easy to get distracted by.

Blake released a husky chuckle. "No, I'm just showing you what *I'd* like to happen."

"Blake," I groaned. Because as much as that was an answer to my question, it was also a way to avoid giving more of one.

"Delaney." He dropped his forehead to mine, and I breathed in his musky, perfect Blake-ness. He cupped my cheek, his hand so tender but so firm. Sure. "I like kissing you. And I'd really like to keep kissing you now that we're home."

"Okay." I could get on board with that. "I hadn't been sure if we were just getting each other out of our systems the last few days, or..."

The hand that had been cupping my cheek fell down my body, his fingertips grazing over my bare skin—from the slope of my neck to the dip of my collarbone to the curve of my breasts. I arched into his touch, my body tingling with longing.

"Does it feel like I'm out of your system, Lane?" he asked, voice gruff.

"I don't...think so." I didn't think so at all, but I wanted to know what *he* was thinking. "What does it feel like for you?"

Blake sat back on the edge of the bed, looking surprised. His touch vanished from my body, making me feel adrift. "Me?"

"Yeah." Gripping the edge of the covers, I pulled them up to my chin. "It's just that last night when I said it was the best sex of my life, you didn't..." I wrinkled my nose before shaking my head and casting my eyes to the side, wishing I hadn't started that sentence. "Never mind."

He stared, seemingly dumbfounded by what I'd just said. But I couldn't imagine why.

"Delaney." His finger slipped beneath my chin and turned it toward him. Brown eyes met mine, ones that were usually so calm but were wild in this moment. "Lane, I..." He broke off with a humorless laugh. "That was the best sex of my life. When you straddled me and I told you that it was the most erotic experience I've ever had, I wasn't lying. It was incredible. You are *not* out of my system. I don't know how to get you out of my system. If I did, I'd—" He bit down on his words before restarting. "If anything, you're embedded deeper into me than ever before."

It was my turn to stare, his words spinning in my mind like gears.

"I didn't say anything last night because I just figured you knew," he added with a touch of regret. "And I was too busy celebrating the fact that it was the same for you as it was for me. I never imagined..." He shook his head and then abruptly stood, walking to the other side of the room where his suitcase was open on the ground. He bent down, rummaging in it for a few seconds until he came back, holding two things in his hands.

"You're not out of my system, Delaney," he said with more finality, handing me a small cardboard box with a picture of tulips on the front. I took it, staring down at the top, where the words *500 pieces* stood out in bold lettering. "But I understand if maybe you're not as sure as me."

He took a deep breath, and I tore my gaze away from the puzzle to look up at him. "Your old puzzle has seen better days, and I thought maybe..." He drifted off, rubbing the back of his neck. "Maybe you need some time with a puzzle today. Maybe it would help you to...piece things together. About everything that's happened."

I went back to studying the box in my hands, speechless. The scenery was a little different from my other puzzle, but it still had rows of tulips and a few windmills scattered in the background. It was so pretty, even prettier now that I knew it really looked that amazing in person. *More* amazing.

"I'm not going to shy away from the things that happened the last two nights," Blake continued. "But it was a lot, Lane. And I know sometimes when you have a lot to process, it helps to put something together that makes sense."

That got my attention.

"Do you think last night didn't make sense?"

"I didn't say that." He shook his head, looking at me with an earnest expression. "I might be struggling to believe it was real, but if I'm being honest, I think it was the most sensical thing we've ever done. But that's just what *I* think. And I know..." He pursed his lips back together, seeming to debate if he wanted to go on.

I swallowed, waiting to hear if he would say more. He didn't.

But he did hold out his other hand, presenting me with carefully wrapped ceramic flowers.

"I also found these when you'd gone off to the bathroom at one of the stores," he said. "I wanted to add a little color to the apartment. Figured you might like that."

I stared at them. Then stared at him, realizing that I was also struggling to believe this was real. That *he* was real. Even though I'd known him for more than a decade of my life, it felt in some ways that I was meeting Blake London for the very first time.

"You found your blue tulips," I whispered.

"Yeah." He looked from the tulips to me. "I guess they do exist."

My lips curved in a small smile. "I'm glad you found your favorite color."

He studied the cornflower-blue ceramic flowers for a second before shrugging.

"I actually prefer a blue that's a little bit darker, but this is close."

"A bit darker?"

"A bit darker." His eyes met mine, boring into them like he was trying to communicate something. But when I didn't seem to get whatever it was, he cleared his throat. "Besides, I didn't give you a 'something blue' for the wedding. I know it's a little late, but—"

"You gave me something blue," I countered. "You gave me the ring."

Blake's gaze dropped to my hand, where my wedding ring was firmly in place on my ring finger. I barely ever took it off.

"I like that you're wearing it even though..." he started but didn't finish.

More thoughts unfinished.

But I understood this one.

Even though I wouldn't have to.

Because there was no one around right now, no one to see us faking it. But I still had it on.

"It's a really pretty ring," I said by way of explanation.

"For a really pretty bride," Blake murmured, his eyes still locked on my hand.

He shook out of his trance a moment later, taking a few slow steps backward, like he wasn't sure he should be so close to me even though last night he'd been *inside* me.

"Take today to think about things, Delaney," he said, clearing his throat. "The last forty-eight hours have been..."

A lot. A lot of change and a lot that we should probably think about. But Blake seemed confident that we could be friends who were married and also kissed sometimes, and maybe that was as complicated as we needed to make it. Maybe it was just as simple as that.

All I knew was that I didn't want to go backward. I didn't want to give up the moments we'd shared in the last few days or the possibility that there could be more of them.

So after Blake left for work, I looked at the puzzle. I studied the picture. I smiled at the sentiment.

But I didn't put it together.

Because I just didn't think I needed to.

I stood inside at Boston Medical, waiting for Blake. The cardiology wing sat to my left, so I hoped that my calculations were correct and the doors I'd planted myself by would be the ones he'd make his way to as soon as he was done for the day.

I took in my surroundings while I waited, making comparisons in my head between Boston Medical and SCMC and all the other facilities I'd worked in. Obviously, it was hard to come to many conclusions just from this preliminary glimpse, but still.

More than anything, I liked that it gave me a picture of where Blake spent his days. I liked imagining him walking these hallways, living the dream that we'd both worked so hard to reach. I liked knowing what his new home away from home looked like.

About an hour passed as I waited, and when early evening hit, I started to worry. But as soon as I pulled out my phone, contemplating if I should call him, footsteps echoed in the hospital hallway.

It was ridiculous that I should be able to recognize someone by their footsteps, but I immediately knew it was Blake. He had a purposeful, confident walk. Especially in hospital hallways.

The steps faltered when they got closer.

"Lane?"

I smiled to myself, pleased that I'd been right.

"Hi," I said, looking up to find my husband a few paces from me, his brow furrowed and hair slightly mussed from a long day at work.

"What are you doing here?" His eyes swept over me, looking for something wrong. "Is everything okay?"

"Everything's fine," I assured him. "Can't I come see where my husband works?" I stood and made my way over to his side. Around us, the hospital's soft symphony kept playing—beeping machines and murmured conversations and ringing phones. But Blake broke the setting's mold, giving me a grin as I approached him. It wasn't Dr. London's usual look. It was *my* grin. *My* smile.

"Of course you can," he said. "But you should have told me you were coming."

I shrugged. "It was kind of an impromptu thing. I had something I wanted to tell you and thought it would be a good time to check out your new digs."

"Yeah?" His grin was cheeky now. I could tell he couldn't decide between asking what I wanted to tell him and asking what I thought about the facility. But he settled on, "And what does my wife want to tell me that couldn't wait?"

"It's about the puzzle."

I reached into the canvas tote I brought with me and pulled out the puzzle from Blake.

His smile faltered, his expression wiping blank. He was steeling himself, and that made my stomach drop.

"I love it," I rushed to say, wanting him to know that above everything else. I loved his thoughtfulness, and I cherished his friendship more than anything.

"I'm so glad," he said carefully.

I nodded before adding, "But I just don't think..." Blake tensed. "I didn't do it. The puzzle. Not today."

Blake cocked his head to the side. "No?"

"No," I confirmed. "I think all the pieces sort of fell into place last night."

Literally. We slid together, we *fit* together like we were...like it was all the confirmation I really needed.

"Last night," Blake repeated, taking a step closer.

"Yeah." I wet my lips, realizing how dry they felt. "It told me everything I needed to know, Blake. I didn't need to do the puzzle today. You're not out of my system, and I like kissing you, too. Wouldn't mind if we kept doing it, either."

Blake took another step. "Just kisses, Lane? Or do you want *more* of last night?"

"More of last night," I said, struggling to breathe because Blake was consuming me now, and his proximity made me think of the things we did the last time he was this close.

"We can do that," he husked. "On one condition."

"What's that?"

"Remember when I said you could see anyone you want when we're married?"

I nodded slowly.

He dropped his voice to a pitch that I wasn't sure I'd truly heard before. "If we're going to continue this, I'm taking that the fuck back."

I couldn't help a grin from creeping onto my face. "That's fine. You've made it pretty clear you don't share, Blake."

He leaned down, his lips finding my ear as he spoke at a gritty

319

volume only I could hear. "No, I don't. Not when it's my ring on your finger and my cock in your pussy, baby."

My lips parted as I felt a flush work up my neck from his words, and when Blake pulled away, a smirk painted his lips.

But a second later, it fell, along with his gaze.

And I immediately knew why.

I'd seen it, too, when I looked in the mirror just before leaving home. I hadn't noticed it this morning, which meant that Blake probably didn't, either. It must have darkened as the day went on.

"Holy shit, Lane," Blake choked, and I lifted my hand to the curve of my neck, tracing where I remembered the purplish bruise to be. Blake watched my finger, his jaw unhinged, his expression horrified.

"Oh, this?" I said with a shrug and a tilt of my lips. "I think this is just what happens when Blake London finally loses a little bit of control."

"I—" Words escaped Blake as he continued to stare at the mark on my skin. His gaze was dark and unreadable. "Does it hurt?" he finally breathed, stepping closer to take over, grazing his thumb over the mark, caressing my skin in small circles.

I shook my head, and he breathed a sigh of relief.

"Are you sure?" he checked.

"I'm sure."

It didn't hurt, and I didn't mind. It felt like...evidence. That I hadn't fabricated the moment when this happened, when Blake had finally unleashed a side of him that I'd never seen before. A side I couldn't wait to meet again.

"I'm fucking sorry, Lane," Blake murmured, still seeming transfixed by my neck. By the mark that he'd made on it.

"No, you're not," I said with a raised brow, knowing that there was more in his gaze than he was letting on. I knew enough by now to understand that.

"No," he admitted hoarsely as he leaned down and pressed his lips to my skin, right where the shape of his mouth was already imprinted. "I'm not."

When he pulled back, I studied him for a moment before musing, "I think *I* know one of your kinks now."

"Is it a kink if it only applies to you?" he muttered, eyes shining bright. "You're the only person I want to mark as mine, Delaney."

"I don't know enough about it." My voice was slow, coated with a thick new wave of want. "But I will say I had no idea you'd become so possessive if I married you."

Not that I was really complaining.

"And now that you've seen this side of me, do you regret it?" he asked, clearly eager for my answer. "Regret letting me slide that ring on your finger?"

He lifted his gaze to mine, and I met it straight on. Because once I decided to go for something, I didn't often back down.

"Not at all."

CHAPTER TWENTY-SIX

blake

RETURNING TO WORK AFTER the honeymoon was abysmal.

I'd always enjoyed my work, even craved it, but now all I craved was more of Delaney. More time with her, more slow mornings, more hot nights, more of everything. I spent the entire day, every day, anxious for the moment when I'd grab my coat, walk through the halls, and see her waiting for me. She'd walk over from SCMC, so we could go home together. Or on nights where I had my CPR classes—well, *our* CPR classes at this point—we would walk there together.

Because that was our routine now, and I felt utterly spoiled by it. Delaney and I had fallen into a pattern that felt so utterly domestic it was hard to remind myself that I *couldn't* have everything, not yet.

Because the reality was that, despite being two friends who were married, shared the same bed at night, and gave each other orgasms, Delaney and I weren't yet where I ultimately wanted us to be. Sure, we were on the same page about sex and kissing. But if I could get her on the same page about wanting this thing for real, wanting that ring to stay permanently on her finger, that'd be great.

I also had to contend with the reality where I had patients to follow up with and friends and family to check in on, and outside of everything involving Delaney, that had been my focus for the last two weeks.

Today, it involved a number of appointments, including one with Grayson and Nessa, where we further discussed their daughter Gracie's potential for inheriting aortic coarctation, like her older brother. They also tentatively brought up questions about what the likelihood might be of any of their future children inheriting a congenital heart defect, and I could tell they were holding their breath the entire time. My chest squeezed for them because ultimately, I couldn't provide them with a guarantee that it wouldn't happen; their oldest Gabriel was proof of that.

I sat in the exam room for a few extra minutes after they left, grappling with my emotions and trying not to think about a scenario where it was me and Delaney navigating through what we might do if it were *our* kids. Which was ridiculous because Delaney didn't want to settle down in a traditional sense. She didn't want marriage. She didn't want any of that.

Was I foolish for thinking that I could make something work between us? For thinking that I could convince her to try out a real relationship? For thinking she might want to stay married after this entire inheritance situation was settled? I badly wanted it to be possible. I didn't *need* kids, but I did need her. I wanted a family with her—even if that family was just the two of us.

After getting through the workday despite feeling tired and Delaney-deprived, I met Natalie and Noah outside a tall, shiny building in Boston's financial district.

They both said I didn't need to come today, but I'd been helping Natalie deal with her custody situation since I'd moved to the East Coast, and I wanted to see it through. Noah had been so busy with becoming a parent lately that he was less familiar with the workings of the bullshit that Natalie had been going through, but he'd connected us with the lawyer we were meeting with today and wanted to be here.

"There's my favorite married brother," Noah called as I walked up.

I rolled my eyes. "I'm your only married brother," I grunted despite the fuzzy feeling I got whenever I received the reminder I was married to Delaney.

"I haven't gotten over it, to be honest," Natalie said with a grin. "That you actually tied the knot. How was the honeymoon? I want to hear all about it!"

"Woah, woah, Nat." Noah raised a brow, putting up his hands to indicate she should slow the fuck down. "I don't know if we want to hear *all* about it."

"No." A smirk slipped onto my lips, unbidden. "You probably don't."

The sound of Delaney moaning my name echoed in my ears, and my body tightened in response.

Suddenly, I wished I was at home. Preferably, at home eating my wife out on the kitchen table like I did last night.

Natalie looked unimpressed. "We talked about this, Blake. Don't forget to *date* your wife, too. Women want more than sex."

That comment snapped me out of it. "I took her on a date first," I said defensively, but my stomach still turned at what she'd said. I didn't like the implication or the thought that my relationship with Delaney had been reduced to sex. I knew, at my core, that wasn't the case, but it still had me itching to take the next step with her and soon.

I wanted to ask her on a date. One that was completely transparent and not at all fake. And I wanted to do it soon.

Natalie sighed. "Well, that's good, at least. I'm so happy to see you married, and I want it to stay that way."

"I want the same thing," I grunted. She had no fucking idea how badly I wanted that. "In fact, this married man misses his wife, so let's get in there and do this thing."

Natalie's face fell, and internally, I berated myself. I knew what her next words were going to be before she even responded.

"You don't have to come with, Blake. I'm good. And I have Noah, too."

"I can handle smart people things sometimes, you know," Noah said, a single brow cocked.

"I know you can," I assured him because even though he'd said it with sarcasm, there was a bit of doubt lurking in the depths of his eyes. "But I want to be here. Just because I'm married doesn't mean I don't have time for my family, too."

Natalie sighed. "Okay, let's go," she said before quietly murmuring, "Thank you."

I grabbed her hand and squeezed it before we followed Noah into the building, up the elevator, and to the entrance of the Gardner Law offices.

A man with a blinding smile and a sharp suit met us by the receptionist.

"Cameron Bryant," he said, his voice smooth and deep. "It's nice to meet you."

"Blake London," I replied. "Same to you. Thanks so much for meeting with us."

I shook his hand before he turned to Natalie, and I couldn't remember ever seeing my sister—highly trained trauma surgeon Dr. London—*blush* at shaking a man's hand before, but I swore that was what happened when she introduced herself. Cameron's dimples indented in response, like he noticed, and I decided it was good I was staying for this meeting. Noah seemed to clock the exchange, too, his eyes darting between Cameron and Natalie.

Once introductions had been exchanged, Cameron led us into the labyrinth of offices in the law firm. But we didn't get very far before we were cut short by the appearance of a tall man with deep auburn hair.

"Not even going to stop to say hi, huh?" Julian drawled, leaning in the doorway of his office. Beside him, a plaque that said *The Briggses* hung on the wall beside the door, and I knew the moment Noah noticed it because a laugh burst through his lips.

"Do they honestly let you two share an office?" he choked through his laughter.

"Sure do," Julian said smugly.

Noah shook his head, pointing to the plaque on the wall. "Did you have to put in a special order for that?"

"Of course he did," Julian's wife, Juniper, cut in from the office. She walked up to stand beside Julian in the doorway and then smiled at Noah and me in acknowledgment before turning to Natalie to introduce herself. "Juniper Briggs. It's so lovely to meet you. I've heard a plethora of nice things about you from Gemma."

Julian's grin broadened at her introduction. It had only been about six months since Julian and Juniper's wedding, which I remembered vividly despite not being in attendance. I'd called my brother that day to find him miserable as he got ready for his best friend's nuptials. Noah didn't know how to come to terms with the fact that he was in love with that same friend's sister, and somehow, I'd managed to convince him to get his head out of his ass and take the fucking plunge.

It was also the day I decided I couldn't survive watching Delaney be engaged to Austin Long.

That was why I'd called Noah that day—to tell him I'd already lined up a job interview in Boston.

"This is ridiculous. I bet the two of you get nothing done. This definitely shouldn't be allowed." Noah tapped on the sign, still stuck on it even after Natalie had greeted *the Briggses* and introduced herself.

This was her first time meeting both of them. Noah had invited both our family and the Briggs family to share a suite at his playoff game last season, but Natalie hadn't been able to attend because of work. I was there but hadn't spent a lot of time with Julian and Juniper, too busy trying to get Theo to behave around the rest of the Briggs sisters so he didn't get any bones broken by Gemma's brother. Julian might be smiling right now, but his eyes had shot daggers that day, his normally pale skin flushing red as he did.

"Nah," Julian replied, ignoring Cameron coughing his agreement with Noah beneath his breath. "It's all very above board. Nothing like when you moved my sister in with you and didn't tell me for three fucking months."

Noah crossed his arms over his chest. "Are we not over this? I thought we were over this."

"We're over it," Juniper pressed, patting Julian's arm to placate him. "Considering how happy Gems is, right?"

Juniper glanced at her husband, and he caught her chin with two fingers, tipping it up. Juniper's lips curved, and suddenly, we were in the middle of an intimate moment no one had invited us to. At least until Noah grunted, "Damn right. Also, if you get to marry your sister's best friend, then she gets to marry me. We're even, Jules."

Julian's brows shot way up—probably because this was the first time Noah had mentioned marrying Gemma in front of him. Or maybe at all. He'd definitely hinted at it but had never stated it so outwardly.

"I'd say so," I cut in before anything else unraveled. "Glad to see everyone is one big, happy family now."

Julian jerked out of the trance that Noah's announcement had momentarily put him in and looked directly at me. "Speaking of happy families, I heard you recently tied the knot. Congratulations, man." He beamed, clapping me on the shoulder.

"Thank you." I couldn't help but grin back. "It's been a whirlwind of a month, but it's been amazing."

"Love to hear that," Julian said genuinely before his eyes darted to Cameron. "Well, I'll let Cam take it from here. You're in great hands, Natalie."

My sister blushed at Julian's words.

Again.

Then she cleared her throat. "I'm sure I am."

Cameron nodded. He ran a hand over his buzzed hair before he unbuttoned his suit jacket like he was suddenly hot. It looked like an expensive suit; the stitching and cut were precise, and the tan color perfectly complemented his light brown skin. If I ever got a chance to marry Delaney again—for real, this time—I might have to ask Cameron where he got his suits. "We'll get this ex sorted out in no time," he said. "I can promise you that, Dr. London."

Cameron's respect for her title did not go unnoticed by Natalie, who looked more warmly at the lawyer than I'd seen her look at any man recently. It was still slight, masked by her usual guarded expression, but it was something. And I knew Noah noticed it, too.

"Looking forward to it," Natalie murmured before we waved our goodbyes to *the Briggses* and followed Cameron down the hallway to his office.

I hoped he was serious about his promise. Because there was no way in hell that Nat's ex-husband deserved what he was asking for in terms of Chloe's custody. And Nat needed a lawyer who'd make sure this man regretted everything he'd done to my sister.

I walked through the door to our apartment after we'd finished up at the law firm, feeling more settled about having a plan for Natalie and also feeling ready to make good on what my sister told me to do in regard to my marriage.

I was going to ask Delaney out on a date. Tonight. Right now.

But then I saw her, and I stopped dead in my tracks.

She sat cross-legged on the couch, leaning forward over the coffee table, which she had pulled as close to the edge of the cushions as possible. Spread across the table were five hundred scattered puzzle pieces. Delaney chewed on her lip as she tried to find where one of the pieces fit. Her face was pale, nearly translucent. Her eyes, red.

My stomach turned. I walked on wooden legs toward her, dropping my keys and phone on the kitchen countertop.

She didn't look up when I approached.

"What's wrong, Lane?"

A single tear ran down her cheek. She bit down on her lip harder. Then, she tapped the puzzle piece on the table repeatedly, staring at the picture on the lid of the box as though it would magically jump out at her where the piece fit.

I crouched next to the table, willing her to look at me.

She didn't. But she sighed.

It was a whole-body sigh. A shudder.

"I like this one." She tapped on the puzzle box—the new one I bought on our trip. "Thank you for getting it for me. I needed to replace the other one."

"Of course." I spoke softly, afraid to spook her, afraid that she might stop talking again. "You don't have to get rid of the original one, though. It carries a lot of memories."

She finally looked up at me. And what I saw in her gaze terrified me because I didn't understand it. "Yeah," she said finally. "It does."

I tucked a limp piece of hair behind her ear and then trailed my fingers down one of the thick braids she wore in her hair. "How was your day?"

She pursed her lips for a moment. "Not great."

That didn't entirely surprise me, but her next comment did.

"I missed you."

My heart leapt into my throat.

"I missed you, too, sweetheart." I cupped her cheek, rubbing my thumb beneath her eyes to wipe away the moisture there. "I'm so sorry it got late. But I thought about you all fucking day. Couldn't wait to get home to see you."

She shook her head. "No, it's good that you went with Natalie. She needed you more than me."

"I'm not so sure about that. Because you haven't told me what these tears are about."

"Thank you for packing me a lunch today," she responded, avoiding my comment. "You didn't have to do that."

"I want my wife to get enough to eat at work, so yes, I did," I said solemnly. "But I'm more than happy to do it. No need to thank me."

She sighed again, but it was heavier. It was *weighty*. Delaney carried so much weight around on her shoulders.

"Lane, please," I pleaded, begging her to let me share the burden. "It wasn't that nurse, was it? Jack or John or whatever? If he got too close to you again, I'm going to—"

"Not Jack." Delaney stared up at the ceiling for a moment. "He's been fine, actually. It's more—" She dropped her gaze again. "It's just that I made you do all this for nothing."

"All...this?"

She waved her hands around like I was supposed to understand her gestures. When I didn't, she added, "The marriage, the honeymoon, everything."

A harsh laugh burst through my lips. "That honeymoon was not *nothing*, Lane. You and I both know that."

Fuck that idea.

"I know, but—" She broke off with a tiny, frustrated growl. "Ophelia let our marriage slip to my parents. She assumed they knew. And I found out today why Anderson was so worried that they knew. Apparently, we need *their* approval in order to get the inheritance. It was included in an addendum that, *fuck*—" She tipped her head back, closing her eyes. "How the *hell* did this slip past me? I looked at that goddamn will so many times. And now there's no hope of me ever seeing that money. Of ever opening my clinic."

Shit.

"You don't think we can convince them that this is legitimate?"

Something inside me hurt. I hated any topic of conversation

that reminded me that this *wasn't* legitimate. It felt so fucking real to me at this point, and it killed me that Delaney might not feel the same way.

"I don't think they care to be convinced." Delaney opened her eyes and stared at the ceiling. "But they still want us to come to dinner on Sunday."

I nodded. "Okay, so, we'll go to dinner on Sunday."

"Blake..." She leveled her head and gaze to meet mine. "You don't understand."

"I do. I do understand. But give me a chance."

Give me a real fucking chance, baby.

"My mom's not going to buy it," she continued to protest—as though there would be anything to buy. I wasn't going to try to sell that I was in love with Delaney. I was just going to walk in there loving her, and for once in my goddamn life, I wasn't going to hide it. "It won't work on her. She doesn't believe in affection. It's not like when we went to dinner with your family."

I smiled at her because she thought I didn't get it, but it was the other way around.

We hadn't tricked my siblings into believing our relationship was real. Our relationship *was* real. Their belief in us had nothing to do with the way she'd sat on my lap or how I'd played with her hair. We didn't fake our chemistry; we just had it. I didn't *make* my siblings think that I was in love with Delaney—I was just in love with Delaney, and they instantly knew it, immediately saw how deeply it ran.

And now, after the honeymoon and everything that had happened between us, our connection was that much stronger.

"It'll work," I promised. "Besides, you're right. It's *not* like when we went to dinner with my family. Aren't things different now? Aren't *we* different now?"

If she denied that they were, I wasn't really sure what I would do, how I'd cope.

But she said, "Of course we're different. But it doesn't matter. They don't actually care how real or not real our marriage is.

They'll be upset about the elopement and the inheritance and, I don't know, *maybe* if we can make them believe that since we've known each other so long that this isn't sudden or for the money...but it probably won't change their opinions."

I thought on that, tipping my head to the side.

If Delaney wanted her parents to think that this had been a long time coming, well, hell...I could make that happen. I could *easily* make that happen.

"I can convince them of that, Delaney. Just let me try."

"You don't have to do this for me," she sighed, looking pained. "You didn't sign up for this."

Finding her hand, I lifted it up, reminding her my ring was on her finger.

"I gave you this, right?"

She nodded.

"I signed up for it, Delaney. I signed up for all of it. And I *want* all of it. This is why I'm here."

Tears pooled along her lashes again, but she didn't say anything. Nothing, except, "Will you help me finish my puzzle?"

Her voice shook as she flashed a wobbly smile.

"Of course, baby." I settled onto the couch next to her. "Can I put a movie on while we work on it?"

Delaney nodded, and I turned on the TV, spending a quiet minute navigating the controls until I found what I was looking for.

Delaney's lips pressed together, suppressing her reaction when *The Lizzie McGuire Movie* started playing.

Then, a laugh hiccupped out of her, and she cleared her throat.

"Thank you, Blake. For everything." She handed me the puzzle piece in her hand. "Can you figure out where this goes? I'm stuck on it."

"I got it," I promised, and that seemed to be a good enough answer for her to finally relax beside me.

Hopefully, *all* the pieces would be falling into place soon.

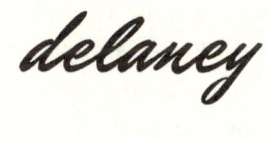

CHAPTER TWENTY-SEVEN

MY PARENTS LIVED ALONG the coastline of Cape Cod—a familiar stomping ground for the upper echelon of society to gather at their country clubs and marinas. Blake drove us there, and I sat in the passenger seat, fidgeting with the hem of my blouse as a way to pass the time, internally cursing out Ophelia. Even though it wasn't *really* her fault.

It was simultaneously the longest and shortest car ride I'd ever experienced. I dreaded arriving, but at the same time, I couldn't wait to get this dinner over with. I wanted to get on with it and experience the disappointment that would undoubtedly be my mother's disapproval so I could move forward and determine a new plan.

Blake seemed confident that wouldn't happen, but he'd never met my mom before. His family was made up of the most supportive people in the world. He shouldn't expect the same sort of situation here.

The first time I'd brought a boy home in tenth grade, my mom's first question was who his parents were. And when she didn't recognize their names because his whole family had only just moved to the Cape, she made a face and said she *supposed* he could still stay for dinner, during which my dad grilled the poor sixteen-year-old about his intentions for after graduation and, more importantly, his financial planning.

I told myself I'd never bring another guy home again.

And here I was, bringing home a husband.

"Give me your hand," Blake said without taking his eyes off the road. I gave it to him, and he took it, lifting my hand to his mouth to press a kiss on the back of it. His soft lips grazed my skin, a gentle caress that sent a shiver through me.

When he did things like that it made me question everything.

There was no one in this car but us and not a single ounce of seduction in what he'd just done. Only tenderness and affection and reassurance and things that might be considered friendly on paper but in real life, in this moment, felt like *more*.

Blake and I had yet to talk about our feelings. As far as I understood, we were married best friends with benefits. But that description was inadequate, wasn't it? It *had* to be. It certainly felt like it should be when Blake did things like use his kisses to comfort me and call me "sweetheart" at the dinner table when no one was around to hear.

We fit together in an inexplicable way; there really was no denying it anymore. But I still couldn't wrap my head around what that meant for me or us, for our future or where this would lead. Maybe it didn't matter, though. Labels were the last thing I should be concerning myself with, and I should just be grateful to have him by my side.

"It's going to be okay," Blake whispered, and I let that soft declaration soothe my nerves.

He tossed a smile at me, and I couldn't help but smile back.

Butterflies fluttered in my stomach.

They didn't have anything to do with my worries about dinner.

The GPS indicated for Blake to turn off the highway as if the stone columns housing the front gate weren't a big enough sign, and I held my breath as we rolled down my parents' dramatically long, curved driveway through a wooded area that eventually ended in a circle drive in front of my childhood home—a coastal traditional with grayish-blue siding and white trim that loomed three stories up, sitting on a rocky inlet. Salt air wafted through the car windows as I rolled them down. And on the oversized wraparound porch was Bryan.

"Laney!" I heard him yell before the car was even in park, and my heart expanded in my chest. Not in a cardiomegaly way, but like a cardiac emergency, nonetheless. Because it was a homesick sort of feeling that I never imagined I'd experience. I'd never longed for being in this house, but I *had* longed for being with Bryan. The dissonance I had with my parents kept me away from him, and a heavy dose of both shame and relief came at the sight of his smiling face.

Bryan bounded down the porch steps to meet us in the drive-way, and as soon as I got out of the car, he flung himself at me, wrapping me up in a bear hug. Considering that my little brother wasn't so little anymore, it nearly took me to the ground. I might be taller than him, but he had a sturdy build that I almost couldn't support.

"Hi, Bry," I laughed before pulling back from the hug. "How are you?"

"So good. So, so good," Bryan responded immediately, speaking in a rushed cadence like he usually did when he was overexcited. "How are you?"

"I'm good, too," I said, and at this moment, I actually meant it. I heard Blake getting out of the car behind me, and I angled my body to include him. "Bry, this is Blake."

I almost tacked on *my husband*, but it felt weird forcing that fact, which was both true and not true, on Bryan. I wondered if this was what Blake had felt when we'd gone over to Natalie's for dinner. My parents were one thing, but it was uncomfortable deceiving people who I had no reason to deceive. People who only wanted our happiness.

"Hi!" Bryan waved enthusiastically at Blake before apparently deciding that wasn't a good enough greeting and that Blake deserved a bear hug, too. And before I could do anything to stop it or throw out a warning, Bryan had nearly tackled Blake to the ground.

But not only did Blake manage to stay on two feet, but he also had a grin on his face from ear to ear. So wide. And I knew it was because Bryan's mood was infectious. He experienced joy in a way that was often considered over-the-top and comical, but it was really just unreserved and real and the way we all should allow ourselves to experience our emotions.

Once Bryan released Blake, they both took a step back, both grinning at each other.

I never realized how badly I wanted this moment to exist until I was living in it. The two most important people in my life, together. I wished we hadn't lived so far from Bryan for so many years in school, so this could have happened sooner.

"It's great to meet you, man," Blake said before clapping Bryan on the shoulder in the same way that he would with his own brothers.

Maybe I *was* experiencing cardiomegaly. My heart felt so big it might burst.

People often infantilized Bryan because of his disability. Even my parents were guilty. My aunts, my uncles, my cousins, too. But he was an adult, and Blake was speaking to him like one, and it was such a little thing that felt really, really big.

Emotion clogged my throat as I stood back and watched as Bryan and Blake chatted. Because of Bryan's hypotonia—his genetic muscle weakness—and how it affected his tongue, among other things, he sometimes struggled to articulate his words clearly. He often used an AAC, augmentative and alternative communication, app to effectively communicate with others, but he must have left his tablet inside. Blake didn't seem to have any trouble understanding him, though. He listened to Bryan talk about his job and his girlfriend before they somehow landed on a critical discussion of a new action movie, the latest in a series that was Bryan's favorite.

I'd always been envious of the loving family that Blake had grown up in. I never stopped to think that because of how Blake was raised and who he was that he could create that feeling for me, too. That being married to Blake meant that he could give me a whole new feeling of family. Because that was what it felt like right now, watching how he was with Bryan. I told him once that it was hard to believe in a lasting love because I never saw it echoed in the way my family treated each other, but I was realizing that I *did* see it in how he treated me. How he treated *his* family. And now, *my* family.

And maybe it wasn't love in a romantic way, but it was still love, right? The way Blake had brushed his lips across my hand in the car was *some* kind of love, wasn't it?

And the feeling bursting in my chest, that was some kind of love, too.

It was, wasn't it?

Love for Blake.

A *desire* for him that oddly had nothing to do with lust.

And had nothing to do with friendship, either.

It was bigger than both of those things.

Scarier, too.

But pieces were clicking together, and it was definitely...there.

Bryan went back inside to tell my parents we'd arrived, and I turned to my husband. My best friend. I took a shaky breath as I looked at him, feeling like I'd just had a veil yanked from over my eyes. Things were clearer than they'd ever been, and it gave me a different sort of hope for the future, my heart traveling down roads despite my brain knowing I was moving too fast.

"Hey, did you mean it when you said that Bryan could move in with us?"

The question was out before I could stop it.

I shouldn't put that kind of pressure on Blake. He'd already done so many favors for me recently; I didn't need to pile on another.

But he just nodded solemnly.

"Of course I did."

"We'd have to share a room," I pointed out.

"Why do you think I suggested it?" His lips curved, and he remained unfazed as I walked forward and elbowed him in response. "I'm just kidding," he added. "But truly, you could move all your belongings into my room tonight if you wanted, Lane. And if living with us was what Bryan wanted—and you—then he could absolutely move in."

"Thank you for that." The aching pressure in my chest grew tenfold. "For considering his wants first and, well, for everything."

"You don't have to thank me. Bryan is a part of you." The salty, early summer air whipped my hair around, and Blake reached out, tucking loose strands behind my ear. "He's a big reason why you are the person you are today, Lane. And I—"

He blew out of breath, cutting himself off. He looked to be finding words—new words than what he'd originally been about to say—but I never found out what they were because I caught sight of my mom lurking in the front door and decided to take advantage of the opportunity. I pushed up on my tiptoes and pressed my lips to Blake's. And even though I'd done that countless times by now, a zap of electricity still shocked me. I leaned into him, and he kissed me back without hesitation, deepening it with a soft moan until I forced myself to break away.

"What was that for?" He released a breathless laugh against my lips. "I need to know so I can do it again."

"Sorry." Heat flooded my cheeks. "I just knew my mom was looking at us."

"Oh." Blake cleared his throat, his eyes sweeping away from my face. After he swallowed hard, he looked back at me with a crooked grin. "Are you going to kiss me like that every time your mom looks at us tonight? Because I might not make it if that's the case."

He was teasing, but his usual accompanying twinkle was absent from his eyes.

I flashed a reassuring smile. "I think you'll survive."

He shook his head. "There's so much you underestimate, Lane."

And with that, he walked away, directly toward my mom. He didn't wait for me to introduce them, didn't hesitate to take charge of a situation he knew I was dreading. He just strode to the front door of the house that had held me captive for so many of my younger years, stuck out his hand, and told my mom how delighted he was to meet her. How much he'd heard about her. How happy he was to be here, to see where I grew up, to have dinner with my family. He thanked her for the opportunity, and all I could do was stare, impressed.

I wasn't sure how Blake knew that my mom was the kind of woman who appreciated that kind of direct hostess flattery, but the little show he'd just put on had been exactly the kind of thing that might win her over.

She was even smiling.

But that faded ever so slightly when she looked over Blake's shoulder and her eyes landed on me.

"Well, are you just going to stand there?" she called.

My stomach plummeted, and I took a deep breath as I forced myself to join Blake in the front entrance. "Hello to you, too, Mom," I muttered.

She raised a barely defined brow. Her hair, like mine, was so fine and blonde that she needed to dye her eyebrows just for them to be visible. "You're the one who's lurking back there like you don't want to see me."

I had to bite my tongue to keep from saying the obvious response.

"My most sincere apologies," I said instead, plastering a smile on my face that she saw right through.

"Don't start with your attitude." My mom glanced at Blake, her lips curving. "Can you believe the attitude on this one?"

"I'm not going to lie, Mrs. Delacroix," Blake started, looking at me with quiet admiration in his gaze, warming me from the inside out. "I'm a big fan of Delaney's attitude. But I would never say she's known for it. In fact, between the two of us, I think I might have the bigger one."

"Really?" My mom looked genuinely shocked at that. She smoothed the pencil skirt that was plastered to her slender frame. "Huh. For a moment there, I mistook you for a gentleman, Mr. London."

"An easy mistake," Blake said with a wink in my direction. I nearly melted into a puddle in my parents' foyer. "Although I did wait over a decade before making a move on your daughter. So I like to think there's hope for me to become a gentleman yet."

"And it's *Dr.* London, Mom," I corrected, to which my mom sent me a withering look that affected me very little. She pursed her lips in thought, but I could tell she wasn't quite sure *what* to think. Her gaze traveled up and down Blake, and I knew even she couldn't deny just how *perfect* he was.

But then, of course, she sniffed and said, "Gentlemen are not made; they are bred," before spinning on her heel and leading us into the house, where we ran into my dad and Bryan in the living room. The space looked nothing like I remembered, which didn't surprise me. She always kept an interior designer on hand to update the house's finishes as styles came and went over the years. God forbid she ever be caught entertaining people in a home that boasted out-of-date design.

Once again, Blake took the initiative in greeting my dad, who couldn't look less interested in meeting my husband for the second time. He also didn't make any indication that he realized he *had* met Blake before, but that didn't surprise me. My dad was simply being the same as he always was, except his hair had grown grayer and his eyebrows bushier, and I felt guilty again about time passing and being absent. Especially when his bright blue eyes lit up a bit at seeing me. I smiled at him, walking straight into his arms when he opened them for a hug.

I wished I had a stronger backbone, more will to resist when my parents offered the tiniest shred of emotion toward me. Instead, I snatched it up and then felt like a fool later.

"Look who's been living on the East Coast for months and finally decided to take the trip down to see us," my dad said, but he was grinning as he gave me a tight squeeze.

Blake side-eyed me, and I bit the inside of my cheek. I'd told him I'd moved to Boston to be close to family, so I was sure that my lack of visits might come as a surprise to him, even knowing what he did about my relationship with them. I'd had dinner once with Bryan and his girlfriend, but beyond that, I'd kept my distance. And I could blame that on how busy it was finding an apartment, and starting a new job, and then marrying Blake. But maybe coming home was a little more painful than I cared to admit.

And perhaps there'd been another reason I'd moved to Boston.

One I hadn't totally admitted to Blake.

Or even myself.

"Well, a new job, a wedding, and a honeymoon have kept me pretty occupied, Dad."

My dad nodded. "Bry showed us the picture of the plane." He switched his attention to Blake. "Where'd ya take her?"

"To the Netherlands," Blake answered. "Your daughter loves tulips, so it felt only fitting."

"Does she?" He looked back to me, his expression a little funny. Like he was realizing for the first time how much he didn't know about me.

"Is it time for dinner yet?" Bryan asked, keeping us all on track. I laughed, and my mom actually smiled because if she did have a soft spot, it was for her son. Not for me, never for me. But I'd gladly give up that position for Bryan.

"Yes." She clasped her hands together. "Why don't we migrate to the dining room?"

I gave a little thumbs-up to Bryan for helping to move this evening along before Blake placed a hand on my back and led me to the dining room table after my parents, as though he'd grown up here and not me. The table was decorated lavishly, even for what I was used to growing up, and I wondered who my mom was trying to impress or what point she was trying to make. Because absolutely nothing she did was ever accidental.

My parents served steak for dinner, and Bryan proudly provided a side of mashed potatoes and grilled asparagus, which were both things he'd learned to make recently in one of his independent-living courses. Everything tasted delicious, and it filled me with pride to see Bryan learning skills that would help him live on his own and chase his dreams one day.

The mood at dinner surprised me, staying light and conversational until almost everyone was done eating. Or until Bryan had finished eating and excused himself. And that was when it took a turn.

"So, Dr. London." My mom cleared her throat, and I knew that whatever came next was not going to be fun. "I know you and Delaney have been friends for many years."

"Yes, ma'am." Blake nodded. "And please, call me Blake."

My mom gave a tight-lipped smile. "Tell me, why have you now decided to take an interest in my daughter? I don't suppose it has anything to do with a certain inheritance that might be awarded to Delaney in the instance that she marries, does it?"

"No, Mrs. Delacroix," Blake chuckled, sounding alarmingly at ease with that lie. I never imagined Blake would be so effortless at delivering outright lies, but here we were. "You've got it wrong. I haven't just taken an interest in Delaney. I've been interested. For a long, *long* time."

His eyes met mine, and my heart jumped into my throat. We sat across the table from each other, which I didn't like. I'd much prefer to have him next to me so I could, I don't know, touch him or something. I just had this feeling that if I could reach out and grab his hand right now, everything would be better. I needed something to ground me in reality. Like the squeeze of his fingers to let me know I should play along. To remind me that we were both on the inside of a little joke, and everyone else was on the outside.

He said he'd convince my parents that this elopement wasn't actually sudden or fake. That our marriage had been years in the making. I was sure that was what he was doing.

"I see," my mom tutted. "So then, why wait? Why wait for such a long, *long* time?" She emphasized Blake's words in the same manner that he did.

But Blake was unbothered by her attack. "I waited because, as you might know, Delaney made it clear to me that she didn't want to settle down. And you could say I'm the settling down type."

"So you're not like your brother, huh?" my dad cut in, chuckling a little to himself as though he made a really funny joke. Then he went back to polishing off his steak.

Blake bristled at that. "Assuming you're talking about Noah, he's actually in a committed relationship. And I don't expect that to be changing anytime soon."

"Well." My mom pursed her lips. "Then do tell. I'd love to know how you got our daughter to change her very stubborn mind about settling down. Since we all know that Delaney is not one to do things she doesn't want to, especially if it doesn't align with her...what do you always call it?" She glanced at me. "*Life vision*, right?"

I snorted. "I don't know how you can honestly sit there and say that when I let you puppeteer me until I moved out. I danced for you, debuted for you, did everything just to make you—"

I interrupted myself, clenching my jaw.

I'd always thought that if I made my parents happy, maybe one day they'd make me feel the same. But that didn't happen. There was never any hope of that happening.

"If you did everything we wanted, you wouldn't have run off to play with people's hearts," my mom snapped back.

I gritted my teeth. She said that like I'd gone off to run a reality dating competition and not become a fully trained cardiologist.

"What was it that you wanted me to do?" I countered. "Stay home and become some investor's wife?"

Beside me, Blake stiffened.

"We would have liked to have some involvement in your marriage pursuits, yes," my dad said carefully before taking a sip of his red wine. "Why do you think we convinced your grandparents to include that addendum before they passed?"

My jaw dropped as my vision went hazy.

So this...this was a *punishment*, wasn't it? For chasing dreams that they never wanted me to have.

"But of course you ignored it," my mom said with a roll of her eyes. "Didn't even think to include us. You can thank yourself that we're here tonight."

"I *scoured* the will I received," I countered. "Trust me, there was no addendum. I had no idea I was supposed to include you in my marriage plans, and I assumed you wouldn't be interested in meeting my husband, considering how much interest you've shown in other areas of my life."

My mom frowned, shooting daggers at me with her eyes before switching to her husband. "Did you not send it to her?"

"Me?" My dad waved the thought away. "I'm sure Anderson would have supplied her with the updated version."

"There was *no* updated version," I insisted through gritted teeth, annoyed that they didn't have anything to say about the part of the conversation where they never cared about me unless it somehow impacted them. "Not that I received."

"Clearly." My mom sniffed and then straightened. "Well, then you might as well tell us more about your...elopement." Her mouth twisted when she said the last word, like it left a bad taste in her mouth.

Blake cleared his throat. "I know the elopement might seem sudden to you—"

"Sudden?" My mom laughed. "Not as sudden as you might think. Despite what we hoped would happen, I always suspected she would do this. Show up with a husband she manifested from thin air just to get our money."

"It's not *your* money," I argued, feeling my blood pressure continue to rise.

"Tell me, how much of a cut is she giving you?" she went on, looking at Blake and ignoring me. "I bet you have your one-year anniversary marked on your calendar, counting down the days until you can divorce. I don't blame you for wanting to detach yourself from her, considering—"

"Stop." Blake nearly bellowed the word, and I jumped in my seat, startled. "Delaney is my wife, and she will *be* my wife for as long as she allows me to be her husband. I refuse to sit here and listen to you disrespect her. She might not be living her life the way you want her to be, but each and every day, she cares more about the people around her than she cares about herself, and your continued insinuation that she is selfishly chasing her inheritance is unacceptable."

I blinked at Blake, shocked and breathless, as my parents struggled with what to say to that. I couldn't really blame them because I didn't have any words, either. Even if I did know what to say, I wasn't sure I'd be able to say anything through the emotion choking me. No one had ever defended me to my parents before. It had always just been me against them, in each and every argument.

"Please." My mom brushed off her momentary speechlessness, but I could tell she was still a bit rankled by Blake's assertion. "I'm sure that ring is from a cereal box or something."

She gave a forced, haughty laugh, but Blake's lips twitched with the slightest smile, surprising me. "Ah, I'm so glad you brought up the ring, Mrs. Delacroix." He held out his hand to me, catching my eye. And this time, I *knew* I was on the outside looking in at something for the first time. Because I had no idea what he was about to say. "Lane, can I see it for a second?"

I nodded, wiggling it off my finger and placing it in his palm.

Blake took it, examining it as he twirled it between his fingers.

Then he leaned forward so my mom could have a better look at it, too. "You might not know much about jewelry, Mrs. Delacroix, but this ring is vintage. Are you familiar with Kashmir sapphires?"

I smiled to myself because I knew how much that comment was going to provoke my mother.

As suspected, she sat straighter. "Of course I am."

Blake nodded. "Then you'll know that they're incredibly rare. Their unparalleled quality makes them highly sought after, but there was only a limited number of these sapphires mined over a century ago. This ring was my grandma's and my great-grandma's before that. She worked as a governess for the Rockefellers when they stayed at their estate in Duluth to tend to the mining on the North Shore, and they became fond of her. So fond that they actually helped arrange her marriage to my great-grandfather, who was a local philanthropist, and even gifted this ring as an engagement present. It became my great-grandmother's wedding ring."

My gaze shifted from my mom's dropping jaw to Blake's intent look, trying to puzzle together fact from fiction as he kept talking.

"My mom never wore the ring once it was given to her," he said. "She tried to pass it down to my sister, but Natalie, like my mom, has never worn much jewelry and said that it should be saved for someone who it might complement better. Who might appreciate it."

Blake looked directly at me, and I suddenly found breathing to be laborious. Challenging at best. Nearly impossible at worst.

"I met Delaney on my first day of med school," he said, brown gaze still boring into me, melting me. "I called my mom that night and said I met a girl with sapphires for eyes and begged her for the ring." He held out his palm, his lips curved as he gestured for me to place my hand in his. I did, and his touch burned its way through me, heating me at my core. "You'd think it was designed for her. But no, it's just a bit of fate. I've been waiting years to see it through. To put this ring where it belongs. See how perfectly that fits?" He slid the ring back onto my finger, and it felt heavier than before. "I didn't even get it resized."

Blake laced his fingers through mine, and I stared at our clasped hands, feeling entranced by his touch and his words and the weight of both of them. They felt unfabricated and unburdened despite the story he was weaving.

"I've been in love with your daughter since the day I met her, and I've been waiting to give her this ring for years," Blake said, directing his attention back to my mom and causing me to jerk my head up. My lips parted in shocked awe as I struggled with what to believe. "We might have eloped, but this marriage is anything but sudden. Proposing to Delaney has been all I've ever wanted. When I saw the very first glimpse of an opportunity, I took it. And you think I'm counting down the days until I can take it all back? Not a chance in hell. I'm staying attached to this woman for as long as I fucking can, understood?"

I stared at Blake, trying to reason with his words and decipher what they meant—if they meant anything at all. I would have realized, wouldn't I? If they were true, I would have realized. He *must* have concocted that story. Had it ready in case my mom pressed him for details about how long our relationship had been going on. It was the responsible thing to do when you were someone who was faking a marriage and trying to make it seem like an elopement hadn't been fake. And Blake had only ever been responsible.

But then Blake turned to look at me, and all of the little reasonings I was making in my head washed away.

And I was left with a pounding, aching heart.

No...it couldn't be. It couldn't all be true.

Because then that would mean that I'd spent the last ten years blind to what was right in front of me. Missing *everything*. We could have been so much more for so much longer, but I'd just had no idea. How could that be? How had I missed it?

I wasn't sure I knew how to accept what Blake was saying and what his eyes were telling me, wasn't sure I knew how to *process* that. My chest tightened. I struggled to get sufficient air into my lungs.

But at the same time, my stomach couldn't stop flipping.

Butterflies hadn't stopped fluttering.

And I knew I was falling, falling, falling.

"I understand," my mom finally relented with a sigh. "I don't appreciate the language, but I understand. And I believe that you're not playing us, Dr. London. But have you ever stopped to consider that maybe *she* is playing *you*?"

Blake opened his mouth, and I could see the fire in his eyes, his eagerness to defend me. But it was my turn to speak up.

"For crying out loud, Mom. I've known about the will since I was twenty. I've known what I wanted to do with that money since I was twenty-two. I've known Blake would marry me so I could get that money since the end of our first med school semester. That was *ten* years ago. There's a reason I never asked him. A reason I never even told him about it."

I expected my parents to counter me, press me for more, but they were silent. Instead, Blake spoke, his voice gentle but demanding.

"What's that, Lane?"

Our eyes met, and I knew, at my core, that we were having a real conversation right now. It wasn't for show or to be convincing; Blake wanted to know. And shit, I wanted to tell him. I wanted to tell him everything.

"I've heard enough." My dad cut off my response before I could even think of it. "Elizabeth, just let them have the damn money or at least ask the important questions."

My mom threw up her hands. "Be my guest, Robert. Ask the important questions, then."

My dad pointed his fork in Blake's direction. "Do you have a good credit score?"

Blake laughed. "I have an excellent credit score, sir."

"Well, there you go. Welcome to the family."

"Robert," my mom chastised. Her eyes cut sharply to him, but he ignored her, too focused on swirling his wine. A muscle jumped in her jaw before she said, "We'll talk about this later. This matter is *not* settled."

"Can't wait," my dad muttered, thick with sarcasm.

I almost smiled.

No, I *did* smile.

Even though my mom had made it clear that the conversation surrounding the inheritance was not done, I felt lighter than I had in years. And while it was my dad's comment that had made me smile, I knew there was only one person at this table who I had to thank for that.

And I was pretty sure I was in love with him.

ten years ago

DELANEY

I stared down the row of seats in the lecture hall at Blake.

We always put a healthy number of seats between us because neither of us knew how to shut up and focus on the lecture if we sat right next to each other. But right now, I didn't need to say anything for him to understand what I was communicating. I shot him a look, and he winked back at me, a tiny smile playing on his lips.

The lecture had barely even gotten underway, and he'd already taken the slides from today, created a Quizlet from the notes, and sent me the flash cards.

I was both irritated and grateful.

I grabbed my phone, ignoring the rules I made for myself about staying off technology during class unless it was relevant to the content.

The rules didn't count when it came to Blake.

> I don't even want to know how you managed that.

> BLAKE: I wanted to see if I could beat how quick you got it done for anatomy dissection.

I wrinkled my nose because anatomy dissection was my least favorite subject at the moment, and then I tapped out a reply.

> If your competitive streak means less work for me, then by all means. Have at it, Blakey.

BLAKE: Never call me that again.

BLAKE: If I could take back the flashcards, I would.

I smiled to myself and tucked away my phone.

I could feel the heat from Blake's glare throughout the rest of the lecture.

But I didn't really mind the warmth.

CHAPTER TWENTY-EIGHT

D ELANEY'S PARENTS ASKED TO talk to her privately for a few minutes after dinner, and given how her mom spoke to her and about her, I was reluctant to walk away. But Delaney gave me a nod of reassurance, and then another when I still hesitated, so I strode out the front door to wait for her in the driveway.

I felt uneasy. And it had nothing to do with the closeness to the ocean or the gray clouds rolling in from over the sea. For once, my mind wasn't dragged into the past. Instead, it was wholly present and completely focused on Delaney.

Her expression at dinner was indescribable, but it infused hope in me all the same. There was something there, something real, when I'd spoken the truth aloud for the first time. I could have sworn I saw it. And *God*, it felt good.

As far as her parents went, it was hard to tell for certain where we landed with them. I thought I'd maybe made an impression, but then again, I didn't know the Delacroix family as well as she did. I only knew Delaney. Was only really concerned about Delaney. How *she* was feeling. What *she* thought about everything I'd said.

I felt her presence and heard her footsteps leaving the house even before I heard her voice.

"Blake."

She said my name on a shaky exhale.

I turned to face her. God, she was gorgeous. Every day, she was gorgeous, but tonight, she had a blue, flowy blouse on that made her look like a summer angel. It brought out the color in her eyes and the sparkle of the ring on her finger. "Lane. Is everything okay?"

She nodded, pressing her lips together and stopping about a foot away from me.

"I owe you," she said. "For everything. Everything about tonight."

I shook my head, tired of this *owing me* shit. Couldn't she see that this wasn't transactional for me? She meant the world to me, and I'd always do anything and everything that I could for her. "How many times do I have to tell you? You don't owe me anything."

"But that was..." She sighed and threw up her hands. "You were right."

That hadn't been what I'd expected her to say. "I was right?"

Her lips twitched. "Don't make me say it again."

"Oh, I definitely want to hear you say it again," I said, the corner of my mouth tugging upward. "I was *what*, Delaney?"

She flicked her eyes up in mock annoyance. "Right. You were right."

I lifted a brow. "About what?"

"About how convincing you could be." She bit down on her lip, avoiding looking directly at me. "That you would convince them. At least, I'm pretty sure you did. Even though my mom says they still have to talk about it."

My smile faltered despite the good news.

"It was...really convincing, Blake," she breathed, so soft that her voice almost got carried away in the wind. "That story that you told. With the ring."

Sighing, I raked a hand through my hair.

So she still thought it was just a story.

Fuck if I wasn't done with the pretense.

"There's a reason for that."

"A reason?" she repeated.

"For why it was convincing."

Because it was all true.

Delaney blinked at me like she couldn't comprehend what I was implying. Like those exact puzzle pieces just didn't fit together. As though me being in love with her for more than a decade was not something she had ever considered possible. *Still* didn't consider possible.

"What's the reason, Blake?" she whispered, almost like she was afraid of the answer.

Little pieces of my heart were chipping away, falling to the pit of my stomach.

How could she still not see things for what they really were?

I truly thought that she'd been starting to realize the extent of our relationship, how it had always been more than we pretended it was. But maybe I was wrong. Maybe it would always be something that only *I* saw.

"I don't understand how it's not obvious." I looked down at my feet, shook my head, and sighed. "But of course it isn't obvious to you. Of course you can't imagine a world where maybe we've always been so much more than friends, Lane."

Delaney remained quiet, and I was terrified of what expression I would find on her face when I looked back at her. So I glanced up at the gray sky instead, wondering if it was going to open up on us. The mood felt right.

Her silence *haunted* me. But it was my fault. A relationship—a *real* relationship—was something she had never wanted, and after years of considering that and keeping all my feelings to myself, I'd spilled them all out onto the dinner table. In front of her parents. On a night where she was already emotional and nervous.

"*Always*, Blake?" she finally breathed, the words coated in disbelief. "Why are you saying it like that? How was I supposed to have known?"

I risked a glance at her, and the mix of pain and shock on her face gutted me.

She was right. For years, I'd purposefully made sure it wasn't obvious. But considering everything that had happened between us recently, I guess I'd been foolishly hoping for a reaction that didn't have so much doubt in it.

"I told you that we needed my parents to believe this was more than just an elopement, that it wasn't something sudden, and you told me you were going to *convince* them, Blake. What was I supposed to think? How was I supposed to know that—" She choked on the final words, almost like she couldn't get herself to say "*you've really been in love with me all this time.*" Delaney covered her mouth with a shaky hand, and I'd never felt a stab to the chest quite like this one.

No wonder she thought it was just a story.

No wonder she'd looked at me at the dinner table like that when I was telling it.

I'd thought maybe there was hope and love and light in her eyes, but she'd just been playing along.

And now I...*fuck*.

"Never mind, Lane." I swallowed past the emotion clogging my throat. "It's fine, okay? Don't worry about it."

I stepped back, putting distance between us, but Delaney stepped forward, chasing me.

"No, Blake. Listen—"

"Seriously, it's okay."

I turned around, ready to get in the car and put this painful moment behind me.

"*Blake.*"

I stopped in my tracks, closing my eyes. The way she said my name was sharper this time, and I couldn't really blame her for being mad. I'd pushed things too far. The difference between reality and fiction had blurred too much, had gotten too jumbled, and it was my fault.

"Laney!" Bryan's voice rang out, coming from the front steps. I looked back to see him waving her over.

"One sec, Bry!" she called before I heard her footsteps following me instead of going to him.

"Go be with your brother, Lane." I shook my head. "You don't get to see him enough, and I know how hard that is for you. I don't mind waiting if you want to spend more time with him. I'll be in the car."

I turned to get behind the wheel, feeling Delaney's gaze hot on my neck. As soon as I shut the door, she turned and walked toward her brother.

Tipping my head back, I closed my eyes and tried to calm the chaos in my brain. I couldn't be entirely sure of how much time passed, but it wasn't long before I heard the door open and smelled the sweetness of Delaney's perfume. Or maybe it was just her fucking essence. I wasn't sure. I'd never actually seen Delaney put on perfume. I just knew she smelled like that. It was mind-boggling and exquisite, and I didn't know how I would ever manage to be less addicted to it and her.

I opened my eyes to find hers on me. It was a mix between a glare and a stare, and I didn't know what to make of it. So I pressed my lips together and started the car.

The ride home began with a quiet roar. The silence and unease was deafening. The hum of the car and the pattering of rain as it began to fall—those were the only sounds until Delaney suddenly broke through the tension.

"I don't understand how I was supposed to know," she said, her voice small but hard. "I don't know how it was supposed to be obvious that you *always*—"

She clamped her lips together, still unable to say it.

That wasn't exactly a good sign for me.

"I know." I tried to focus on the road, but fuck, it was hard. "And I'm sorry," I added, despite badly wanting to clarify whether she was just stunned by how long I'd loved her or if she truly hadn't seen my feelings for what they were at all, even in the last couple of weeks. But all I did was try to reassure her by saying, "It's okay, Lane."

"But—"

"We can just forget about it. Really."

I hadn't made it this far just to lose her because I'd said too much.

"You want to forget about it?" she echoed.

The stark emotion in her voice remained unnamed.

"That might be for the best," I cemented, keeping my eyes on the highway.

It actually sounded like the worst.

A roll of distant thunder filled the silence that followed. Delaney didn't say anything else, and I didn't dare open my mouth again. Not right now, not when I was feeling too many things so intensely.

Neither of us spoke again until we were almost home, and then all Delaney said was, "Thank you for coming with me tonight."

"You're welcome." I dared to look at her for the first time since we'd pulled out of her parents' driveway, and the unreadable look on her face was almost too much for me to bear. I needed a fucking minute to get a grip and reassess all of this. So I took a breath and said, "I think I'll head to the gym. Get a quick workout in before the workweek."

Delaney didn't look too happy about that, but I couldn't figure out why. She pressed her lips together and remained silent for a moment before giving a curt nod.

Her response made me hesitate, but fuck, I knew I needed to work out some of my pent-up emotions so I didn't do something else I regretted tonight.

Delaney opened the car door, and she had one foot out of it when I grabbed her wrist to stall her. Feeling her soft skin beneath my fingertips made my heart burn up.

"Text me when you get into the apartment, okay?"

She glanced back at me, her eyes finding mine, making it momentarily hard to breathe. She looked like she might say something but then shook her head and turned away.

"Okay."

And then she was gone.

I watched her walk away. Every step she took stomped on my heart a little bit.

Once she disappeared into the elevator, I grabbed my phone and texted Noah. I wasn't sure if he would be available, but I wouldn't mind the company. And the distraction from my own fucking head.

By the time I'd shot him a text and gotten a reply that he'd meet me at the gym, Delaney had messaged that she'd made it upstairs. So I took off and thanked God I kept an extra gym bag in my trunk for emergencies like this.

Somehow, Noah showed up only about twenty minutes after I did, and I was grateful because even though I'd been destroying the same punching bag until I had sweat dripping down my temples, the gym was empty except for the owner, Zach, and being alone with my thoughts wasn't helping my fucking headspace right now.

"What's going on?" Noah burst through the doors, panting as though he'd run here.

"Nothing." My glove connected with the bag, and the chains rattled above it. Noah lifted a brow at me but seemed to understand. He threw his stuff down and then got ready in silence before joining me at the bag next to mine. He gave me a look, which I understood.

He was here.

When I was ready to talk, he'd listen.

Until then, he'd be waiting.

He worked on some of his footwork and approaches while I continued to take my frustration out on the swinging bag. When Zach noticed that Noah had shown up, he swung by to let us know that he wanted to head home because of the incoming storm but tossed us a set of keys to say we could lock up when we were done.

I knew Zach pretty well by this point, but Noah's presence always helped with shit like this. And this time, I wasn't complaining. I wasn't ready to go home yet and face reality.

Once Zach was gone, I sighed and turned to Noah. "I think I fucked something up with Delaney."

Noah cocked his head to the side, observing me. I could tell he wanted to say, "*Already?*" but kept his lips sealed. Instead, he adjusted the straps on his gloves until they were just right and then turned to face me straight-on.

"Fine." He sighed and threw up his hands. "You can punch me in the face. I'll tell Gemma it was for a good cause."

I rolled my eyes. "I don't want to punch you in the face. I wouldn't mind if *you* punched *me* in the face, though. Knock some fucking sense into me."

Noah sighed. "You wanna tell me what you did?"

"The marriage isn't real," I blurted, and Christ, saying that aloud really fucking hurt. But at the same time, it felt so good to get off my chest.

"What?" Noah frowned. "You're not married?"

"No. We are, just...it's complicated."

"I see."

He didn't *really* see.

"It's a convenience thing," I tried to explain. "For her inheritance."

I didn't really have it in me to go down the long rabbit hole of our situation. Hopefully, that would suffice.

Noah's brows shot up as more understanding washed over him. "A convenience thing," he repeated. "And you've just, what, been *pretending* to be in love with her while *actually* being in love with her and hoping she doesn't notice?"

I glared at him, annoyed at how ridiculous it sounded when he put it that way.

But I couldn't really be mad, considering he wasn't *wrong*.

"Yeah, that was pretty much the plan. Until tonight. When we had dinner at her parents' house," I said before turning back to the bag and serving it a right hook.

"I take it dinner went well," Noah said dryly.

A dry laugh slipped out of me. "Her parents aren't...entirely supportive of us. With the elopement and everything. Didn't believe any of it was real, so I tried to tell them the truth."

"Like the real truth?"

"Yeah, the real truth."

"I take it that was what didn't go well?"

"I think it went well with her parents." I threw another punch. "But Delaney...I don't think she ever expected to hear me say what I did, and I think I made her uncomfortable, which I'd been trying so goddamn hard not to do this entire time. I've been so careful, man. Because I am well aware that I want her in a way that she might not be ready for. Might not *ever* be ready for."

"For fuck's sake, you didn't make me uncomfortable."

The sound of Delaney's voice—her stilted breathing and forceful words—caused me to whirl around with my heart in my throat.

She stood there, the front door to the gym closing behind her, looking like she'd run through the rain to get here. It pounded harder against the pavement outside, a depressing backdrop for the most beautiful woman I'd ever seen and ever known. The damp ends of her hair were dripping onto my old U of M alumni shirt. It was half-soaked, sticking to her skin. Her chest heaved, her eyes bright as she stared me down.

"Delaney...*God*, Lane, did you walk here?" I scanned her from top to bottom, inspecting every inch of her to make sure nothing was wrong. "Are you okay?"

"No, I'm not okay!" she cried, and alarm spiked through me. I lurched toward her, but she put a hand out. "No, stop."

I stopped, even though it felt wrong. So, so wrong. "Lane—"

"Just stop and let me talk. Without interrupting me and

without telling me it's fine and assuming what I'm going to say before I say it," she pleaded before inhaling deeply. "Christ, Blake, I know I told you earlier that you were right, but you're not right about everything. Okay? Because I *don't* think we should just forget about this. I *don't* think that would be for the best."

My jaw dropped; my heart pounded. I did as she asked. I was quiet, waiting for her to go on, and every second that passed was torture. It felt like my heart was in a vise, and I needed her to release the tension pushing in on me from all sides.

"I'm *not* uncomfortable," she said finally. Forcefully. It should make me feel better, but relief was hard to come by when she looked at me like that. "You've never once made me uncomfortable. In fact, I'm so unbelievably comfortable with you I never ever want to *not* be with you. And I'm only pissed because I was trying to tell you that, but you wouldn't let me. I was confused, Blake. You made me think that you'd say anything to convince my parents, so I didn't know what to believe at first. And just because I didn't immediately know how to put my feelings into words after learning the truth about *everything* you've been keeping from me doesn't mean I don't have things I want you to know, too."

Pain leaked from her eyes on the last words, and I felt both elated and like something had crumbled into pieces inside me.

"I thought you—"

"I know what you thought, but you were wrong, Blake."

My lips parted, but words didn't come out.

I'd never experienced such happiness and such guilt at the same time.

"Yes," she emphasized, seeing my expression. "For once in your life, you were wrong, Dr. London."

Noah chuckled at that, and I shot him a glare. "Shut up."

"What?" He shrugged. "I like her."

"I'm going to punch you in the face after all." I sighed before looking back at my wife. "Delaney—"

"No, I'm not done talking," she interrupted, putting her hands on her hips. Her expression grew twisted, and I could *feel* the choked emotion in her voice. "Blake, do you..."

She had to pause, gasping for a breath as a shiver racked through her as she stood there in soaking clothes, and my limbs shook, too, needing to go to her.

"*Please*, Lane," I whispered, hoping she'd understand. "Let me—"

But she shook her head and cut me off, speaking in a tortured whisper back.

"Do you even know?" I watched her throat work as she swallowed. "Do you even know how frustrating it is to be trying to tell someone you love them and they act like they don't want to hear it?"

"*What*?" I breathed, not quite sure I'd heard her right.

I felt dizzy, the gym spinning around me while Delaney's face stayed still. She was the constant in my life. And I never dared to imagine—

"Well, I think that's my cue," Noah said before shuffling off, grabbing his gear, and slipping out the front door, throwing me a smirk and a wink before leaving me and Delaney alone.

"Please just talk to me," she said, her voice suddenly small. But it echoed in the empty gym anyway, reverberating through my body. "Was it really the truth? What you said to my parents?"

I didn't know how to simply continue our conversation after she'd just said what she said. And I really needed to make sure I hadn't just made it up, fabricated her saying those words. Those perfect, magical, goddamn words.

"Delaney, did you just say—"

"Answer the question first. Please, I just need to hear you say it."

She was killing me. Christ, she was killing me. But I owed her at least this much. Fuck, I owed her the whole world.

"Every word." I held her gaze, that gorgeous sapphire gaze. "Every word was true."

Her breath visibly hitched. "Always? From the very beginning?"

I nodded slowly. "From the very beginning, Lane."

She stared, taking that in. Rain began pelting against the front windows of the gym behind Delaney as the moment stretched between us. She was making me suffer, and I deserved it, but that didn't mean I wasn't dying inside as I watched her fully comprehend the truth.

She held up her hand. "The ring?"

"Has always been for you."

"Blake." Her brows furrowed adorably as she walked forward with determination in her step, and I thanked God for every step she took closer to me. And I kept being grateful, even when she reached out to give me a little shove. I took the opportunity to keep her close, grabbing her by the wrist as soon as her hand hit my chest, tugging her into me. Her wet clothes against my bare skin never felt so good. Fuck, I loved this woman. Even when she was mad at me. Even when neither of us knew what the hell was going on.

"Why?" she cried, not resisting but pounding her free fist on my chest. "Why have I never known? Why the *hell* didn't I know?"

"Because you never wanted that." I spoke softly, my chest feeling like it was cracking open. "You had no interest in dating or marriage, and I wanted to respect that. You grew up never getting to experience life the way you wanted, and the last thing I ever wanted to do was take that away from you."

Her lashes fluttered as she looked at me without responding, her chest rising and falling against mine, in time with mine. Thunder clapped outside, but it was nothing compared to the resounding roar of my pulse in my ears, thumping loudly.

"Why do you think I turned down the attending position at Mayo and moved away when I found out you were engaged, Lane?" I added, my voice full of gravel and emotions as I brushed her damp hair out of her face. "Why do you think that hurt so hard? I spent years keeping my distance because I thought you didn't want to settle down and then found out you were marrying some guy who you barely even knew, and it fucking *killed* me. I couldn't stay and watch you attach yourself to someone who wasn't me. I just couldn't do it."

Delaney gasped like she'd never in her wildest dreams imagined that her engagement might have hurt me. Like she was horrified that it had. She blinked at me, those long, wet lashes taunting me as her lips parted. I counted the number of heartbeats until she responded.

"Blake...I'm sorry." Her expression crumbled, and I knew she meant every word. "I'm so sorry. It wasn't real. It was never real."

"I know that now, baby." I released her wrist and cupped her face with both hands. My gaze dropped to her lips because hell, I wanted to kiss her. *Fuck*, I wanted that so bad, but I also wanted other things. Wanted to know other things, wanted to hear other things. "But why didn't you ask *me*? You said you'd always known I would marry you. You should have come to me from the beginning."

She bit down on her lip, chewing on it for a moment before admitting, "Because I think I always knew."

Tears had welled along her lash line, slowly leaking down her cheeks. I brushed them away with my thumbs. "Knew what, sweetheart?"

"That it was inevitable what it would do to me to be married to you. And I didn't know...I didn't know how you felt. I was scared, okay? Scared to feel something real when I'd run away from it for so long."

Now I knew how she felt earlier, when she'd learned a new reality about us. And I understood why that had knocked the wind out of her to the point where she hadn't known what to say right away. Because I was speechless. A part of Delaney had always known we were inevitable? Fucking speechless.

But I did have one question. One question that everything depended on.

"Are you still scared?"

"A little." She exhaled a shaky breath. "It's not you. It's them. It's reframing what family and love means and seeing it through your eyes. It's just new for me, Blake. But today, I saw what it might look like."

"I don't blame you for being scared, Lane. We can take this one step at a time, okay?" I could do slow. As long as we were on the same page about the direction we were moving, I could do slow. "Let me keep showing you what love means, what love is. Let me prove to you that I can give you all of it, baby."

"I want that," she whispered, and hearing her agree so simply made me feel like I was soaring. "As long as you know this—me and you and this marriage—is real. It might be unconventional, but this is real for me."

Holy hell.

Real. This was real. We were real.

Delaney London. Delaney London. Delaney London.

"Say that again," I begged as my hands began to move, needing to feel every bit of her, assure myself that she wasn't just a figment of my imagination and she was here in the flesh, saying all the things I'd always wanted her to say. "I want to hear it. I'm sorry you felt like I didn't earlier. I'm so sorry. I want to hear everything you have to say. Everything. Say it, Lane. Please."

My thumbs brushed over her mouth, her soft lips, wanting to feel the words as she spoke them.

"This is real, Blake." More tears lined her lashes, making them glisten. "I love you, and this is real."

Nothing in this world had ever felt as good as the shape of Delaney's lips saying I love you.

"Oh my God," I groaned, dropping my forehead to hers and bracing myself for an explosion. Because my heart was on the brink of one. Bending down, I scooped my hands beneath her legs, lifting her into my arms. She wrapped her legs around my waist, clinging to me, and I felt her tears roll down my cheeks. "I love you, too. Baby, I have loved you since the very moment you came into my life. It's unbelievable how ingrained you are in me. You are *everything* to me, Lane. Absolutely fucking everything."

Delaney nodded, accepting my words as the truth, her forehead pressing against mine as we stayed locked together.

"You moved here because you couldn't watch me marry someone else," she whispered, her voice wavering through gasping breaths, "but you didn't realize I've only ever been attached to you, Blake. I've only ever been drawn to you, only want to be with you, only ever want to call you on a hard day, only look for *you* in a crowd. It's no wonder I spotted you so easily that day in the SCMC lobby. I just didn't realize...for so long, I didn't fully realize what that meant."

Her confession stunned me into silence. She exhaled, and I inhaled her breaths, if only to collect that much more of her.

"Why do you think I moved to Boston?" Delaney tipped her head, and her lips grazed mine as she spoke things that made my head spin faster, my heart beat louder, even louder than the storm crescendoing outside. "There were reasons. So many reasons I told myself. Reasons I told you. But there was only ever one real one. *You.* It's because of you, Blake. It's because I didn't know how to be in a place where you weren't. It's because the only heart I've ever been attached to is yours."

"Fuck, Delaney." I tightened my grip on her, reeling from her words. "I don't want to interrupt you if there's more you want to say, but I really fucking need to kiss you. Tell me I can kiss you now, baby."

She nodded, and my mouth captured hers in seconds. Goddamn, this mouth. This mouth and all the things it had just said. It tasted so fucking good. Those words tasted so good. She tasted so good—unbelievably real and perfect and *good*. Fuck, I'd never get over it—never get over her. This kiss was the kiss I'd always wanted, and it was better than I ever could have imagined.

Delaney moaned, and my whole body, my whole being, was at her command.

"The answer is always going to be yes," she whispered against my lips. "For you, it's always yes."

Every time she opened her mouth, she opened my world just a little bit more. I didn't know existing could feel like this until right in this moment.

"Only for me, right?" I gasped, not needing the reassurance but wanting to hear it anyway.

"Only for you," she murmured before I slanted my lips over hers again and got lost in the feel of them. My tongue dove into her mouth, tasting and exploring and never wanting to come up for air. Especially not when she was kissing me back in the exact same, greedy way—like she would never get enough.

But then her body started writhing against mine as I held her, and I knew she needed more. Fuck, *I* needed more.

"And what if it's not enough right now for the way I need you?" I nipped at her lip, tugging on it because I couldn't keep away from the feel of her mouth for long. "What will the answer be if I ask for more? Will that be a yes, too?"

She whimpered. And then, "Always."

"Thank God, Lane. Because *fuck*, I want you right now in ways I can't even describe."

A second later, Delaney whispered words I should have expected in my ear.

"Then put me out of my goddamn misery and take me."

CHAPTER TWENTY-NINE

B LAKE HAD ME BACKED up against the corner post of the boxing ring within seconds, my legs wrapped around his hips and one of his hands clutching my ass. His lips hadn't left mine; our mouths were inseparable. Blake kissed me in a way that, until this moment, I hadn't realized I wanted so badly. *Nothing* was left out of this kiss. He wasn't holding a single thing back, and it made me understand how much he'd withheld before.

His kisses ravaged me: rough and tender, quick but slow. He groaned into my mouth, and heat flooded between my legs. All I wanted was to clench my thighs together in response, but they were held open by his broad body, and I almost cried when he seemed to read my mind, grinding up against me to give me the friction I was seeking. His erection hit me just right, even through our layers of clothes, at an angle that might have me coming embarrassingly soon if he kept at it. And God, I hoped he did. My fingers dug into his shoulders, hanging on with desperation as I tried to tilt my hips and match his movements.

"Blake, I—" I started, trying to warn him what he was doing to me and how quickly he was doing it, but Blake cut off my words with a needy thrust against my body, and stars burst in my vision.

"Delaney." He shuddered my name, kneading my ass like he couldn't get enough. And then, without warning, he smacked it, causing me to jerk forward and collide with him in such a sweet, sweet way. A pleasure-filled gasp flew out of me, breaking our kiss. But Blake seemed to appreciate my response, his growly voice echoing in my veins. "*Fuck*, baby."

"Fuck," I echoed, looking up at the ceiling and feeling like I was going to float up to the top of it. "Blake, oh my God."

"I know, Lane," he hummed. "I know how you like it."

"Yes." My head spun. "Don't want you holding back."

"Never again," he promised, dragging his lips to the curve of my jaw, peppering kisses across my skin. "Going to make sure you know you're mine every fucking day from here on out. Been holding back for way too goddamn long. Never again."

He sucked on my pulse point, and I released a breathy "Good boy."

That was what I wanted. A version of Blake London who didn't hold back.

"Holy—" Blake choked on the rest of his thought before grabbing at my leggings, trying to find the top of them. "Need more. Need these off."

I kicked my sandals to the floor and tipped my hips toward him, arching off the post and wrapping my arms around the back of it for support, trying to make it easier. Blake eventually found what he was looking for, ripping the fabric down my legs as I held on and watched him.

Now that I could stare at him, I wanted to *stare* at him, appreciate him, take in his broad, shirtless shoulders and defined muscles that, to this day, still surprised me. His sharp jaw ticked as he focused on his task, and strands of his wavy hair hung over moody eyes. Lightning flashed through the front windows behind him, casting a magnificent glow, illuminating every perfect inch of him as he threw my leggings to the floor.

When he looked back up, his expression was fierce, telling me he'd be keeping his promise tonight. There was no more holding back. None at all.

My breath vanished.

His lips tilted with a smirk as he realized I'd been watching him, and then he slowly brought his body back to mine, dragging his hands up my bare legs to hitch them back around his hips.

"I love you," he mouthed, not actually saying the words but making me *feel* them. His love made my whole body pliant and warm, and I found it difficult to speak.

Blake didn't wait for my reply anyway, capturing my lips with his again, drugging me with a deep kiss that only made his words feel that much more profound. I wanted this kiss forever and ever.

But the skies intervened.

A sharp clap of thunder knocked us both back, shaking the building and then sending it into darkness a second later.

"Shit," Blake muttered, swiveling his head around to assess the gym. The current between us momentarily severed as he let me slide down his body and back to my feet. "One second, baby. Don't move."

He regrettably walked away, over to the front door to survey the block. It had also grown dark, save for one streetlamp, which cast through the gym's windows—the only source of light in the building. It shone onto the middle of the boxing ring.

I decided to follow it while I waited, feeling drawn to the spotlight. Adrenaline pumped through my veins, still coursing from the run here, the heart-pounding confessions, the kiss before the crash, and I just—I *needed* to move. Blake told me not to, but I didn't know how to just stand here and wait while my emotions felt so trapped by my body. So I climbed through the ropes of the boxing ring onto the padded arena.

By the time Blake turned back around, I was experimenting with the feel of the floor beneath my bare feet, wondering what it would feel like to dance on. The sound of my old ballet instructor, Ms. Sylvia, rang in my ears, yelling at me to "feel the floor!" as I spun across it. I dragged my toes over the soft, elastic material, testing it out before settling in first position.

My feet had never completely healed from the damage that had been done to them at my mom's insistence. And I think that resentment caused such a resistance to ever acknowledge the dancer in me. There *were* parts of ballet that I missed; there was connectivity, there was expression, and that all felt so integral to being human, being alive.

I learned that in Amsterdam. And I felt it right now, too.

When Blake and I had been at that club, I thought my desire to dance, to move, had been caused by the atmosphere, something to do with the ambience, the music, the lights.

But here I was, standing in the middle of a dark room with only a streetlamp for light and only the sound of the rain as my backdrop melody, and I still felt that urge.

It had nothing to do with where I was or what was going on around me.

And everything to do with the man watching me with heat in his gaze.

Blake was my muse.

And I didn't just feel the need to dance; I felt the need to dance for him.

I transitioned from a tendu into an arabesque, catching how Blake's gaze darkened out of the corner of my eye. Vaguely, I remembered that I was half-naked, with only my bra, underwear, and his alumni T-shirt covering my body.

It was all I could feel against my skin—this half-soaked shirt, the one I wore to sleep night after night because it made me feel more attached to the man who gave it to me all those years ago.

I'd been frustrated with Blake for never telling me the truth about his feelings for so many years, but why hadn't *I* known? *I* should have realized the strength of my attachment for him, should have come to know it for what it was.

That was on me.

I played a part in this, too.

And like him, I'd do my best to make up for it. I didn't want to take another day for granted.

I was still reeling from his confessions, still absorbing them and fully realizing them. I felt them move through me as *I* moved, balancing my foot up on the top rope of the boxing ring as I faced my best friend, my husband. Even in the darkness, I caught the way Blake tracked my movements. Then, he started toward me, climbing into the ring and sinking into the chair in the opposite corner, draping one arm over the rope in a slight mimic of what I'd done.

"I told you not to move," he said without a single ounce of irritation. He didn't care.

"Had to," I breathed as I leaned forward in a stretch. Blake's eyes traced my body, and my eyes remained glued to his gaze, wanting to see his reactions. I only took my attention off him for a moment, spinning to stretch the other leg, giving him a nice view of my backside.

When I checked over my shoulder, I found Blake staring at me hungrily.

"I know." He sounded starved. My lips curved. He caught it, his brow raising at my expression. "You like having an audience, don't you, Lane?"

"I like having *you* as my audience," I corrected.

"Only me." It was a soft promise. "I'm the only one allowed to see you like this." His eyes flicked around the building before returning to me. "The power outage made sure of that. No security cameras. No lights. Doors are locked. Just you and me, baby."

"I like that." The way he was looking at me made me shiver. He was half-covered in shadows, and I wasn't used to seeing a side of Blake that could be a little bit dark, but I liked it. God, I liked it so much. "I think if I had you to watch me, maybe I never would have quit ballet."

"I could watch you forever, Lane." He ran his hand over his jawline, like he couldn't believe what he was seeing. "You're so fucking beautiful."

"I think you just have a thing for this T-shirt," I teased before leaning down to stretch the other side of my body.

"I definitely have a thing for *you* in that T-shirt," he said. "But I think the T-shirt itself would look even better on the floor."

I glanced back at him. "You think so, huh?"

"Yeah." His eyes flared as I lowered my leg and faced him, toying with the hem of the shirt and pretending to debate, even though I knew what I was going to do. "I think so."

I lifted the shirt over my head with a single swoop of my arms, tossing it to the side, over the boxing ring ropes, and Blake's pupils widened. His breathing quickened, his chest visibly rising and falling as he leaned forward to rest on his knees, watching me with an intensity that made my heart pound in my chest like I was preparing for a performance at Carnegie Hall and not nearly naked in a boxing ring on a tiny side street in Boston.

Blake lowered his voice and ordered, "Dance for me."

So I did.

I danced for him like this boxing ring was my stage, and he watched, enraptured by a truly sub-par show. My movements weren't fluid, and my limbs weren't capable of half of what they used to be, but it didn't matter. I felt connected in a way I never had before. I felt every beat of Blake's gaze. It radiated through me, causing my skin to flush and my nipples to harden against the lining of my bra.

When I paused with my leg raised and smiled at Blake, he rasped, "What is that called?"

"This is just a leg extension."

"One day, I'm going to fuck you in that position, Mrs. London. I don't think all that flexibility should go to waste."

"One day?" I questioned.

He shook his head. "I'm enjoying the show too much right now to interrupt it."

I lowered my leg and raised my hands above my head instead, letting my fingers trail my arms as they raised in a sensual, slow exploration. "I thought you wanted me, Mr. London."

"Oh, I do," Blake said, running his tongue over his bottom lip as he surveyed me. "I want to worship you from head to toe, Delaney. Appreciate every fucking inch of you. Right now, I'm doing it with my eyes. Soon, I'm going to do it with my hands. And then my mouth. And finally..."

He leaned back in the chair, leisurely throwing one arm back onto the ropes while he used his other hand to stroke his cock through his shorts.

My breath caught in my throat.

"You like that plan, don't you?" he asked, his lips cocking to one side.

"I'm a little impatient for the last part, if I'm honest." My attention remained fixed on his hand as it moved up and down his length. My mouth watered. "Maybe you should give me a sneak peek."

Blake's mouth transformed into a wicked grin as he yanked the waistband of his shorts down to let his cock spring out.

"This what you want, Lane?"

I bit my lip, transfixed by how he stroked himself. My arms fell limply back to my sides. "It's a good start."

Suddenly, things were moving too slowly for me.

"Delaney..." Blake stood, and my stomach flipped as he closed the distance between us, kicking his shorts to the ground and off to the side. "How long have I wanted you?"

"For a long time." My voice shook as I heard myself say that truth aloud. *For a long time.* Blake had wanted me for a long time. My head spun at the notion, but at the same time, it was so *comforting*.

When Blake got within reach, he rested his hands on my hips, his touch branding me. Hot. I was so hot.

"Be more specific."

His fingers found my hip bones, his thumb rubbing in tantalizing circles. I arched forward, wanting more of his touch, wanting to feel him. His other hand reached around my back, expertly undoing my bra. It loosened around my body, the straps sliding down my arms. My nipples brushed against his chest, and he moaned. I gasped.

"Since the day we met," I breathed, still dazed by those words.

I let my bra fall to the floor, forgotten.

"That's right." His hands wandered up my sides and then flattened on my abdomen, smoothing over my skin until he had my breasts in his palms, squeezing gently. I melted into him, and he stepped forward like he'd known I would need more of his support, like he'd known his touch would turn me into a puddle. "I've been a patient man, waiting for this day. It's your turn now, sweetheart."

Abruptly, he reached down and ripped the sides of my underwear in two pieces. Then, he dragged the fabric from my body, throwing the discarded material behind him. We'd littered the boxing ring with our clothes and stood naked in each other's arms. And God, I shook from how much I wanted him.

So much that relief flooded me when Blake tilted his hips and the tip of his cock nudged between my legs. Instinctively, I parted my thighs, and he wedged between them, sliding his cock against the outer lips of my pussy. I widened my stance further, and Blake pressed upward, making sure his length dragged over my clit, just like he had on the plane. My jaw dropped, my hips flexed, and I braced my hand on his chest before dragging it down, lower and lower. His muscles rippled beneath my fingers, and I wanted more of that, more of him.

"My turn to touch you?" I asked breathlessly.

But he shook his head. "To be patient."

"But Blake..." I tipped my head back as my body responded, fluttering to life with the feel of him as he gave a tiny thrust. "Oh my *God*."

"I'm not God, baby." Blake's breath flirted with my ear. "I'm your husband."

I clutched his shoulders with a sigh, urging my hips forward to try to chase more of him. "Please," I begged.

"Please what?"

I could *hear* his smirk but didn't even care enough to comment on it. He could be cocky about what he did to me because fuck, did he do things to me.

"Just...more. I want more."

Blake nibbled on my earlobe before murmuring, "If you want more of this cock, you can get on your knees."

Maybe I should be mad that he was denying me, but I was too eager to please, too giddy at the thought of exploring more of him. As long as I got to experience him in some capacity, I didn't care.

"It's going to be worth it, Lane," Blake promised, as though I needed encouragement. "The wait will be worth it. Just like it was worth it for me when I finally got to taste you for the first time."

"The kiss at our wedding?" I asked as I dropped to my knees in front of him, bouncing on the rubbery material beneath us.

Blake nodded, his gaze blazing as he watched me.

"That was a real kiss, Delaney." His voice was raw as he cupped the back of my head, fingers gently playing with my hair. "It was as real as I dared to make it."

"I know," I confessed. I'd always known. "It felt real."

Blake stilled at my response, and he looked like he wanted to ask more. But then I pressed my lips to his stomach, and he zeroed in on my mouth. On how I traced a path down his abdomen with my tongue, savoring the slightly salty taste of his skin. The heat of his body, the pulse just beneath his skin, I reveled in all of it, in all of him. And then when I fisted his erection without warning, a violent shudder ran through him, and I reveled in that, too. In what I could do to him. I licked at his tip, and Blake made a deep, guttural noise, causing that satisfaction to sink deeper inside me.

"Suck, Lane." He looked down at me with reverence in his eyes despite his brusque command, which was punctuated by another boom of thunder. "See how good my cock tastes with you all over it."

I did as he directed, looking up at him through my lashes as I sucked him slowly into my mouth, inch by inch. I could taste the muskiness of his scent combined with a hint of my own arousal, and there was something about it that made me feel tortured, made the agony of want and desire flow faster through my veins.

"Oh, hell." Blake pushed his fingers through my hair in an almost compulsive way, like his hands needed the reassurance that I was real. "You have no idea how satisfying it is for me to know, after years of having to sit back and watch other men flirt with you, that no one else will ever get to see you like this." His lips parted in awe as he looked down at me. "Isn't that right, Lane?"

I nodded, feeling more confident about that fact than ever, and then slipped his cock out of my mouth to answer him, even as he groaned at the pause. "The only man I get on my knees for is my husband."

Possession spiked in Blake's eyes. Lightning flashed across his face. "And who is your husband, Delaney?"

My lips curved. "You."

"That's a good little wife," he praised. It shot right through me.

I sucked him back into my mouth without delay, using one hand to twist around the base of his erection while the other reached between my legs, desperate for something to ease the ache, the unrelenting pulse that kept growing stronger and hotter.

"You can touch yourself," Blake grunted, watching me with his own brand of desperation. "But you can't finish."

I whimpered around his cock.

"I know, sweetheart," he soothed. "But trust me. Don't you trust me?"

I nodded.

More than anyone.

"That's my girl." He tipped his head back with a groan. "Fuck, you feel so good, Delaney. You're so, *so* good. And God, I need to come. I need to come so when I fuck you, I can take my goddamn

time. Your pussy always makes me lose it, but today, I need to—"
I took him all the way to the back of my throat, and Blake choked
on air, unable to speak until I popped him back out of my mouth
again.

"So you get to finish, but I don't?" I challenged, lifting a brow.

"You will, Lane." He raised a brow right back. "I thought you
trusted me."

I rolled my eyes and then returned to lavishing my tongue
around the tip of Blake's cock. He swallowed a moan and then
started speaking in a softness that made my body crawl with
need.

"Roll your eyes all you want, Mrs. London. I've never told you,
but I think that attitude you give me is hot as fuck. I want it *all*."

"Is it attitude?" I flicked my fingers between my legs faster,
feeling like something was clawing at my insides, needing to be
released. "Or have I just been secretly flirting with you all along?"

"Wasn't secret to me, baby." Blake's lips were soft as they
curled. "Glad you finally started to see it for what it was, though."

"Have you always known about my feelings?" I asked, pausing
all of my movements, too stunned by what he'd just said. "Even
when I didn't?"

He cupped my chin. "I always knew we had chemistry that
went beyond friends. Knew you acted on that chemistry from
time to time. But also knew you didn't see it for what it really
was."

"Not anymore. Now I know. Now I see it." I drew him back
into my mouth, and Blake cursed roughly, raking a hand through
his hair before it flopped back down over his forehead.

"That's it, sweetheart." His words were like velvet, but his
body was taut, like steel. "I want to feel the back of your throat."

I introduced him to it without a second thought, blinking
through the tears that sprang to my eyes. When he hit deeper
than he ever had before, I choked a bit, and Blake seized up,
gasping for air, same as me.

"*Shit*, Lane. I'm going to—" He couldn't even finish his

sentence. I nodded anyway, as if to say I was ready, but he shook his head. "Want to—" A groan interrupted his thought, and then he tried again. "Want to see how good your tits look with my cum on them. Can I?"

My brows shot up, but something bloomed inside me. Something that made my fingers crawl back between my legs, massaging the ache that suddenly had intensified.

I nodded again, and Blake released a hushed "*fuck*" like he hadn't actually thought I'd say yes.

A second later, he pulled out of my mouth with a grunt, stepped back, and shot his release across my body, coating me with it. His cum dripped down my chest, exactly the way he wanted it to. It was obscene, the way I loved it, loved him like this. I fought to catch my breath while obsessing over, well, Blake—the way shadows emphasized the lines of his body, how intoxicating his expression was while taking in the sight of me, getting drunker and drunker off it by the minute. His eyes devoured me, and he seemed unable to look away. But I didn't really want him to.

"Marking you as mine is never going to get old," he rasped. "I want you like this all the time." He swiped his fingers across the tips of my breasts, spreading his cum around my nipples. They tightened in response, pebbling from the desire that continued to bloom inside me, deeper, stronger. "Unbelievable," he breathed, barely audible.

His slow, hot perusal finally made its way to my face, and I lost my breath at the depth of his gaze. He looked *ruined*. And utterly delicious.

Blake began to trail his fingers up my body, and I instinctively opened my mouth. His eyes sparked, his lips curved, and he gave me what I wanted, sliding his fingers between my lips so I could taste him.

"It's so fucking hot the way you always want more of me, Lane."

He sounded disastrously awed.

I sucked around his fingers, and he moaned as he drew them out of my mouth.

"But now it's my turn, okay? Let me see those fingers that have been buried in your pussy."

I slipped my hand from between my legs, swallowing a needy noise as I grazed my clit one final time. Blake watched eagerly, hungrily, gripping my wrist as soon as I held it out for him and bringing my fingers to his lips. Without another word, he sucked them into his mouth, licking each finger clean with a moan of appreciation that I felt deep in my bones.

"*God yes.*" His grin made my stomach flutter when he flashed it at me, his eyes hooded with lazy desire. "Thank fuck it's my turn to get you in my mouth, baby. Because that taste is so fucking good."

I watched wordlessly as he sank to his knees. We faced each other, eye level, on equal ground. Cupping my cheek in his palm, Blake leaned forward and brushed a tender kiss across my lips, making me shiver.

"Blake," I whimpered.

"I'm here, sweetheart."

"Always?"

"As long as you want me to be."

"So always, then."

He looked at me like I was the pinnacle of his existence. "Say it again."

"Always, Blake," I whispered. "I always want you to be here."

"Then that's where I'll be. Here." He raked his gaze over my face and then let it drop, along with his voice. "And right now, more specifically, between your legs."

He used a single finger to push me onto my back, and I unfolded my legs so they were bent in front of me. Meanwhile, Blake kissed his way down my body, pausing to suck a nipple into his mouth, causing me to arch against his lips with a cry. I'd been dying for this, been aching for this, for the heat of his mouth, for the wetness and the warmth. Then he moved lower, swirling his tongue around my belly button, nipping at my lower stomach, and kissing my inner thighs. And all the while, he was chanting praises about how beautiful I was, how much he loved me, and I wanted to cry. By the time his mouth made it between my legs, I shook beneath him.

"*Please*," I begged.

"Patience, Delaney," he ordered like it was the simplest thing in the world.

"I can't wait any longer."

"Yes, you can." He kissed the spot just above my clit before dragging his tongue lower and then stopping. *Goddamn him.* I chased his mouth with my hips, bucking upward to get more.

"You're so fucking incredible," he mused, sounding only half-conscious, like part of him was stuck in a dream. "So fucking responsive. It's because it aches, doesn't it?" He traced his tongue in a featherlight pattern, tracing everywhere except where I really wanted him, and sounds came out of me that I didn't even know I could make.

"So bad," I panted.

He pulled back, spread me open, and spat on my clit. "I'll make it better, but you have to be good for me."

I gasped and repeated for what felt like the millionth time, "*Please*."

He swirled his spit around my pussy and then abruptly sucked my clit into his mouth in response, making me throw my head back with a scream. It echoed off the walls, mixing in with the sounds of the rain pounding against the windows. Blake didn't stop, either. He tongued my pussy relentlessly, until I was writhing against him, *so* close to the edge, and then, to my utter despair, he stopped.

As quick as the pleasure came, it left. I looked down to see Blake sitting back on his heels, looking at me with an unreadable expression. His lips cocked to one side before he wiped at his mouth with the back of his hand, and I'd never felt more attracted to him and frustrated with him before in my life.

"Are you trying to edge me?" I cried.

Blake grinned.

"No, baby. I *am* edging you."

I stared at him, momentarily speechless, and his grin simply grew.

"If it's too much, you can tell me. At any time, okay?" I nodded, and he checked, "Is it too much?"

Slowly, I shook my head, even though I really wanted to tell him it was. It was too much, and my body pulsed in ways that I didn't fully understand. But earlier, I promised him that I trusted him. And I did. I trusted Blake with everything in me.

"Good girl." Blake gave me an appreciative once-over before he leaned forward, pressed a kiss to my temple, and nuzzled his lips close to my ear. "On your hands and knees, Lane."

I hesitated for only a moment before adjusting my position, desperate for a release, *needing* it, however he wanted to give it to me.

"Fuck, look at you," Blake rasped, tracing the length of my spine with his fingertip. Goose bumps broke out across my body. "You can grab onto the ropes if you need."

"If I need?"

"If you need something to hang on to while you sit on my face."

He gripped my hips before I had time to comprehend his words, tugging me down toward the floor at the same time I felt his breath tease between my legs. And then the flat of his tongue returned to lapping my clit, and I gasped, throwing my head down with an unrestrained moan.

Blake echoed my moan, releasing his own between my legs as he savored me. The vibrations from his throat bounced inside me, creating a palpable effect of how badly we both ached. How intense our connection was. And if the way he was eating me wasn't enough, that sure did it.

Especially when he tightened his grip on my hips and dragged me lower. "*Sit*, Delaney."

His demand was muffled but clear in its interpretation.

I dropped my weight down, letting my pussy drag over his mouth as he sucked and licked and lapped, and *fuck*.

"*Yes*," he grunted, but it was barely audible. Because I'd done what he asked, and I'd *sat*. Blake's face was my personal throne at the moment, and I was taking my rightful seat on it.

And *God*, did it feel good.

One of his hands trailed to my ass, giving it a little smack that sent a jolt of nuclear pleasure through me. And when I whimpered in response, Blake did it again. And again, until I'd undoubtedly soaked his face, and I was so, *so*—

Blake suddenly disappeared, and I collapsed forward with a sob.

Too lost in the ghostly sensations of what I'd been so close to feeling, I was barely conscious of the fact that Blake was flipping me over, not until his handsome face appeared above mine. He breathed ragged reassurances as he gazed down at me, his expression both carnal and tender at the same time. He took one of my hands and anchored it above my head and then did the same thing with the other one until he had me pinned beneath him, our bodies flush.

It was the safest I'd ever felt.

"Please tell me you're going to fuck me now," I pleaded, feeling accomplished that I'd strung together so many words.

"Is that what you want?" He swirled his hips against mine, rutting his erection between my legs in a teasing sort of way. "You want my cock in your tight little pussy?"

"Want that." I spread my legs, just in case it wasn't obvious. "Please."

I was so sure that I'd cry if he didn't give it to me. It was unbearable, the way I wanted him. The way I *loved* him.

"Oh, baby." His voice was husky. I wanted to drown in it. "I want it, too. You have no fucking clue the way I want you."

I tipped my hips up to feel again how hard he was. "I think I do."

But Blake shook his head, squeezing his eyes shut for a moment like he couldn't look at me like this for too long without losing it. "You asked me before, you wanted to know why I haven't slept with anyone since med school," he rasped, his words coming out stilted, like he hadn't parsed them out first but needed to say them. "It's you, Lane. It's because I met you. And I couldn't imagine ever being with someone who wasn't you."

My heart lurched in my chest.

I gaped at him, breathing his name because it was the only thing I could get myself to say. And then my jaw dropped further when the blunt head of his cock nudged between my legs, slipping inside me. I braced myself, feeling the tingle of anticipation, the delicious stretch of my body accepting him. But then he stopped.

I knew immediately that this wasn't like the other times Blake had left me on the edge tonight. This was different; Blake's shallow breaths and the tautness of his mouth as he gritted his teeth told me that much. There was no smirk, no gleam in his eyes.

"*Fuck*, Delaney," he swore, hanging his head as he squeezed his eyes shut again.

"Don't stop," I begged, inhaling shakily. "Just let go, Blake. You told me you would."

"I will." Blake opened his eyes, sending an electric current through me when they collided with mine. He shook his head before dropping to give me a fierce kiss. "Nothing's stopping us now, baby. Nothing. Just—give me a second."

I wiggled my hips because *a second* sounded like a really long time, and I was desperate for friction.

"*Delaney*," he growled.

"I don't think I can wait." I needed to feel him inside me, needed that connection. "I don't think I can do it anymore."

He sucked in a breath. "Now you know what it's been like for me," he said, and he was right—I could *feel* his agony. But then he abruptly thrust his cock the rest of the way in, making me cry from the ecstasy of it. He was so deep and so perfect, and it was everything I'd ever wanted. "For so *fucking* long, Lane."

I gasped before whimpering, "I'm sorry."

"Fuck, don't apologize. Just—" He broke off with a groan as I clenched around him, feeling greedy for the feel of it.

"I love you," I whispered.

Because that was all I could do, wasn't it?

I couldn't change the past, but I could love him fully now, love him out loud the way he deserved.

"Oh my God." Blake laced our fingers together and gripped tight as he drove his hips home, smacking them against mine. My eyes rolled back, but then I quickly found his gaze again, needing to see the warmth of them, the fervor in them, the glow and warmth. "I love you so much, Delaney." He thrust again, harder. "So." And again. "Fucking." And again. "Much."

He snapped his hips one more time, and I crumbled, reaching my climax and then falling over its peak in a way that was a shock to my system. The orgasm blazed through me, setting fire to everything I'd ever known about Blake and me and letting it burn into something new. It went on and on, spasms of pleasure reaching parts of me I didn't know existed. Blake pushed me further, thrusting through my downfall and wringing every ounce of satisfaction from it that he could, until I was spent.

"That's a good girl." Lips grazed mine, and my eyes fluttered shut. "Love feeling you come on my cock, baby."

I tried to catch my breath, tried to slow the heartbeat I could feel in the tips of my toes and pads of my fingers. Blake slowly rolled his hips over mine in a lazy, unrushed way as I came down and found myself again. One of his hands let go of mine and snaked down my body instead, like he wanted to both soothe me and resurrect me. He palmed my breast, kneading it while brushing his thumb over my nipple. A breathy mewl left my lips as I pushed myself up, wanting more of it, more of his touches.

"Beautiful," Blake breathed. "Just beautiful."

He made me feel it.

I tipped my hips, experimenting with fucking him back, loving the friction of our bodies sliding against each other, in and out.

Blake swore softly before pushing himself upward and onto his knees. He grabbed my hips to help me find the right rhythm and then increased his pace, letting our bodies slap together as his breathing grew ragged. I watched as Blake dropped his eyes, studying how we fit together, how his cock drove in and out of my body, the perfect two pieces of a puzzle. Each of us tethered to the other. A litany of curses fell from Blake's lips, a chant that told me this was what would send him over his own edge, seeing this, watching us.

His gaze pierced me when he looked up. I nearly choked on the raw emotion in its depths.

"Are you going to take my cum in your sweet cunt, Lane?" he asked, his voice full of gravel and grit.

I nodded. *Yes*, yes I wanted that. "I'm still on the pill," I reassured.

But Blake shook his head and leaned back down over my body, his thrusts hitting harder and deeper and faster as he found my ear with his lips. "I wish you weren't."

I groaned. I wasn't sure why or what was happening, but those words shot straight to my core, and I felt my body tightening around him again.

"You liked that," Blake muttered, more to himself than to me. He sounded awed, like my reaction was unfathomable. But I could tell the moment he comprehended it completely because a rough "*shit*" left his lips, and he drove into me with renewed passion.

"You're so *fucking* perfect for me, Delaney." He sounded utterly destroyed by that thought, and I understood. Christ, I understood.

Everything about the moment spurred me back into action, meeting each of his thrusts with a renewed desperation. Blake's eyes rolled back into his head, and I could practically feel his pulse radiating inside me, how it increased, crescendoed with every movement, with each collision of his hard body and my soft one.

"*Again*," Blake demanded—the only word he seemed to be able to get out as he pounded me against the floor of the boxing ring. But I knew exactly what he meant.

He came violently, and I followed him, gasping for air as I hit an even higher peak than I had before.

My name left Blake's lips in a stream of words I didn't fully catch, too busy crying my own vocal cords raw. But I did hear when Blake pumped his hips one last time and murmured, "You take me so good, Lane. You're so good to me, letting me fill you up."

All I could muster was a soft whine as a response.

"Yeah?"

I felt his gentle chuckle brushing against the skin of my neck before he kissed my pulse point.

"So good," I repeated on a sigh.

Blake rearranged us, and somehow, my head was suddenly being cradled against his chest.

I heard distant thunder.

But I wasn't sure if it was from the storm outside.

Or the roar of Blake's heart, pounding against my ear.

Steady.

Strong.

An echo of mine.

Forever attached to his.

CHAPTER THIRTY
blake

D ELANEY FELL ASLEEP IN my arms before I could even pull out of her, and all I could do was stare at her. Touch her. Run my fingers through her hair. Watch the rise and fall of her chest.

The idea that maybe I would get to love her like this for the rest of our lives blanketed me. What a concept, a comfort, a dream.

No wonder she could sleep so peacefully, knowing the same truths as me.

I wasn't sure how long we lay on the canvas of the boxing ring, entangled and sweaty and messy, but I could have stayed there all night.

When the rain reduced to a soft patter and the power flickered back on in the gym, I gently shook Delaney, rousing her just enough to quickly clothe her. And then I let her crash into my arms again, carrying her out to my car and driving us home.

She fell asleep against the window.

Garbled words fell from her lips as I brought her into our apartment, carrying her bridal-style like that first night she came here. The first night she came home.

"Baby," I whispered over the top of her head. "Can you wake

up enough to let me wash you?" She buried her face deeper in my chest, and I chuckled. "If you just stand in the shower, I'll do the rest of the work."

"That still sounds like a lot of work," she said, her voice muffled against my shirt.

"Lane, I made a mess out of you," I pointed out, feeling my cock stiffen again at the thought.

"Mmm," she hummed as though she liked the thought of that just as much as me. As though she was debating how she really felt about it. Like maybe she wanted to stay like this. Like she wanted to be mine in every single fucking way.

It was painful, the way my body reacted to that.

"Fine," Delaney sighed eventually, but she wasn't acting like she was happy about it. She disappeared back into my shirt and then reluctantly slid to the floor once we made it to the bathroom.

I turned the shower on, and once it was warm enough, I stripped Delaney's clothes off and guided her inside.

Washing her body as she smiled sleepily, her blue eyes twinkling, was quite possibly the most relaxed and at peace I'd ever been. I only had to pretend that just being near her like this, feeling her curves beneath my hands, and seeing her slowly awaken beneath my touch didn't make me feel like I was just a walking bottomless pit of desire when it came to her.

Lucky for me, Delaney noticed me hardening and slid her hand over my erection, pumping it up and down. And then she turned around and let me fuck her slowly against the shower wall before coming around my cock for the third time tonight.

She slumped against me afterward, murmuring that she loved me, and I didn't know if I would ever recover from what had happened in the last few hours.

Our tether pulled tighter.

From my heart to hers.

Delaney laughed that she could handle walking to our bed, but I didn't want to lose the chance to carry her over every threshold the way a husband would, without any pretense or lies.

So I lifted her in my arms and walked her through the apartment to our room.

It was our room now.

Our bed.

I'd settle that in the morning, just in case she had any funny ideas about still living out of the guest bedroom.

That was for guests.

But this was her home.

Until we picked out a new one together, somewhere down the line.

Reason and logic told me I was rushing things in my mind, but my heart said otherwise. My heart told me that this was right. The timing was right, everything was right.

"Thank you," Delaney whispered to me once we were wrapped around each other in bed.

I shook my head. "I don't even know what you're thanking me for this time, but you've got to stop. 'Thank you' is for favors, and absolutely nothing I have done for you has been a favor. It's all been things I've wanted. If anyone should be saying thank you right now, it should be me."

Delaney's lips curved in a smile, unfazed by my sharp insistence. Same as usual.

She didn't say anything for several long moments. We sort of just stared at each other, stuck in a dazed existence. Her mind whirred, but the pace was slower than normal; I could see it in her eyes, a slow settling of reality.

"I don't know what I'm going to do if my parents refuse to approve the inheritance," she said, momentarily sobering.

My stomach dropped at the reminder. "Well," I started, grabbing her hand from beneath the covers and pressing a kiss on the back of it before brushing my lips across her ring. It pained me to say, but... "We could sell this. It would give you a good amount to start your foundation on, and then we could seek out investors or—"

"What? *No.*"

Delaney snatched her hand back like she thought I might take her ring off and pawn it right this very second.

My lips stretched in the start of a smile. "No?"

"No, I'm not—" She frowned, looking down at the ring before tucking her hand close to her chest, keeping it away from me. "I'm not selling it."

I lifted a brow. "It's worth a lot of money, Delaney. I wasn't lying."

"Yeah, but—" She thought about it. For just a moment, she thought about it. But then she settled on an emphatic "*No*."

I put my hands up in mock defense while my grin grew unrestrainable. "Okay, okay."

She swatted at my chest. "Stop it. It's not funny. I don't know why you're smiling."

I grabbed her hand and kissed her palm. "You're right. It's not funny. But it makes me happy you want to keep the ring. And even more than that, it makes me happy that you're choosing yourself for once. I'm so proud of you for being selfish."

Her brows furrowed. "I don't know how to feel about that statement."

"Good," I assured her. "You should feel good."

Delaney sighed, looking up at the ceiling. "I still very much want to open this clinic, Blake. It's the mo—" She cut herself off, biting down on her lip before glancing over at me. "It's one of the most important things to me."

It was amazing that I hadn't yet gone into cardiac arrest tonight.

"Tell me more about these important things."

"Well...there's you."

A rattling in my chest made it hard to think. "There's me."

"You come first, and this ring..." She slipped the band off to study it. "It has too much of you in it to ever give up."

Funny that she thought it had too much of me when I'd begged my mom to give it to me because it had so much of *her*. It was made for her.

Made for us, I suppose.

"What else is important to you, Delaney?"

I wanted to know everything.

"Other...things." She chewed on the inside of her cheek as she thought. "Things I'm still trying to puzzle out."

I nodded. "I'll be here when you do."

I had a suspicion of what they might be, but I wasn't going to push her.

"Also." Delaney perked up. "I think I'd like to travel more."

"Yeah?"

"Yeah," she repeated shyly. "Our trip brought me more joy than I can honestly ever remember experiencing before."

All I could do was smile, feeling like I was going to burst. The rattling in my chest intensified.

"What?"

"Nothing." I shook my head. "That's just, that's all I wanted for you when I planned it. All I've wanted you to have."

She laughed. "A work-life balance?"

"Something like that, yeah."

"Thank—"

"Don't." I pressed a finger to her lips. "Don't you even dare."

Moonlight streamed through the bedroom window, making her eyes glitter. Her lips tempted me, swollen from all the time I'd already spent kissing them tonight. But I knew I shouldn't interrupt this conversation. Nothing was more important than the thoughts, the words, the worries she had right now. And I didn't want to do anything to push those down when they were just coming up to see the light.

"Everything will work out, Delaney. If we can't get your inheritance money, then we'll find another way. There's always another way." I shrugged. "I do have a massively wealthy brother who has been known to make philanthropic donations. Mostly to animal shelters, but I think he might be open to adding a new foundation to his list."

Delaney laughed but immediately shook her head. "Absolutely not. The last thing I will ever do is become one of those women who dates you and also wants something from your brother."

"*Dates*?" I repeated with a scoff. "Baby, we're married."

She rolled her eyes. "You know what I mean."

"I do. I do know." I grinned. "And actually, I've been meaning to ask you if you'd let me take you out soon."

"Take me out?"

"On a date." I brushed my fingers over her lips, tracing them lightly. "I'd really like to take my wife on a date."

"Okay." She nipped at my fingertip teasingly. "What dress would my husband like me to wear on our date? The red one from Amsterdam or the black one from graduation?"

Flashes of Delaney stripping that red dress off her body danced through my head, and I had to swallow hard before I could talk.

"Fuck, I have to choose?"

"Yeah." Her grin was wicked. "You have to choose."

I pictured the black dress next. Pictured it on Delaney. Then pictured it on the floor for the very first time and sucked in a breath.

"I think maybe I'll just have to take my wife on two dates, then," I decided.

"That would work, too."

"Glad you agree." My fingers moved to trace her jawline. And then her neck. And her collarbone. I wanted to commit the lines of her body to memory. "And then I can buy her more dresses."

"And go on more dates?"

"Exactly." I still hadn't wrapped my head around the fact that this wasn't a dream. "It's like you can read my mind."

She pursed her lips before correcting, "I think I can finally read your heart."

Finally.

"You have always been a very talented cardiologist, Dr. Delacroix."

Delaney shook her head, and when she spoke, her voice was thick.

"Why the hell did it take two cardiologists this long to figure out the way each other's hearts worked?"

I was speechless for a moment, swallowing regret, pushing it down and refusing to let it sour this moment.

"That sounds like the beginning of a joke," Delaney added, a shaky laugh following her words. It didn't sound convincing.

"I don't know if I find it funny."

"No, maybe not funny." Delaney sighed, snuggling in closer to me. "But at least it has a happy ending."

"Yeah, baby." I kissed the top of her head. "It does."

one year ago

DELANEY

I thought I'd caught a glimpse of Blake at least five times since walking into this football stadium, but as it turned out, there were a lot of men over six feet tall with dark, wavy hair in Minneapolis.

But I knew he was probably here somewhere.

His brother was playing in town tonight.

I was sure he wouldn't miss it.

Honestly, it felt weird not knowing whether or not he was here. But it wasn't really any of my concern since I'd come with Austin. The man I was engaged to. The man I'd be married to for a whole year—if only in a legal sense. He said he had tickets, and I jumped at the opportunity.

I wasn't really a fan of football.

But it was a good chance to get to know Austin a little better ahead of our impending nuptials. Because either way, even if my engagement to Austin was fake, I should likely spend time focused on him.

And less time searching for Blake London in the crowds.

But even as I told myself that, I saw him.

He was surrounded by two guys—his other younger brothers. All three of them were staring intently at the women's bathroom like they were waiting on someone.

I wondered who it was.

Blake did a double take when I walked up to him, like he hadn't expected to run into me at a football game of all places, and I couldn't really blame him.

"Lane," he breathed, his brows furrowing.

His two brothers stood taller, turning with a bit of surprise to look at me, too.

I was pretty sure the blonder one's name was Sully and the other, Theo. We'd only met once or twice before. They both lived in the cities, a little more than an hour from where Blake and I lived in Rochester.

"I have to go find Austin, but I saw you in the crowd and just wanted to say hi!" I said, knowing my voice sounded overly bright.

Maybe that was why Blake's frown deepened.

Then he cleared his throat.

"You're here with Austin."

"Yeah, he's a big...fan."

Of which team, I honestly wasn't sure.

Blake nodded. "Right."

This was feeling a lot more awkward than I'd expected.

"I hope Noah has a good game," I said with a smile, looking between Blake and his brothers. They flashed me polite smiles between continued glances at the women's bathroom. Huh.

"I think he's going to have a great game, considering the company in the stands tonight," Sully said before snickering to himself like there was an inside joke that I didn't fully have the context for.

"I'm sure he's happy to have you all here." I looked back to Blake. "I'll see you soon, yeah?"

I needed that reassurance. It had been a few days since we'd talked. I didn't like it.

"Yeah." Blake swallowed and smiled at me, but it seemed forced. Like the smile he gave other people. Not the smile he gave me. "I'll see you soon, Lane."

Something seized up in my chest as I walked away—some kind of malfunction that I was sure textbooks wouldn't be able to diagnose.

But I was sure it was nothing.

Just a bit of nerves. For meeting with Austin tonight.

It was a nervous system problem.

Definitely not a cardiovascular thing.

Definitely not.

CHAPTER THIRTY-ONE

A FEW DAYS LATER, I learned that for once in his life, my dad stood up to my mom on my behalf. It was not something I'd expected, and I was sure it hadn't gone over well.

My grandparents made the inheritance decision contingent upon my parents' approval, but knowing what a pushover my dad had always been when it came to matters involving my mother's wishes, especially regarding their children, I never thought his opinion would be the important one.

But it was *his* parents' will. And apparently, he'd told my mom that enough was enough.

I could have my inheritance.

My dad called to deliver the good news, which was doubly shocking. I'd expected an email. But he said something that made me think he'd been a little hurt by the notion that he hadn't been there for my wedding, even if it was an elopement.

He said he didn't want to miss anything else.

He knew if they denied me this, he'd miss everything.

I wanted to ask where he'd been when I had my college graduation or when I'd celebrated getting my first job but held my tongue. I knew it was because my ambitions didn't align with the ones he'd arbitrarily created for me, but marriage was something that had traditional value to him. And so that was what he cared about.

He also admitted to liking Blake. He appreciated his honesty at dinner and said that his job was respectable.

Which I found ironic.

Respectable *for a man*, I suppose.

He wanted us to come to dinner more often, which surprised me the most out of everything.

I said I'd think about it.

I wasn't sure I was ready for that kind of commitment, considering how the last one had gone and the odd, resentful heartache of simply visiting home, but I'd think about it.

Blake and I went out to dinner to celebrate the news—our first official date, outside of the evening in Amsterdam. Because Blake had since made it clear that that *had* been a date.

He decided on the black dress, saying he'd already gotten a chance to peel the red one off my body, and now he wanted to do the same with the black one.

I couldn't argue with that logic.

On our second official date, Blake surprised me by booking us dancing lessons. He claimed they were mostly for his benefit; he wanted to be able to keep up with me on the dance floor.

I cried when he told me.

Maybe a little dramatic, but he'd broken through a dam. He'd found the parts of me that I'd walled off because I didn't think I wanted them. But I did. I just wanted to experience them on my own terms, in my own way, with people who didn't pressure me and fought for me instead.

For our third date, I asked Blake to teach me how to box. I thought it was only fair. And the smirk that had slipped onto his face in response had made my request worth it, even if I soon learned my punching aim was awful.

"Do you know why I got into boxing?" he asked me as we walked out of the gym afterward and onto the Boston streets, where brick buildings lined the cobblestone. Humidity soaked the midsummer night air, making me stickier than when we'd been working up a sweat with the bags.

I shook my head, and Blake sighed.

"I needed a distraction," he admitted. "Needed something to obsess over that wasn't you."

My steps faltered; my breathing hitched. Everything about my existence seemed to skip a beat. It was painful knowing that Blake had gone through that. That I'd put him through that unknowingly. I suspected I'd always feel guilty about what I hadn't known, what I probably should have figured out years ago.

"Did it work?" I asked.

He responded with a low, rumbling chuckle. "I'm always going to be obsessed with you, Lane."

My stomach betrayed me, flipping and turning.

"But it did help me channel some of my...frustrations," he added carefully.

"Yeah?"

"Yeah." He glanced down at me. "Which was especially helpful once you moved in with me. Sometimes you walked around in your fucking towel, Lane. Christ, it was like you were trying to kill me."

I bit down on a guilty grin.

"I realized I liked it more than just being a distraction, though," Blake went on. "It was good for my body, good for my mind. I needed that. Something I could do for me, to be better. I spent a lot of time visualizing what my perfect future might look like without doing the work to create it for myself. I needed to try something new, push myself a bit and live outside my carefully constructed patterns."

"So you decided you wanted to punch people?"

Blake's lips twitched. "It's not about punching but learning to take calculated risks. Sometimes it's okay to let things get a little messy. Coloring inside the lines doesn't always create a pretty picture."

"Calculated risks, huh?"

"Yeah." Blake's eyes wandered my face. "Calculated risks."

"Would you consider asking your best friend to marry you a calculated risk?"

"It was definitely a risk." Blake nodded. "Not sure how much time I really spent calculating it, though. I was too worried you'd end up engaged to someone else again if I didn't get that ring on your finger as fast as possible."

"I'm glad you took the risk," I said, meaning it with every ounce of my being. "Even if our relationship did get a little...messy there for a bit."

"I was scared of that," Blake confessed. "For so many years, I'd been scared of blurring the line of our friendship. And that was exactly where we ended up anyway. For a terrifying few hours, I thought I ruined everything."

"I think we've always been a little blurry, Blake. Has it ever *really* been clear?"

He shook his head. "No, not before now. But I think I *wanted* clear. Watching my parents' divorce scared me away from the messy bits of a relationship. I hated the thought of getting messy with you and losing you. God, losing you was all I was ever worried about. Even if that meant I only got to have you as a friend."

"I get it," I assured him. "But I don't think you realize, Blake."

He paused on the street corner, giving me his full attention. The streetlamp behind him created a halo around his frame, making him glow. "What?"

"If you want to get rid of me, you're going to have to cut me loose," I warned. But it wasn't really a warning—more like an attempt to dispel any remaining fears he might have about us. "I'm too tied up in you to break free, even if we get pulled in different directions again."

Blake's gaze warmed. He stepped forward, backing me against a brick wall and bracing his hand against it so he could lean in, showering me with his stomach-flipping intensity. "I'm going to hold you to that."

I blinked up at him, feeling my throat tighten. "Just don't let go, okay?"

"Never, Lane." He rested his forehead against mine. "Fucking never."

"Things might get messy every now and again, Blake." This time, it really was a warning. "I'm not as perfect as you. And—"

"Shut up," he grunted, shaking his head.

"I mean it. If you're still scared of what might happen—"

He pressed a finger to my lips. "I'm not scared anymore."

"No?"

"No," he said firmly. "Because getting messy with you was the best thing that ever happened to me, Delaney. And I'm never going to let my hesitation and fears get in the way of us again."

"Me either," I whispered against his touch.

Blake replaced his finger with his lips, and I silently vowed to myself that I'd never let my own fears hold me back, either. From Blake or anything.

Blake and I celebrated our first anniversary by driving to a very important plot of land.

It wasn't much to look at right now, but someday, it would be a clinic. Our clinic.

There was a lot of hard work ahead of us, a lot of preparation and long hours. The groundwork itself was daunting. But exhilarating at the same time. And the most exciting part was getting to have Blake by my side.

He'd assured me that he hadn't been lying the day he'd proposed at Giovanni's; he wanted to expand the medical community and work together to do it. He wanted to surround himself with the best of the best and then create a place of hope for patients. He wanted to save lives; I knew he did.

And this was where we were going to do it—in the outskirts of Boston, settled not too far from the bay.

I stared at the water, watching it lap against the shore, our feet grounded in soil where one day our front entrance might be.

"Are you sure?" I asked.

I didn't have to explain my thinking. Blake stood beside me, staring just as intently at the ocean. But his expression was calm, his body relaxed. Stoic, despite the energy that hummed between us. I wasn't really sure what it meant, but it felt good.

"I'm sure," he said simply.

"You'll have to see it every day," I pointed out, even though we'd had a conversation like this before.

I just needed him to be sure.

Nothing was more important than this.

Than Blake.

"I know." He cocked his head to the side, considering the water. "I like to think it's honoring her. It's honoring how many people who will be helped or saved because of her and the path she inspired me to take. Because of her and because of Bryan."

Warmth filled me.

"Do you still dream of her?"

"Sometimes," he admitted, which surprised me.

He'd never told me. And I'd never woken up to find him like I had that night on our honeymoon.

But then Blake added, "It doesn't always end the same way, though. Sometimes taking a risk and jumping into the water to try to save her...it works. It's a bit cruel because when I wake up, I'm reminded of reality. That she's gone, and I failed. But I also think it's a reminder that sometimes the risk of doing something is better than the risk of doing nothing. In the end, I'm still glad that I jumped into the water. That risk was still worth it, and in another scenario, taking that risk might have changed everything."

"I like that." I surveyed the land around us. "We're definitely doing something here, Blake."

"We sure are." Blake cleared his throat. "Hey, Lane?"

Something about the emotion in his voice made me spin toward him, a swiftness in my bones. And a second later, I knew why.

Blake was on his knees.

"What—what are you doing?" I choked, the wind knocked out of me.

His grin had a softness to it. "You wouldn't let me do this the first time around, so I had to sneak down here before you stopped me."

"The first time around?" I repeated.

Finding new words? Impossible.

"Proposing, Delaney." The corner of his mouth quirked. "I'm proposing."

All I could do was stare at him. "But we're already married."

He sighed. "I was really hoping that there'd be less arguing if I did this properly."

"I'm not—" I hiccupped into a laugh and then covered my hand over my mouth, sealing my lips shut.

Blake's lips curved into a full-fledged smile. And then he readjusted himself a little bit, leaning one of his elbows on his knees and piercing me with a gaze that took my breath clean away.

"This all started so that we could get here," he said. "To this day, to this point. But now that we're here, I need to make it clear right now that this is not the end. This is just the very beginning, baby."

I swallowed and managed to whisper, "I like the sound of that."

He closed his eyes momentarily, like he was savoring my response. "You don't know how fucking happy it makes me to hear that."

"Yes," I blurted, wanting to skip to the part where I got to say that.

"I'm not done," Blake said, giving me a look that seemed to be a warning. "There's more."

"More than getting to stay married to you?" I countered, clutching a hand to my chest. "That's already a lot. That's already perfect."

"Yeah, Lane," he insisted. "Because I don't just want to stay married to you. I want to remarry you."

"You...what?"

"I want to remarry you," he repeated firmly. "I don't care where or when or who comes. I don't care if it's in the same court-house or at a vineyard with endless bottles of your favorite white wine. I don't care if our whole family comes or if we don't invite anyone at all. I don't care if it's tomorrow or in a year. But I want it to be on our terms. I want to buy you a wedding dress that you *love*, Lane. I want to take you on a honeymoon that isn't a single bit fake. I want to say 'I do' and then fuck you in a bridal suite like it's our first time. I know you've never wanted to get married, but goddamn, marrying you is all I've ever dreamed of. I chose to go on this wild ride with you because I wanted to, so fucking much. You did it because you felt like you had to. I want you to get a chance to choose this time. I want you to decide if marrying me is really what you want, and then I want to do it the right way if it is."

He'd rendered me powerless to my own body, his words breaking down functions inside me. My heart roared, my breathing stuttered, my vision blurred. He'd said so many things, and I couldn't think of one coherent thought, one single thing that could even begin to convey how he made me feel.

"Delaney, I love you," he said in a final sort of way.

I dropped to my knees, meeting him on the ground. On *our* ground. "I love you, too. I love you so much, Blake."

"And that's all I really need, sweetheart." He cupped my face between his hands. "Your love. But if you want more than that..."

I nodded aggressively. "I do."

"Stop skipping ahead," he said cheekily, giving me a wink. Then he released my face and fished in his pocket for something, pulling out a small jewelry box.

"Blake…" I shook my head. Because he'd already given me the most gorgeous ring in the world. "What's that?"

"It's a wedding band. But if you want to put it on now, you can put it on now. You're already my wife. But I'm still going to ask." He popped the box open to reveal a perfect single band. "Will you marry me? Marry me again, Lane."

"Yes," I breathed as tears filled my lash line.

"Yes, what, Lane?" he pressed gently. "I need to hear more."

"Yes, I want to marry you, Blake." The tears had broken free, streaming down my face. I wiped at them, but it was no use. "Again and a million times over. I'll choose you every single time you ask, okay?"

He was smiling at me. It was *my* smile. "More than fucking okay."

I watched as Blake lifted the ring, holding it out to me as if checking whether I wanted to wear it now. And fuck yes, I wanted to wear it now. At the very least, try it on. I held out my hand for him, and he slid it onto my finger.

Unsurprisingly, it was a perfect fit.

My mind reeled as I thought back through everything he had said, imagining a wedding. A full-blown wedding where I got to marry Blake. *Re*marry Blake.

"I get to pick out my own wedding dress?" I asked, still processing this reality.

He nodded. "I thought that might make you happy."

"*You* make me happy, Blake."

It wasn't about the dress. It was about the choices. And I knew he understood that.

"I know, baby," he reassured. "But it's okay to want the whole experience, too. To want more for yourself and for us."

I worried my bottom lip as my brain continued to race through the future, thinking about the things that lay ahead for me and Blake. I loved every bit of it. And I just wanted to make sure *he* loved every bit of it, too. He was letting me choose. I knew in my bones he deserved that same right.

"What?" he probed, studying my expression carefully.

"What about...kids?" I ventured, sitting back on my heels and considering him. "I know you want them, and I—I'm still thinking."

"I want a family," he said like it was a correction. "Delaney, it's only ever been you. I only want kids if it's with you. And if that's not what you want, then we'll create our own family. Our family is us. It's me and you and Bryan and all my siblings and all the kids they're going to have. Our family can be whatever we want it to be."

I stared at him, in awe of who he was and how much he meant to me. And not for the first time, I saw myself thinking that it would be a damn shame if I didn't let this man give me the kind of family I always wanted to have myself but never dared to dream about because I didn't trust anyone enough to give it to me. But after everything we'd been through, and especially recently, I trusted Blake. With my life, with all of it. That much I knew.

"You'd be a really good dad, Blake." The words carried in the wind. "Sometimes I think you were born to be a dad."

"You'd be an amazing mom, Lane." He swallowed, and I saw something shine in his gaze. "And I know I was born to love you. And every part of you. Maybe that includes your kids. Maybe not."

"Our kids," I amended. I wouldn't be having my kids; I'd be having our kids.

"Our kids," Blake repeated, looking like he was struggling to contain himself at the thought.

My heart damn near exploded.

"I have so much I want to do." I stared at the empty plot of land, letting my eyes trace every rock, every pebble that lay upon it. "This clinic might be my baby for a while, but then..."

"Babies grow up," Blake said softly, finishing my thought.

"Become self-functioning," I added. "And then maybe..." A smile lit up my face.

"Maybe," Blake agreed, matching my grin. He looked at me

like *maybe* was just fine with him. Like he was content with imagining possibilities and getting to explore all of them with me, even if some were just ideas. "You can have it all if you want it all, Delaney. You don't have to pick, sweetheart. We'll just take on one dream at a time, okay?"

A dream.

Having a family with Blake really was something out of a dream, something I didn't think was possible. I grew up thinking I could never be a mom when the only example I had of motherhood was a painful one.

But that day with Blake's family, when I'd walked into Natalie's home and saw how love could be shaped differently, changed things. When I'd held Delilah and seen the way Gemma looked at her, like she'd do anything for her. When I'd experienced how Blake and his brothers had rallied for Natalie and Chloe in the last year. That was family, that was parenthood, that was a redefinition of my upbringing.

I took a deep breath. "Okay."

"You have time to think about it." Blake spoke the words I needed to hear. "Just let me know when the puzzle comes together for you."

I nodded, knowing I had all the pieces. He'd given me all of them. I just needed to line them up in a way they fit. And I knew they would soon.

"Have you thought of a name for your baby yet?" He changed the subject, pointing to the ground beneath us.

I cocked my head to the side. "I like to think that this one is *our* baby, too."

"Yeah?"

Blake's brows raised. He hadn't expected that.

"Yeah, Blake." I nodded, feeling sure that this was the right move. I had for a while. "That's why I was thinking that The London Cardiac Center sounded like a pretty perfect name."

Blake's lips parted, a suspended moment of awe until he leaned forward and pressed those lips to mine. He'd run out of words, and since I knew the feeling, I didn't press him for any. He'd already given me so many today. And all I needed now was him. So I returned the kiss eagerly, tangling my fingers in his hair and dragging him closer. Our knees banged against each other as rocks dug into our skin, a branded reminder of what this soil would grow. And how we would nurture life together.

"Perfect," he whispered against my mouth.

And it really, really was.

epilogue

ON OUR SECOND ANNIVERSARY, Delaney and I celebrated our marriage in a vineyard along the coast, surrounded by family. She wore a stunning dress. A stunning dress for a stunning woman. Classic and sleek without a lot of frills, perfect for my Lane. It fit her like a glove, in a way that had my mouth watering and my hands itching to take it off her. I'd been deprived of that the first time around, considering our wedding night was simply pizza on the couch.

Tonight was going to be nothing like that.

And I absolutely could not wait.

I'd flown my mom out to go wedding dress shopping with Delaney, which I think helped to fill the hole of her own mom's absence. My mom adored my wife. She'd been silently cheering us on from the sideline for years, ever since I asked for that ring, and she couldn't be happier that we'd made it here today.

Gemma had tagged along dress shopping, too, as well as Delaney's cousin, Ophelia. Both of whom were walking toward me right now, giving me a look like I'd done something egregious.

"Did you know your brother is trying to persuade the DJ to let him take over?" Ophelia demanded, all fiery, which I'd learned was just Ophelia's personality. "And I think the poor man's considering it just so he'll leave him alone."

Oh good. *I* hadn't done anything. Just Sully.

That checked out.

I glanced over at Gemma, and she immediately put her hands up.

"Don't look at me. *My* London brother is over there." Gemma pointed to Noah, who was holding Delilah on his hip while trying to intervene between Julian and Theo since Theo was, once again, being very indiscreet about his obsession with a certain red-haired woman with the last name of Briggs. And not the one who stood right next to me.

Julian looked on the brink of losing it, considering one of his twin daughters, either Lily or Rosie, was simultaneously crying in Juniper's arms while the other was strapped to his back. He reached out to take the wailing child from his wife, pressed a kiss to her forehead, and then started bouncing up and down as he continued to watch Theo closely.

Despite the chaos around us, I smiled. We hadn't all been together since Noah and Gemma got married about a year ago, and I felt so lucky that everyone had been able to make it to the East Coast again for this.

I shook my head. "No, I know it isn't *Noah*. I was just going to ask if you've seen Delaney. She was with you last, right?"

"She's trying to ward Sully off the DJ at the moment," Gemma said. "But I don't think she's being very successful, which is why we came to get you."

"Got it." I shook my head with a laugh. "I'll be right there."

"Okay." Gemma nodded and then gave me a soft smile. "I promised I'd help Chloe with her wardrobe malfunction, so I'm going to run to do that quickly before everyone is seated for dinner. Nat couldn't find any safety pins, but I think I have some in my bag."

"Thanks, Gemma." I wrapped my arms around her shoulder

and pulled her in for a brief side hug. "Thanks for everything you do for our family."

"I love you guys," she said, her voice barely a whisper. "And I'm so happy for you."

Emotion coated my throat as I swallowed, but I let her go and watched her walk off in search of my oldest niece.

"You know…" Ophelia started, and I turned to look at her. "I wasn't so sure of you before, but I think you're okay."

A snort of laughter escaped me.

"Did you just decide this now, Ophelia?"

She shrugged and inspected her nails, remaining silent.

"Why weren't you sure of me?" I pressed, not truly caring but curious all the same. "We didn't even meet until after Delaney and I got married. The first time."

"That's *exactly* why I wasn't sure of you." She pointed her manicured finger at me, an accusation. "I wasn't sure if you were the real deal or not."

My brows pulled together. "I married Delaney without a moment of hesitation."

"Still." She shrugged again, waving her hand. "You could have been love bombing her or something."

I shook my head with another laugh, considering the reality of what happened. "It was actually a bit of the opposite."

She had no idea how much restraint I'd used over the years *not* to bombard Delaney with my feelings.

"Well, I know that now. But before, I had no clue about the whole inheritance thing." She shot me a glare as though it was my fault she didn't know. "*Obviously*, or I never would have mentioned to Elizabeth and Robert that you eloped. I wish Laney would have explained everything to me. I mean, I'm *all* for taking money from my grandparents. They certainly don't need it anymore."

I chuckled, understanding why, of everyone in her family, Ophelia was the only person Delaney remained close to outside of Bryan.

"Well, everything worked out," I said. "Robert and Elizabeth even made an appearance tonight."

I was worried about Delaney's parents coming, but it had gone well. Her mom acted cordial, and her dad had seemed truly happy to be included. It wouldn't repair the years of damage they'd done to their daughter, but it was something.

Ophelia rolled her eyes at the mention of her aunt and uncle. "They'll leave when the wine runs out."

I raised a brow. "Who said the wine is going to run out?"

"See?" She smirked. "I knew I liked you."

"Actually, what I think you said was that you weren't sure if—"

"You should really go find your wife," she cut in, her lips curving further. "And do something about your brother."

"Shit. Right." I stood straighter, immediately twisting around in search of Lane. Darting away from Ophelia, I rounded the corner of the winery to where a big tent had been set up. The DJ and the dance floor sat in a large open spot between the canvas structure and the vineyard, surrounded by bouquets of tulips. I hadn't been able to grow a tulip field in Massachusetts in time for today, but I had been able to buy as many tulips as my credit card would allow for the occasion.

I spotted Delaney standing next to the DJ booth. And holy shit, she took my breath away. How was it even possible that she was real? I'd asked myself that a million times over in the last year, but today especially. Our life was a thing of dreams. Truly, undeniably, unbelievably perfect.

The cardiac center was well underway. We'd rented a space in an established clinic while we got on our feet and continued putting things in place to open our own doors. We now housed our free CPR clinics there as well. A small portion of the inheritance had been saved for a tiny but homey brownstone, which sat perfectly situated between Natalie's place and Bryan's new supported-living apartment. Despite everything going on with the clinic, our schedules were still a bit more predictable than a trauma surgeon's, so Chloe usually walked over to our house after school and hung out until dinnertime, or later sometimes. She *loved* Bryan, who came over equally often.

I smiled at Lane as I walked up, struggling to take my eyes off her. But then Sully's face wormed its way into my vision, and I narrowed my gaze.

My brother sat behind the DJ booth, a goofy grin on his face. And the DJ was nowhere to be seen.

Jesus Christ.

"Oh my God, did you really chase him away?"

I should have run over here faster.

"Nah." Sully waved off my concern. "I just told him to go get some snacks and wine for a bit."

"So you told our DJ to go get drunk?"

"No." Sully drew out the word. "I just told him I'd keep an eye on things for him while he took a short break. But now that you're here..." Sully stood, clapped a hand on my shoulder, and flashed me a smile. "Happy for you, man," he said before striding away and leaving me with Delaney.

Delaney,

Delaney London, Delaney London, Delaney London.

Today, that became doubly true.

How lucky was I that I got to marry the love of my life *twice*?

I looked her up and down, appreciating every inch of this woman, even the odd expression on her face that seemed to match Sully's suspiciously well. Music started playing behind us. Sully must have pressed Play before leaving, but it was so soft, so quiet, I could barely make it out.

Reaching out, I laced my fingers through Delaney's. "Have I told you how stunning you look today, sweetheart?"

A flush worked its way up her neck to her face. "A few times, yes."

I opened my mouth to throw more compliments at her, not knowing how to stop gushing over everything about my best friend, when the song grew louder, interrupting my thoughts and cracking a smile onto my face instead.

Delaney laughed and tugged on my hand, pulling me closer. "Dance with me? I wanted one dance, just you and me."

I shook my head, my grin so wide it hurt. "I will dance with you to *The Lizzie McGuire Movie* theme song any fucking day, Lane."

"This is why I love you."

Wrapping her in my arms, I led us in a gentle sway. "Oh, really? *This* is why?"

Her cheeks indented adorably. "And a lot of other reasons."

Still couldn't quite believe that, but I'd spend the rest of my life getting used to it, and I was plenty okay with that.

I held Delaney against my chest, enjoying having her close enough that I could feel her heartbeat. Then I spun her out onto the dance floor, and she twirled on my fingertip.

"This really is what dreams are made of," I said as she danced back into my arms, and I cradled her against my chest again.

Delaney blinked up at me. "It really is."

"Are you ready to go to Italy next week for your real Lizzie McGuire moment?"

We'd booked our honeymoon months ago, right after we'd nailed down the dates for the wedding reception. I kept picturing Delaney lounging in the Italian sun, a hat shading her shoulders and a glass of wine in her hand. I couldn't wait to explore a new country with her. And then explore *her* at night, just like I had on our first honeymoon.

Delaney bobbed her head, an eager nod. "Very excited to be back on a Vespa with my hot husband."

She placed a hand on my chest, and a whole-body shudder worked its way through me from her touch. And how she'd said the word *husband*.

I lowered my voice. "Are you going to wear your hair in braids again, Lane?"

She gave a sheepish little shrug that I didn't buy for a second.

At this point, Delaney was anything but inexperienced and naive about the way I wanted her. I brought my mouth to her neck, brushing kisses up the length of it.

"If you want me to," she breathed.

"Oh, I want you to," I whispered in her ear.

She melted against me, locking her hands at the nape of my neck. "You like a hairstyle with built-in leverage, don't you?"

I nipped the shell of her ear and started moving my hands, dragging them up her body, needing to feel her. "You know I do."

Delaney made a tiny whimpering noise that had my body reacting instantaneously. "Sorry if the wedding updo is disappointing, in that case."

"Not even a little bit." I raked my eyes over the elegant bun her hair had been swept into. Absolutely nothing about her and nothing about today was disappointing. "I can be creative."

The song changed, and I realized that Sully had prepped the entire soundtrack for us. It rolled into another title from the movie.

But we were barely listening to it anymore.

Delaney twisted her fingers into my hair and whined my name. "Blake."

"I know, baby."

I more than understood. I felt how much I wanted her in every breath I took.

"Can we sneak up to that bridal suite a little early?"

I groaned. "I think they're planning to seat everyone for dinner in like five minutes."

"Sully can distract them, can't he?"

She pressed her lips to my pulse point, sucking lightly.

I hoped she left a mark.

Fire licked my veins.

"*Fuck*, I can't say no to you."

I grabbed Delaney's hand, leading her inside the back entrance of the winery. Sully stood just inside the door, twiddling his thumbs, and I might have called him out for spying on us if I didn't need him to do exactly as Lane had suggested.

"Distract them," I grunted as I hurried Delaney up the back stairs, which were tucked right near the door, grabbing her train behind her so she didn't fall.

"Distract who?"

"Everyone. Give me ten."

"Ten?" Sully scoffed.

"You're right. Probably more like five."

With the way I wanted Delaney right now, I didn't think we'd need long. I demonstrated absolutely no restraint anymore when it came to my wife, and I knew that was exactly the way she liked it.

"Not what I meant," Sully called after us, already halfway up the spiral staircase. "Take your time."

As soon as we made it to the landing at the top of the stairs, I gripped Delaney's hip with one hand and wrapped my hand around her throat with the other, pulling her back into me and bringing her ear to my lips. "I'm not taking my fucking time."

"I don't want you to," she replied, her voice thick with want.

"Good answer," I grunted, releasing Delaney to let her walk the rest of the way into the bridal apartments that were created for the use of wedding parties on the day of events at the winery. The rooms were littered with makeup and hair tools and garment bags, and I had to watch my step as I followed Delaney through the doorway.

As soon as she heard the door close behind me, Delaney spun and grabbed me by the front of my jacket, yanking me toward her. *God yes*. I responded just as eagerly, crashing my lips to hers despite the makeup I knew I was smearing, longing to taste her fully. And *hell*, did she taste good. Like everything I had ever wanted.

"Later tonight, I'm going to take my time peeling this off you, baby," I murmured against her lips, sculpting my hands over her dress to feel her curves.

"And now?" she gasped.

"Now?" I paused to give her a deep, all-consuming kiss before growling, "Right now, you're going to get fucked in your wedding dress, Delaney London."

"Mmm," she hummed, her body molding to mine at the words, seeking mine. "Is my husband going to fuck me?"

"He's going to fuck you so goddamn hard," I promised as I cupped her face in my palms and pulled back to look at her, wanting to see her expression. "Is that what you want?"

"Yes," Delaney said without hesitation, her voice strong even as her body trembled. She raked her fingers down my chest, and I felt like I could jump out of my skin.

Knowing we didn't have a lot of time—before dinner and before we both lost it—I urged Delaney further into the room, not stopping until I had her up against the back of a couch and she was perched atop it. I tried to step between her legs, needing to be closer to her, but her dress made it difficult, and I groaned in frustration.

Meanwhile, Delaney kept running her hands over my body, trailing lower and lower. She ran a single fingertip down the length of my erection, and I thought that might be it for me, absolutely destroyed at the sight of Delaney touching me like that while wearing a white dress. Because she looked a whole lot like mine. *My* wife. *My* best friend. *My* business partner. My fucking everything.

Mine.

Delaney's touch switched from featherlight and teasing to a tight squeeze, and I cursed in surprise, undone by the feel of her hand cupping me.

"Delaney Rose London." I moaned her name, and it echoed in my brain, a sweet symphony that I could play over and over again. "If you touch my cock one more time, I'm going to have to find something to bend you over."

Delaney's lips stretched in a slow smile at my threat. "I've heard that before." She leaned closer. "This time, I'd like you to make good on your threat, though."

"Holy shit, Lane," I groaned before grabbing her hips and spinning her around. She backed her ass into me, grinding it against my crotch and making me gasp for air as I bent her over the back of the couch. "With fucking pleasure."

Delaney glanced over her shoulder. "And what are you going to do now you've got me bent over?"

"Fuck the little tease right out of you," I grunted, lifting my hips just enough that she'd feel how ready I was to do that.

Delaney's eyes rolled up, her lips parting, and seeing her reaction caused me to hasten my actions, grabbing the bottom of her dress to peel the layers up and over her hips.

And good Lord, Delaney wasn't wearing any underwear.

"Are you trying to fucking kill me?" I choked.

"Definitely not." But I could hear the amusement in her voice, mixed with the desire. "I need you alive right now, Blake. Alive and—"

A sharp gasp cut through her words when I swiped a finger along her soaked pussy.

"My wife gets so fucking wet for me, doesn't she?"

She nodded while whining for more.

I'll give you more, baby.

"She wants me to touch her." I thrust two fingers inside her, and I almost fainted from *hearing* how wet she was for me. "Wants me to lick her." I leaned down to taste her while I slowly pumped my finger in and out. In and out. "Wants me to fuck her."

"Yes," Delaney cried and then cried even louder when I suddenly withdrew my fingers, sucked them into my mouth to clean them off, and then nearly lost it from her taste. *Fuck.* I swallowed, savoring the moment for a split second before I got enough of a grip to unbuckle my pants and get into position, dragging the tip of my cock through her pussy.

"Yeah, Lane?" I checked. Because I wanted to hear it. I'd never get enough of her saying yes to me.

421

"Yes," she hissed, glancing back to glare at me despite being suspended over the couch. And then I watched as her glare turned into a look of wondrous pleasure as I thrust inside her, hard, fast, bottoming out within fractions of a second.

Unbelievable. God, she was unbelievable.

"Blake," she cried. "Oh my God, Blake."

Delaney threw her head back, not caring if anyone heard how fucking good I made her feel, and shit, did I love that. Love her.

"I know, baby." I sucked in, trying to steady myself for a second. That first moment of being inside her was *so* fucking good I didn't know how to handle it sometimes. "I know."

She arched her hips, trying to get more as she backed up, needing another dose of my cock.

"Not such a little tease now, are you?" I smirked, pulling back only a fraction before driving forward, causing Delaney to tip over the couch.

She made an unholy sound that I wanted to record and play on repeat.

"I didn't hear you, sweetheart. What was that?"

"No," she cried as I pulled out further and slammed into her again.

My lips curved. "Didn't think so."

I looked down, taking in the scene. Delaney in this dress. The white fabric bunched around her hips. Me driving into her from behind.

It was an image from my goddamn dreams.

Which meant I had no hope of making it last.

Delaney's gasps grew louder, and I suspected it had something to do with the angle we were at as I thrust into her repeatedly, rocking her hips against the corner of the couch. Needy pants fell from her lips with every slam of our bodies, and I realized I was wrong—I'd never experienced anything like this, not even in my dreams. This was better than *anything*, real or fake.

"You're going to spend dinner with my cum in that tight cunt of yours, Lane," I rasped, swallowing a moan as I pictured it.

Prepared myself for it. "And then later tonight, I'm going to clean my wife up before taking her to bed and filling this pretty pussy again. And again. And—"

"*Blake.*"

She nearly screamed my name that time, her walls tightening around my cock as she danced along the edge of an orgasm.

My pretty little wife, my sweet dancer.

"Tell me I can, Delaney," I begged, needing to hear her say it so we could both let go.

Her head tipped back and forward in a wordless nod, and it was good enough for me.

"Fuck, I love you, Lane," I cried as my release overwhelmed me, my climax hitting hard and fast, my vision blurring. Delaney squeezed around me, strangling my cock as she came at the same time, sending me through another wave of blinding pleasure. "*I love you, I love you, I love you,*" I chanted, collapsing forward until I could feel her skin on my lips.

"I love you, too, Blake. So much." She sounded broken, but I knew it was just because she trusted me enough to fall apart in my arms. I knew how to put her back together again. Knew what all her perfect pieces looked like.

She looked back at me, and her blue eyes shone.

"I needed this," she said.

I flashed her a smile. "Needed my cock, baby?"

"No," she started before amending when she saw my affronted expression. "Well, yes, but no, that's not what I mean."

I pulled back, drawing out of her slowly. Her eyes fluttered shut for a moment until we were separated, and as hard as that was, I knew we'd be together again soon. "What'd you mean, sweetheart?"

"I needed this," she said as I helped her fix her dress. She turned to face me. "I needed today. To choose."

Emotion clogged all of my senses. "I'm so proud of you for choosing, Lane."

So ridiculously proud of the life she'd built for herself. So proud of the things she chose to do because she wanted to. So grateful she chose to do all those things with me.

"It helped," she whispered. "It helped the puzzle."

"Yeah?"

Delaney nodded, biting down on her lip. I could tell she was fighting tears, but they were good ones. I knew they were good ones. "Everything fits together now."

I'd waited years for her to say those words, and all I could do was smile at her, overcome with a happiness that felt a lot like peace. "It's a pretty picture, isn't it?"

Delaney smiled back.

"The prettiest, Blake."

THE END

acknowledgments

THERE'S NOTHING quite like finalizing a book and seeing all the pieces come together on something you've worked so long and hard to finish. It's emotional and joyous and also a time to share gratitude for the people who helped me get to this point.

To my readers, first and foremost, thank you for being here. To those who have been here since the beginning, I can't thank you enough. And to those who have just joined me, thank you for being here! Your support is so very appreciated!

To Nate, my number one cheerleader. Thank you for believing in me and encouraging me every step of the way. Thank you for always supporting me in chasing my dreams.

To Caitlin, thank you for doing everything under the sun, as usual, to help with this release and thank you for being the best friend I could ever ask for.

My alpha readers, Kelsey, Reilly, Deidre and Hanna, you all deserve the world!! This is the first time I wrote a book without sharing it online as I went, and having you all to bounce ideas off of and provide feedback was so very important and helpful. I will forever be grateful to you all.

To the most amazing crew of beta readers: Belinda, Sevval, Nikki, Alyssa, Emma, Madison, Stephanie, Brianna, Lilly, and Rebeka. Each of you brought such important perspectives to the table and really helped to shape this book into what it is today! Thank you endlessly for your time and support.

To Ruby, thank you for navigating this author life with me from the very beginning! I can't believe how many years have gone by since we stumbled into the same internet space, and I couldn't be more grateful for that or for you. Seriously. Can't wait to give you an IRL hug soon!

Sandra, thank you for continuing to work with me and providing your editing expertise once again! I appreciate you so much.

To Alie, the drawing you did of Blake and Delaney is my absolute favorite yet! Thank you so much for always bringing my characters to life in the most fantastic way.

To my fellow authors and friends in the book community, I'm so honored to experience this space with you and to interact with you all. I'm so lucky to get to be a part of such a thriving community. Thank you for making this job the best!

To my friends and co-workers who have been nothing but supportive as I transition into my new author era, I appreciate you endlessly. Taking risks is so much easier when you have people around you who will back you up.

And last, but definitely not least, thank you to my family. (You caught the part where I said *definitely not least*, right? I was just saving the best for last!) Wholesome and loving fictional families are always so easy to write for me, and you're the reason for that. So, thank you.

about the author

AMELIE RHYS is a romance author with a love for writing swoony stories packed with tension and heat. When she's not daydreaming about fictional characters, Amelie loves to travel new places (so she can write about them) and find new coffee shops and bookstores (so she can curl up and read in them). Amelie also likes spending time at the lake with her family. She lives in Minnesota with her husband and two rescue dogs.

Books by Amelie Rhys
Alive at Night
Awake at Dawn
Attached at Heart

Information about Wildflower book 4 coming soon!

Made in the USA
Las Vegas, NV
17 March 2025

19678187R00256